my
mother
cursed
my
name

my mother cursed my name

a novel

ANAMELY SALGADO REYES

ATRIA BOOKS

NEW YORK   LONDON   TORONTO   SYDNEY   NEW DELHI

ATRIA
BOOKS

An Imprint of Simon & Schuster, LLC
1230 Avenue of the Americas
New York, NY 10020

First Atria Books hardcover edition July 2024

ATRIA B O O K S and colophon are trademarks of Simon & Schuster, LLC

Simon & Schuster: Celebrating 100 Years of Publishing in 2024

For information about special discounts for bulk purchases, please contact Simon & Schuster Special Sales at 1-866-506-1949 or business@simonandschuster.com.

The Simon & Schuster Speakers Bureau can bring authors to your live event. For more information or to book an event, contact the Simon & Schuster Speakers Bureau at 1-866-248-3049 or visit our website at www.simonspeakers.com.

Manufactured in the United States of America

1   3   5   7   9   10   8   6   4   2

Library of Congress Cataloging-in-Publication Data

Names: Salgado Reyes, Anamely, author.
Title: My mother cursed my name : a novel / Anamely Salgado Reyes.
Description: First Atria Books hardcover edition. |
New York : Atria Books, 2024.
Identifiers: LCCN 2023058292 (print) | LCCN 2023058293 (ebook) |
ISBN 9781668038000 (hardcover) | ISBN 9781668038017
(paperback) | ISBN 9781668038024 (ebook)
Subjects: LCGFT: Magic realist fiction. | Novels.
Classification: LCC PS3619.A4375 M9 2024 (print) | LCC PS3619.A4375
(ebook) | DDC 813/.6—dc23/eng/20240112

ISBN 978-1-6680-3800-0
ISBN 978-1-6680-3802-4 (ebook)

To my mother, who blessed my name.

part
one

part
one

chapter 1

Angustias

For generations, the women in the Olivares family attempted to change the course of destiny through the power of names. Despite being renowned experts on stubbornness, each of the Olivares women underestimated the extent to which destiny shared this trait. As a result of their oversight, the Olivares women failed to control their lives and, most importantly, their daughters' lives, in every single attempt.

The Olivares women's unsuccessful efforts began on the 18th of June 1917 when Justa Olivares, a quite cruel and unjust woman, decided to name her daughter Calamidades. Justa believed that if life had been unkind to her, there was no reason for her daughter to have it any better. Justa chose not to see the wickedness in her name choice. In fact, she convinced herself that it was a gift, for calamities could bring wisdom and resilience if one put in enough effort to see beyond the pain.

Calamidades Olivares did not experience a single calamity in her life, except for the night of her birth when her mother passed away with Calamidades sleeping in her arms. Calamidades was adopted the very next day by her wealthy and lonely aunt, Daría, who appointed her as the sole beneficiary in her will. Because Daría provided her niece shelter, wisdom, and love, the three ingredients needed to prevent a bitter heart, Calamidades grew up without resentment toward her mother and her name. Justa, Calamidades believed, had been right. Calamities could be a gift, but it was one she never received.

Life made a point of protecting Calamidades from disaster. When a hurricane hit the northeast of Mexico, Calamidades's coastal hometown, Matamoros, remained completely untouched. Ten years later, when a five-year drought hit the region, rain fell over Calamidades's house, and only her house, once a month without fail. Six years after the end of the drought, a swarm of deadly wasps invaded the county, but if you asked the people of Matamoros what the monstrous insects looked like, they could not say. The wasps flew right around the city's outer limits, leaving no victims or remnants of despair.

At the age of twenty-six, Calamidades was blessed with a beautiful daughter whom the doctor declared to be the healthiest baby he had ever delivered. Calamidades named the baby Victoria so that she could triumph in every task she set out to complete. With the belief that her daughter was safe and sound and destined to be victorious, Calamidades passed away peacefully in her sleep on her thirtieth birthday.

Victoria Olivares was not successful in anything that she did, which was quite unfortunate when the stakes were high. She failed almost every exam in school, was always chosen last when forming teams in the playground and lost every game of damas chinas she played with her great-aunt Daría in the ten years she got to spend with her before the woman passed away from old age. No matter how much effort she put into a matter, and it was quite a lot of effort considering how much her spirit should have been crushed by the circumstances of her life, Victoria could not help but fail. At the age of five, she attempted to fly, fell, and broke her arm in three places. At the age of fifteen, she attempted to cook for herself for the first time and burnt down her house. And at the age of eighteen, Victoria became addicted to gambling and lost every single cent she inherited from her great-aunt.

Because Victoria had done so poorly in school, she was unable to find a job that paid enough to help her pay her gambling debts. Loans became her lifeline, and when she realized they would also be her ultimate demise, Victoria sought divine aid.

To change her fortune, Victoria named her daughter Olvido, after the saint Nuestra Señora del Olvido, so that all her sins, worries, and most importantly her debts, could be forgiven and forgotten. But they were neither forgotten nor forgiven, and Olvido was forced to immigrate to the United States to escape the loan sharks who demanded more and more money even after Victoria's death.

With the repercussions of her mother's mistakes looming over her head, Olvido grew up to be a very unforgiving woman. She did not forgive nor forget life's injustice, her mother's selfishness, her husband's imprudence, and later on, her own daughter's blunders. The only mistake Olvido learned to accept was Americans' mispronunciation of her name. "Old-vee-dough," she grew accustomed to saying to the restaurant customers she served. "But without the D in Old."

"Ol-vee-do," the customers would repeat. "So beautiful. What does it mean?"

"Oblivion."

The customers would exchange curious glances and chuckle. "That can't be a real name."

"It is real," Olvido assured them by patting her name tag. "Go to Mexico. You'll hear worse. Now, would you like corn or flour tortillas?"

To ensure that her daughter did not become as reckless as Victoria Olivares, Olvido named her Angustias. Olvido hoped that a constant state of uneasiness would force her daughter to think twice before acting and prevent more misfortune in the family, but the opposite occurred. Angustias Olivares grew up to be a joyful and carefree girl. While other students cried on their first day of kindergarten, worried about the prospect of leaving their parents, Angustias comforted her mother and assured her she would be all right. While the neighborhood children panicked before a hurricane, discussing to no end how their parents had bought an infinite amount of food and boarded up their houses to survive the end of the world, Angustias played outside until the wind began to drag her feet. On the evening of Angustias's first hurricane, Olvido had to carry a kicking and screaming Angustias back into the house and tape the door locks to prevent her from escaping.

Angustias always arrived at school at the last minute, studied for exams at the last minute, and apologized to teachers at the last minute, barely saving herself from a trip to the principal's office all without an ounce of worry in her heart. Angst was a foreign concept to Angustias, so when her sixteenth birthday rolled around, and she discovered she was pregnant, Angustias was ecstatic. Olvido was mortified.

Angustias's daughter's name came to her through divine intervention. She was sitting in the passenger's seat of her boyfriend's car rambling about the movie they were on their way to see when she had a sudden craving for sour pickles, sour gummy worms, and a jumbo sour slushy. She ordered her boyfriend to stop the car and turn around—they had passed a gas station a few miles back. Her boyfriend refused—they would be late for the movie.

Frantic, Angustias unlocked the car door and made a show of pulling the handle toward her. She didn't push the door open, but she had every intention of doing so. Her cravings had become so intense, she threatened to jump out of the car and walk all the way to the gas station if he did not take her there immediately.

"No quieres que tu hija salga con cara de pepinillo, ¿verdad?" she warned.

Her boyfriend stared at her perplexed. He understood Spanish fairly well, but Mexican sayings always went over his head. "If you don't satisfy your pregnancy cravings," Angustias explained, "your child will be born looking like the food you desired."

Angustias's boyfriend scrunched his nose. "That doesn't make any sense."

"Yes, it does," Angustias argued. Mexican sayings sometimes sounded silly, but they carried the wisdom of a hundred generations. One could not possibly fight a hundred generations worth of wisdom unless they were dumb and reckless, and Angustias was reckless but not dumb.

"So, let's say you're craving mangos."

"The baby will have jaundice."

Angustias's boyfriend laughed.

"That's not funny. This," Angustias said, pointing at her belly to indicate both the baby and her stomach. "Is a serious matter."

"So, if you think the baby will look like a pickle, it'll . . . have acne?" he reasoned.

"Perhaps," she said. "And what if she gets bullied for it? Will you be able to live with the guilt?"

Her boyfriend rolled his eyes but shook his head.

One illegal turn and ten dollars later, Angustias had her hands full of sour delicacies. With her brain empty of desperation, she was able to consider the meaning of her cravings more thoughtfully. "Maybe it's not literal," she said between slurps of her jumbo sour slushy. And, just as abruptly as her cravings had appeared, she was struck by the meaning of her sign. Angustias gasped with such horror, her startled boyfriend swerved into the left lane and came inches away from hitting an oncoming car.

The universe or God or whoever is in charge of signs, was informing Angustias that her daughter was going to be a sour person, quite sour, judging by the intensity of her cravings. Angustias could not bear the thought of such a dreadful prophecy being fulfilled, so she decided right then and there that her daughter would be named Felicitas.

Felicitas Olivares did not grow up to be a grumpy child as the divine sign had indicated. However, she was born with a sour face. On the day of her birth, when she looked upon Felicitas for the first time, the obstetrician felt an immediate sense of judgment and wondered if the baby had not wanted to be delivered just yet. While bathing and clothing Felicitas, the nurses constantly doubted their techniques. They must have been doing something incorrectly for the baby to have looked so upset. One of them vowed to think twice before having a child of her own. If she could not handle the dissatisfied and disappointed look of a stranger's baby, how would she handle the disapproval of her own?

Now, at least three times a day, Angustias has to rub her daughter's forehead to remind her to remove her frown. "You will be the first girl in the history of the world to develop wrinkles at the age of ten," she says to Felicitas one morning before she leaves for school. She reaches over the kitchen table and pushes against the crinkle between her daughter's brows.

"That's fine," Felicitas says, swatting her mother's hand away. "Wrinkles are a sign of wisdom."

"And how would you know?" Angustias asks. Ignoring her daughter's protests, she runs her thumbs over Felicitas's brows to separate them. The frown reappears as soon as Angustias sits back down. She's not too worried. Felicitas's morning frown is a bad habit, but not a sign of anger. Angustias can tell by the cool, pale-yellow cloud that hovers over the crown of her daughter's head. A warmer tone would be ideal, but it's early and a school day. Any shade of yellow is a blessing.

"Abuelita Olvido is a very wise woman," Felicitas explains. "Or so she claims, and she's more wrinkly than a dried prune. The bus is here. I gotta go."

Felicitas carries her dirty dishes to the sink, plants a kiss on her mother's cheek, and runs out of the apartment, leaving the door wide open. Usually, Angustias yells after Felicitas to remind her to close the door and to have a nice day at school, but something feels different today, something Angustias can't explain. A small seed of concern sprouts within her. Its leaves push against the inner walls of her gut and makes her wonder if she's going to be sick. She sniffs the leftover milk in her cereal bowl. It doesn't smell unusual. This isn't food poisoning.

Angustias sits in the kitchen and watches as Felicitas runs toward the school bus parked on the opposite side of the street. She remains in that position even after the street becomes deserted and all she is left with is the view of her neighbor watering his plants. The neighbor waves at Angustias. She stares back blankly.

The banging of the rebounding door brings Angustias back to reality, but only for a moment. As she carries her own empty plate to the sink and washes the dirty dishes, she goes right back to questioning how it is possible for Felicitas to know what her grandmother looks like. Felicitas has not seen Olvido since her first month of life. The only mental image Felicitas can possibly hold of her grandmother is that from an old photograph of Angustias's first birthday. Olvido was thirty-six years old at the time. Not a wrinkle in sight.

Perhaps she misinterpreted Felicitas's cloud and mistook a pearl-white indifference for the pale yellow that signaled the brink of joy. Is that how Felicitas felt about her grandmother now, indifferent? Indifference was good, much better than resentment. And what was that at the border of Felicitas's cloud? The gradation was so soft, Angustias cannot be sure, but she thinks she observed the appearance of a slight mischievous red orange when Felicitas mentioned Olvido's looks. Maybe that was the joke. Felicitas cannot know what Olvido looks like, so it is funny that her guess is a face "more wrinkly than a dried prune."

Angustias's trance is broken once again by the shrill ringing of her cell phone. Grateful for the distraction, she merrily reaches for the phone and does not bother checking the caller ID before answering. It takes only a short exchange of words for Angustias to regret her actions.

"Oh," she gasps. Her hand shoots up to her trembling lips. "Yes. Yes, I'm here. I— I understand."

With every burning tear that rolls down her cheeks, Angustias wishes for a change in circumstance that can take her out of that moment. She wishes she could rewind time. She wishes she could tell her past self to not answer the phone, to not wake up, to pretend that her hearing had momentarily failed her. But Angustias answered the phone and heard the dreadful news that made her drop to her knees and cry out in pain. She cries until a puddle forms beneath her. The puddle transforms into a pond, and the pond becomes a lake. It is a miracle she stops crying. Three more tears and she would have flooded the neighborhood.

Angustias remains on the floor for what could be fifteen minutes or fifteen hours. Once her clothes have soaked up every drop of her sorrow and no more tears spill from her eyes, she stands up, walks into the bedroom, makes a few calls, sends some emails, and packs all of her and Felicitas's belongings. She moves on to the kitchen and living room, packs the remaining items around the house, and carries six boxes, two suitcases, and a dying plant out to her rusty but trusty green car.

She drives off and stops only twice, once to drop off the apartment keys with her furious and confused landlord and again to pick up Felicitas from school. By the time Angustias reaches the pick-up area where Felicitas stands carrying her black backpack and an armful of library books, the tears on her clothes have evaporated. The sadness she carries in her heart has not.

"What's going on?" Felicitas asks as she clasps her seat belt.

Angustias gives her a reassuring smile and looks into the rearview mirror before backing up. There is danger behind her. Impatiently sitting in the backseat is a threat to her peace of mind, the one who cursed her heart, but she is invisible to Angustias's eyes. Nonchalantly, Angustias blows a kiss goodbye and presses down on the accelerator.

chapter 2

Felicitas

"You couldn't wait for the final bell to ring?" Felicitas says, glowering at Angustias. Despite her mother's disdain for her frown, Felicitas believes there are three advantages to her sour face. One: she is less likely to be abducted. Kidnappers seek cute, naïve children, words that would never be used to describe a girl with a frown as deep as hers. Felicitas's face says, "I am aware of all that's wrong with the world. I see danger coming a mile away." Two: she can always win a sour candy eating contest. No one notices pain when you look upset to begin with. Three: it allows her to show her mother she means business. While other kids pout, an adorable gesture that scares no one, Felicitas scowls, a real grown-up level of intensity scowl.

"You don't even like school," Angustias says dismissively.

"I do when we get to watch movies based on books I like," Felicitas says, deepening her frown.

"Oh," Angustias says, glancing at her daughter. "Right. Today was Tuck Everlasting Day." Felicitas nods. "Okay, I understand. I'm sorry." Felicitas softens her expression. "I'll tell you what. As soon as this trip is over, we'll have a movie night. It'll be a smaller screen, but at least you won't have to sit on a metal desk."

"Trip?" Felicitas turns so that her knees rest on the car seat and her head pokes out above the headrest. Sitting in the back are one large blue suitcase with gray duct tape covering a hole on the front flap and a smaller black suitcase with a bat keychain hanging from its side. The teeth of the zippers brace each other for dear life, fighting the garments threatening to pull them apart. Pepe, their dying devil's ivy, rests on top with a seat belt around his ceramic pot. And then there's that pesky intruder sitting behind the driver's seat.

Felicitas sits back down and readjusts her seat belt. Her eyebrows furrow again. "That looks like a lot for a weekend."

"We're not leaving for a weekend," Angustias says, and winks at her. Felicitas whips her head back. The intruder shrugs.

"How long?" Felicitas can barely hear her own question over the sound of her rising heartbeat.

"Forever," her mother replies.

Felicitas involuntarily smiles. Angustias spots the rarity, and a smile begins to form on her own lips, but it's doomed to be short-lived. Felicitas's frown returns.

Nothing sounds as wonderful to Felicitas as the possibility of leaving Oakhill, Arkansas, forever, but this is not her first rodeo. She knows there are things one must think about before uprooting one's life to an entirely new place on a random Friday morning, things that her mother most likely did not think about.

"What about her job?" the intruder asks. "Ask her."

Felicitas wants to shush her. She's perfectly capable of redirecting Angustias toward reason, thank you very much. "What about your job?" Felicitas asks.

"I sent them a nice email letting them know I was quitting."

Felicitas gasps. "You can't just do that!"

Angustias shrugs. "But I did. And it's fine. I got paid on Monday."

"What about her apartment?" the intruder asks.

Felicitas glares at her through the corner of her eye. "What about the apartment?"

"I returned the keys and paid off this month's rent," Angustias says. "Thank God I hadn't signed a lease. I didn't get the deposit back, though. I should have known."

"What about school?"

"Oh, you'll definitely continue to go to school."

"But where?"

"Wherever we go."

"Where are we going?"

"Right now? Grace, Texas."

"Stop the c—"

Felicitas sprints out of the parked car and throws up her lunch right beneath the "Come back soon!" sign that marks the outer limits of Oakhill. She looks up, reads the sign, and throws up some more at its suggestion.

The jolly sign is right. They will have to come back soon if her mother comes to her senses and realizes it's best not to quit a decent paying job. Are there any secretarial positions in Grace? Will Angustias qualify for any of them? Will Angustias's coworkers let Felicitas stay in the break room or sit behind Angustias's desk whenever school is closed for holidays or bad weather days? Will Angustias's new boss let her arrive late when Felicitas misses the bus?

No, they will not, because they won't trust them yet. They'll be new in town, outsiders once again.

And what about school? Will Felicitas's new school make a fuss when they see her history of truancy? And where will they live? Will they be able to afford an apartment, a nice one without funky smells and creaking pipes?

Felicitas asks Angustias all of this once she gets back into the car. Her nausea returns when her mother responds "I don't know" to every single question.

"Don't look at me like that!" Angustias says, straightening her back and lifting her chin. "I don't know because it doesn't matter. We're going to Grace, but we're not staying there. It's just a stop until I know where we're actually going to stay."

"Why Grace?" Felicitas asks despite having a good guess for the answer.

"That's where Abuelita Olvido lives—Lived." Angustias's voice cracks on the last syllable, and for a fraction of a second, Felicitas feels a laugh bubble up in her throat, but such a reaction would be cruel and suspicious. Felicitas presses her lips together with her teeth and hopes her mother mistakes it for an indication that she's trying not to cry. It doesn't matter. Angustias is too busy looking up at the car's ceiling, attempting to keep a tear from falling. "Abuelita Olvido passed away this morning," she musters up the strength to say. "Do you understand what that means?"

Felicitas rolls her eyes. "Yes. I'm ten, not five."

Angustias nods. The movement betrays her attempts to hold back her tears. Salty, scorching rivers make their way down the mountain of sorrow she's become.

Felicitas has seen her mother cry a handful of times. Most of these instances have involved Olvido in some way. A conversation on the phone, a letter in the mail, an old object triggering a memory. Reminders of Olvido and by Olvido never fail to turn Angustias's happy-go-lucky self on its head. That's how Felicitas knew Angustias loved Olvido. It was strange and nonsensical. Angustias cried when she cared. She didn't cry when they were evicted in Tennessee, or when she got fired in Louisiana, or when she found out that her boyfriend in New Mexico was cheating on her. Angustias didn't care about those things. She said so herself.

"It doesn't matter as long as we are together and we're healthy and happy," Angustias always recites after a particularly worrisome event. Felicitas supposes that when it comes to matters of Olvido, this rule does not apply, especially now that Olvido has passed away.

Felicitas knows exactly what "passing away" means. Mr. Campbell, their next-door neighbor in Redpoint, Oklahoma, explained it to her when she asked him why so many people dressed in black were entering his house. "It's for my funeral," he explained calmly. She was four years old at the time.

Mrs. Reed, Mrs. Thompson, and all the dead people Felicitas encountered throughout her life insisted on explaining to her what it means to die even after she told them she was well informed of the matter. Old people love to explain things, Felicitas learned early on, and dead old people are particularly determined to have their explanations heard, probably because it is an almost impossible task to accomplish. They can speak and sign all they want, but their loved ones cannot hear them. They won't even turn in their direction. They'll simply whisper the names of their dearly departed and run their fingers over their faces, immortalized in photographs, leaving the dead frustrated and lonely. Feeling pity over the recent tragic events they've encountered, Felicitas courteously lends them her ears, her eyes, and an understanding heart.

Over the years, Felicitas learned how to explain death in various ways, explicitly and implicitly, religiously and scientifically. Her mother has no way of knowing this, however. Felicitas never discusses her ability to see spirits. She fears the possibility of Angustias worrying about her, or worse, not worrying at all.

But she must definitely, absolutely under no circumstances tell Angustias about what, no, *who* she saw that morning. There's no way to appropriately explain that, neither explicitly nor implicitly, neither religiously nor scientifically.

Felicitas woke up early, as she does every day, to make coffee for her mother, a gesture Angustias believes Felicitas does out of love. She is only partially correct. Making Angustias's coffee every morning allows Felicitas to steal some for herself. No cream and no sugar for her. She doesn't like to mask the bitterness that runs down her throat and tingles the tips of her fingers and toes.

"Why don't you just serve yourself a cup?"

Felicitas spun to find the source of the voice. Hot coffee splashed against her black dress burning the skin between her sternum and belly button.

"Did that not hurt?"

Mouth slightly open, Felicitas shook her head. She'd expected to see a complete stranger, a spirit that had accidentally wandered into the house. Instead, the woman who sat before her was only a partial stranger, one whose heart Felicitas did not know but whose eyes had often infiltrated her dreams. Even framed with creases, those brown eyes were unmistakable. Hundreds of hours spent staring at a single picture had ensured they were.

Felicitas's hands shot to her belly. The coffee spread and dripped as she pressed against her soaked clothes. *Don't throw up*, she demanded. *Don't.* Her stomach rumbled in protest. It needed to get her worries out.

How? Felicitas's body asked. *How will you break the news to your mother?* Before Olvido, all of Felicitas's spiritual encounters had been coincidences. Spirits had not sought her out, required her help, or asked her to inform their loved ones about their death, a fact Felicitas is thankful for. She presumes being the bearer of bad news is a difficult task, especially if one can't explain how they obtained such information.

"Hello?" Olvido said. "Can you not hear me?"

Felicitas sucked in a deep, shaky breath, further realizing that if she were to tell her mother about Olvido, she would also have to reveal her ability to see dead people, which was another conversation she was not ready to have. Suddenly, Felicitas understood why the protagonists in her books were dumb enough to keep a diary too easily accessible to be pried open by nosy people. Some secrets are too big to keep in your heart but too complicated to tell your mother.

After an extremely brief introduction that involved stating their names and relation to each other, and responding "I know" to what each said, Felicitas informed Olvido that she could not talk for long. She did not want to be late for school. Olvido said she understood. She only had one request.

"Dime," Felicitas said.

"¡Dígame! Háblame de usted."

The demand to be spoken to in a formal manner was expected. It had occurred the very few times they'd spoken on the phone, but this morning, Felicitas refused to obey. Grandmothers were supposed to be nice, kind ladies who force you to eat too much food and give you loose change to buy candy even though you cannot buy candy with a few coins anymore. They were not supposed to be mean ladies who make your mom cry and force you to speak formal Spanish. If Felicitas was going to do Olvido a favor, then Olvido was going to have to cater to Felicitas's wish for some normalcy, even if it had to be fulfilled in the afterlife. They continued the conversation in casual Spanish.

"I need you to make sure that your mother buries my body in

Mexico," Olvido said. She did not say "please." She did not smile. The lines that formed between Olvido's eyebrows remained in place. The ones on Felicitas's did as well.

"Why?"

"As you can see," Olvido said, extending her arms and moving them up and down in front of her torso. "I have not gone to Heaven, and I believe it is because my body is not yet where it needs to be." Olvido raised her chin and puffed out her chest. "I am Mexican by birth, upbringing, and now, death."

Felicitas took a sip of Angustias's coffee and grimaced. Her beloved dark brew tasted extra bitter and not in a wonderful, electrifying way.

"Did your mother ever play 'México lindo y querido' for you?" Olvido continued, frowning at her granddaughter's lack of attention.

"Yep," Felicitas responded, staring at her feet.

"Do you know the lyrics? 'México lindo y querido,'" Olvido began to sing.

"Yeah, yeah. I know what line of the song you're talking about," Felicitas interrupted.

"Don't you think it make sense—"

"Is that it?" Felicitas said. "Is that all you want me to do? Take you back to Mexico pretending you're still asleep like the song says?"

Olvido hmphed. "Yes. That is it. You don't have to follow what the song says word for word, though. And it's not polite to interrupt when someone—"

"Well, I need to get ready for school. I'll let my mom know, and I'll see you at your funeral if we go."

Olvido's jaw dropped. "*If?* Well, now I can't leave." She let out a small laugh that carried no amusement. "I have to make sure you get there."

"Suit yourself," Felicitas said, and casually moved on to her morning duties, referring to Olvido only once. She relished seeing her grandmother's face light up when she called her wise, and then darken when she called her wrinkly.

With a sharp stab to Felicitas's chest, guilt quickly killed her amusement. For hours, Felicitas rubbed the spot over her heart where she'd been hurt. It was what she deserved, she knew. Whatever pain guilt had given her paled in comparison to what Angustias would be feeling at some point in the day. After Felicitas left for school, Angustias would receive a phone call and hear about Olvido, and she would be in mourning for the rest of the afternoon and possibly several days. Unlike Felicitas, Angustias would cry.

And cry, Angustias does. Felicitas takes off her seat belt, reaches over to the center console, and wraps her arms around her. She pats her mother's back the way Angustias does when Felicitas comes home from school teary-eyed. Her hands switch between pats and circles and light squeezes on the shoulders. "You can pick the playlist this time," Felicitas whispers in her mother's ears.

Through her sobs, Angustias smiles. "I know just what we need," she whispers back, already typing a playlist title into her phone.

With a better attitude and less stressful music, the Olivares girls head south. Felicitas sticks out her tongue at the farewell sign before it's out of sight. For a moment, her eyes flicker toward the intruder. She should stop calling her that. Soon, they'll be in *her* hometown, planning her funeral, surrounded by a world that she never let Felicitas into. Felicitas will be the intruder, and maybe Angustias will see her as one, too.

chapter 3

Olvido

Upon realizing she was dead, Olvido's first thought was, *The laundry!* She finds this fact embarrassing. One would think that there was nothing going in her life more memorable than house chores, but there was. Of course, there was. There was . . .

There was . . .

"Taliah," Olvido exclaimed when she saw her friend peeking in through the kitchen window. Her hands shot up to cover her mouth as if Taliah could hear her. Could she?

"Hello?" Taliah called, looking in Olvido's direction. "Olvido? Are you there? Is this a bad time? I can come back later if you want."

It was, indeed, a terrible time. Twenty minutes before, Olvido had woken up from a nap and realized she'd overslept by fourteen hours. At least her headache was gone, but so was the saliva in her mouth.

And the rise and fall of her chest.

And her pulse.

"Actually, can I use your restroom?" Taliah yelled. "You were right about bladders and aging."

Olvido rolled her eyes. Taliah was only forty-nine. "Tell me about it when you're in your sixties," Olvido yelled back.

"Listen, I'm going to come in anyway because I need to use your restroom, okay?"

Olvido took a step back. Her heart beat rapidly, but it was just a phantom sensation. How useless.

"Hope I'm not waking you from a nap," Taliah said as she set down on the kitchen counter the house key Olvido always hid underneath the smallest flowerpot on her front porch. "Your lawn is looking a little dead, by the way," she said scrunching her nose.

Taliah did not do well with dead things. Seeing dead animals on the side of the road brought her to tears. Dead silence in a large crowd made her so nervous she began to hiccup. She thought there was nothing worse than a dead party, and one of her biggest fears was only finding dead batteries in the middle of a power outage. Surely, she would enter a state of shock or faint from fright if she found Olvido's dead body. Who would find her?

"I'm also going to borrow some detergent," Taliah said coming out of the restroom. "Well, not borrow—" She came to a halt in the middle of the hallway, took a step back and craned her neck to see into Olvido's bedroom. "I knew you were here! Why are you still—"

Olvido grimaced and ran out of her house. "God," she said, not as an expression of frustration, but a direct call to Heaven. "God—" The potential questions and remarks were infinite. Most began with *what* and *why.*

What were You thinking taking me during a day as beautiful as this? Couldn't You provide something more appropriate? A storm? A light drizzle? At least one dark cloud?

Taliah slowly opened the door, walked out the front steps and hic-cupped.

What a relief to die in my sleep. Although, you did go overboard with the pain level of that headache.

"Yoo-hoo! Taliah," Samara, Olvido's neighbor, called from across the street.

Why am I here? Is this normal? Where is my angel, my light, my tunnel?

"Is everything all right?"

Taliah responded with a hiccup.

Where is Thelma? And Cecilia? Where is my mother?

"Olvido," Taliah croaked. "Um. She—"

*I didn't take the towels out of the washer. They're going to stink up. And
I have underwear in the dryer, old pairs. Who's going to find those?*

Angustias.

Olvido does not know why she appeared in front of Felicitas at that
moment. Perhaps God wanted it that way. He knew of the girl's ability.
Perhaps it was because when Olvido visualized her daughter, she saw her
granddaughter cuddled up in her arms, her face scrunched up into a cry.

Olvido did not fret. She figured she could think of home and disappear, but in a fraction of a second, she realized she didn't know where
home was. No one was waiting for her at her house. The lights were off.
The doors were closed, the curtains drawn. All that was left was dead
silence, unless Taliah was still hiccupping.

Angustias's apartment was not home, even if her family was there.
Olvido didn't know where the cups and plates were stored, how the
shower worked, where the spare key was hidden. She didn't have house
slippers waiting for her by the front door or a favorite blanket enticing
her to take a nap in the living room there.

Home had to be further away, in both time and distance. It had to
be Mexico. It was where she took her first breath and first steps and
babbled her first word. It was where she learned how to write her name
and dismiss its meaning, where she last saw her mother, where she
realized she had the guts to embark on the longest, most strenuous
journey of her life. In Mexico, she would not have to relive late-night
arguments and lonely mornings and watching Angustias drive away.

Now, Olvido has a front-and-center view of her daughter's drive
back. Unfortunately, Felicitas's scowl is in the picture.

Fortunately, she should say. Anger fuels action, and whatever her
granddaughter is feeling is not the abandon-your-mother type of anger
that Olvido knows so well because there is no reason for Felicitas to
feel that way toward her. Angustias could not have told her about the
past, what Olvido asked her to do. If she had, Felicitas wouldn't be able
to look at Olvido in the eye, would she? Mindlessly, she picks at a leaf of
the devil's ivy sitting beside her.

She hates me.

She hates me not.

chapter 4

Angustias

Angustias has not been back in Texas in a little over nine years. She hates to admit it, but she missed the state. She never thought she would be one of those people who misses a state. A state is nothing but lines on a map. Land is land and people are people and buildings are buildings no matter where you are. She would know. She's been everywhere. Seeing the "Welcome to Texas" sign, however, makes Angustias's heart skip a beat, literally.

Angustias stays mum as she cannot discern whether this jolt is good or bad. Since the moment she realized she was pregnant, Angustias began to worry more often. Are the baby's kicks a sign of happiness or discomfort? Is the blood in her urine normal or is the baby dead? Why is she getting so many nosebleeds? Is she dying? She can't die. If she dies, the baby could die, too.

It's a good heart skip, Angustias decides, as she lets out an irrepressible squeal of joy when they stop for dinner. There is one place that she can't deny she's missed.

"It's okay, I guess," Felicitas says as she puts down her burger on the yellow wrapper that serves as her plate.

"Felicitas Graciela Olivares, I will disown you and abandon you right here in this Whataburger if you say that again. We're in Texas now, you must respect its national treasures." Angustias reaches over and drags the yellow paper with the rest of Felicitas's fries toward her. In exchange, she pushes her milkshake across the table.

"It's not a national treasure if it doesn't pertain to the nation. And you can't abandon me here because someone will call child services and you'll go to jail, and I don't have money to bail you out."

"Pertain? Bail? Big words!" Angustias mocks even though she feels a little jolt of pride at hearing Felicitas's advanced vocabulary, but with it comes concern. It is a foreign, unpleasant feeling that has not loosened its grip on her gut all night.

Angustias pops a fry into her mouth and feels a burst of cold oil. It tastes disgusting. Angustias doesn't blame her beloved fries for her vanished appetite. It's her stomach. It's full. Angustias finished almost all of her and her daughter's orders, but her hands can't stop shoving food in her mouth. They know what she needs. If they stop, her mouth will not be able to avoid Felicitas's questions, neither the frivolous ones nor the ones about Olvido. Felicitas doesn't mean to upset Angustias. Her innocent curiosity is evident by the tangerine orange of her cloud, the same color that formed when she first asked why the sky was blue and why she shouldn't pronounce the *s* in *island*.

If Angustias could see her own cloud, if she even has a cloud, she is sure it would be dark brown, one shade lighter than her hair. It probably started out light when they walked in the restaurant, the color of coffee with four tablespoons of powdered creamer, but every question has sucked the creamer out spoonful by spoonful. So far, Felicitas has asked:

1. *What was Olvido like?* Strict. *I know that, but what else?* Grumpy.
2. *What did she do for fun?* Mmm, she liked to play damas chinas, but I thought it was a boring game, so we didn't play often. *What else?* Uh. Oh! She loved taking care of her plants.
3. *Why did she move out of the Valley?* She never told me. *Did you ask?* Yes, but she changed the subject.
4. *What did you love about her?* She was my mom, duh. *But what else?* Are you going to eat that?
5. *Is Grace in the Valley?*

Angustias sighs with relief. There is no trace of Olvido in the last question. "No," she says. "Not even close. It's relatively close to the border, but further north along the river. See?" Angustias's cell phone displays a map. She zooms in until the destination's name takes up half the screen. Felicitas moves the map around with her finger. The word "Grace" lies on the corner of two intersecting blue lines. One line reads Rio Grande River and the other reads—

"Devils River! Cool!"

Confused, Angustias takes back her phone and moves the map around. "That's so strange. I didn't even know that existed. Of course, you think that's cool," she says, rolling her eyes.

"Of course, you didn't know it existed. Have you never checked where she lived?"

"Hmm, it's pretty ironic," Angustias says, ignoring Felicitas's comment, "that your grandma chose to live near a river with a name like that." She looks up from her phone, one eyebrow raised. "Do you know what *ironic* means?"

It is Felicitas who rolls her eyes this time. "Yes, mother. I heard the Alanis Morrison song loud and clear the five times you sang it in the car. Off-key, by the way. Why is it ironic?"

"Morissette," Angustias corrects. "Your grandma was very religious, very Catholic. Every time she saw something she disapproved of, she would say, '¡Esas son cosas del diablo!' That's the devil's work."

Felicitas throws her arms up in the air and slides down her seat. "You don't have to repeat things for me in English! I understand and speak Spanish just as well as you."

"Okay," Angustias says, throwing her arms up in surrender even though Felicitas is mistaken. Her Spanish is quite good. She can understand it and speak it, and she can read and write basic sentences, but she does not do any of this perfectly. She misgenders certain nouns, places emphasis on the wrong syllables, and accidentally uses similar-sounding English and Spanish words with vastly different meanings.

Angustias is perfectly content with her daughter's level of Spanish. It's outstanding considering the fact that Angustias doesn't speak to her in Spanish every second of the day. "It's okay to make mistakes," she once said to Felicitas after she suggested they vacuum the carpet and Angustias explained that *carpeta* meant *folder*. *Carpet* was *alfombra*. "You're learning and that's all that matters."

An angry crimson border appeared on Felicitas's burgundy cloud of frustration. Felicitas doesn't like not knowing things. So, instead of constantly correcting her, Angustias now repeats phrases in English and in Spanish. According to the internet, Felicitas's brain will naturally notice patterns and absorb appropriate translations.

Olvido did not employ this teaching method on Angustias. She was an avid fan of pointing out mistakes. "What do you mean 'te quiero bien mucho'?" Olvido said when Angustias tried to tell her that she loved her very much. "'Te quiero mucho.' That's it. 'Bien mucho' is what Mexicans here say." She signed air quotes around the word *Mexicans*.

Angustias wanted to point out that she was a Mexican "from here," which meant that it was acceptable for her to say "bien mucho," but she did not because when Olvido told her, "Te quiero mucho," she was correcting her, not saying that she loved her back.

Eventually, Olvido told her "Te quiero muchísimo," and Angustias understood that *muchísimo* meant very much, but somehow the translation of "Thank you very much" was "muchísimas gracias" and not "gracias muchísimo." Spanish, like Olvido, was difficult to understand.

"Felicitas," Angustias says, and points to her own forehead to remind her to unknit her brow.

Felicitas doesn't follow her advice. Instead, she grows quiet. When Felicitas speaks again, she doesn't look Angustias in the eye. "Was I 'una cosa del diablo'?"

Angustias jumps back in her seat. The lines on her face mirror Felicitas's. "What? Of course not!"

"Then how come she never visited us, and how come she never invited us to visit her? And it always seemed like she didn't want to talk to me whenever she called. If she wasn't angry at you anymore for having me, how come she still hated me?"

"She did not hate you," Angustias says, wagging her finger. "And she was still angry at me, but it was not your fault. She only called from time to time because completely abandoning your child is—"

"'Cosas del diablo,'" Felicitas concludes with narrowed eyes and pursed lips.

Angustias mindlessly reaches for the wrapper in front of her. She looks at the window to avoid staring at the slate-colored cloud over Felicitas's head, but its reflection forces her to see her deepest fear. She shuts her eyes tight. Her fingertips feel nothing but greasy paper. Panicked, Angustias looks down and sees she has no more fries that can save her from further questioning, not just from her daughter but from herself. Was Angustias una cosa del diablo? Angustias cannot ask her mother about it now, but if she could, she is sure Olvido would say, "Yes."

It doesn't matter. Angustias can live with her mother's negative perception of her. The coldness will roll off of her like the snow that melts with the arrival of spring, but Felicitas already lives in a perpetual winter. Olvido's disdain, the frozen chip on her shoulder that she carried to the grave, will give Felicitas's heart frostbite. Felicitas can survive a suspicion, but not a confirmation. She is just a child.

But Olvido is dead, and Felicitas is safe from the truth, and Angustias is safe as well since it appears her daughter is not going to continue the interrogation. Angustias taps Felicitas's hand and joyfully announces that it is time to hit the road again.

Felicitas remains quiet the entire walk back to the car. The crackling of the restaurant's faulty neon sign fills the space between them. Although silence is typical for Felicitas, Angustias can tell this was not the casual type. Her daughter's face doesn't hold its usual frown, but there is tension in her jaw and cheeks as if she's holding in a secret or a scream. She's not angry, though. There's no crimson in her cloud.

"Hey," Angustias says in an attempt to distract Felicitas from whatever it is that is bothering her. "Since Grace is a border town, most people will speak Spanish, which means we can't use it to talk about people behind their backs, but—"

"Other kids won't call me Felicity?" Felicitas says, lethargically opening the car door and stepping inside.

"Exactly!" Angustias beams as she turns on the ignition and backs out of the parking lot. "And people won't call me Angie."

"Or Angus."

"Or Angus Beef." Angustias's "moo" fails to make her daughter laugh.

Felicitas appears to consider her mother's comment and sinks further into her seat. Her cloud is slightly bluer than it was inside the restaurant, but still in the family of grays. "It doesn't matter. They'll make fun of me for other things. They always do. Besides, we're not staying there, right?"

"Right. But maybe, we can go to the Valley afterward. Settle down there? Maybe forever?" Angustias drags out the last word and spreads her hands out across the air in the shape of a rainbow. Unamused by the theatrics, Felicitas turns and stares out the window, letting Angustias's *forever* linger in the air.

chapter 5

Felicitas

Felicitas knows that forever is unquantifiable, and unquantifiable things don't exist.

The weak foundation of her mother's promise is obvious despite the honesty and hope in her voice. They have moved nine times in Felicitas's ten years of life, twice without warning. It will take divine intervention to get her mother to stay put, but considering how terrible the previous nine places were, she isn't sure she actually wants such an intervention to occur. She begged Angustias to stop moving the summer they lived in New Mexico, before school started and she realized she lacked the friend-making skills that all kids seemed to possess.

"Fine, we may move to a different state," she said two weeks into sitting alone during lunch and recesses.

"When did I say we were moving?" her mother asked.

"You didn't, but you will. Soon."

One month later, they packed their suitcases and headed to Wyoming where Felicitas spent her lunch and recess periods hidden in the book stacks of the school library.

Angustias always manages to fit in easily. Within a few days of moving, she receives invitations for various parties and a couple of dates, and she joins their neighbors' book clubs, cooking clubs, and knitting clubs, despite not enjoying any of those activities. Felicitas, on the other hand, never makes friends, not even the kind who you do not see after school but sit next to everyday at lunch. There's always something about her that her classmates can laugh at: her name, her clothes, her tendency to use certain Spanish words that cannot be translated to English.

"I . . . I . . . Me empalagué," she said to Mrs. Cox when she insisted Felicitas finish her slice of end-of-year party cake.

"Mindy's mom bought that cake for the class," Mrs. Cox argued. "It's rude to throw away food other people spent money on."

"But, ¡me empalagué!" Felicitas insisted, not knowing how to say that her taste buds had had enough and were begging her to stop coating them in sugar.

"I don't know what that means," Mrs. Cox said. "Speak English."

"It's too sweet," Felicitas finally said. She could tell by Mrs. Cox's tight lips that the translation had failed to convey what she truly felt. She didn't mean to criticize the cake. She wanted to criticize herself and her weak sweet tooth.

"Next time, you can buy a cake for yourself," Mindy hissed. "Oh, wait. You can't. You're poor."

Felicitas finished her slice of cake in silence as her classmates snickered around her, occasionally chanting deliberately bad pronunciations of "me empalagué."

Angustias tells her that mockery is a sign of jealousy, but Felicitas knows there's nothing to be jealous about. It's simply fun to bond over a shared hatred of someone else. Even when there are other children in school who are exactly like Felicitas—weirder, if you ask her—they are fortunate enough to have their New Kid status dethroned by her arrival.

If there is anyone who is jealous, it is Felicitas. She is jealous of her mother's ability to not worry, of the ways things inexplicably work out for her, of how everyone instantly likes her. Most of all, she's jealous that Angustias is an adult who doesn't have to follow her mother's orders.

Felicitas promises herself to never make any of the exasperating decisions Angustias has made so far. She will not run away. She will not act on her feelings, especially those that come in waves.

Stay.

Leave.

Stay.

They're just feelings. Felicitas knows they'll pass like the raindrops that soften toward the end of a storm. She thinks they will, at least. She's never remained in one place long enough to determine if a rippling of emotions can come to an end. But it must, otherwise everyone would be either miserably living in one place or happily bouncing around like Angustias, and no one Felicitas has met has looked as miserably stagnant as herself or as happily mobile as her mother.

"Which of these towns sound better for our next home? McAllen? Brownsville? Weslaco?"

Felicitas doesn't comment on her mother's proposition and instead covers her ears by folding her pillow around her head. Closing her eyes won't trick her mother into thinking she is asleep, but it will signal that she wants to end the conversation. Angustias respects these signals eighty-five percent of the time.

Olvido, who quietly sat in the backseat throughout their conversation, doesn't take the hint. Unaware of the social rules this particular Olivares duo has formed without her, she pokes her head out from behind Felicitas's seat, and says, "What does she think she's going to do in the Valley? Does she even have money to get you all the way there? How much do these secretary jobs pay? Does she have money right now? Ask her."

Felicitas presses the pillow around her ears and shuts her eyes tighter.

"Go on," Olvido insists. "Ask her! You cannot just let your mother run around carelessly. What if you have no more money for food or you run out of gas? You have to make sure you at least make it to Grace. Ask!"

Felicitas shakes her head slightly enough for her mother to not see. It appears her grandmother does not see the gesture either. *Maybe she's blind*, Felicitas reasons, choosing to be the bigger person and give her grandmother the benefit of the doubt. *Maybe she needed to get glasses before she died.*

Angustias's purse falls over from the car's center console and spills its contents into Felicitas's lap. Among the pens, notepads, tampons, and an absurd number of receipts is a flat wallet with a small amount of cash and two credit cards. Felicitas frowns at her grandmother. Olvido frowns back and points at the items in her lap.

Do it, she mouths. *Now.*

"How much money do we have left?" Felicitas sighs as she holds up the wallet.

"Don't worry about that." Angustias tries to snatch the wallet, but Felicitas draws it back.

Olvido scoffs. "Pues alguien tiene que preocuparse."

"Well, someone has to worry about it," Felicitas echoes as she reorganizes her mother's purse.

Angustias laughs but there's no joy in the sound. "You sound like my mom."

"Well, maybe you should have listened to her because I'm tired of it!" Felicitas snaps. She clicks off her seat belt and climbs into the backseat, leading Olvido to move forward in the process. Pushing the too-heavy suitcases aside, she makes space for herself beside Pepe and plops down.

"Tired of what?" Angustias asks her daughter's reflection in the rearview mirror. "Hello? Felicitas? Tired of what?" Felicitas frowns at her mother's reflection and throws her blanket over her head like a vampire using its cape to disappear into the night. Beneath the cover, Felicitas can still feel her mother and grandmother's irritating concern. It is uncomfortably hot, like standing near a stove with boiling broth on a warm summer day. What is supposed to be a sign of love and care is simply bothersome.

Because she can't scream in frustration, Felicitas does the next best thing. She cries silently over the dying devil's ivy until she falls asleep. By the time they arrive in Grace and Felicitas awakens, the plant has grown three inches.

chapter 6

Olvido

Olvido moved out of the Valley five years after Angustias's departure. She woke up one morning with a familiar emotion in her heart, an urge to escape, but fused to it was a less familiar feeling: libertad.

Olvido opened her eyes at six in the morning and laid in bed staring at the ceiling 'til eight. She turned on her side at nine and laid facedown 'til ten. Then, at eleven, the corners of her lips turned up ever so slightly to create the saddest of smiles. She could finally run away. There were no responsibilities holding her back. She had gotten fired from Sunrise Diner the night before for no reason other than being considered old.

"I'm sixty-two, not ninety," Olvido had argued to the new manager. "My mind works better than yours, and look, my hands don't tremble at all. I can carry the trays just as well as I did twenty years ago. Better, actually."

The new manager, a kid straight out of high school, nephew of the owner, refused to hear her out. Olvido's age was a liability, and it didn't fit with the modern, hip look he envisioned for the restaurant.

"Hip? Modern?" Olvido had screamed in his office. "The customers here are closer to death than the Devil."

"And that is why we needed to make changes," the manager had argued. Who would dine at the restaurant once the regulars were gone?

Olvido didn't pack her belongings. She didn't expect to be gone for too long. She just needed to get away for a moment; a long moment but a moment, nonetheless. She could only drive west. If she drove east, she would hit the ocean within an hour and that was not enough time. If she drove south, she would hit the Mexican border within fifteen minutes. If she drove north, she would hit a customs checkpoint within an hour, and Border Patrol would ask for her driver's license. She could lie and say she's a tourist, but she wouldn't have proof, and they would question her until she broke down and—

Olvido drove west. She ran out of gas when she reached Grace. Don Tiberio found her on the side of the road, patiently waiting for no one in particular. She sat on the edge of her pickup truck's box, back hunched, feet swinging, a lit cigarette between her fingers. She hadn't called for help, but she wasn't avoiding it either.

"Excuse me! Ma'am! Do you need help?" Don Tiberio shouted, poking his head out the window of his truck.

Olvido turned to him and shrugged.

"Are you lost?"

Olvido shrugged.

"Is there a problem with the truck or did you just run out of gas?"

"Gas," Olvido shouted back, her voice weak and raspy from thirst.

"Okay. We can help. There's a gas station about two miles that way. Would you like to wait here or come with us?"

Olvido shrugged.

Don Tiberio nodded, stepped out of his truck, walked around to the passenger side and held the door open for Olvido. Olvido threw her cigarette on the ground, dragged her feet along the dirt road, and thanked Don Tiberio before pulling herself up.

A young boy about Felicitas's age who was sitting in the middle of the bench seat looked up at her. He scrunched his nose with disgust. "What's wrong with your face?" he asked.

Olvido turned to him and jumped back, feigning surprise. "What's wrong with yours?"

The boy frowned. "Nothing's wrong with my face."

"Are you sure about that?" Olvido taunted.

"Dad!" the boy shouted.

"Mike, stop screaming."

Olvido stayed at the motel in Las Flores that night. She didn't feel the need to keep driving west anymore, but by the time she filled up her truck's tank, it had gotten too dark to drive back. She returned to Grace the next morning to attend Sunday service with Don Tiberio and his wife. There, she met Mrs. Cecilia, who insisted on having Olvido over for dinner.

"Stay," Mrs. Cecilia suggested over dessert.

"I already paid the motel for the night," Olvido said, taking a bite of Mrs. Cecilia's flan.

"No," Mrs. Cecilia laughed. "Stay aquí en Grace."

Olvido shook her head. "There are no motels here."

Mrs. Cecilia rolled her eyes. "¡Ay! You are so dense. Stay in Grace, ¡permanentemente!" she said, shouting the last word.

Olvido frowned. "Why would I do that?"

"¿Por qué no? You don't have anywhere else to be. You're not needed anywhere," Mrs. Cecilia said matter-of-factly.

Indignant, Olvido shoved a loose strand of hair behind her ear. "I'm not needed here either," she pointed out and stuffed her mouth with more flan.

Mrs. Cecilia wagged her finger at her. "That is not true. Grace always needs good people. And you, corazón, are good people."

Olvido laughed dryly. "How would you know?"

"I saw you take money from the ofrenda basket this morning," Mrs. Cecilia said. Olvido's fork froze mid-cut. Her shoulders tensed. "And you gave it to Mike."

Olvido looked down at her hands. Her fingers played with the corner of her blouse. "He wanted ice cream," she explained, unable to look at Mrs. Cecilia. "His parents refused."

"I know," Mrs. Cecilia said. "That boy is always hungry. He's growing too quickly. Little brat."

"You don't think that was wrong?" Olvido asked, glancing up with fearful eyes. "I stole from God."

"Ay," Mrs. Cecilia scoffed, swatting away Olvido's assumption. "God doesn't need that money. He's God! You think God put riches on this Earth just so He can have something shiny to look at? No! That's what the universe, with all its pretty little stars and planets, is for. Money is for *us* to use. *We* are his real treasures."

Olvido pressed her lips together to hold back a torrent of tears, but they burst out of her like a gusher. *Just as if I'd made this myself,* she thought. "I'm sorry," she said as her cries turned into deep sobs. "I'm sorry."

Mrs. Cecilia knew the apology was not meant for her. "So?" she asked.

With puffy eyes and tear-streaked cheeks, Olvido nodded. She would stay.

"Not just for the end of the summer, though," Mrs. Cecilia pushed. "Para siempre."

Olvido nodded again, but she did not mean it. Forever was too immense to visualize. If she did not stay in her hometown nor her first home-away-from-home forever, how could she possibly live in Grace until the end of her days?

"Dios dirá," Olvido said, and this was not a lie. God did have the final say. It was He who chose to end her journey in Grace, a place with kind, considerate, and generous neighbors, devout believers. Although, it would have been more convenient to have her die in Mexico. Getting her granddaughter to voice her wish will not be simple. Felicitas keeps putting barriers between them, an excuse about needing to go to school, refusing to look at her, a literal blanket.

"Felicitas," Angustias whispers. "Wake up. We're here."

Through the front windshield, Olvido can see her house waving hello with the blowing branches of its only surviving tree, a short mesquite with dry leaves and a bent trunk. Bigger and bigger it grows, until it seems to stand in front of her with open arms, waiting for a hug. Only Olvido can see it in the darkness. Angustias is distracted by the beautiful, lit house across the road.

Olvido snaps her fingers to get her daughter's attention, but only her granddaughter turns, giving her a glare as fierce as only Olvido can make. This resentment, wherever it is stemming from, cannot last forever. Olvido will eventually go home, to her real home. Dios lo permita, hopefully sooner than later.

chapter 7

Angustias

Angustias's favorite part of moving is the drive. The highways that connect cities and states take her through the most deserted parts of the country. Without tall buildings and blinding city lights, the sky can bare its beauty. At first, it is vast, then endless. Earth's curve is almost visible. If she drives a bit further, the car will lift off and carry them into outer space. Then, without fail, red brake lights and white headlights extinguish the fantasy.

The limitless sky returns when Angustias draws near to the address her mother's neighbor gave her. There are no cars or businesses, just one small house hidden in the darkness of the night and a large, bright house that at first glance looks like a mansion. Compared to the shoebox apartments they've lived in and—

"Hi! I'm Samara!" a woman yells into Angustias's window. Angustias jumps and accidentally presses the car's horn. "You must be Angustias, and you must be Felicitas! Welcome, welcome!" Samara wiggles her perfectly manicured fingers at a groggy Felicitas. She runs around to the left side of the car, opens the door, and begins to take out their luggage. A mix of colors looms over her head. An excited and curious salmon pink. A tired baby blue. And deep gray. For mourning.

Angustias looks at her own cloudless head in the rearview mirror. With a sigh, she opens the door but is only able to take one step out of the car before she's attacked with a kiss and a hug. Despite how bony Samara is, her embrace is warm and comforting.

"I'm so glad you made it home safely. Was there a problem getting here? I know we're not on any physical maps, and I don't remember how we look on those satellite ones," Samara says.

"No, there was no problem," Angustias says, attempting to pull back. "Um, are you the person I spoke to on the phone?" She shifts her weight from one leg to the other. Her nails drum against the faux leather flap of her purse.

"Yes! That's me. I'm so sorry the call was so short, and I'm so sorry about your mother." Samara hugs her again, this time with less enthusiasm.

"Uh, that's okay," Angustias says when she's been released and quickly realizes how her words sound. "I didn't mean—I meant—Uh, is this my mom's house?" She glances over Samara's shoulder to gain a better view of the picture-perfect residence behind her, the kind of house that appears at the end of those remodeling shows Angustias is obsessed with, the kind she dreams they'll be able to afford one day. Even in the darkness of the night, it's easy to detect its beauty. White brick, black shutters, a bright red door, and a dark wood porch. The lawn is just as perfect. Grass that is even in hue and length, flowers of all kinds and colors, each in its own section, symmetrical on both sides of a stone pathway that lead up to the porch.

The contrasting door brings back a memory. They were living in Missouri in a small apartment complex with very strict rules that Angustias didn't bother to read. One day she came home with a bucket of orange paint and two fat paint brushes. She told Felicitas she'd always wanted a colorful front door so that when she came home from a long, difficult day, she could be greeted by the happiness of color and not the drabness of a beige block of wood. "Yellow says 'Welcome!'" Angustias explained to Felicitas. "Color says, 'Here, you can have fun!'"

She'd stopped by the hardware store to pick up some hinges for a cabinet she needed to fix and saw that the paint was on sale. "It's a sign from the universe!" Angustias shouted and proceeded to change herself and Felicitas into clothes that they could ruin.

Painting the door took them all night. They fell asleep, cheeks pressed against stained hands. The next morning, they woke up to the hilarious sight of stubborn, yellow streaks on their faces and a less hilarious note from their landlord taped to the door. They were fined for destroying property and lost half of Angustias's monthly paycheck. Displeased, Angustias thought it would be best to move to a cheaper apartment and then decided they should move to a whole new town while they were at it since they had taken the trouble to pack all their belongings. They never painted an apartment door again.

"Oh, no," Samara laughs. "This is my house. I wanted you to arrive here first so I could give you the key to Olvido's house and show you how to get in. La puerta tiene maña. You have to jiggle the key a certain way to get it to open. Her house is right across the street from mine. See!" she says, pointing beyond the car.

Felicitas and Angustias turn to find a much smaller, blander house. Brown and beige brick, brown roof, brown and yellow grass surrounded by a chain-link fence.

Angustias gasps and reaches for Felicitas's hand. "She built it to look just like the one I grew up in?" Her eyes survey the scene in front of her, searching for an explanation. She never imagined Olvido loved her house so much she would want to reconstruct it down to its most minute detail. The lights are off, but with the moonlight and a bit of memory, she can visualize the house's defining characteristics. On the bottom right of the front door is a smear of blue paint. Even at five years old, Angustias was obsessed with the idea of having a colorful door, but she only had five bottles of different shades of blue nail polish to work with, and she only reached a certain height.

To the left of the door is a window covered in bubble wrap and tape. Angustias broke it after she got into a fight with Felicitas's father. She threw her hair straightener at it in the hope that the neighbors would hear the shatter and run in to help.

Outside of the fence is the mailbox, still dented on its side. Angustias crashed into it as she backed out of the driveway one last time before she left home with a suitcase in the trunk and Felicitas strapped into her baby car seat.

"No," Samara says with a smile "It *is* the house."

Angustias's gaze leaves the house for a second to look at Samara, to ask her if she has lost her mind, but instead she says, "Excuse me?"

"It's the same house. When she brought her belongings, the house came, too. One cannot just abandon their home, can they?"

Angustias smiles tightly. She really hopes that Samara's question is rhetorical. "How did she move—" Angustias's inquiry is interrupted by an irrepressible long yawn. She places her hand over her mouth as if she can push the yawn back into the pit of her stomach, but it stretches further like a decade's worth of yawns are simultaneously making their escape.

"Oh, you must be so tired!" Samara says after she finishes yawning herself. "Here, I'll open the door for you." Samara steps forward, and Felicitas attempts to follow, but Angustias holds her back. The phone call with Samara was short, but Angustias remembers everything that was said, including the fact that her mother died at home, apparently the same home Angustias grew up in, the home that still carries millions of wonderful memories and an equal number of painful ones. Her head hurts, and Angustias fears the pain will never subside.

"Actually, I was thinking we could stay at a hotel," Angustias says.

Samara wags her finger. "Oh, nonsense! You wouldn't be comfortable there. Besides, we don't have one."

"You don't—What? There's . . . there's no hotel in this town?"

Samara shakes her head, still beaming her polite smile. "No."

"No motel or Airbnb?"

"No," Samara repeats. "The town's too small. No one comes here unless they know someone or they're just passing through to get gas."

"There's a mall but no motel?" Angustias questions.

"In Las Flores. It's the town right next to ours, thirty minutes north."

Unbelievable, Angustias wants to say, but it isn't. From where they're standing, she can discern that the town is quite empty. Samara's and Olvido's houses are the only structures they can see for miles. Everything but the land where the houses rest and the small patch of green that surrounds Samara's home is dry, yellow grass. Even the dirt road that divides the two neighboring houses is infiltrated by some patches of yellow weeds.

"Well, if that town is big enough to have a mall, it must have a hotel, right? We can stay there," Angustias suggests.

"Nonsense! It's close enough, but it's so late, and you're so sleepy. Listen, if you truly can't stay at your mom's place, you can stay with us."

"No!" Felicitas shouts. Angustias stares at her, perplexed. "I mean, I don't want to bother you—"

"You wouldn't!" Samara says, dismissing the idea with a wave of her hand. She picks up Felicitas's suitcase with her free hand before Angustias can protest again. "There's only a few hours left until sunrise, so you'll barely be here."

"Well," Angustias says, hesitation slowly leaving her voice. "I guess if you put it like that."

"Wait," Felicitas says. She pulls on the back of Angustias's shirt and beckons for her to move closer. Angustias obeys. "I think we should stay at Grandma's house," Felicitas whispers.

Angustias glances up at Olvido's house and shakes her head.

"Yes, we have to," Felicitas insists. "We need to sort through her things."

"No," Angustias whispers back. "We can do that later. I'm tired. It's three in the morning."

Felicitas sighs and frowns as if she wants to agree, but she continues to fight. She moves Angustias by her arms so that they're huddled like football players discussing their next play. "El muerto y arrimado, a los tres días apestan," she says.

Angustias stands, looks back at the house and then her daughter. "Who taught you that?"

"I read it somewhere. It doesn't matter. You understand, right?"

Angustias pouts and nods. She feels Felicitas's fingers intertwine with her own. "You want to learn another saying?" she says. Felicitas squeezes her hand to indicate that she does. "When I left the house, your grandma estaba como agua para chocolate."

Felicitas narrows her eyes. "She was like water for chocolate?"

"Yes. Do you know what that means?"

"That she was sweet?" Felicitas guesses.

"It means she was really, really mad," Angustias explains. "Boiling mad." Felicitas stares blankly at Angustias. "To make hot chocolate, the water has to be boiling," Angustias clarifies.

"Oh," Felicitas says. "Who uses water to make hot chocolate? Doesn't it taste better with milk?"

"Some people don't have money for milk."

"Oh."

"I was also really, really mad," Angustias admits, remembering how certain she was that her invisible cloud was a rich shade of scarlet, darker than Olvido's. "That's how we last saw each other."

"But it's not how you last talked to each other," Felicitas points out. "And it's not how you two remember each other."

"Well, how I remember her, at least. I don't know how she remembered me."

"Right." Felicitas frowns. "Well, if she was mad, she's not here to yell at you anymore. There's nothing in that house to be scared of, and if there is, I'll scare it away first."

"You are kind of scary," Angustias teases. Felicitas lifts her chin up proudly.

Angustias squeezes Felicitas's hand and informs Samara that they will be needing the keys to Olvido's house. Samara smiles and nods.

They cross the dirt street, walk through the metal chain-link fence, and up the stone path in the front yard and the two steps of the front porch. It's an arduous journey for Angustias, but she manages to keep a straight face by entering a staring match with Olvido's house. She dares the windows' dusty curtains to blink first. Move, rustle, swing. Show me that death and stillness aren't all that's left.

There's movement in the house, but it's a scene that plays out only for her eyes. The window shatters. The door slams. Her car speeds away.

Angustias shuts her eyes tight.

"The trick is," Samara says once they are gathered around the front door. "You twist the knob to the left as you move the key to the right."

How long did she deal with this problem? Angustias thinks. *How many things are broken in this house? Why did she never fix them?*

"And you have to pull the knob toward you the entire time. Like this." The door opens wide, and Samara steps aside. She moves her arm up and down the door frame as if displaying an exquisite work of art, but what Angustias sees holds no appeal.

Felicitas steps inside. Angustias does not.

"Mamá," Felicitas says, extending her hand toward her. With a deep breath, Angustias takes her daughter's hand and steps through the front door.

chapter 8

Felicitas

Felicitas has always wondered what her mother's childhood home looks like. In tales of her youth, Angustias described the kitchen where Olvido made buñuelos for Christmas Eve, and the living room where she watched bad reality TV marathons on Saturday afternoons, and the bedroom she locked herself in for hours after a fight with Olvido.

Descriptions were not enough. Olvido's house looks nothing like Felicitas expected. She imagined an old lady's house with knitted tablecloths on every piece of furniture and antique figurines on every surface. She imagined embroidered pillows and arrangements of artificial flowers. She imagined the smell of cinnamon and perfume. She imagined a house fit for a storybook.

But Olvido's house is only old in its wear, not its style. This, she should have expected because Olvido was, in fact, not very old. Sure, she had a few wrinkles here and there, and she had let her white hair grow out, but she was not "more wrinkly than a dried prune" as Felicitas had said the day before. She was only sixty-two at the time of her death, not as old as eighty-nine-year-old Mrs. Reed, who needed dentures to chew her food, or seventy-three-year-old Mr. Kelley, who only had a few white hairs left on his shiny head.

"I'll come by in a couple of hours to bring you two breakfast," Samara says, putting a hand on Angustias's shoulder.

"Oh, no. That's okay," Angustias says with a grateful smile. "We'll probably be asleep until lunchtime."

"Okay! I'll come by with lunch then."

"No, thank you," Angustias maintains. "How about we walk over to your place for dinner?"

"Wonderful! We usually eat at six but come by whenever you're hungry. Should I help you to get settled—"

"No," Angustias says, quickly blocking Samara's path. "You must be so tired, too. Besides, I know my way around this house."

"Are you sure—"

"Yep," Angustias says. "Thank you. For everything."

Samara nods. "I'll be right next door if you need me, and don't forget about dinner."

"Are we really going over there for dinner?" Felicitas asks Angustias once the door is closed.

"We'll see," Angustias says, and shakes her head in disbelief. "It's so strange hearing English being spoken in this house."

"We can speak Spanish if you want."

Felicitas hopes her mother will reject the offer. Spanish has always been their secret language, but now, it is the opposite. If they speak Spanish, Olvido will understand what they say perfectly, and Felicitas wants to keep her conversations with Angustias to herself. She wants to keep her mom to herself.

"No. It's okay. Let's change into pajamas. It's late . . . or early. It's bedtime."

"Where's the bathroom?"

"First door on the left," Angustias says. "But let's make a deal right now. No going into any of the bedrooms yet, all right?"

Felicitas frowns. "Then where are we going to sleep?" she asks.

"The living room." Angustias yawns either to end the conversation or because she's truly tired. Felicitas doesn't put up a fight. She's fought enough in the last twenty-four hours. They should have just slept over at Samara's.

The Olivares girls quietly change into their pajamas, a pair of equally distressed oversize T-shirts and basketball shorts with waistbands that don't stretch properly anymore. They brush their teeth, crawl onto separate sofas, and close their eyes, but despite their exhaustion, neither one falls asleep. Felicitas can feel her grandmother's eyes on her, ready to pounce on her like a tiger as soon as Angustias falls deep into slumber.

A whimper forces Felicitas's eyes to open. She rolls over and finds Angustias staring at the ceiling. Silent tears run down her face and fall to her ears. Her bottom lip quivers, and her shoulders shake every which way.

There's no need to ask what's wrong. Felicitas walks across the living room, lays beside her mother, and rests her arm around her waist. The touch unleashes Angustias's cries. Angustias slaps her hand over her mouth to muffle them, but it's an unfair fight.

"I didn't even wear black today," Angustias whispers between sobs.

Felicitas pats her mother's arm. "You can wear black tomorrow."

They remain embraced until Angustias falls asleep. The tears drying on her cheeks reflect the moonlight as it slips through the window's blinds. A hand reaches out to touch them.

Felicitas jerks her hand forward to slap it away before it makes contact, but the outstretched palm is too quick for her. "Did you just hit me?" Olvido asks, incredulous.

Felicitas glowers at her grandmother. "I didn't touch you." She moves over to her own couch and throws a blanket over her face.

"Do not fall asleep now," Olvido exclaims. "You've slept plenty."

But Felicitas feels as if she hasn't slept since the day she was born. She wishes Olvido could go to sleep, eternally, forever, because forever is unquantifiable, and unquantifiable things should not exist.

Yet, they do. There she is, calling her name. It's inexplicable, like how Felicitas can see people that should not be seen and how she misses the warmth of someone who never gave her anything but frost.

chapter 9

Olvido

Felicitas remains motionless with her head fully covered by the blanket. Olvido attempts to peel it back and force her granddaughter to face her, but her fingers pass through the fabric as if it weren't there. It is not the comforter, Olvido knows. It's her. She's not fully there.

Olvido refuses to tell Felicitas about her tactile issues for fear of appearing weak. Children do not respect and help weak grandmothers because they have yet to develop empathy. They only understand fear, a hard hit to their bottom with a stern hand or with the sole of a shoe. Her granddaughter does not suspect that the purse that fell on her lap was not pushed by Olvido but rather toppled over by Angustias hitting a pothole. Olvido put her hand forward in an attempt to get the natural world to react to her touch. She failed, but at least she was able to put on an act.

She won't be able to pretend for long. Felicitas seems smart. She clearly inherited her genes, hopefully, not just irritability but intelligence as well.

Olvido leans forward and whispers in her ear.

"Felicitas. Felicitas. Felicitas." She does this for fifteen minutes, then worries that the sound has actually lulled the young girl to sleep, but Felicitas grudgingly sits up at the one hundred and eighty-first mention of her name. She motions for her grandmother to speak.

"You are too rude! I should not have let Angustias raise you so far away from me." Olvido realizes she has walked herself into a conversation she does not want to have, so she pushes back a strand of hair, smooths out her blouse and quickly changes the subject. "At least you wore black in my honor."

"I wear black every day. What do you want?" Felicitas whispers. Her tone is low, but the irritation rings loud and clear.

Olvido stands defiantly. "I want to know why you didn't tell your mother what I asked you to tell her. You had so many hours to do it," Olvido whispers back even though no one but her granddaughter can hear her.

"My mom doesn't know I can see spirits, and I don't want to tell her," Felicitas says. Not telling Angustias things seems perfectly reasonable to Olvido. She spent twenty-seven years not telling her daughter about her own thoughts and feelings, or secret hopes for the future, and especially not about reminders of the past, and she will not tell Felicitas things either. Olvido's past actions will float up to Heaven with her, and Felicitas will remain on Earth with a saintly image of her grandmother, as she should.

Olvido has already asked God for forgiveness. She does not need her granddaughter's pardon, just a decent enough perception so she can help Olvido convince Angustias to carry out her final wish, and perhaps to light a candle for her from time to time in case Heaven is dark and confusing during thunderstorms and hurricanes.

"Well, you have to."

"No."

"Yes." Olvido balls up her fists and tries to punish her useless palms with her sharp nails.

"No. Unless . . ." Felicitas glances at her sleeping mother and turns back to Olvido. "Do you want to talk to her? If I tell her I can see you, she'll want to communicate with you. I bet you two have so much to say to each other."

Olvido remains quiet, and Felicitas smiles presumably at her victory. What Felicitas is not aware of, however, is that the stubbornness she inherited from her mother, her mother inherited from Olvido.

Olvido has many years of experience above Felicitas when it comes to having the last word.

"Well, if you don't inform her that my body needs to be taken to Mexico, I will never cross over to Heaven, and if I don't go to Heaven..."

Felicitas clasps her hands and lifts her shoulders with joy. "You'll go to Hell?" she says.

Olvido fumes. "I will stay here."

"I'll be in Hell."

Olvido wants to call out her insolent behavior once again, but this is the exact mentality she needs Felicitas to have. She draws close to her granddaughter's face, and with the same tone she used to employ on Angustias to warn her of an impending spanking, she says, "Yes, you will be, so you better find a way to tell her and make sure I'm taken to Mexico. Do you understand?"

Felicitas huffs and rises. "Can you lift things with your ghostly hands?" she says, wiggling her fingers in front of her face.

Olvido scoffs. "Do not call them 'ghostly,' and yes, I can," but she crosses her hands in front of her instead of putting her claim into action.

Felicitas narrows her eyes and reaches for the decorative pillow beside her. "Catch," she says as she releases the pillow into the air and observes with mischievous fascination how it goes through Olvido's chest, right through her heart.

Despite the lack of pain, Olvido is horrified. "How dare you?"

"Would you like to try again?" Felicitas teases.

"What?"

Felicitas throws a second pillow. Olvido dodges it. With a naughty grin, Felicitas prances into the hallway. Olvido follows. "You lied!" Felicitas says cheerfully once they're out of Angustias's earshot. Olvido scoffs but does not try to lie again. "Well, there goes my plan."

"Which was?" Olvido says, refusing to look at her.

"For you to write my mom a letter."

Olvido rolls her eyes. "If I could do that, don't you think I would have done it without asking you for help?"

Felicitas sighs. "Do you have a pen and paper? I'll write it for you."

Olvido eyes the journal suspiciously. "I think she'll be able to tell the difference between my handwriting and that of a five-year-old."

"I'm ten."

"Your behavior says otherwise."

"I have perfect handwriting," Felicitas insists. "All my teachers say so. And I can make it look different, shaky. You're hella old, so my mom will believe you couldn't write well anymore."

Olvido's eyes narrow. "Fine. Let's try it," she says pointing toward the door to her bedroom. "If your mom doesn't believe it, it will be you who will have to figure out an explanation." Careful to avoid loud creaks, Felicitas gently opens the door. Olvido peers in with curiosity. Her bed is made. Her pillows, fluffed.

"Where?" Felicitas asks.

"Nightstand. First drawer. There are pens and paper. No, do not use that. That's my phone book."

Felicitas rolls her eyes and digs for loose sheets. "It's not like you're going to use it anymore." Using the nightstand for support, Felicitas carefully writes onto a torn envelope.

I am begging you. Please leave me alone.

Olvido leans over her and squints. The sentence is in English. "What does that say?"

Felicitas smirks. "Don't you know?" she asks innocently. Olvido knows exactly what she means. Felicitas is worse than a stranger. She is an unexplainable phenomenon. Angustias would have never dared tease Olvido over her reading skills. How could she have raised such an insolent girl?

"I don't have my reading glasses on," Olvido explains tersely.

"Shouldn't death have fixed all your medical problems?"

Olvido knew it. Felicitas has no empathy, no respect. It's too bad she can't take her shoe off and threaten Felicitas with a spanking. "I wouldn't know. This is my first time being dead," Olvido says, straightening her back. "Now focus. Here is what I want you to write."

chapter 10

Angustias

Angustias began to see people's colors on the evening of her eleventh birthday. She can't remember if there were instances before this date when colors appeared over people's heads like the halos of her mother's saints, but she's certain that on her eleventh birthday, five minutes 'til seven, when the sun began to trade places with the moon, the colors remained.

It began with her father.

Angustias's father was not a terrible person, but he wasn't a great one either. His absence and disinterest never bothered Angustias, a wonderful side effect of her cursed name. When he lied, however, Angustias couldn't help but wish she could kick him in the shins, step on his feet, and scream, "You're the most terrible person to ever be born," even though it was a lie. "Don't ever come back."

In Angustias's point of view, lies are only told to people you believe are stupid enough to believe them, and while many believed Angustias was stupid, her father should not have been one of them. Fathers are supposed to believe you can grow up to be the next president, discover a new planet or create a cure for cancer. Fathers are not supposed to expect you to believe they're going away on a business trip for a few days when you know for a fact that they don't own a business and can barely hold a part-time job for a few months at a time, so no sane businessman would ever send them away on a trip on their behalf. This is the second-to-last lie Angustias's father told her.

A cloud of rusty brown appeared at the crown of his head before the lie fully escaped his lips. Angustias didn't know what the cloud or its color meant, and she expected the enigma to roll off her like raindrops dripped off the edges of a plant's leaves. But there was something about that rust color that sparked her curiosity.

Rust is not good. Rust indicates that something is old and not taken care of. Rust is dangerous if it's on a nail, and the nail pokes the bottom of your foot, and your mother discovers that the reason why a nail was so easily able to bite through your dirt-covered skin was because you were not wearing any shoes, which she told you time and time again to never do.

"It is called tetanus," Olvido had told her while cleaning up a cut on her knee. Angustias had tripped on a cement block at the construction site behind her house. According to Olvido, the half-built building was off limits for young, barefoot girls whose names began with the letter *A*. The construction workers had not bothered putting up a sign to let people know of this rule because they trusted mothers to inform their daughters and for daughters to obey. "It's not the rust that causes it. It's the little bacteria that travels through the wound, up to your body. They row their boats up the red rivers in your veins, up and up and up, and when they reach your brain and tie their rafts to the pier where your cells work hard to tell you to breathe and move and play, BAM! You drop dead."

Angustias's bottom lip quivered as she whimpered, "I can die?"

"Well, not necessarily," Olvido admitted. "First, your body will bend in all sorts of strange ways." Olvido contorted her arms and hands and bent her spine so that her head was at an angle in which she could only peer at Angustias from the corner of her right eye. "Then it will lock, so that it stays like that forever. And you know where the problem will begin?"

"Where?"

"Your jaw. You won't be able to talk."

Angustias gasped. "I love talking."

"I know you do. And if you don't treat it, then you can die."

Angustias stared up at her mother in horror.

"So, what are you never going to do again?" Olvido asked.

"Run around barefoot," Angustias responded. This had been a lie but an acceptable one because Angustias didn't think Olvido was stupid. She simply didn't have the heart to tell her that her shoes no longer fit.

"What's wrong?" Angustias asked her father when she heard his second-to-last lie.

"What do you mean?" he responded.

"Something's . . . not right." She waved her hand at the space over his head to bid the color farewell. Her father's eyes blinked rapidly as if they couldn't stand to meet Angustias's skeptical ones for too long. Angustias leaned in. "Are you lying?" she whispered.

Angustias's father stumbled back, dizzy with booze and shock, and stuttered, "N-no." That was the last lie Angustias's received from her father. She kicked him in the left shin, stepped on his right foot, and yelled. "You're the most terrible person to ever be born! Don't ever come back!"

Angustias's father obeyed, but not because of her command. A few days prior, several gossip-loving churchgoers had informed Olvido that her husband was seen late-night drinking at Don Gregorio's bar. After a few hours, he drove off with a woman dressed in the highest of heels, the shortest of skirts, and a shirt so tight even the holiest of men could not help but stare at her, with disgust or desire, only they and God knew.

"And it was not the first time," Doña Josefa had said to Olvido. "And not the same girl." She had not bothered to whisper nor hide how the corners of her mouth twitched with amusement.

Angustias's father was allowed to visit Angustias on weekends and holidays if he asked for permission from Olvido days in advance. He visited Angustias four times the year after his final lie, twice the following year, and made one phone call two years after that. Drunk and desperate, he begged her for her birthday money, but Angustias had no money to give him because all she had received were shoes.

During the year in which the colors first appeared, Angustias made five hundred and seventy-five corrections to her cloud guide, which she drafted in the margins for her science and history textbooks. Through interactions with her mother, neighbors, teachers, classmates, supermarket workers, and the mailman, Angustias slowly deciphered the meanings of colors. She learned that navy blue and midnight blue were not the same. Salmon and bubblegum pink both signaled excitement but differed in energy levels. Brown revealed fear even though so many wonderful things were brown like coffee and cinnamon and her skin after an afternoon at the beach. Yellow always indicated joy, and different shades signified different intensities of the feeling. Most clouds were rarely a single color. Some were more opaque than others, few contained colors Angustias had never seen, and none ever appeared over her own head.

Angustias can't help noticing colors just like she can't help misconstruing their meaning. No, Felicitas's crimson was not anger over Angustias's decision to move. It must have been frustration at her inability to obtain perfect attendance, a goal she set for herself at the start of the third grade. No, Felicitas's cloud was not a melancholic slate when Angustias told her Olvido hung up before she could reach the phone. It was different, more blue than gray, more disappointment than abandonment. Felicitas can't possibly feel abandoned by her grandmother, by a person she saw for no more than a few weeks with a brain that could not retain memories and a heart that was too innocent to feel anything but love.

Luckily for everyone but Angustias, on the day after Olvido's passing, her unconscious color misidentification aids her family. When Angustias wakes and finds Felicitas with eyes wide open staring at the ceiling, she mistakes her sky blue of determination for tired baby blue. "Couldn't sleep?" she mumbles.

"I slept okay," Felicitas responds.

Angustias sighs. "I barely slept."

"Yeah, right. You snored like a bear."

"I don't snore," Angustias shrieks and throws a pillow across the room. Felicitas catches it in the air.

"Whatever. Are you hungry?" Felicitas jumps off the couch, revealing that she is already dressed. Black shorts, black tank top, black scrunchy.

Angustias rolls over, wrapping her blanket around herself, and falls to the floor. "No. I don't want to eat. I don't want to do anything," she whines. "Although, I do want coffee."

"There's none here. I checked. We can go to Mrs. Samara's house, but you'll have to change clothes or at least put on a bra."

Angustias lifts her head to look at Felicitas. "Or you could go get some for me," she says batting her eyes.

"Fine," Felicitas says, already heading toward the front door. "But you have to start cleaning while I'm gone. Maybe check the washer first."

Angustias starts with the kitchen but not until Felicitas returns with a hot cup of coffee and marmalade-cheese toast. Then, it takes her two hours of work to deem the kitchen clean, a baffling amount of time given that all nooks and crannies were spotless before their arrival. They sweep the floor, store the clean dishes in their proper place, wipe down the counters, and polish the cabinet handles. They open the pantry and check the date of every can and box. Nothing is expired. "Let's double check," Angustias says. Felicitas obeys with a frown.

Eventually, they move on to the refrigerator. Inside they discover stacks upon stacks of labeled plastic containers with names Felicitas does not recognize. Emilio. Estefanía, Salomón, Raúl, Gerónimo. Taliah.

Felicitas checks the contents through the clear bottom. "It's picadillo and rice."

"Free lunch," Angustias sings as she does a dance with her shoulders.

Felicitas smiles and nods, but her face drops quickly. A maroon red of annoyance fills her cloud. "It doesn't belong to us," she says. She places the containers back in the fridge and closes the door before Angustias can protest.

When Angustias becomes preoccupied with scrubbing the mold off the edges of the kitchen sink, Felicitas announces that she will be taking a restroom break. Angustias doesn't look up and barely mumbles an "okay," as if her brain can only focus on one task at a time.

Back.

Forth.

Her pace is quick, and her arm shakes from the force, but she could keep scrubbing forever. She could scrub until the house is nothing but a wooden skeleton and a cement base, and even then, she would not be satisfied with the lingering mold of her memories.

But the pain forces her to stop for a moment. She rests her back against the kitchen counter and lets her weight drag her down until she feels her bottom hit the cold tile. "Felicitas?" she calls out to the hallway.

"Coming!" Angustias hears her daughter respond. She sees her cloud before her face. It's a cobalt blue of concentration, the kind that appears over Felicitas's head when she's working on her math home-work or reading a mystery book with an unsolvable case.

"What were you doing in there?" Angustias asks.

Felicitas frowns. "What was I doing in the bathroom?"

"Never mind," Angustias says, holding out her hand for help. *She needs to eat more fiber*, she thinks, and adds All-Bran to her mental grocery list.

"Are we done with the kitchen?" Felicitas asks eagerly. Her face lights up when Angustias responds that they are, but dims when she hears that it is time to clean the living room.

Angustias walks cautiously out into the hallway. In its current state, the house appears as fragile as her mother's patience once was. It is dark and silent. Any movement, she suspects, will cause the windows to shatter and the walls to cave in.

This is not Angustias's house. There is no music; there are no screams, no cries. There is no smell of reheated leftovers wafting out from the kitchen or of incense dancing around the living room. This is Olvido's house, and Angustias is an intruder, and not a curious one.

While dusting the end tables, Angustias is careful not to linger too long around the photographs. Just a quick glance and she can remem-ber every detail. There's one of Angustias with streaks of chocolate cake on her clothes, mouth, and cheeks. It was her first birthday, and she was left unattended for just one second too long. Her mischievous smile insinuates that that was exactly what she wanted. There's one of Angustias's kindergarten graduation. She isn't smiling. Olvido, looking uncharacteristically proud, hugs her tightly with both arms. There is one of Angustias's quinceañera. The party was in the backyard. People sat in plastic chairs and ate off paper plates, very informal, yet Olvido insisted Angustias wear a puffy pink dress and a tiara. The dress was a loan from her second cousin Martina. The tiara was from the dollar store. Olvido and Angustias fought for three days about her outfit. Exactly one year and five months later, they were fighting about Angustias's pregnancy.

"I think it's time to go into the bedrooms," Felicitas says, slamming her duster onto the coffee table. Frustrated burgundy floats above her.

"No," Angustias says nonchalantly. "You missed a spot there."

"No," Felicitas says dragging out the word. "I think we should go into the bedrooms. We've cleaned everything but that. You can't avoid it forever."

Angustias doesn't look at her when she speaks. "What about the hallway bathroom and the backyard? Didn't you say something about the washer? And I'm not avoiding anything."

"Your bedroom or Grandma's? Those are the only two options."

"Felicitas, I said no."

Felicitas stomps her foot and crosses her arms defiantly. "Well, I said yes."

Angustias pivots toward her daughter. "Well, I said no," she snaps.

In three quick strides, Felicitas is out of the kitchen. She runs down the hallway, her dark hair flying wildly behind her like a flag crying "War!"

"Felicitas, no!" Angustias yells, but it is too late. Felicitas reaches Olvido's bedroom and leaps inside.

Angustias slowly inches toward the entrance, careful to not disturb her mother who sits on the edge of the bed, smiling as if she's been patiently waiting for her return for the last ten years. And there she is, calmly reading the Bible by the window. And brushing her hair in front of her vanity. And folding clothes on the bed. Even her cloud is there with its ever-changing borders. Pink, red, yellow, always mixed with gray.

"I read that when someone dies, you need to show the morgue their birth certificate," Felicitas says. "Where do you think it could be? Maybe the closet?"

While Felicitas digs between coats and dresses, Angustias can't help but drift around the room. There are bits of Olvido all around. She's in the hairbrush next to the mirror, the rosary hanging on the bottom edge of the glass candle, the fallen lipsticks, and the compact blush.

But Olvido is not there. If she were, she would be pointing out the million and one things Angustias has to do. "Do you have a plan? Have you not given any thought to my funeral? Oh, you're not worried? What a surprise."

Angustias moves to the nightstand and opens the top drawer. Her fingers rummage through the mess, pushing and tossing receipts and notes, broken pencils and dried pens.

"Mamá, what was that?" Felicitas leans over Angustias, takes a folded, cream-colored paper Angustias tossed to the side. "Querida Angustias, tengo el presentimiento—"

Angustias snatches the paper out of her daughter's hands. "Sorry," she says, and silently reads to herself. She doesn't notice when Felicitas leaves the room. The words in front of her devour her senses. She feels nothing but the smooth paper between her fingers, and she hears nothing but Olvido's final words.

chapter 11

Felicitas

Felicitas's experiences with letters have never been good. Letters from landlords and the government indicate trouble. *I'm raising the rent!* Letters from teachers bring about expenses. *Please have Felicitas bring cupcakes for our end-of-year party. No nuts or dairy, please.* A lack of letters on Valentine's Day publicizes her lack of friends, and a lack of letters on her birthday highlights how small her family is. Letters, like Olvido, are bothersome, so Felicitas should not be surprised that letters written by Olvido are so exasperating they can even make perpetually-cheery Angustias mad.

But she is surprised. Everything about Olvido is so new to Felicitas, her grandmother is constantly startling her.

"¡Niña!" Olvido shouts and flinches when Felicitas spits water through her face. "Something's wrong," she says, wiping away where the drops should have landed. "She threw the letter away."

Felicitas doesn't hear the last sentence. She is already running into Olvido's bedroom. "Mamá, what happened?" she asks as she walks over to Angustias, who sits beside the nightstand, the letter is no longer in her hands.

"In here," Olvido calls from a corner of the room.

Taking the letter out from the trash can, Felicitas pretends to give it a quick read for appearances and tosses it back in. "Imagine having to read it a million and one times," she wants to say, but she bites her tongue just as she did the night before.

She wrote as quickly as she was permitted by Olvido's multiple interruptions. "That's not how you spell *cieló*. That last word has an accent over the *o*. I would never cross my *T*s like that."

Felicitas pressed down on her tongue. Staying quiet increased the possibility of Olvido following suit.

"Did your mom not teach you to dot all your *I*s?"

Harder, she pressed. One more comment from Olvido and she would draw blood.

"What, you don't find my joke funny? Are you sure you're your mother's daughter?" Press down. Bury the anger.

By the time Olvido said, "Okay, I guess this will do," Felicitas could taste metal in her mouth. When she wiped away the tears brimming her eyes, Olvido didn't notice. She was too busy pointing out the missing accent in *México*.

Four times. She mentioned Mexico four times. God, three.

Dear Angustias, the letter began.

I have the feeling that I will not be here much longer. Sometimes God's signs are very direct feelings, and this is one of them. There are many things I want to say to you, but there are two that I will write in this letter, and the rest, I will tell you when we meet again in God's home.

The first thing I want to say is that I forgive you. I understand why you left, and I hope you don't feel too guilty about everything that happened. I am not angry at you for walking out. I hope you figured that out by the many phone calls I've made out to you over the years. No matter how far apart we are, no matter how little we talk or how much we fight, I will always love you. God put me on this Earth to be your mother, and that is what I will be even as I watch over you from Heaven.

The second thing is that I have a request. I need you to bury me in Mexico. Do you remember 'México lindo y querido'? Follow the lyrics. Take my body back. Matamoros would be ideal, but any place in Mexico will suffice. It's been so long since I've been home, and if I

can only make it there in death, then so be it. I know this will make it
more difficult for you to put flowers on my grave, but this will give you
a good excuse to visit Mexico. I always felt bad that you could only
visit with your aunts and uncles and never with me. By the way, the
family phone numbers are in my phone book in the bottom drawer
of my nightstand. Call everyone and inform them of my passing. If
they can't make it to the funeral, I really don't care. Just please fulfill
my wish. It's a matter of death or death. You see. You always said I
couldn't make jokes.

With immense love,
Mom

Mexico, four. God, three. Felicitas, zero.

"We need to take Grandma's body to Mexico," Felicitas says.

Angustias turns to her, perplexed. "Why?"

"Because it's what she wanted." And it is the only way Felicitas can
get rid of her.

"So?" Angustias says. "She's gone. It doesn't matter where her
body is."

Olvido gasps. "How can you say that? How can she say that? Felicitas, ask her."

"The plans are set," Angustias declares. "The funeral will be on Sunday. Samara will help me let her friends know, since she actually knew
your grandma's friends. I'll call your grandma's cousins tomorrow. The
funeral will happen, we'll leave, and that's that."

"No," Felicitas protests. "We need to take her body to Mexico. That's
that."

Angustias presses her fingertips against her temples. "Why?"

"Because—because I want to honor her," Felicitas lies. "Honor your
father and your mother. It's in the Bible, isn't it? Not honoring your parents son cosas del diablo."

Just like she was una cosa del diablo. If she hadn't been so preoccupied with burying her emotions and remaining civil, she would
have admitted that with every sentence Olvido ordered her to write,
something boiled within her heart. It was hot and icky and terrible. It

was anger and disappointment and shame. "Tell me exactly what you would have liked to say," she told her grandmother. "Exactly. It's your last chance."

Olvido is forever. Felicitas is a zero. To her grandmother, she does not exist.

"When did you read the Bible?" Angustias asks.

"We need to take her body to Mexico," Felicitas repeats with desperation.

"I have no idea how you ship a body to another country," Angustias says, shaking her head as if she can rattle out the answer like a coin from a piggy bank. "What kind of paperwork do I have to fill out? Who do I talk with to get a spot in the cemetery?"

"¡Ay, excusas!" Olvido exclaims, putting her fingertips to her forehead and rubbing her temples.

"We can google it," Felicitas suggests.

"We ran out of data getting here. And your grandma doesn't— didn't have internet."

"We'll go to Samara's," Felicitas says. "She definitely has Wi-Fi."

Angustias closes her eyes for so long, Felicitas takes it as a sign that her mother wants to drop the topic completely, but Angustias eventually rises to her feet. "Okay," she says with a sigh. "But don't get your hopes—"

A doorbell interrupts her. Even the universe knows there's no need to warn Felicitas about getting her hopes up. Such an occurrence is as rare as a girl who can see ghosts.

"Maybe that's Mrs. Samara," Felicitas says. She runs out, eager to escape the stuffy, crowded room.

"Hello!" a statuesque lady greets when Felicitas opens the front door. "I'm Taliah." The woman's curls shake with every syllable as if her body has so much energy, it must be in constant movement to release it. "You're Felicitas, right?" Felicitas nods. "That's wonderful!"

Felicitas shrugs. "It's all right."

"Oh! And you must be Angustias."

"Yes," Felicitas hears her mother say, but she doesn't turn around. She's too busy examining Taliah's denim overalls. There's splattered paint on them from the straps to the legs' hems. Some spots are traced over with marker, creating a wild mix of shapes. Flowers. Hearts. Cats and dogs.

"My name is Taliah," Taliah repeats, reaching into her oversize canvas bag. "I'm a friend of Olvido's—was. I'm so sorry for your loss." She smiles apologetically and pulls out two small metal dishes. "I brought over some Parmesan chicken and a green bean casserole for you two. Olvido used to say Americans are obsessed with casseroles and that she didn't see the appeal, but between you and me, that was before she tried mine."

"That's true," Olvido says, appearing behind her friend. "Don't be rude. Let her in."

"Would you like to come in," Angustias offers before Felicitas gets a chance. "I think we have something that's yours." Angustias rushes into the kitchen and digs around in the fridge. "Here it is. Taliah with an *H*?"

"That's me. Oh," Taliah says as Angustias places the Tupperware with her name on it in her hands. "I can't believe—I—" Taliah's sniffles grow into sobs. "I—"

"No. I cannot do this." Olvido says walking out into the hallway. "I cannot see her cry."

Felicitas does not wish sorrow upon anyone, with a few exceptions, of course. Taliah, she believes, does not deserve to be an exception. She seems kind and generous, but if her cries scare away Olvido, would it be too horrible to keep the tears flowing? Just for a little while, a few minutes, an hour at most. "Would you like to stay for lunch?" Felicitas asks.

In the time it takes Taliah to cease crying, Felicitas sets the table and reheats Taliah's casserole. Angustias stays by Taliah's side, patting and rubbing her back. She whispers "Mhm," and "I understand," and "Just let it out."

Felicitas doesn't mean to interrupt, but they're closer to dinner than lunchtime. Her stomach voices her thoughts to the room.

"Oh my," Taliah says with a laugh. "You must be hungry. I know I always am."

"Ms. Taliah," Felicitas says halfway through their meal. "Did my grandmother cook for you often?" She's genuinely curious. Olvido refused to say anything when they discovered the perplexing contents of the fridge.

"Well," Taliah says, cleaning the corners of her mouth with a napkin. "I wouldn't say often, but yes, she did cook some dishes for me when I needed them. Gorditas were my favorite. Straight off the pan? Oh, so good. Fideo, too. And you must think, 'Fideo? That's so simple. Couldn't you make it yourself?' But the way she made it, my goodness. Out of this world, really. Or should I say, Heaven-sent?" Taliah winks at Angustias. Felicitas nudges her mother to be let in on the meaning, but Angustias shrugs, confused.

"And she cooked for other people, too?" Felicitas says.

Taliah nods eagerly. "Yes, she told y'all about it? What she'd created for people here?"

"No," Felicitas says matter-of-factly.

"No?"

"No," Angustias repeats.

"Well, yes," Taliah says, with her left palm to her chest. "She cooked for some townsfolk from time to time. She could remember everyone's favorite dish off the top of her head, but you know what's funny? I can't remember hers."

"Barbacoa," Angustias says as she cuts through her chicken. "She liked to order it for Sunday breakfast. Never made it herself. 'Too difficult,' she always said. Was my mom selling food? Is that what she created, a business?"

Taliah's jaw drops, appalled by Angustias's suggestion. "Selling? No. Olvido would never charge. That woman was a saint."

Angustias rolls her eyes at Felicitas. Felicitas widens her eyes in reproach. "What do you mean it was Heaven-sent?" Felicitas persists.

"Oh, you know." Frown lines form on Taliah's forehead when she sees Angustias's blank stare. "Don't you?" she says with a hiccup.

"Uh, that . . . it was really good?" Angustias guesses and passes her a glass of water.

"Yes, just that." Taliah agrees. "It was just really good."

"And it was 'Heaven-sent' in the sense that it was free, right?"

Taliah nods. A sad smile replaces her perplexed frown. "But it was more than that, really. She would invite us over to her house, and just—" Taliah's voice cracks. "She gave us a space to speak frankly and offered patience and empathy. She never judged. She simply gave. She seemed so grateful to have us over, too. We knew she was lonely."

Felicitas stabs at her green beans. Cream bleeds through their wounds. Olvido never judged. *Stab.* Olvido was patient. *Stab.* She was lonely. *Stab. Stab.* How can Angustias speak with such confidence when she assures Felicitas that Olvido didn't hate her? If Olvido didn't judge, she wouldn't have judged Felicitas for being born at an inconvenient time. If she was patient, she wouldn't have kicked Felicitas out before she gave her a chance to grow up and prove her worth. If she was lonely, she would've called Felicitas. She would've waited until she reached the phone and begged her to visit her.

A piece of chicken flies across the kitchen when she attempts to swat her mom's hand off the space between her brows. Angustias waves her hands in front of her own face. *Remove that frown.* Felicitas imitates the gesture.

"Could you help us with something?" Angustias says, standing up and walking toward the fridge. "Do you know these people?"

"Yes," Taliah says as Angustias reads out the names on the containers. "Well, there are two Gerónimos here, but I think I know which one she was referring to. I'll let them know Olvido left something for them so they can stop by the house later. No sense in letting all that food go bad."

"Thank you," Angustias says. "And there's one more thing. Could you let people know my mother's funeral is postponed until further notice? We have something to sort out."

As she washes the dishes, Felicitas considers what drew Taliah to Olvido. She supposes opposites balance each other out. The sky is most beautiful between sunrise and sunset. The best desserts combine salty, sweet, and sour flavors. Olvido isn't entirely sour, Felicitas learns later that night. When Angustias falls asleep, Felicitas searches for Olvido around the house. She's not concerned, certainly not. She simply wonders where ghosts go to hide. She finds her grandmother sitting at the edge of the bathtub, silently crying, and swaying her head. Felicitas didn't know spirits could shed tears. She didn't know Olvido had a heart.

chapter 12

Olvido

Olvido finds it devastatingly embarrassing to cry in front of children and especially distressing in front of Felicitas. Children can perceive differences between themselves and adults. Adults are bigger and should be wiser and more responsible. When children sense that an adult is not what they should be, they feel superior and smarter, and in those unfortunate moments when they are, they are also burdened. Olvido knows from experience.

Victoria Olivares was nineteen years old when she became pregnant with Olvido. At that point in time, most women in their early twenties were already well into their second or third baby. They knew how to take care of their children and their husbands, their houses, their fields, their small businesses, and themselves. Most importantly, they knew how to be good neighbors. You can't produce milk? Don't worry, I'll give your baby breakfast, lunch, and dinner. You'll be back from work late? I'll watch your kid for you. I'm already watching six. How much trouble could one more be? Your daughter's clothes don't fit her anymore? Here take this. After my daughter, I only birthed sons. I wanted to save money and reuse her dresses, but their daddy wasn't too happy about that choice.

Olvido grew up observing her neighbors take care of their own children and herself. Each woman had a slightly different technique to get her to obey. Some would leave her to starve if she complained about the saltiness of their beans. Others would hit her with a belt if she refused to stop putting bugs in her mouth. One neighbor, Doña Ginebra, sweetly explained why it was a sin to play with saints as if they were dolls, and another neighbor smacked her in the back of the head with a Bible for eating before praying.

These observations informed Olvido when it became imperative for her to take care of her mother. She never used any of the physically painful methods, but she did mimic her neighbors' strict tone and threatening poses. She would stand in front of the doorway, feet apart, hands on her hips, and look her mother in the eye when she demanded, "Return that lottery ticket. You were supposed to buy maíz," or, "Tell Don Fabián that your game of chess was a mistake. You'll give him ten tomatoes from our garden if he returns just half of what you gave him," or, "Give that ring back to Don Pancho. He's not going to save you from debt, and I don't like the way he looks at my legs."

Olvido became a mother before she conceived a baby of her own. She vowed long before she met Angustias's father that she would do everything in her power to never let her child feel what she felt when she saw her incompetent mother stumble through the front door late at night with empty bottles and emptier pockets, but imperfection was inevitable. Olvido depended on Angustias from time to time, usually when English-language documents and new technology were involved, but Olvido refused to let her dependency become habitual. Angustias needed to worry about certain things like doing well in school and not straying from the path of the Lord but not about grown-up matters. She didn't bite her nails thinking about how they would pay their house bills. She didn't experience insomnia due to overthinking about her mother's health. She didn't develop a stomach ulcer from the worry that one day she would come home and her mother would be gone.

"Who took her?" Olvido asked Doña Ginebra about Victoria on a random Monday evening.

"The loan sharks. They came while you were at work," Doña Ginebra explained. "I won't say which ones, though. It is for your own good."

"Who took her?" Angustias would have had to ask if Olvido hadn't been careful.

"La Migra," someone would tell her. "Don't go to the police. It's for your own good."

Felicitas does not appear to worry about Angustias as much as Olvido needed to worry about Victoria, but it's enough to make Olvido shake her head in frustration. Angustias's name failed her. Olvido failed her. Angustias hadn't grown up like Olvido, but she had grown into a Victoria. There were no empty bottles or staggering debt that Olvido knew of, yet there were empty pockets and a daughter sick to her stomach with concern.

What would have happened if Angustias had listened to her before she ran away? How would her life be different? Olvido has asked herself this a million times, but it's not until Felicitas whispers, "¿Abuela?" that she asks herself something new. Would her granddaughter's life be different? Better? Happier?

"¡Abuela!" Olvido flinches as perfume droplets pass through her cheeks. "Are you okay?" Felicitas asks, her eyes wide with worry. Olvido nods, and Felicitas sets down the perfume bottle she held out as a weapon like a crucifix to the Devil. "Well, then, hurry up. I'm tired." Olvido's frown returns to match Felicitas's.

"Hurry up to do what?"

"Practice. I'm not going to be writing notes and picking things up for you forever."

"Writing that letter was your idea," Olvido points out.

"Yeah, dumbest idea I've ever had."

"I agree."

Felicitas smiles sarcastically. "The quicker you learn to be independent, the less I'll have to interact with you."

Olvido laughs. "*You* are going to teach *me* about independence? I've been independent since the day I was born. I practically had to cut my own umbilical cord." Felicitas sticks out her tongue in disgust. "Más sabe el diablo por viejo que por diablo," Olvido says, pausing between words and dragging out the word "viejo." "Do you know what that means?"

"The Devil knows more," Felicitas cautiously translates.

"Yes. Go on."

"From being old than for being a devil."

Olvido nods. "Exactly. It means that experience can bring far more wisdom than inherent intelligence. You may have a big brain, but I have sixty-two years' worth of knowledge."

Felicitas crosses her arms. "Isn't that grammatically incorrect? Shouldn't it be 'el diablo sabe más'? The subject comes first."

Olvido shakes her head. "Not necessarily. I don't know about English, but in Spanish, you can play with the order of words and not change the meaning, but you can change the beauty of the sound, the feeling you convey." Olvido spreads her arms forward and to the side like a poet or an opera singer.

"That's not really true, though. Is it?" Felicitas taunts. "I'm not old, and I'm teaching you something right now." With the tip of her index finger, she presses down on the nozzle of one of Olvido's perfume bottles. Fragrant droplets fly toward her and disappear before they land on her shirt. "Aren't I?" Felicitas pushes down again. "Aren't I?" And again. "Aren't I? Aren't I?"

"Yes!" Olvido shouts. "Now stop it! You're wasting a very expensive perfume." She reaches for the bottle, forgetting that her fingers will go right through. The bottle moves half a millimeter, a distance so small that the average untrained eye, the kind that can't detect ghosts, would've missed it.

"Doesn't smell expensive," Felicitas continues. "It kind of smells like old people."

"It does not. Stop it."

Felicitas scrunches her nose and reaches for the bottle. "Yes, it does. Eew. I hope I never smell like that. I hope I die young."

"Stop it!" Olvido screams. Her clumsy fingers wrap themselves around the perfume bottle and move it toward her, but they fail to stop its momentum. The bottle flies through her waist toward the wall. Felicitas manages to catch it before it shatters.

"God is always listening," Olvido reproaches, ignoring Felicitas's own reprimand of her carelessness. "Con la muerte no se juega."

Felicitas frowns. "If I shouldn't play with death, shouldn't you say 'Death is always listening'?"

"What? No. There's no Death. There's only God."

"So, God kills?"

"Yes!"

"So, God killed you?"

Olvido's response comes out sounding like an interrupted sneeze. She fakes a cough to conceal the shock. "No!" she eventually answers. "God doesn't kill people."

"But you said—"

"You are just like your mother!" Olvido shouts, pressing her fingertips against her temples.

Felicitas narrows her eyes. "Which part of my mother?" she challenges. "The part that you dislike or the part that you hate?"

Olvido frowns in confusion. "I don't hate your mother."

"So, you dislike her?"

Olvido sighs. Of course, Felicitas has an affinity for misinterpretation and arguments. She is Angustias's daughter. "No. I meant—every time I tried to teach her about God, she asked me unanswerable questions. Why did He only save Noah's family? Why did He create a son and not a daughter? How do we know He is a he? The answer is, I don't know. Understand? I. Do. Not. Know. But as I said, más sabe el diablo por viejo que por diablo."

Felicitas stomps her foot. "Well, *vieja*, can you tell me how you were able to move this?" she says, holding up the perfume bottle.

Olvido's eyes move from the bottle to her hands and back. "I don't know, diablita," she says. "You tell me. Teach me something."

Felicitas paces around for a few seconds and stops. "Anger," she declares. "Your anger fuels your movement. But," she says, stopping Olvido's comments by lifting her index finger. "I don't think anger by itself is enough. You're always angry, and you haven't been able to move things so far."

"I am not always angry," Olvido protests.

"This bottle. What's special about this bottle?" Felicitas bends down and moves her head to inspect the perfume from different angles.

"Nothing," Olvido says.

Felicitas scratches the bottle's logo. It's flimsy aluminum. "Didn't you say it was expensive?"

"I lied."

"Hmm." In a sudden move, Felicitas sprays the perfume in Olvido's face. "How do you feel?"

"Angry," Olvido barks.

"Good! Grab my hand." Reluctantly, Olvido reaches out to Felicitas's outstretched hand. Her fingers pass through without difficulty. "Interesting," Felicitas says, tapping her chin. "Follow me."

Olvido obeys and follows her out to the bedroom and toward the nightstand. "Pick up your Bible," Felicitas orders and adds, "Please," when Olvido refuses. "But concentrate. Imagine yourself grabbing it as if it was any other day, as if you weren't dead."

"It's rude to remind dead people that they're dead," Olvido reproaches but reaches for the Bible. She conjures up the memory of its texture, soft leather, rough at the edges where her fingers have damaged the material and created rivers of gray in the black sea of the cover. She can feel the golden valleys of each letter.

"I can feel it!" Olvido beams.

Felicitas's face remains serious. "Great. Now try to grab my hand. Concentrate again. Picture your fingers touching mine. Imagine what they feel like."

Olvido's fingers fail her. Felicitas claps her hands behind her back and paces about the room like a detective in a black-and-white film. She comes to a sudden stop and turns swiftly for dramatic effect. "Do you know what muscle memory is?" she asks. Olvido nods. "Are you sure? Muscle memory is when—"

"I know what it is."

"You see. You're angry again. 'I'm not always angry,'" Felicitas mocks with a whiny tone. "Is that perfume bottle something you touched a lot?" Olvido nods. "Well, then, case closed. Your body, or whatever is left of it, only remembers how certain things feel. You never grabbed my hand, so you don't remember how to grab my hand."

Olvido isn't sure, but Felicitas's statement sounds like an accusation. "What about all the other items around the house that I wasn't able to hold on to?"

"Maybe you weren't concentrating?"

"I wasn't concentrating when I reached for the perfume."

"You kind of were. You really, really wanted to take it away from me, didn't you? You were so annoyed." Felicitas smiles impishly.

Olvido sighs. "So, I will never be able to touch things I never touched before?"

Felicitas shrugs. "I don't know. Here, give me five."

Olvido takes a deep breath and imagines her palm pressing against Felicitas's. She knows what a hand feels like. She's shaken every hand in Grace, big, small, soft, rough, clean, and dirt-stained, but her hand passes through her granddaughter's.

"Keep trying," Felicitas encourages.

Olvido imagines their pressed palms again, their fingers lined up perfectly, Felicitas's hand should take up half the area of Olvido's, but is Felicitas's hand cold or warm? Is it dry? Is it sweaty? Are her fingertips rough from playing an instrument? Does Felicitas play any instruments?

The lack of knowledge brings an uncomfortable, phantom warmth to her cheeks, so Olvido doesn't ask. She prefers to spend half an hour in silence trying and failing to touch palms than to admit she doesn't know simple facts about the girl who shares her last name and face.

"Did you not play patty-cake when you were little?" Felicitas asks, moving to sit on the bed. Her chin rests on her unoccupied hand. Her eyes struggle to remain open.

"Patty ¿qué?"

"Never mind."

An hour passes. Felicitas is unable to keep her eyes open for more than two seconds at a time, but her hand keeps moving back and forth in sync with Olvido's. "Why are you helping me?" Olvido asks.

"I told you. The sooner you learn to do things yourself, the sooner you'll leave me alone," Felicitas mutters with her eyes closed.

"You are too rude," Olvido snaps. The embarrassment she feels deep in her stomach reaches up her throat and snatches back her words of gratitude.

"Where do you go when you're not here with my mom and me?" Felicitas asks, pausing to rotate her wrists.

It's a simple question with a simple answer, but with Felicitas, Olvido has noticed, knowledge is power. "Why don't you want to tell your mom about your sight?"

"My sight?"

"Your ability to see spirits."

"None of your business," Felicitas says, putting her hands up to continue their practice.

Olvido mirrors her movement. "Then it is none of your business where I go."

"Fine."

"Fine." Olvido's hands pass through Felicitas's own. If only she could hold on to the real world, she could have Felicitas confessing in less than an hour.

It's better this way. Questions lead to answers, and answers lead to fights. They often did with Angustias. And Felicitas is correct. Her relationship with Angustias is not Olvido's business. Felicitas is not her daughter, not her responsibility.

"Fine," Felicitas repeats, wanting to have the last word. Olvido lets her win.

When Felicitas's hand movement slows down to an awfully slow pace, Olvido decides to quit. "Go. I don't want you to fall asleep here. Your mom will panic if she wakes up and you're not next to her."

Felicitas nods in agreement and stands. "Keep practicing," she says as she walks toward the door.

Olvido follows her out into the living room and watches her slither underneath her blanket. When Felicitas's chest begins to rise and fall in a steady rhythm, Olvido moves toward Angustias. She reaches out to touch a strand of her daughter's hair, but her fingers pass through like a whisper of wind. That's not right. Her fingers should remember. For seventeen years, her fingers brushed that hair, caressed those cheeks, patted those shoulders. They did look different, she will admit. That hair was thicker. Those cheeks were fuller. Those shoulders were not as strong. This is not the same Angustias who ran to Olvido when she had a nightmare. This Angustias checks for monsters under the bed and scares them away with a shake of her finger.

Maybe Olvido was wrong. Angustias isn't anything like Victoria, and Felicitas isn't as burdened as Olvido once was. Maybe raising Felicitas has been good for Angustias. Motherhood has forced her to mature. Still, Olvido stands by the benefits of the alternative. Angustias could have entered motherhood at a more appropriate age and matured at a slower pace.

But Felicitas is here now, and because she is, Olvido is able to return to her bedroom, open up the Bible to Proverbs 17:9, and read, "Love prospers when a fault is forgiven, but dwelling on it separates close friends."

"Love prospers. Love prospers," she repeats until the sun rises, ignoring the forgiveness that must occur for her wish to come true.

chapter 13

Angustias

Angustias discovered her daughter's coffee addiction seven months, two weeks, and four days late, but she kept her knowledge a secret for over a year. One July morning, Felicitas informed Angustias that they had run out of coffee and asked her to stop by the grocery store after work to buy more. Only coffee, nothing else.

Angustias didn't need to see the rust-colored cloud over her daughter's head to know that request was odd. Coffee was a desire, not a necessity. At the time, Felicitas had acquired a second terrible habit although not through observations of her mother. She'd become obsessed with the idea of keeping track of expenses, just the idea, no execution. Her capabilities were limited as she was only eight years old, but she never missed an opportunity to say that she had "made calculations" and found that they needed to "spend less and save more." Angustias blamed *Sesame Street* and their headache-inducing lessons on saving money. She knew her daughter had no clue as to how much she earned and spent, but she pretended to take her advice. Eventually, she did more than pretend. By the time of the coffee request, she had already convinced Angustias to cut back on ice cream, nail polish, and body lotion.

After Felicitas left for school, Angustias dug into her purse and took out her last grocery store receipt. She had bought a tub of coffee not too long ago, and she had most certainly not drunk enough for the container to be empty. There was only one other person in that house who could contribute to the coffee's depletion.

Angustias bought the coffee and did not say a word. She wasn't too concerned. Olvido had gotten her into coffee pretty early on, and in Angustias's opinion, she'd turned out all right. She knew her awareness of her daughter's secret would come in handy someday, and it does.

Now, in Olvido's living room, Angustias wakes up to the sound of her phone alarm at 6:30 a.m. She turns it off before it wakes Felicitas. Quietly, she rises, puts on her bra and shoes, and fetches two mugs from the kitchen. She walks to the neighbors' house and rings the doorbell. As expected, when Samara answers the door, she has a bright bubblegum pink cloud above her head. She's been awake for hours, she says. "Come in. Come in. I'm glad you're here. There are some things we should discuss."

"How long do I have?" Angustias inquires when Samara asks if she's given some thought to the funeral. "Oh, you mix cinnamon into your coffee grounds, too?"

"I taught her that," Doña Sarai, Samara's mother, brags from the dining table. A watermelon pink of pride brightens her cloud.

"At most a week," Samara says as she pours water into the coffee-maker. "But the funeral home charges per day." Angustias's eyes grow wide. "But don't worry!" Samara assures her. "We can help with the cost. And I'm sure other people will want to help, too." Doña Sarai nods in agreement.

"Other people?" Angustias questions, looking back and forth between the women.

"Yes. Other people in town."

Angustias drums her fingers to the beat of the dripping coffee. Even though Samara's coffeemaker looks like the expensive café kind, it is unusually slow. "I'm sorry," she eventually says. "But why would people in town want to help pay for my mom's funeral?" She knows the question sounds harsh, but it's early. She doesn't have the energy to sweeten her words.

"Well," Samara says as if the answer is obvious. "Because we loved her."

Angustias eyes Samara warily. "But . . . why?" Olvido was not the type to befriend her neighbors. The only neighbor she ever developed a good relationship with was Doña Telma, and that friendship blossomed by accident.

One morning the year Angustias turned seven, Doña Telma's son kicked a soccer ball over the fence and broke one of Olvido's potted plants. It was a young gardenia Olvido was planning to transfer to open land. Olvido found its corpse that afternoon when she got back from work. Every inch of it had been damaged beyond repair. Carrying her precious dead plant in one hand, Olvido marched over to Doña Telma's and knocked until her neighbor opened up.

"You should put your son in soccer lessons," Olvido advised before she left. "He has a strong kick but terrible aim."

"Better than good aim and a weak kick, don't you think?" Doña Telma laughed.

Olvido frowned. "No," she said. "I don't."

To repay the damage, Doña Telma agreed to watch Angustias for one Saturday while Olvido was away at work. A few days later, Doña Telma's son broke a second plant, so Doña Telma watched Angustias for a second Saturday, and a third Saturday, and a fourth Saturday, until Olvido had no potted plants left. By then, Doña Telma had grown accustomed enough to Angustias that she kept an eye out for her without needing to be asked, and Angustias had accepted that under Doña Telma's watchful eye, she couldn't get away with her usual forms of entertainment like decorating the mailbox with glitter stickers she'd stolen from Hillary Guerra in Language Arts class or catching stray cats to play with as if they were her babies.

Despite certain limitations, Angustias liked being watched by Doña Telma. She liked knowing that if she fell and hurt her knees or accidentally lit the house on fire, someone would be there to help. Most importantly, she would have an adult who could testify that Angustias did not mean to cause any trouble. Before Doña Telma, when Olvido left Angustias without adult supervision, Angustias had to be as responsible as possible. She couldn't eat candy for lunch because Olvido would check that the leftovers in the fridge were gone and not in the trash.

She couldn't climb the tree in the backyard because if she got stuck, Olvido would come home and find her there, and she would know Angustias spent the day playing instead of finishing her homework or cleaning the house. Doña Telma still didn't let her eat candy for lunch or play outside all day, but at least if she disobeyed, Doña Telma could make her some tea to cure her stomachache or help her out of the tree before Olvido arrived.

Doña Telma's son confessed to Angustias later that summer that he had broken the flowerpots on purpose so that Angustias could go over to their house on the weekends. Angustias thought it was somewhat sweet, but when he leaned in to give her a peck on the lips, she punched him in the face out of loyalty for her mother and her beloved plants. She broke his nose.

At that point, not even a hospital bill could put a dent on Doña Telma and Olvido's friendship. The two of them had grown close over the trips Olvido would make across the lawn to pick up Angustias after work. Doña Telma would offer Olvido a nice, cold drink. Olvido would offer her leftovers from the restaurant. The two women would sit on the porch all evening until the sunset transformed into a diamond-filled sky. Drunk on laughter and Doña Telma's cheap beer, they would forget about going to bed early. The responsibilities of the next day did not yet exist.

Olvido told Doña Telma wild stories about picky, entitled customers, and Doña Telma filled her in on the gossip of the neighborhood. Olvido complained about her ex-husband. Doña Telma confessed she still missed hers. They each recounted their less-than-ideal journeys from Mexico. Doña Telma promised Olvido they would return one day.

Angustias never saw her mother cry as much as she did when she heard the news of Doña Telma's passing one year before Angustias left her house for good. A tear would escape Olvido every time she accidentally turned in the direction of her friend's house. "I can't even send her flowers," Olvido would say softly. "They took her to Veracruz. It's too far."

Angustias can't imagine Olvido having made genuine friends through her own efforts, especially not a town full of them, especially not close ones that would consider paying for her funeral. Despite the opportunities to build relationships that church and Angustias's school provided, Olvido never behaved with others as freely as she did with Doña Telma. She never made humorous remarks, only laughed politely at other's jokes. She didn't join in on post-service chisme, neither with eagerness nor slight curiosity, and she didn't rebuke cruel and overly invasive comments, although she did complain to Angustias on the drive back to the house. She interacted with other parents just enough to keep getting invited to social gatherings but never went above and beyond to deepen any relationships. She only attended parties if she received a personal, formal invitation, she left parent-teacher nights early, and she never invited nonfamily members over to the house. This behavior worried Angustias for brief moments, specifically on days when Olvido laid in bed for too long or stayed out in the yard well after the sun had set. Then, she would forget about it the way one forgets why they walked into a room or opened the fridge.

"I don't understand," Samara says cautiously. "Sorry. She did tell me you two didn't talk very much."

"No," Angustias admits. Exemplifying the statement, she remains quiet. Samara and Doña Sarai's pitying indigo clouds tell her that any attempt at lightening the mood will fall flat although Angustias doesn't need colors to know that. Their faces, the slight downturn of their mouths and upturn of their inner brows say it all.

Then, a joyous expression spreads across Samara's face. "Oh, I just remembered the day she moved here!" She giggles at her own thoughts. "Sorry, it's just a funny anecdote. Mom, do you remember—"

"Yes," Doña Sarai laughs. "The cat?"

"Yes! It's because when she—" Samara erupts into a fit of laughter. "When she moved in—"

Angustias tries to remember a funny anecdote about Olvido. She tries and tries. There are none. Her head hurts.

"You know," she says, pushing back her chair. "Felicitas is probably wondering where I am. Could I have a glass of milk? I promise to bring it back. The glass not the milk."

"Of course, but you don't want to eat first?" Samara says as she stands. "Or bring Felicitas over? Y'all don't have to change out of your pajamas. My son, Gustavo, he refuses to change out of this new Star Wars set I bought him."

"No, no. That's fine," Angustias insists. She contorts her finger to secure the two mugs and glass between her hands. "I want to hurry to get to the funeral home as early as possible."

"Oh! I can drive you. Felicitas can stay here and play with Gustavo."

"Thank you," Angustias says, already making her way out the door. "Felicitas isn't the playing type, though, unless you have some murder mystery board games."

"Oh, um, no. I don't think we—"

"A Ouija board?" Doña Sarai gasps and signs a cross over her chest. Tight-lipped, Samara shakes her head. "Then, yeah. I think she'd rather spend the day with me. Thank you for the coffee!" Angustias shouts from across the lawn.

When she arrives to her mother's house, she heads straight for Felicitas. "Wake up," she whispers into her daughter's ear, "Wakey-wakey." Felicitas shows no signs of consciousness, but her hair is tangled with a mischievous red orange. "Despierta. I brought you coffee."

Felicitas's eyes shoot open.

"I knew it. Get up. We're going into town." Felicitas sits up and eyes her mother suspiciously. Her gaze slowly shifts toward the steaming mug on the coffee table. "It's for you. Go on," Angustias encourages. "Yes, that's right. I know you've been drinking coffee. Don't give me that look. I'm your mother, Felicitas. I know everything."

Felicitas innocently stares at the mug but eventually accepts that there is no use in pretending. "Why now?" she asks between sips as Angustias digs through her suitcase in search of the right outfit. What does one wear to plan their mother's funeral? Not a thong, that's for sure. "Or have I always been allowed to drink coffee?"

"No. Coffee is bad for you. It's a drug. You're too young to do drugs. I thought I had washed the stain out of this."

"So, I'll be old enough to do drugs one day?"

Angustias laughs. "No. Well, I guess you'll eventually have to make your own decisions. Fine, you have permission to do drugs on your hundredth birthday, but no hard drugs."

"What are hard drugs? Are there soft drugs?"

"Oh my God. Have my slacks always looked this worn?"

"So . . . why now?"

"A-ha! This works," Angustias says, lifting a knee-length black dress. "I'm letting you drink coffee today, and only today, because I'm trying to buy back your love. I know you're not happy about the sudden move."

"I'm never happy about sudden moves."

"Yes, but I know you've been feeling overly annoyed lately. I'm sorry. I'm not particularly thrilled about this trip either. So, is it working? Are you still mad at me?" Felicitas shrugs. "Success!" Angustias shouts and runs to hug her.

Felicitas pushes her away. "You haven't brushed your teeth, have you?" Angustias shakes her head and prances to the bathroom. Felicitas joins her a while later, a towel in one arm and clean clothes in the other.

"What did you mean by 'We're going into town'? Where are we going exactly?" Felicitas asks as she slips out of her pajamas and steps into the shower.

"We need to go to the library to do some research. You want us to figure out how to take Grandma's body to Mexico, remember?" Angustias shouts so Felicitas can hear her above the water. "Or are you no longer adamant about that?"

"No, no," Felicitas yells back. "We have to do that."

"I thought so," Angustias sighs. "Well, afterward, we have to go the funeral home to tell them our new plan."

"Weren't we going to go to Mrs. Samara's house to do that?" Felicitas says once she shuts off the water. Angustias waits for her at the edge of the bathtub with an outstretched towel, the way she used to do when Felicitas was five. Felicitas scrunches her nose and takes the towel she set out herself.

"Yes, well, I thought about it," Angustias says, throwing her towel over Felicitas's head and ruffling her hair. "And I just think we should try to do this on our own first, you know? Let's be independent. Who knows how many other favors we're going to need to ask of her later?"

"Later?" Felicitas questions. "Aren't we leaving?"

"Yes, we are, but between now and the funeral I mean. Samara already stayed up all night to greet us, and she helped us into the house, and she's given us coffee two mornings in a row, and she's offered lunch and dinner—"

"Okay, okay," Felicitas says. "I get it."

Angustias was sure she did not. She barely understood herself. The feeling in her stomach is a painful mixture of shame and annoyance and guilt. The unusual emotions have given her heartburn and prevented her from enjoying her morning coffee.

"So, we're just going to skip breakfast?" Felicitas asks while Angustias dries her hair.

"Of course not," Angustias says. "We'll go out to eat. My treat."

"Who else's treat would it be? I don't have any money."

Angustias jokingly pushes her away and heads toward the shower where she takes the longest bath of her life. She feels bad about wasting water, but she can't bring herself to shut it off. Every few minutes, she turns the valve and raises the temperature until the water is scalding. Her skin turns a concerning shade of pink, then red. Too distracted by the conversation unfolding in her mind, she does not feel any pain. *Do you think . . . ? No. But what if . . . ?*

Angustias wonders how it is possible for Samara to merrily laugh at a memory of Olvido while she cannot. She's her daughter, for God's sake. Did Olvido ever laugh at a memory of her? Did she recall anything about Angustias with fondness? She must have. Angustias did, after all, give Olvido seventeen years' worth of happy memories.

Tolerable memories.

No. Happy memories. Angustias was happy. *I was happy*, Angustias repeats to herself. *I was happy. I loved my mom. My mom loved me. I loved my mom. My mom loved me.*

Of course she did. Angustias explained it to Felicitas the previous evening. Olvido had simply been angry. One can be angry with someone they love and love someone they are angry with. Felicitas had gotten mad at Angustias plenty of times. There were days when Felicitas didn't want to talk to her or even look at her, but she didn't love Angustias any less. If Olvido had truly hated Angustias, she wouldn't have called her every month. If Angustias had truly hated Olvido, she wouldn't have answered the phone. Yes, she'd been hurt by her mother's actions, but what daughter hadn't been a bit hurt by their mother at some point in their lives?

Angustias had heard all sorts of heartbreaking stories about her school friends' mothers. About their bodies. *She called me fat. She called me anorexic. She keeps pointing out the bump on my nose. How much do you think a nose job costs?*

About privacy. *She made me give her my phone so she could read through my texts. She flipped over my room because she's convinced I'm on the pill.*

About violence. "She swears she didn't mean to slap me that hard," her friend Leslie once cried to her in the privacy of the school restroom. "But I don't know. I—I—I need more concealer."

I loved my mom. My mom loved me. But she didn't love Felicitas, did she?

Angustias jerks back when the scorching water slaps her face. The abrasive wake-up call saves her skin from a burn, but it doesn't save her heart. The line she's kept repeating to herself has washed away.

chapter 14

Felicitas

Felicitas's love of reading began the day she discovered that books are free, at least the ones in libraries are. Because Angustias earned just enough to pay rent and put food on the table, they could not afford internet, cable, video games, or any sort of escape other than the radio, which repeated songs far too much for both of their liking, and basic television channels, which only had good programming on weekdays. Trips to the movie theater were rare. Vacations were out of the question.

Felicitas was in kindergarten when she first visited the school library and after borrowing a book and reading it in the span of a single night, she realized she didn't need to watch people, hear people, or pretend to be other people to escape her reality. Then, she found out public libraries existed. The possibilities were endless.

Finding the public library is Felicitas's favorite part of arriving in a new town. As she walks between the stacks, she envisions herself visiting every day, growing up and advancing from the children's section to the young adult section to the fiction section. She grows taller and the stories grow longer, and one day, with Angustias still at her side, she returns to the children's section and reads to her own daughter.

Felicitas does not envision herself growing up in the Grace Public Library as there is no possibility that she will stay in the town, so she enters the building in the same way she carries out almost any task, with a frown on her face. It quickly transforms into amazement.

The Grace Public Library is smaller than any library that she has ever been in. However, the amount of books inside seems to out-number the catalog of any other. On every bookshelf, paperbacks are jammed between hardcovers. Magazines are crammed between the bookshelves and the ceiling. Encyclopedias are stacked between cook-books, and a stack of dictionaries create a display for *The Very Hungry Caterpillar*. Most books are sideways, slanted, and upside down. Some are on the brink of falling out of their bookshelves. There are so many books yet no people.

The Olivares girls hear rustling paper and mumbling coming from behind the front desk. Felicitas stands on her toes to look over the wooden counter. She can see a head full of curls and lean hands that rummage through loose sheets.

"Excuse me," she says. The head of curls shoots up and accidentally hits the underside of the countertop.

"Are you okay?" Angustias and Felicitas rush around the front desk and find a man bent over, forehead against the floor and hands behind his head. He nods though his lack of words suggests he is anything but. Angustias and Felicitas each move to either side of the man, grab his arms, and attempt to help him up.

"Are you Olvido's daughter?" he asks when he looks up and sees Angustias's face. Angustias lets go of his arm, letting him fall back to the floor. "Yes. Listen, we—"

"I'm Emilio. Nice to meet you." The man awkwardly stands and shakes both Angustias's and Felicitas's hands, twice each. "Truly. It's nice to meet you. I heard so much about you. Both of you." Felicitas doubts Emilio heard anything about her other than the fact that she exists if Olvido admitted to that at all. Suddenly, her eyes widened at a realization.

"Great," Angustias says. "Listen—"

Felicitas pulls her mother toward her and cups her hands around her ear. "Isn't Emilio one of the names on the list?" she whispers.

Angustias looks up at the young man and whispers back. "Yes, but we shouldn't say anything right now. What if he starts to cry like Ms. Taliah?"

"Is something wrong?" Emilio asks.

"Yes, actually," Angustias says, standing back up. "We're in dire need of a computer and internet connection. Have we come to the right place?"

Of course not, Felicitas thinks. The library is so tiny and overstuffed, she doubts even the thinnest laptop could be shoved onto a shelf.

"Yes, of course!" Emilio responds. He quickly searches through the papers on his desk until he finds a green sticky note. "There's a code. The computers are this way. Follow me."

Emilio takes the Olivares girls through a labyrinth of bookshelves until they reach the back wall where two computers rest on a cramped desk. "What are those?" Felicitas asks.

"Computers," Emilio answers warily.

"They look ancient. Like, from the nineties."

"Well, I think they're from the mid-aughts but—" A screen lights up when Emilio moves one of the mouses, and a desktop background appears when he types in the code. "They work just fine. Anything else I can help you with?" he asks. Angustias smiles and shakes her head. "Okay, well, I'll be in front. Let me know if you need anything."

Felicitas and Angustias thank him and get right to work. It's much easier, Felicitas determines, since she doesn't have Olvido speaking over Angustias. She hadn't seen her grandmother since the night before. Felicitas doesn't understand why. Is she angry? Of course she's angry. She's Olvido. Still, shouldn't she be here, acting a little thankful? Felicitas stayed up all night helping her even when Olvido kept treating her like a wad of gum stuck to the bottom of her shoe.

Concentrate, she tells herself. *Map out her escape.*

She starts the search with a general topic: how to transport a deceased individual to another country. There are four million two hundred and seventy search results.

Angustias and Felicitas dig around for an hour. On a notepad, Angustias writes down what Felicitas reads out, including the basic process, the state the body should be in, who needs to approve of the transportation, whether and how the government is involved, where the body needs to arrive, how they can contact the cemetery and buy a lot, and most importantly, the total cost. They are one question away from getting all the information they need when a bright message pops up informing them that the computer will shut down in five minutes. Felicitas runs to the front desk and drags Emilio to the back to fix the problem.

"Sorry," he says as he types a code into the computer. "It's been so long since someone has used these, I forgot there was a time limit." When the message disappears, Emilio can't help but see the last web-page the Olivares girls opened. He glances down and scans the infor-mation written on Angustias's notepad.

"It's okay. We're actually not going to need the computer anymore," Angustias says, tapping her pen against the piece of paper.

"What?" Felicitas says, her frown deepening.

Angustias circles the number at the bottom of the sheet and holds up the notepad. "I'm sorry, mijita. That's too much. We can't afford it."

"But—"

"But nothing. Look." Angustias points to the paper again. Ten thou-sand dollars. Angustias, Felicitas knows, doesn't have, has never had, and will probably never have that kind of money in her wallet or bank account. "I'm sorry," she repeats, taking Felicitas's hand. "We can't take Grandma back to Mexico. She'll have to stay here like we originally planned."

"No," Felicitas snatches her hand away and takes a step back. "We have to. We promised."

"We didn't promise anything, and we can't afford it."

"But it's what she wants—wanted," Felicitas contends. "You're going to sell the house aren't you? Can't we use that money? Or we can ask people around town. We can hold a fund-raiser."

"If what we want is to fulfill Grandma's wishes, we should definitely not raise money for her funeral. She *hated* being on the receiving end of charity. And houses don't sell in a day, especially not old ones like your grandma's."

Felicitas paces back and forth. "Did Grandma have any savings?"

Angustias laughs. "I wish! Any money she left is in between the cushions of her sofa."

"We can cook! We can make dishes like her and sell—"

"You know I'm not the best cook, and that would still be a fund-raise—"

"I can figure the cooking out—"

"Felicitas, stop." Angustias keeps her tone calm, but Felicitas can detect its seriousness. "She's staying here. That's final. Felicitas, stop frowning right now."

Deliberately, Felicitas scrunches up her face more. She looks up at Emilio. "Is there a restroom here?" she grunts.

Emilio points down a narrow hall of books. His finger shakes with fear and embarrassment over witnessing the argument. Felicitas storms down the hall until she finds the restroom sign, walks in, and slams the door shut.

Leaning over the restroom mirror, Felicitas stares at Olvido's face. Her grandmother isn't present, but she might as well be. The anger she incites in Felicitas's heart is more than felt, and her face is there, glaring at her with hateful eyes. Felicitas pinches her cheeks and moves them around in patternless circles, distorting her reflection. She hates how her face is identical to her grandmother's. She hates her eyes, her nose, her lips. She hates her frown, and the hate intensifies it.

She wishes she could look like her father. He didn't want her either, but at least she never got to experience his lack of love. He didn't kick her out of his home. He didn't call Angustias and pretend to be busy as soon as Felicitas reached for the phone. He didn't die and seek her out only for his own benefit, ignoring the prior ten years of silence and disdain, all the moments they could have shared but preferred to experience alone. Her father's face is a clean slate. With it, she can be anyone she imagines him to be. But she is Olvido's granddaughter and has Olvido's face. Bitter. Cold. Undoubtedly angry.

"Why can't you just leave?" Felicitas snarls and splashes water onto the mirror. The reflection disappears before Felicitas moves away.

chapter 15

Olvido

Olvido knows Angustias is not familiar with traditional funerals. In the seventeen years they lived together, she only attended two, one for Olvido's friend, Telma, and the other for Doña Rocío, a church acquaintance. Family funerals, Angustias had experienced plenty, but none of them are a good example of what Olvido expects for her own.

With the exception of Olvido's sister-in-law, Rosa, Angustias and Olvido's entire family lived in Mexico—aunts, uncles, cousins, and people they called aunts, uncles, and cousins but were not actually related to them by blood. When a family member passed away, Olvido and Angustias were always unable to attend their funeral. Olvido had entered the country on a tourist visa and stayed a little longer than what was permitted. If she traveled to Mexico, there was no coming back. But Olvido quickly found a way around her dilemma. She could hold her own funerals at home.

Olvido's home funerals were small and unconventional, but full of heart and respect for God, which is what funerals were supposed to be about. At the entrance table, she set up an altar with mismatched candles, flowers from her garden, and a picture of the recently deceased. Dressed in appropriate black attire, Olvido and Angustias stood in front of the altar, prayed, and read a few Bible verses. They ended their ceremony with amens and goodbyes. In subsequent visits, Olvido gave her family members money so they could buy flowers and decorate the departed's tomb on her behalf. She could not ensure they carried out her request, but at least God knew she tried.

Despite how unique funerals were at the Olivares household, Olvido and Angustias never discussed what each wanted for their own burial. When it comes to Olvido's wishes, Angustias is, as usual with all things Olvido, completely lost.

"So, you don't want to change anything?" the funeral home director, Mr. Sosa, asks.

"Yes," Angustias says, nodding. "I want for whatever plans you already had to move forward."

"So, you came here to . . . ?"

"To tell you that, and I want to know, what *are* the plans that you have? And how much will everything cost? And what do you need from me? Other than money, of course. And . . . my mom's here, right? Well, her body. Of course, you know I meant her body."

"Yes, to your last question," Mr. Sosa says, putting his hands up to stop Angustias. "But let's start with the first."

As Mr. Sosa throws around dates and numbers, Angustias nods incessantly. "This Tuesday. Does that still work for you?" Nod. "Open casket." Nod. Nod. "Would you like to see the options we have available?" Nod. Nod. Nod. Olvido nods along with her. Perhaps it was pointless to show up for this. No. There must be something they're forgetting.

"Ask who's doing my makeup," Olvido says to Felicitas. "Carla or Miranda? I somewhat trust Carla, but Miranda? Nope. That girl cakes her face every day with so much makeup, I'm surprised the circus hasn't recruited her."

Felicitas frowns, but Olvido can see a smile creeping up her lips.

"I'm not saying this to amuse you. I don't want to look ridiculous in front of everyone. Go on. Ask. It's the least you can do since you failed to convince your mother to carry out my last wish."

Felicitas rolls her eyes but asks, "What about her makeup?"

"What?" Mr. Sosa says.

"Her makeup. You guys paint corpses' faces, right? My grandma liked to keep her makeup minimal." Angustias turns to her, perplexed. "I mean, I'm assuming she did. She seemed . . . dull." Olvido gapes at her.

"Felicitas," Angustias reproaches.

Mr. Sosa nods. "I'll let our staff know."

"What staff—" Olvido begins.

"To keep the makeup minimal or that my grandmother was dull?"

"Felicitas," Angustias repeats more harshly.

For the rest of the meeting, Olvido remains quiet except for making the simple request that they leave her hair down. Soft curls would be preferable.

"You also do hair, right?" Felicitas says. "You should tie her hair up. It will pull her skin so she doesn't look so wrinkly."

Olvido storms off and finds an empty office where she will not have to hear more about the disaster awaiting her corpse. To practice her sense of touch, she repeatedly and unsuccessfully attempts to pick the lint off a chair's seat. "Sí puedes," she chants to herself. "You can do this. You need to do this." Felicitas, like Angustias, is unreliable, but it's fine. Olvido will take matters into her own hands. She just needs to make them work first.

chapter 16

Angustias

Throughout the drive back to her mother's house, Angustias bites her tongue. Asking why Felicitas spoke so rudely of Olvido back at the funeral home could begin a conversation she doesn't wish to have. She's so carefully avoided it so far. She's stayed mum about certain things and lied about others. But Felicitas must sense the truth. The slate color above her head won't brighten. And there's that tired baby blue. Maybe Felicitas is simply being a preteen. She needs guidance. "You shouldn't have said those things about your grandmother to Mr. Sosa," she says calmly when she parks the car on Olvido's driveway. "It was very rude."

"Maybe I got it from you," Felicitas says. She sounds exhausted. This is not the sassy comeback of a tween.

Angustias turns to her perplexed. "What's that supposed to mean?"

"Or maybe I got it from her."

"If you knew your grandmother," Angustias laughs, "you would know that she always strived to seem polite."

"Seem," Felicitas says, dragging out the word and tapping her chin with her index finger.

"Felicitas," Angustias reproaches.

"I think those people are waving at us," Felicitas interrupts. Angustias's reprimand catches in her mouth. Felicitas is not attempting to get out of an argument. There is, in fact, a middle-aged couple with dark gray clouds above their heads walking toward them.

Angustias slumps into her seat. It's going to be a long evening.

Angustias and Felicitas are unaccustomed to having guests in their home. They have no family, and in Felicitas's case, no friends to invite over. While Angustias accepts invitations to grand parties, small gatherings, and the occasional date, she only goes out and never invites people in. She doesn't want to disrupt Felicitas's privacy.

The years of hosting experience the Olivares girls lack is made up for in a matter of hours at Olvido's house. Taliah was a quick informant. Felicitas and Angustias's evening is taken over by the recipients of Olvido's dishes. Each visitor gives Felicitas and Angustias a hug and a kiss and a hard pat on the back, and waves to them as they walk out the front porch with a labeled container in their hands.

Angustias has no help as Felicitas refuses to look up from the book she checked out at the library. A permanent crimson cloud looms above the chilling hardcover. She speaks only to comment on what's happening.

"Your phone's ringing."

"Someone's outside."

"One dish left."

"I think Mrs. Samara is coming over."

Angustias doesn't bother smoothing out Felicitas's frown. It is plastered on tighter than the polite smile Angustias has held all afternoon and will have to hold until Samara's family leaves.

"I really wanted Gustavo and Felicitas to meet," Samara whispers to Angustias as her family settles down in the living room. "Isn't the best part of moving making new friends?"

"Uh-huh," Angustias says. With an eager grin and brows that rise high above his wire-rimmed glasses, it is obvious that Gustavo agrees with his mother. Felicitas, on the other hand, looks like she's never heard of the term *friend*. Her brows are set low. Her lips are ever-so-slightly downturned. Yet, at the edge of her now pearl white cloud of indifference is a hint of tangerine. She's curious.

"Hi. I'm Gustavo," Gustavo says when Felicitas sits down. "And you're Doña Olvido's granddaughter, Felicitas?" Felicitas nods. "Do people ever call you Feliz or Felix or Lizzie?"

"Not if I can help it," Felicitas responds.

"No one ever calls me Gus. Not that I want to be called Gus. I actually don't like nicknames, and I think people use them too much. People don't usually think that around here 'cause everyone is Mexican, but if you tell people that you don't want to be called something, they *do* listen, and it's not like that in other places, and I know that because before here, we lived in El Paso. Over there, they called me Tavito. I didn't like that name, but people didn't stop calling me that even when I asked them to. What's your take on names?"

"We all have them," Felicitas says dryly.

"True. You like R. L. Stine?" Gustavo says, pointing at the book Felicitas left open on the coffee table next to Pepe. "My friend, Estela, loves R. L. Stine, and she loves telling me his stories because I refuse to read them, and she especially loves telling me his stories because she thinks I'm scared, but I'm not. I haven't been scared since I was seven."

"How old are you now?"

"Nine."

"You look younger."

"I know," Gustavo says coolly. "It's even worse because I skipped a grade, so I'm much shorter than everyone in my class."

"'Kay."

"Okay!" Angustias interrupts. "I don't think anyone else is coming." She suppresses the urge to say, "Thank God." "Should I go pick up a pizza, then? Sorry, I don't have anything prepared for dinner, and well, everyone took basically everything in the fridge."

"Oh, I think the meat loaf and rice we brought should be enough, no?" Samara says.

Angustias smiles and nods, glancing at the burnt meat loaf and dry rice Samara set on the kitchen counter. "You know what? Yes. You're right. And we're not that hungry—"

"I'm starving," Felicitas says loudly.

"So, we'll probably not eat that much. If we have leftovers—"

"Pack them for lunch," Gustavo suggests, looking at Felicitas. "That's what we always do. You'll need lunch for school tomorrow."

"What?" Angustias and Felicitas say simultaneously.

"Gustavo," Samara reprimands. "I'm sorry. He gets ahead of himself sometimes. We were going to ask you, Felicitas, if you would like to go to school this week with Gustavo. It's the last week of the school year, so you really wouldn't be doing work."

"And you'll get to meet everyone you'll go to school with next year," Alberto, Samara's husband, adds.

"And maybe play with this summer. That is, of course, if you're fine with that, Angustias."

Angustias smiles politely. Internally, she's screaming. Summer? Next year? They will be gone by the weekend. She's not going to force Felicitas to interact with hundreds of strangers just to keep her occupied.

"I don't know," Angustias says. "My mom's funeral is on Tuesday, and—" She stifles a sigh of relief as the doorbell rings. "And we still have people showing up wanting to pay their respects. Hi!" she says with genuine enthusiasm when she finds Emilio patiently waiting on the porch, picking at a stain on the front of his shirt. He gives a small jump when he sees her. "Are you here for your food? Come in. Do you know my neighbors?"

"Hi, Emilio," Samara's family greets in a chorus.

"Of course, you do," Angustias says under her breath and hurries back into the kitchen. "I thought maybe Ms. Taliah forgot to tell you, and we left the library in such a hurry even I forgot to say something." She runs back to the entrance of the living room, two containers in hand. "Here," she says, shoving them into Emilio's hands. "She must have really liked you. She even left you a piece of cake for dessert. Fun fact, my mom preferred cooking over baking."

"We know," the guests say at once. Angustias smiles tightly at Felicitas. Her daughter does not return the gesture.

"I wasn't in need of food, you know," Emilio says as he softly pats the plastic lid. "She just thought I looked too skinny."

You kind of are, Angustias thinks and quickly shakes the thought away. Is the house slowly turning her into her mother?

"Y'all know how she was," Emilio continues. Samara's family nods, nostalgically. "And she knew I ate all of my meals alone since my family doesn't live near here, and she would—she would prepare food and come eat lunch with me at the library or invite me over for dinner. That's how I got to meet other people in town."

"Oh," Angustias says. She knows she is supposed to say more to comfort him, but she's too exhausted to think of the right words. For hours, she has had to look at indigo clouds with dark gray centers and listen to stories of what a great person her mother was. She learned about the time when Olvido cooked the Romano's Thanksgiving feast because the whole family was down with a bad cold, when she delivered food to Doña Salazar in the hospital because she refused to eat anything but gorditas de azúcar, and when she treated Mr. James's son's food poisoning with teas and soups. Never charged a cent, not one penny. Apparently, she let Doña Guerrero sleep over for more than a week when her house felt too cold and empty after Don Guerrero's passing. She tolerated her sleepwalking and picky eating habits. She listened to Mr. Dominguez talk for seven hours straight about his life regrets, which included everything from rejecting Yisel Estrada's kiss in the elementary school playground to majoring in business instead of fine arts.

"And she did not interrupt me," Mr. Dominguez marveled. "She even refused to take a sip from her drink so she wouldn't have to go to the restroom. People just don't listen like that anymore, don't you think?" Angustias nodded and smiled and agreed. She patted backs and offered hugs, hot tea, and coffee.

There are no more smiles or comforting words left in Angustias to lessen the gray over Emilio's head. If she's supposed to try to make Emilio feel better, she doesn't want to do it, but perhaps she doesn't have to. Emilio isn't crying. Then again, he is also not leaving.

"Sorry," he eventually says. "It's just, um, since buying food isn't a problem, I thought that, instead, I could pay Olvido back and give you two something to eat." He bends down to pick up a plastic bag containing two Styrofoam containers and holds it out to Angustias. The delicious, intoxicating scent emanating from the bag hits her nostrils, and her stomach roars in response. She can feel it churning inside, imploring her to eat. "Sorry. I would've brought more if I'd known y'all would be here."

"Thank you," Felicitas says, appearing beside Angustias and taking the plastic bag from Emilio. "Would you like to stay for dinner?"

"Felicitas," Angustias reproaches, attempting to pry the bag out of her daughter's hand.

"Yes, stay," Doña Sarai says eagerly. Angustias figures that even she is aware of how terrible her daughter's dishes look. Her stomach stirs with disgust at the memory of the meat loaf's scent.

Angustias steps aside to open a path to the kitchen. "Please stay," she says.

Emilio shakes his head apologetically. "No, it's fine."

"Please, come ea—"

"No, really—"

"Just do it!"

"Okay."

Emilio steps further into the house and follows the Olivares girls and Samara's family into the kitchen. Angustias's hunger has reached such great heights, she wants to rip open the bag and eat the food straight out of the container with her hands, but she resists the urge. Her mother probably made a big deal about taking out nice plates and setting the table for her guests. Angustias has never felt the need to live up to those expectations, but she's already been compared to Olvido so much that day, she can't help but put in a little effort. She sets seven ceramic plates and neatly places a metal fork under a napkin beside each. *I'm not my mom*, she thinks, staring at the setup. She snatches the napkins and throws them casually over the utensils. *I'm not her, and she's not here.*

chapter 17

Felicitas

Felicitas, like most Olivares women, believes in signs, but only when it is convenient for her. If she finds money in a pocket and then stumbles upon a Girl Scout cookie sale, clearly, she is meant to buy a box. But if they only have lemon flavors left, then the stand is a coincidence and she is supposed to save the money for something more important like soap or eggs. If she can't find one of her shoes when she's running late to catch the bus, she's meant to skip school. But if it's a "the substitute wasn't given a lesson plan and will let Felicitas read the entire period" type of day, it was not a sign of anything, and she needs to be more organized.

Olvido believes in signs, Felicitas knows. Her mother told her that much. "But only when it was inconvenient for me," Angustias said. "Always trying to prove she was all-knowing."

"Do not eat with your elbows on the table!" Olvido snaps.

Felicitas's meat loaf–filled fork freezes midair. The corners of her lips twitch with a smile. *It's a sign*, she thinks, setting down the mystery meat. *I can't eat this*. Angustias taught her to never ignore signs no matter how rude it would make her look, and wouldn't it be more discourteous to vomit in front of the guests?

"Did you— ¡Ay, Emilio! Mijo. It's so good to see you. Oh," Olvido tsks. "You've gotten so skinny again." She pats his curls with her translucent hand. Emilio doesn't react. "And everyone else is here, too? Is this a pre-funeral funeral?" she beams.

Felicitas rolls her eyes. Her grandmother's love of attention is obnoxiously obvious.

"Niña," Olvido abruptly barks. "What did your mom say? Did you try to convince her on the drive back?" Felicitas shakes her head slightly. "What! What do you mean no?"

"Mamá," Felicitas says casually. "Are you sure we can't take Grandma's body to—"

Angustias slams her fork down. Only Emilio tenses up. "Please, Felicitas," Angustias says. "I don't want to hear about that crazy idea right now."

"What crazy idea?" Gustavo asks.

"I wanted to give my grandma a proper, extravagant farewell," Felicitas says, looking at her mother. "Maybe shoot her into outer space or combine her ashes with dynamite powder for a fireworks show."

"Really?" Gustavo marvels.

"No." Felicitas shrugs at Olvido and serves herself a giant spoonful of Emilio's chilaquiles.

Olvido scoffs and paces around the room. "Tell her you can see me," she says. "Tell her you can see me right now. I want to have a word with her."

Felicitas pretends she cannot hear her and sips her water. Her grandmother doesn't really want her to do that, she's sure. She would have already done something to make her presence known. The fear that flashed on Olvido's face when Felicitas said, "I bet you two have so much to say to each other," the night before keeps reappearing on the curve of her inner brows and the tightness of her lips.

Olvido brings her hand down on the table with a force Felicitas didn't know she held. Plates and utensils bounce up, and bits of food fly onto the tablecloth. Olvido jumps back in surprise.

"Felicitas!" Angustias gasps. "Did you just kick the table?"

Felicitas can't respond. She is having a hard time concentrating on a single voice.

"That's how it's going to be then?" Olvido booms. "Fine! If you won't make her listen, I'll do it myself."

"I didn't. I didn't kick the table," Felicitas says but does not elaborate.

It's not the right time to tell Angustias the truth. She will think she is lying, that she is finding ways to get out of the trouble her anger has gotten her in.

Angustias's mouth opens to speak again, but her words are interrupted by the sound of a familiar tune. The notes to "México lindo y querido" dance into the kitchen. A deep voice follows the guitars and trumpets' rhythm and demands their attention.

Seven heads snap toward the living room. Angustias quickly looks away.

"'México lindo y querido, si muero lejos de ti,'" a recording of Vicente Fernández's voice sings.

"It's a sign," Felicitas exclaims. Her mother believes in signs. Signs are safe.

"It's a ghost!" Gustavo shouts. Felicitas attempts to kick him under the table, but her leg doesn't reach.

"A sign of what?" Emilio asks.

"Do you know Spanish?" Felicitas asks him. Emilio moves his hand side to side, so-so. "The song is saying," Felicitas explains, delicately moving her arms as she speaks as if she were reciting a poem. "Mexico, beautiful and dear, if I die far away from you."

"I didn't know you didn't know Spanish," Gustavo says to Emilio. "Aren't you Mexican?"

"Gustavo," his parents reproach. Doña Sarai laughs.

"'Que digan que estoy dormido y que me traigan aquí,'" the mariachi continues.

"Have them say I'm asleep and bring me to you," Felicitas translates.

"Here," Angustias says. The anger in her voice has been replaced with confusion and fear. She stares attentively at the food in front of her as she swings her fork around creating a storm of sauce and meat.

"What?"

"Bring me here. The song says *aquí*, *here*, not *ti*, *you*. You've always sung it wrong, and I never corrected you because I liked your version better," she explains, but she looks like she wants to rip her ears off to never hear Felicitas's version, or any version, ever again. *I don't want to be here*, she seems to say with her silence. *And I don't want to be with you.*

Felicitas puts her hand over her mother's, but Angustias draws hers back. She throws her napkin on the table, scoots her chair back and marches into the living room where a vinyl record spins around as the mariachi's voice grows louder and louder. Suddenly, the song comes to a halt. "That was not funny, Felicitas," she hollers.

"It wasn't me," Felicitas shouts, running into the living room. "I was sitting right next to you. It was—It was a sign! Do you believe me?"

Angustias says nothing.

Does Olvido know the consequences her actions have on Felicitas's relationship with Angustias? Does she care? Is this some master plan? If Olvido couldn't keep Angustias, neither would Felicitas.

"What happens when we don't listen to signs?" Felicitas says, reminding Angustias of the countless anecdotes she recounted over the years, tales of life-changing signs, of consequential disregards and misinterpretations.

Angustias pauses and takes in a deep breath. "Fine. I'm listening," she says. "What do you want me to do?"

chapter 18

Olvido

It is impossible for Olvido's mind to not wander into the past as she hears Angustias hum "México lindo y querido." It is in the name. Mexico. Home. Far in space and time. The day Olvido accepted that she needed to migrate, she told herself she would return to Matamoros. She would cross the border as soon as she heard from her cousins that the loan sharks had calmed down or moved, or better yet, died. But that never happened. Instead, the news she received about the state of her country became worse and worse. Extortion intensified. Violence rose. Death became unpredictable and common. There was no going back for Olvido, not within a year, a decade, or perhaps even a lifetime, not with her daughter at least.

Now her daughter has a daughter of her own, and they are listening to a song they cannot possibly identify with in the way she does. What do they know about missing home? They have never yearned for an opportunity to reunite with their friends and family. They only know this country, and they have each other.

When Angustias left her house the summer after her high school graduation, Olvido felt it was the perfect time to return, but she could not bring herself to do so. She got in her truck, turned on the ignition and sat in her driveway for an hour, contemplating how her daughter was doing out in the world completely alone. Worse than alone. She was with an infant, a baby that needed to receive but could not give.

If Olvido was in Mexico and something happened to Angustias, she would not be able to get to her as quickly as she would if she stayed. Olvido needed to stay. Now that Olvido is dead, going home is not a matter of when but how.

"Okay, read the options back to me," Angustias instructs.

Felicitas picks up the notebook, clears her throat and reads. "Number one. We pay for the legalities and hire the funeral home to take the body across the border."

This was Emilio's suggestion. He sat with them for a couple of minutes trying to come up with a solution after Samara's family left and Felicitas explained their dilemma. Then, Felicitas suggested that they smuggle the body across the border, and it all became a bit too much for him. He excused himself and let them know that if they ever needed his help, they could find him at the library. He also gave them his phone number and asked them not to call him if what they needed involved illegal activities. Felicitas said they could not make any promises. He smiled nervously and left.

"That sounds good to me," Olvido says.

Angustias shakes her head. "No money. Next."

"Number two. We sit Grandma up in the backseat of the car, and we drive down to Mexico. If someone stops us, we say that she's asleep, like in the song."

Olvido laughs. "Ridiculous! But," she says somberly. "If it's the only way..."

Angustias taps her index finger against her chin. Olvido tries to guess what is going through her mind, why her brows draw together with concern. Perhaps it is too morbid for her. This option would require them to touch a corpse. Felicitas must be loving it.

But how will they sneak her body out of the funeral home? Mr. Sosa will not release her just like that. Olvido imagines Angustias making a run for it. Her body falls out of the wheelchair and hits the pebbled floor, scraping her skin.

Olvido and Angustias shake their heads simultaneously. "Nope. I don't like that. Next."

"Number three. We push her body down a river. We can't access

Devils River, but Emilio said there are other creeks and streams that connect to it. We can put it on a nice raft or something. Not a coffin, though. It might be too heavy and sink."

The third option would not solve the fact that they would have to sneak the body out of the funeral home although it would potentially save them from legal issues with border patrol. But it wouldn't save Olvido. Her lifeless body would be exposed to the scorching sun and freezing water and the vicious vultures waiting around the corner for their next meal. The hideous creatures would land on her torso, piercing her skin with their claws, and with their razor-sharp beaks, they would gnaw at her face, ripping the skin off the flesh and pecking her eyes.

"No!" Olvido screams, covering her eyes with her hands.

"Never mind," Felicitas says before Angustias can agree.

Angustias shakes her head. "I don't want to see her like that, floating down a river," she says. "Even if she is covered in pretty flowers on a nice raft."

"You agreed to an open casket," Felicitas points out.

"Yeah," Angustias says. "But I wasn't going to look in. And the coffin would float, by the way, because there's air inside, like a ship."

Felicitas narrows her eyes and pouts as she taps her chin. "You're right about the coffin," she says. "But it would still be a lot harder to sneak out a coffin than a body."

Angustias melts into her chair.

"I think she's actually thinking this through," Olvido says leaning in to inspect her daughter's face. "She's worried. Angustiada."

"I'm getting dizzy," Angustias says. "I need something sweet."

Angustias and Felicitas dig into Olvido's peach cake that Emilio left for dessert. They each throw out ideas as they chew on the sweet nectar of the fruit. Still amazed by Angustias's uneasiness, Olvido forgets to stop them. The Angustias she knows, or knew, would have accepted the first option given to her, whether it was an easy or difficult one, it wouldn't have mattered. Why worry? Just do it. Is what Olvido suspected last night true? Did motherhood bring about maturity in Angustias? No. It was simply age. Even Angustias could not escape the anxiety brought on by adulthood. She had bills to pay and mouths to feed. Perhaps she was imitating Olvido. She'd accepted that her mother was right, and it was time to think things through. Olvido had taught her well.

"We could fund-raise to pay for the first option. I know you said Grandma wouldn't have liked that—"

"She's right," Olvido interjects. Asking for charity after people had already gifted her so much when she was alive? It was impolite. Embarrassing.

"But who cares about—I mean she's not here, and it seems like people here *loved* Grandma, right?" Felicitas says, rolling her eyes. Olvido scowls.

Angustias pauses and rubs the back of her neck. "Right, but to be completely honest, I don't want to do that. I don't want people to think we're . . . needy."

"That's right," Olvido says. "Very good."

Felicitas slowly puts down her fork and leans over the table to place her hand over her mother's forehead. "Are you sick?" she asks.

"What?"

"You never care what people think. You always tell me not to care what people think."

"What terrible advice," Olvido scoffs.

"I care," Angustias says, lightly pinching her daughter's hand and removing it from her face. "Sometimes. And yes, you're right. I mean, I'm right. Ugh, you know what I mean. It's just . . . I don't know. Maybe it's because we're here," she says, her eyes sweeping across the room. "Being here makes me care about what people think. Your grandma always cared about what people thought, and she always told me I should care, too."

"I did not," Olvido objects. Not always, just when it was appropriate and imperative.

"And she always told me to stay quiet. No digas nada. Calladita te ves más bonita."

"I meant for you not to comment on other people's business," Olvido rebuts. "And our own business, sometimes."

Did their church need to know Angustias was pregnant before her belly even showed? Did all the parents at Angustias's school need to know her father had left before his scent had washed off their sheets? And what if in one of those moments where she talked on and on, she divulged Olvido's secret to the wrong person? She needed to practice self-control, put in some thought, a bit of apprehension.

"But she was wrong. It's not always good to stay quiet. What kind of life is that, never sharing your thoughts and opinions? Boy, she was wrong about so many things."

"That's enough," Olvido says.

"It was always about appearances for her," Angustias mocks, feigning a prissy voice.

"That's enough!" Olvido repeats. Her voice cracks at the last vowel.

"Be prim and proper. Una señorita."

"I did my best," she contends. "I always tried my best." Angustias was a mother now. She was supposed to understand.

"But you don't have the autonomy of una señorita. You're still a child."

She hadn't matured. She was just like Victoria.

"Mamá," Felicitas says in a somber voice so low, Olvido can barely hear her.

"You can have opinions, but don't speak on them because if they're the wrong ones, you'll go to Hell."

Olvido stomps her foot. "That's it. I don't want to hear this anymore. Make a decision so I can finally leave. For good. That's what you want isn't it?" Olvido's words are meant for her daughter, but she is looking at Felicitas as she speaks. She needs to be seen at least once, even if she looks weak and messy and hopeless.

chapter 19

Angustias

Angustias can't help rambling and oversharing the same way she can't help yawning in the middle of a long workday or laughing at her own jokes.

"And things are what they are simply because that's the way they've always been. God forbid we try to change our values."

Since becoming a mother, Angustias has become more conscious about what she says and how she speaks.

"And by change, I mean improve, but she didn't see it as an improvement."

Road rage is acceptable to a degree, but cuss words are not allowed. Always be polite to restaurant servers and retail workers. Set a good example.

"I mean, she was a working woman. She understood the importance of freedom and independence. But when it came to *my* freedom—oh, suddenly a girl's place is in the house under lock and key."

And under no circumstances speak *too* ill of her mother. Esas son cosas del diablo. But "too" is such a subjective measurement.

"Can you imagine living like we're in the fifties? She wasn't even alive in the fifties!"

"Mamá," Felicitas says once again, her voice only slightly higher than before.

"And God forbid you make a mistake once because there is no forgiveness," Angustias continues. Her throat is dry but her cheeks are damp with tears. "There is no room for mistakes in this—"

"Am I the mistake you're talking about?" Felicitas interjects. Despite her frown, her voice is cool and level.

"What?" Angustias turns to her daughter, shamefaced. "No."

"Then what mistake are you talking about?"

Angustias's mouth opens and closes. "Just . . . just everything I did, like, like little thi—"

"No. You're talking about getting pregnant, aren't you? Pregnant with me."

Angustias laughs dismissively. "Well, yes. But she was mad at the fact that I got pregnant, in general. Not pregnant with you, specifically. She was mad at something I did, not something you did."

"Well," Felicitas says, standing up and pushing her chair in. "You are no longer pregnant, and I'm still here. And you are both still angry, so what or who do you think the mistake is?"

Felicitas marches to the living room, turns off the lights, and throws herself on the couch. She wraps a blanket around herself and turns to bury her face into the space between the seat cushions. She doesn't respond when Angustias asks, "You both?"

Angustias does not attempt to fall asleep. She knows she will not be able to even if she tries. To tire out her mind, she busies herself recleaning the clean kitchen, and when that fails to distract her, she walks out onto the back patio and sits on the metal rocking chair that faces the dead garden.

Angustias is the mistake. She never stops and thinks about what other people hear when she talks. Her mother was right. Calladita se ve más bonita.

As she swings back and forth, propelling herself with the tips of her toes, she notices an upside-down ceramic pot sitting on the edge of the cement floor. Angustias rises, reaches forward, and lifts the pot. Ashes cascade down. Some fly away into the garden, carried by the light spring breeze. Her mother was smoking again.

Olvido was very honest with Angustias about her smoking days, and she proudly showed off that she was capable of quitting cold turkey when she got pregnant. Angustias reprimanded her when she first heard of her old habits. How was it possible for her to warn Angustias about using drugs if she had been a smoker?

"It was a different time," Olvido said. "And I haven't touched a cigarette since then."

Angustias's chest tightens as if her lungs are caving in. *When did it begin?* She wonders, moving the ashes around with her finger. Had it been when she left the Valley, when Angustias left home, when she told her of her pregnancy?

Angustias's tears fall and accumulate in the cement until they can't contain themselves within a single drop. Breaking into a stream, they carry the ashes down the back porch's floor, dripping down into the grass.

Drip.

Drip.

Drip.

An idea floods Angustias's mind and drowns out her cries. She considers waking up Felicitas but doesn't want to risk another fight. Instead, she calls Samara, who gets to work as soon as Angustias hangs up. As instructed, Samara calls everyone in town and informs them that Olvido's funeral is postponed until further notice.

In the spot where the tears and ashes landed, tiny blades of grass begin to sprout, pushing the dry brown leaves aside. By the next morning, Olvido's garden is green, vibrant, and alive.

chapter 20

Felicitas

Felicitas feels anything but vibrant when she wakes up Monday morning. The lights are out and the sun's still down, but an alarm is ringing, and she needs to shut it off before it wakes up Angustias. Felicitas reaches across the coffee table, grabs her mother's phone, and cuts the noise. Angustias remains silent and still, but only for a few minutes.

"Why are you up so early?" she asks by the time Felicitas is almost fully dressed, ready to take on the day alone. With her eyes still closed, she feels around the couch until she realizes her phone is on the table. A bright, white light shines on her half-asleep face. "It's not even seven."

"I'm going to school with Gustavo," Felicitas says as she ties her shoelaces.

Angustias stands so fast, she takes a moment to balance herself. "What? Why? That's crazy. Why would you go to school today? You're not even enrolled, and I didn't give you permission."

"I didn't give you permission to take me out of school," Felicitas shoots back.

"I didn't need your permission. I'm your mother. And I didn't do it on purpose. Your grandmother died."

Felicitas is well aware. That's the problem. She can't stand to be Olvido's messenger, personal assistant, and punching bag any longer. Olvido won't follow her to school. She'd much rather be around her daughter even if she's angry at her.

"You didn't delete your weekly alarms," Felicitas says as she walks toward the door. "If it makes you feel better, maybe that's a sign I'm meant to go to school."

"Or it's a sign that you're ready to spend the day with me," Angustias says, shuffling behind Felicitas. "I'm going back to the funeral home later. I'm changing the burial plans. I know how we can get your grandma to Mexico."

"Great," Felicitas says unenthusiastically, stepping out of the house. "Let me know the new plan when I get back."

"Felicitas," Angustias yells from the front door.

Felicitas, already in the middle of the street, pivots on her heels. "Do you really want to be the type of parent that tells her child not to go to school?" she shouts so the neighbors can hear. "What's next? You're going to give me alcohol and drugs, the hard kind?"

Angustias rolls her eyes and slams the door, but Felicitas can sense she's staring at her through the window. Sure enough, when Samara opens the door and learns that Felicitas wants to go to school with Gustavo, she looks over Felicitas's shoulder and flashes the same wide grin she greeted them with two nights before. She waves with her whole arm and stands on her toes. Felicitas turns. Her mother, with her face half covered by the rising sun's glare on the window, is not smiling.

"Have you had breakfast?" Samara asks. "Is your mom not coming over?"

"No to both questions," Felicitas replies. "She's not feeling well. She's…sad." Samara nods apologetically. "I think she wants to be alone."

Samara continues to nod as she leads Felicitas into her house and says, "I'll text her." Felicitas can't help but feel a bit jealous. She wants to be alone, too, but to escape the company she doesn't want, she must throw herself into a crowd, the worst kind of crowd, a sea of schoolchildren.

Felicitas has experienced six and a half first days of school as the New Kid. The half occurred in the second semester of the third grade when her mother's car broke down before they fully made it out the driveway. By the time Angustias gave up trying to fix the problem and called a local cab, four hours of the school day had gone by.

First days are not too terrible, Felicitas has learned. Taunting begins a few days into her arrival. First days are simply long and lonely. Felicitas is what Angustias calls "reasonably quiet," but other kids mistake her for being shy or stuck up or strange. It does not help that she dresses head to toe in black every day of the week, the one thing she refuses to change no matter how much teasing it causes, and that her clothes are clearly secondhand. Angustias tries to mend the clothes they buy at the thrift store, but she is a terrible seamstress and there is nothing she can do about the discoloration of the fabric.

Felicitas knows the solution to her predicament: put in a little effort the way her mother does. That is what Mrs. Thompson said to her before crossing over. They sat on the doorstep of Felicitas's apartment, staring out at Mrs. Thompson's as they wheeled her body out on a stretcher. "Just do what your mother does, baby. Smile a little. Talk a little," Mrs. Thompson suggested. "And you'll see how people smile and talk right back."

Felicitas can't bring herself to follow the advice. She finds no reason to smile and there is nothing she wants to say. She doesn't know how to start a conversation or insert herself into one, and the pessimistic side of her knows there is no point. They will move again and again and again. Today, she will experience her eighth first day of school, and by next week, she will experience her ninth.

Felicitas holds her breath as she and Gustavo make their way into the Grace Elementary School building. With every classroom they pass, at least one kid looks up at Felicitas. They narrow their eyes as if trying to place her in their memory, and when they realize that they are unable to do so, they go back to paying attention to their books, their cell phones, or their friends. The sound of a familiar melody drifts into her left ear. It's fast, upbeat. It's in Spanish. The chatter around her buries the music as she moves farther away. "Did you hear that?" she asks Gustavo when they sit.

"What? Did someone fart?" Gustavo says, already searching for a culprit.

Felicitas scrunches her nose. "No. Forget it."

"Who's your new girlfriend, shrimp?" A tall, lanky boy with spiky black hair steps in front of them. He points a finger at Felicitas so that his dirty fingernail is millimeters away from her face. "What's wrong with her face?"

"Nothing," Gustavo snaps. "And she's not my girlfriend. She's Doña Olvido's granddaughter. Show some respect."

The lanky boy withdraws his finger. "Oh," he says. Pink splotches appear on his cheeks. "Sorry," he mutters and moves out of the way. A couple of seconds later, they hear him roar with laughter behind them. He found a new victim.

"Wow," Gustavo says, cocking his head to the side and pushing up his glasses. "I can't believe that worked."

"Who was that?"

"Mike Herrera. He's a bully, but he won't hurt you, not too much at least. He stopped hitting kids last year after he tried to punch Andrew Perez in the face, but Andrew moved his face, and Mike's hand accidentally struck the pavement. He broke three bones!"

Felicitas winces at the imagined pain. "You didn't seem scared."

"I told you. I haven't been scared since I was seven."

Felicitas nods with respect. "And he also knew my grandmother?"

"Yes. We all knew your grandma. Everyone knows everyone, but we definitely knew your grandma."

Felicitas narrows her eyes. "Why?"

"You know, 'cause of her cooking," Gustavo says.

"Right," Felicitas nods even though she doesn't fully understand what he means. "What does it have to do with that guy?"

"Well, last summer, every day, Mike would stop by your grandma's house in the mornings to pick up lunch because his parents didn't give him lunch or lunch money for summer school." Gustavo's eyes grow big. He checks his surroundings, looking twice in Mike's direction. "Don't tell him I said that."

Felicitas crosses her arms. "I won't, but you shouldn't talk about people's personal business if it's not your own."

"Sorry. You asked."

"Well, yes, but don't repeat what you said to me," Felicitas commands, as the memory of Mindy chants, "You're poor."

"I won't." Gustavo traces a cross over his heart with his index finger.

Felicitas uncrosses her arms, but her expression does not soften. She can't believe it. Her grandmother did a good deed for a random boy who is not very nice. She did good deeds for other people who were not her own family. Strangers tasted her grandmother's home-cooked meals before she ever got the chance to do the same. Strangers got to know Olvido, maybe even love her, and maybe Olvido loved them back. Or maybe Felicitas was getting ahead of herself. She shouldn't care. Olvido won't be around much longer. Felicitas will carry out her dying wish. Last evening's fight seemed to change her mother's mind about it.

"We're here," Gustavo says, coming to a stop at the end of a line of kids and leaning against a wall. "Estela, this is Felicitas, my new neighbor." Gustavo pushes up his glasses and smiles at the two grim-faced girls. "Felicitas, this is Estela, my annoying friend."

Estela sticks out her tongue at Gustavo and eyes Felicitas up and down. Felicitas mimics the gesture. The two girls look unusual standing next to each other, Felicitas dressed in black from head to toe and Estela dressed in various shades of pink. She wears a pink tulle skirt, pink sneakers, a dust-rose colored cardigan with pearls for buttons, and a pearl encrusted headband that sweeps back her brown curls.

"Are you going to a funeral?" Estela sasses.

"I will soon. Are you playing dress-up?" Felicitas shoots back.

"Perhaps."

"I knew you two would get along," Gustavo says gleefully and rambles on about how he has a sixth sense for finding friends as they scatter into the classroom. Estela and Gustavo separate and move to their assigned seats. Unsure of where to go, Felicitas stands to the side. She turns to find the teacher already making her way toward her.

"Hello. I'm Mrs. Luna," the teacher says softly, slightly bending her knees so that she's closer to Felicitas's eye level. "You're Felicitas?" Felicitas nods timidly. "It's very nice to meet you, Felicitas. The principal and I spoke to Gustavo's parents about your visit, and we're very happy to have you. Would you like to introduce yourself to the rest of the class?" Felicitas shakes her head. "I see. Well, you can take one of those chairs and sit next to someone, anywhere you want, okay?"

Felicitas nods and walks toward an empty desk in utter disbelief. The teacher actually gave her the option to not humiliate herself in front of the whole classroom. Adults, with the exception of her mother, tended to disregard her desire for silence. Felicitas has never understood why grown-ups can't make up their mind about kids talking when they don't want to and staying quiet when they have something to say.

"Mrs. Luna, who's that?" someone shouts from the back of the classroom, killing Felicitas's small but impressive victory. Her mouth goes dry. How many times will she have to repeat her name? How many new variations of its pronunciation will she encounter?

"Her name is Felicitas, and she'll be visiting us for the day," Mrs. Luna tersely explains. "You know who else will be visiting us? C. S. Lewis!" The class groans. Relief washes over Felicitas once again.

For the next four hours, Felicitas attentively listens to lessons on symbolism, fraction addition, and the water cycle. During group activities, people ask her who she is, what she's doing in their school, how long she will stay, and if she is not too hot wearing a black jacket in hundred-degree weather. No one asks her to repeat her name more than once and most pronounce it correctly on their first try, just like Mrs. Luna. A few people ask her if she has a nickname, but they don't force one on her when she tells them that she does not. Then, they leave the safety of the classroom.

"Is your name really Felicitas as in 'felicidad'?" one boy questions as they walk out. Felicitas nods. A hint of smile forms on her lips. He knows what her name means. "Then why do you look angry?" The corners of her lips drop back to their usual place.

"She doesn't look angry, stupid," the boy's friend interjects, whacking him with his backpack. "She looks sad. Maybe we can call you Tristecitas."

The first boy laughs and suggest an alternative. "Tristitas."

"Enojaditas," his friend shouts.

Their laughter pushes Felicitas back, but an arm interlaces with her own and drags her forward. "Her name is Felicitas because parents don't name their kids after what they really are, Ángel," Estela declares, chin up, eyes fierce. "If they did, your mom would have named you Pendejo instead."

"Estela Diaz," a voice booms behind them.

"Yes, Mrs. Hart?" Estela asks innocently, turning with Felicitas's arm still locked with hers.

"This is your third strike. I'm going to have to call your parents, and we're going to have a very serious discussion about your inappropriate language."

"That sounds wonderful, Mrs. Hart. Will you discuss your support of bullying?"

"Excuse me?"

Estela stomps her foot. "You don't want me to call Ángel the *P* word because you don't support students standing up against bullies, and that means *you* support bullies."

Mrs. Hart lets out a deep exhale. Felicitas imagines fire blasting out of her nostrils. "I will have a conversation with Ángel's parents as well, but this is the third time this month that I have heard you using inappropriate lang—"

"Why is it inappropriate?" Estela demands. "Is it because it's in Spanish? Mrs. Hart, are you racist?"

Felicitas's smile returns. She can make it through the rest of the day on her own. Almost.

In the cafeteria, Felicitas sits with Gustavo and Estela and discusses R. L. Stine. Gustavo eventually becomes bored, at least that's what he pretends to be, and moves to a different table with other friends.

"If you like Goosebumps, you should read Fear Street," Felicitas says to Estela when Gustavo leaves. "The characters are older and the stories are less childish."

"I've heard of Fear Street. I saw the movies." Estela pushes her plate to the side and leans over the table. "Do you like scary movies?" she whispers.

"I love scary movies," Felicitas whispers back.

"Me too! But they are all rated PG-13 or R. It's not as fun to watch scary movies on a TV screen at home as it is to watch in a movie theater."

"How would you know?"

Estela moves back on the bench and crosses her arms. She smiles, but her voice tells Felicitas she is anything but happy. "My older sister used to sneak me into the movie theater. We bought tickets for a different movie and waited in the restroom until the one we wanted to see began to play."

That sounded exactly like something Angustias would do. In fact, Felicitas recalls, Angustias did just that when she was a teenager. She told Felicitas all about it during one of her reminiscing episodes. Angustias, however, snuck in to see comedies where the chances of people dying were low. Horror was not her cup of tea. She only watched those kinds of films when Felicitas begged her to. Felicitas never bothered asking Angustias to take her to see a horror movie because she knew she was not allowed, not by her mother's rules but by the theater's restrictions. She didn't want to break the law and risk getting her mother in trouble.

Estela looks down at her plate and pushes around her food with her spork. "She moved away last year, though. She decided to go to college and totally abandoned me."

"My mom can sneak us in."

The spork stops. Estela glances up. "Your mom would sneak us into a movie we didn't buy a ticket for?" she asks skeptically.

"Yep. She would probably want to throw me a whole party to celebrate my rule breaking."

"She sounds cool."

"She's a mom," Felicitas says with a shrug.

"Well, I already know what movie we should see. *Dead at Midnight*. Have you heard of it? It looks so creepy."

Felicitas had indeed heard of it and knows that it will not be released until the middle of summer. She will be long gone by then. She offers Estela a small smile. Knowing that the plan is a bust, she can't bring herself to give more. "Yes, I have."

"Oh my God! There's this other movie by the same director." Estela fills Felicitas in on the history of the movie and the horror universe the story is set in. She tells her of her all-time favorite horror movies, and

Felicitas tells her of hers. During History, they talk about their favorite books and TV shows. During Spanish, they debate whether black is better than pink. During Art, they discuss how one can believe in the effectiveness of mood rings but not horoscopes or prophecies, and by the time they part ways to get into their respective school buses, Felicitas wants to cry. Luckily, no one notices.

"Bye!" Felicitas calls out to Estela as she heads toward bus number twelve. Only she can detect the tremble in her own voice.

"See you tomorrow," Estela shouts back before stepping into the yellow monster's mouth. It swallows her whole, but she doesn't seem afraid. She doesn't know that her journey has come to an end in Felicitas's grander story.

Felicitas's sadness turns into anger, anger toward herself. She has been crying too much lately. What she hasn't been doing much of is making friends, and she has just made a friend she does not want to leave. Maybe her mother doesn't want to leave either. What reason is there to run away from Grace? None other than Olvido's house makes her act strange, but they don't have to stay at Olvido's. They can stay at Samara's for a while, just until they find a house or an apartment to rent. And Felicitas can attend Grace Middle School in the fall and the spring and the year after that and the year after that and the year after that. If they stay, she can hang out with Estela and Gustavo in the summer and meet other kids, and maybe she'll like them, and they'll like her back, and she can have a whole group of friends. Angustias will see that Felicitas is happy, and she'll want to stay. Forever.

No. Forever is unquantifiable, and unquantifiable things don't exist. The only real thing is the present in which she had a good day, just one good day, an accident. Tomorrow will be a new day, a terrible one no doubt. Olvido's nagging and yapping will have her wishing she was anywhere but here in no time. *Just one more day,* she tells herself. *Don't think about friends. Don't think about goodbyes. Don't cry. Don't cry.*

chapter 21

Olvido

Olvido, as Felicitas predicted, stays by her daughter's side despite her dissatisfaction with her. It's what she has done since the day Angustias was born. Old habits die harder than resentment. Angustias is living proof.

"What do you think, Angustias? Angustias?" Samara smiles apologetically at Mr. Sosa and gently pushes Angustias's shoulder. "Angustias."

Angustias responds with a "Huh?"

"Huh?" Olvido repeats dumbfounded. "Se dice, 'Excuse me. Can you repeat that, please?' You weren't raised by wolves." She's glad Samara accompanied Angustias to talk to Mr. Sosa. She's a smart girl. Not that Angustias isn't, but she is clearly not mentally present. Funny. That is all Olvido can be.

"The urn?" Samara says.

"Huh?"

Shaking her head, Olvido steps out of the office and rattles her open palm at the door as if she could give everyone inside a simultaneous spanking. When she turns, she finds the strangest of sights. A petite, old woman in a flower-print nightgown runs from one end of the hall to another. She jumps, stretches her arms and laughs, amused by her flexibility. She stops when she notices Olvido and pushes her white, tangled hair out of her face to get a better look. Olvido's heart sinks to her feet. It's Ramona, a friend who moved to Grace last November. She shouldn't be there. No one whom Olvido cares about should be there, not in the same state she's in.

"Olvido?" Ramona exclaims. Her smile reveals various missing teeth. She must have died before putting in her dentures.

Olvido smiles tightly and nods. She should be shouting Ramona's name back with as much joy, but her throat is desert dry.

Ramona runs to her and embraces her like a child who's spotted a friend at the playground. "What are you doing here?" she asks.

Olvido swallows. "Huh?"

"Wait," Ramona says, stepping back. "A few days ago . . . I heard the news. Aren't you . . . ?"

Olvido nods apologetically. Shaking her head, Ramona takes a step back. Olvido nods more intensely. With a deep inhale, Ramona burst into sobs. No tears spill from her eyes. It is very unusual. She can run and jump, but she cannot cry properly. Is crying another special ability only Olvido holds? How useless.

"I'm sorry," Olvido says. Ramona's wails grow louder. "When— When did you . . . die?"

Ramona abruptly stops crying, her shoulders still up, ready to launch another cry. "I'm dead?" she says softly.

Olvido grimaces, mortified over her imprudence. "Oh, I'm so sorry, Ramona," she says. "I didn't know—I didn't mean to—"

Ramona laughs, a deep belly sound. "I'm just kidding," she says. "I know I'm dead. I was just trying to lighten the mood. How are you? Don't answer that. What are you doing here? Not in Heaven, I mean. Wait, let's go into one of the rooms. More privacy."

Panicked, Olvido looks around her in search of other spirits. She hopes no more friends appear any time soon. "When did you, um, pass away?" she says as she follows Ramona into the chapel and takes a seat beside her on a pew. "And how, if you don't mind me asking."

"Oh, you're not going to believe this," Ramona laughs. "I fell out of a tree this morning."

Olvido's hand shoots to her chest. "Ramona, what were you doing in a tree?"

Ramona shrugs. "I can't remember. I think I hit my head so hard, I got amnesia, but I know I fell out of a tree because I overheard my son talking about it on the phone with his wife. I lasted a couple of hours in the ICU."

"Your son is visiting? That is terrible timing."

"Isn't it? He found me. My poor boy. He's in shock, hasn't eaten all day. Well, he ate a sandwich and some soup and a bag of chips, but that's hardly anything."

Olvido knows she should not feel glad in such a heartbreaking moment, but she is. It was not Angustias who found her. Her daughter avoided that trauma.

"I'm happy, though," Ramona says with a toothless grin. "I escaped!"

"Escaped who?" Olvido whispers, her eyes shifting from side to side.

"The nursing home. My son never approved of me moving here all by myself. I'm sad it was for such a short amount of time. He arrived yesterday, came to convince me to go back to Chicago with him, but not to his house, no. He took out a pamphlet. Gave me a whole presentation. An assisted living facility is what he called it. When have I ever needed assistance? Don't answer that. I'm only eighty-eight not a hundred. My mother lived to nighty-nine, you know. My grandmother, one hundred and two. We have wonderful, ever-youthful genes.

"I guess I have no choice but to go back with him now. That's where they'll hold my funeral. He already stopped by to talk to Mr. Sosa about shipping my body. Shipping! Like I'm some piece of mail. It's all moving so fast, but I guess he wants to get out of Grace as soon as possible." Ramona giggles. "You know what I hope my last words were?"

"What?" Olvido says.

"You'll never catch me alive!" Ramona shouts and breaks into a sprint between the pews.

"Ramona," Olvido laughs. "That's horrible."

"Run with me, Olvido," Ramona says as she leaps across the air. "Nothing hurts anymore."

Olvido knows that isn't true. Her heart still aches.

"When do you think we'll see the light?" Ramona says, collapsing beside Olvido.

"I don't know," Olvido says. "I'm starting to think I never will."

"Oh, don't be so dramatic," Ramona says, hitting Olvido's arm. "You died, when? Friday?"

"Maybe Thursday."

"And it's only Saturday."

"It's Monday."

Ramona slaps her cheeks in horror. "I missed Sunday service again?"

"Yes. Don't worry. I did, too."

"You know what I'm really going to miss?" Ramona says, leaning in. "Your machaca con huevo. Más machaca—"

"Que huevo," Olvido says with a laugh.

Ramona sighs and turns to her with a serious look. "Olvido, may I make one last confession to you?" she says.

Olvido straightens her back and takes Ramona's hand. "Of course."

"Oh, I don't know if I can," Ramona laughs halfheartedly. "I really wish I could take a bite of that machaca right now."

Olvido nods. "Close your eyes," she instructs. "Go on, close them."

Ramona complies reluctantly. "I feel silly."

"You're not. If you're silly, so am I, and I would never want to be described as such."

"Oh, trust me," Ramona says. "No one has ever called you silly."

Olvido pats her hand. "Ready? Clear your mind. Now, imagine you're in my kitchen, sitting at the west-facing window. It's a clear day. The room is a bit hot because of the lit stove. You can smell the coffee brewing and the tortillas puffing up with hot air. You scoop up a forkful of machaca con huevo and take a bite. You crush the beef between your teeth. The salt explodes up to the roof of your mouth and down to your tongue."

Ramona smiles. "I love salt. It's so bad for my health."

"The egg keeps it from being overbearing. It's hot, practically burning your mouth."

"Nothing worse than cold eggs."

"You feel the heat of the salsa you poured on top. You taste tomatillo and serrano and fresh cilantro."

"Ugh, I hate cilantro."

"And? What else do you hate?"

"I hate," Ramona says, her voice trembling. "I hate being afraid."

"What are you afraid of?"

"I'm afraid of being dead. I'm afraid of seeing my family cry at my funeral. I want to be gone by then, but I'm not sure how to leave. Do you?" Ramona says, opening her eyes.

Olvido shakes her head. "Why are you afraid of seeing your family cry?"

Tears roll down the creases of Ramona's cheeks. "Because it's painful," she says. "I don't want to be in pain."

"Their sadness will not last forever," Olvido says.

"But *my* pain will," Ramona says, tightening her grip. "If they're sad, I'm sad. If they're happy . . . I think I'll still be sad. I know it sounds horrible, but what if they forget me?"

"You know that won't happen."

"I'm not afraid of what will happen, I'm afraid of what it *feels* like is happening. The brain and heart are two separate things. I know that better than anyone. My brain sometimes forgot my grandchildren's names, but my heart didn't love them any less."

Olvido pulls her hands away and massages the areas Ramona dug into with too much force. "We won't be here forever, Ramona. If you don't want to witness how life goes on without us, you don't have to."

"Where will we be, then?"

Olvido frowns, confused. "Heaven, of course." Ramona knows this. Perhaps, amnesia made her forget about God. That is why she's afraid. Without God, without faith, there is no refuge from fear.

"Are you sure?" Ramona whispers. "What if there is no Heaven?"

"Don't say that," Olvido snaps. "I'm sorry," she says quickly. With one hand, she pats Ramona's leg. With the other, she plays with the edge of her shirt. "You said, you were afraid of pain, correct? Isn't fear itself painful? Fear makes you unhappy. It hurts to be unhappy. It's a vicious cycle. I've lived my life afraid of so many things, things I had no control over, and that made me miserable, and I was afraid that I would be miserable forever. I'm still afraid of that." She is still in pain. Her death did not end motherhood. As long as Olvido has a conscious, she will worry about her daughter's well-being, and that is fine. She chose to be a mother, but she did not choose to be dead. What good is it to still be able to see the living if she cannot help her daughter, if she can only hear how much she resented her? It is not good. It is torture. Only divine intervention can put her out of her misery. "I know that I have no way of knowing if Heaven is real or not, but if I remain hopeful about it, I won't be afraid, and I won't be in pain."

Ramona shakes her head with pity. "Didn't you hear what I said? The brain and heart are two separate things. I can tell myself that God will take me soon, that Heaven exists, and it is a wonderful, painless place, but my heart won't believe it."

Olvido stands. Her hands close into tight fists at her sides. "How can you abandon your faith so quickly?"

"Look at the evidence, Olvido," Ramona says, standing to face her. "We're still here."

"Well, I won't be for long," Olvido says confidently. "I'm going home soon, and so will you. And when we give a proper goodbye to our respective homes, we will be taken to our new one. I hope to see you there." Olvido steps around Ramona and marches to the entrance.

"Olvido," Ramona calls. Olvido turns reluctantly. "I'm surprised you spoke to me like that. It's a sin to disrespect your elders."

Olvido shifts her weight as she thinks. "I passed away first," she says. "I'm older in dead years." Ramona's laughter follows her out of the room, forcing her to quicken her step. She was wrong. Ramona is silly, but Olvido is not, and neither is God nor Heaven, because without Heaven, there is no Hell, and Hell is something she is already experiencing.

chapter 22

Angustias

Felicitas was born at exactly 12:00 p.m. on a humid, cloudy Tuesday. Angustias remembers this fact every day on the hour. She calls it the Felicitas Hour, the time of the day in which she misses her daughter the most when they are apart.

Angustias steals a quick glance at her phone. How long can she hide in the restroom before Samara and the funeral home director begin to suspect that she ran away?

11:59.

12:00.

Angustias feels the urge to hug Felicitas, to tell her how much she loves her, how much she wants them to go home, far away from Grace. She might as well just tell the mirror. Every feature she has, passed on to her by Olvido, was gifted to Felicitas. Her thick eyebrows. Her almond eyes. Her brown skin. The only difference is her hair. Her stick-straight strands transformed into loose curls after her pregnancy. If she straightens it for Olvido's funeral, will people think she's her mother's ghost? Maybe she'll spook everyone away and they'll let her mourn in peace.

Tugging at the ends of her hair, she leans toward the mirror. "Would that be okay, Mami?" she asks. "Or would that be disrespectful and shameful?" With wet fingers, Angustias pushes and pulls her cheeks and chin and stretches the skin on her forehead and eyelids. Her touch lingers on the dark crescents beneath her eyes.

"I think they make you look cool, like a vampire," Felicitas once told her.

"A vampire? You mean hideous and creepy?" Angustias replied, sticking out her tongue.

Angustias knows that was not what Felicitas meant, but it's how she feels sometimes. She feels hideous. She feels tired. She feels like her mother must have felt while raising her. Angustias used to think Olvido was born tired, that simply being conceived had been too much for her to handle. Her mother must have been born with a baby blue cloud over her head the way Felicitas was born with a frown. Angustias revised her conclusion shortly after giving birth herself. It was Angustias who had been too much to handle. She ran too much, yelled too much, jumped too much.

Felicitas is definitely not too much to handle but life is. Rent breathes down her neck as she pushes her shopping cart down grocery store aisles. "Why buy that brand of bread when that other one is two dollars cheaper?" Rent whispers. "Sure, your taste buds will be satisfied by the expensive option, but what about me? You can't forget to feed me. You know what happens when I'm left hungry at the end of the month."

"I don't care if you're late," her car insurance shrieks as she drives on the expressway. "I will not cover whatever accident you get yourself into." Angustias doesn't ask what it *will* cover because she's asked many times before. It simply shouts, "I won't cover it. I won't. I'm not responsible. I'm not."

"Turn me off. Turn me off," the heater sings on cold, winter nights. "You can't afford me. Just put on two pairs of socks." Angustias obeys. She lays an additional blanket over Felicitas and tucks it around her feet. Weather has become exponentially unpredictable. Maybe there will come a time when she'll have to fall asleep to the heater's song no matter how unpleasant it is. She'll just deal with the consequences later.

"What happened to you?" she asks her brain in the nights when it keeps her up, flashing reminders of the cost of life. "You never worried like this. *I* never worried." She knows the answer and repeats it to herself, hoping that it will lull her to sleep. *You are not just you. You are a mother. You are Angustias* and *Felicitas.* The chant works its magic far too slowly. She wakes up exhausted. Fatigue is not a good look on her.

Angustias dries her hands and sighs as she walks out of the restroom. She hopes Felicitas is having a better day than her in school. It was just a little quarrel, not enough to be traded for schoolwork. If anyone knows how bad mother-daughter fights can get, it's Angustias, and the one she had with Felicitas was nothing. Yet, Angustias continues to check the time until they are out of the building, counting down the hours and minutes until she can see Felicitas again and check that her cloud is not permanently crimson.

"I can't believe Mr. Sosa gave me such a long extension for the payment," Angustias says to Samara as they walk along the main street of town. Her comment is interrupted three times by passersby. "Good afternoon, Samara. How are you? How's your mom? And who is this? Wait. Don't tell me. Oh, my goodness. Are you Olvido's daughter? You look just like her!" Their voices remind Angustias of how she used to coo at Felicitas in her first years of life, but Angustias spoke with love. These people's voices express nothing but indigo.

"Well, believe it," Samara says to Angustias. "I told you people would want to help. Are you hungry? Should we eat a snack before we meet the kids at home?" Angustias nods with desperation. Her stomach is begging to be filled.

"But I'm still confused as to why?" Angustias says. "Was she in need of money? Was she selling her dishes? Are there even enough people here to sustain such a business? Maybe a home-based business would have been a smart choice since she wouldn't have had to pay additional rent. But wouldn't she need a business license?"

"Oh! Taliah!" Samara calls out waving her arms over her head. "Yoo-hoo!"

Across the street, Taliah waves one arm back. She speedwalks toward them, ignoring the oncoming cars that are forced to brake for her. Her overfilled paper bags force her to shift her weight, causing her to wobble like a penguin, but despite the struggle, she makes it through with a bright smile garnished with a daffodil yellow.

"It'll be on Wednesday at 9 a.m., and then we'll probably head to Nuestra Señora del Carmen at noon," Samara tells Taliah once they finish recapping their respective weekends minute by minute. "We still have to talk with Padre Alfonso, but I think he'll accept that plan."

"I'm sure he will," Taliah says with a nod.

A sudden, inexplicable wave of judgment washes over Angustias. She smiles to hide the discomfort. Her attempt is in vain. The hot, icky feeling seeps into her skin and tries to escape the same way it came in, bringing a red tint to Angustias's cheeks.

Where is the judgment coming from? Angustias wonders. Not Samara. She's guilty of pity but not criticism. Not Taliah. Her cloud is still bright as sunshine. Could it be . . . ? Angustias inconspicuously looks up and jerks her gaze back down. No. She must be judging herself.

It's okay, she thinks to herself. *This is a difficult time. You're doing your best.* But she's not so sure. It's her mother's funeral. She should be the one inviting people. She should be the one informing them of the details, but she doesn't know who Padre Alfonso is or even where Nuestra Señora del Carmen is located.

"You know what," Angustias interrupts. "I forgot I have to stop by the library. Felicitas asked me to pick up a book for her."

"Oh, I'll go with you," Samara says, readjusting her purse.

"No, no. I can go by myself," Angustias says, already a few feet away from Samara and Taliah. "I'll meet you back at the house to pick up Felicitas."

"But how will you get back home?" Samara shouts.

Angustias wishes she had an answer. Maybe she won't find one until she's dead. Felicitas will be left to figure it out like Angustias has to do for Olvido.

There she is again, slowly transforming into her mother. Angustias must not wait around for a full conversion. Soon enough, she'll sprout fangs and commence her days at nightfall. At least Felicitas will think she's cool. That is until she realizes Angustias isn't hungry for blood. If she truly is like Olvido, Angustias will suck her daughter dry of energy, patience, and a belief in unconditional love.

chapter 23

Felicitas

The full extent of Felicitas's knowledge on the subject of funerals is based on fiction. Television shows and movies taught her that funerals are quick and organized. They consist of attendees talking and walking around a spacious, somber house, or silently sitting in the pews of a church while tearfully staring at a giant portrait of their loved one, or crying in a green, freshly cut field of grass as a casket is lowered into the ground. Burial ceremonies do not last long, just a scene or two, and they don't take long to plan.

Real funerals turn out to be nothing like the ones on television. As she patiently waits for Olvido's to be over, Felicitas wonders if she should have watched something other than American programs to get a better understanding of mourning rituals. "Maybe a telenovela would have given me a better idea," she tells Olvido in the privacy of the funeral home's restroom.

Olvido shakes her head. "No. It would not have made a difference. I saw plenty of novelas in my lifetime and attended plenty of funerals as a child, and I never witnessed one quite like this, so rushed and . . . ugly."

Felicitas frowns and splashes water at her grandmother's face. "We tried our best."

"I know," Olvido sighs, wiping where the drops should have landed. "That's what makes it so sad."

Felicitas's first funeral experience begins with numbness in her legs, a consequence of sitting in a funeral home for what Felicitas is sure is an eternity even though eternity cannot be measured. Breakfast, brunch, and lunchtime come and go. Guests bring food to share, but bad communication leaves them with fourteen foil pans of barbacoa, three pounds of tortillas, three plastic cups filled with salsa and zero utensils.

At the start of the ceremony, the main room of the funeral home appears ridiculously empty with just a tiny black and gold urn propped up on a table in the middle of the center stage. Flower arrangements come in one by one throughout the morning and help fill the emptiness, but they emphasize the smallness of the urn. Eventually, the flowers overtake everything, the stage, the hallway, the seats. It appears that every family in Grace ordered a flower spray for Olvido. Gardenias interlace with aves del paraíso, which tower over sunflowers, which push against red roses that lean on baby's breath cradled by bundles of leaves. Once all the seats have been taken over by plants, people head out to make room for more incoming sprays.

At some point, only Angustias and Felicitas remain in the main room. They sit in the first row to the right. Angustias stares straight ahead. At her side, Felicitas holds on tightly to her hand, refusing to lose the fight against the petals and leaves that push against her. Wrapped up in her own sorrow, Angustias doesn't notice her body becoming one with the plants behind her. Leaves and stems twirl around the strands of her hair. Petals frame her face like long, delicate earrings with a necklace to match.

"This looks absurd," Olvido says to Felicitas as she slowly walks around the room, her body passing through the flower sprays, her gaze lingering on the signed cards. She pauses to point to the middle of the stage. "I should be in an open casket, not in an urn. Whoever heard of such a service for a box of ashes? At least people sent flowers. Grace has such good people, don't you think?"

Felicitas gives a small nod. She restrains herself from rolling her eyes at her grandmother's complaints. It is her funeral after all. She deserves a bit of compassion.

Felicitas has been so good about remaining respectful, she didn't even roll her eyes when Olvido began asking questions about Angustias the moment she noticed Felicitas was awake. "Is your mom awake? Has she eaten? Make sure she doesn't forget to put on perfume. And why are you wearing pink? I can't rest in peace seeing such a disrespectful act. Do you not want me to rest in peace? Do you want me to stay?"

Instead of saying, "Please, don't," Felicitas rushed to the bathroom to change. The demands continued all day.

"Fix your mom's makeup. It's running." Olvido says, making her way between the jungle of flowers surrounding her urn. "And fix her hair. Yours, too. Has your mom eaten? She's gotten so skinny. It's the crying. She's dehydrated. Make sure she eats. I think there are some—"

Felicitas squeezes her mother's hand more tightly with every command. The pain finally forces Angustias to look up and notice the lack of people around them. Every guest has been replaced by a floral arrangement. "Where did everyone go?" she asks. It's already one in the afternoon.

When the ceremony at the funeral home ends, the townspeople head to the church to hear the priest deliver his hour-long sermon. Due to her lack of experience, Felicitas doesn't know whether this length is standard. She hopes for the sake of others' sanity that it's not.

Every time the priest says, "En el nombre del Padre y del Hijo y del Espíritu Santo," which seems to be after every other sentence, Olvido repeats the phrase in Felicitas's ear and makes a point of showing her where to place her hand with each word. By the fourth try, Felicitas gets the order right.

"I'm glad your mom hasn't forgotten Catholic prayers and hymns," Olvido says. "Although she should have at least taught you the basics. You should tell her to go to church more often, at least on the holidays, especially during Semana Santa. And don't forget to tell her to wear black for the next six months. That's tradition, but really you should continue after six months. Maybe a year? Has your mother—"

"Amen," Felicitas shouts along with everyone's more calm repetition of the word. Angustias fails to suppress her laughter. Giggles turned into a deep laugh that rises from the depths of her belly. A wave of laughter spreads throughout the church. It begins with Doña Regina and ends with the priest. To Felicitas's surprise, Olvido smiles, but when she does, she looks only at Angustias.

By the time they arrive at the river, it's already twilight. Purples, blues, and yellows ripple beneath the sky in the currents. They overlap, but do not mix, racing each other to reach the intersecting river, then the gulf and the ocean. The leaves of the low trees dance to the rhythm of the townspeople's hymns, asynchronously and off beat. The funeral attendees gather as close to the water's edge as possible. Angustias and Felicitas stand in front of the priest who looks out into the crowd gathered behind them.

As the townspeople end their song, Felicitas lifts herself on her toes and extends her neck to get a better look at the river's southern end. The land bends and breaks, blocking her view of the full extent of the waters. She has seen the map, though. Olvido's ashes will have to make a difficult journey to reach the Rio Grande.

The priest begins his speech with a joke about Olvido's name, a play on words about how she will never be forgotten. Olvido shakes her head but chuckles. It's the happiest Felicitas has ever seen her, not that she's spent much time with Olvido. Less than a week. Just a few days. Insufferable days, but . . . not even days. Hours because she slept for at least a quarter of the day each day. And she continued going to school the whole week, and Olvido didn't follow. And when she was in Olvido's house, there was all the time she spent in the restroom, which she prohibited Olvido from interrupting. All in all, if Felicitas lives to the age of ninety or above, her time with Olvido will be relative to the blink of an eye.

When the priest opens the urn and spills Olvido's ashes into the river, the cold water will wash away more than a body and soul. Down will flow all the memories and secrets Felicitas never had access to. What part of Mexico were her ancestors from? Angustias cannot remember beyond a few generations back. Why did Olvido come to the US? Did she regret it? Should Felicitas go to Mexico, too?

"Make sure she eats well," Olvido says as the priest rambles on. "None of those spicy chips that have probably given her an ulcer by now. And make sure she gets off her phone from time to time. And make sure she doesn't walk around barefoot. She's going to catch a cold, and then what will you two do?" On and on she goes. "Now that I'm gone, you are all she has, so take care of her, okay?" Olvido instructs.

What do you think I've been doing this whole time? She wants to ask. *I'm all she's had for the last ten years.* But these are not questions that need to be answered. What burns white hot in Felicitas's mind, she would never say out loud even if she and Olvido were alone. *Are there any instructions about me? Do you not care if I catch a cold? Did you ever love me, even for just a moment or the blink of an eye?*

chapter 24

Angustias

Angustias doesn't have a eulogy prepared. When the priest asks her to say a few words, she instinctively takes a step back. Calladita se ve más bonita.

Had she been asked to speak about her mother the day she heard of her passing, Angustias would have only spoken flattering words. Olvido was hardworking, resilient, brave, smart, selfless. Loving. *I loved my mom. My mom loved me.*

A week has passed. Her grief has cooled just one degree enough to allow hot memories of resentment to rise above the rest. She doesn't feel any less mournful about her mother's absence, but she doesn't feel any more nostalgic about the past either. Hearing the townspeople's recollections of Olvido has only proven that her mother was capable of gentleness and sympathy. Withholding that from Felicitas was not a personality fault but a choice, and now Angustias can choose to be just as cruel. She could point out every single mistake Olvido ever made, divulge the last threat she made before Angustias left. But she can't. Her mother isn't there to witness her revenge. She would only be hurting Olvido's friends, and most importantly, Felicitas.

"Actually," Angustias improvises. "I think my mom would have loved to hear from y'all." Yes, that sounds right. Funerals are, after all, mostly for the living to let out their grief, to let go of their gray and make room for whatever other color gives them the strength to carry on. Besides, the only thing Olvido wanted to hear coming from Angustias's mouth was an apology, which Angustias can't bring herself to give, especially not in front of a crowd of strangers.

The funeral guests don't need to be asked twice. One by one, they walk up to where Angustias is standing and face the crowd. With tears in their eyes but a smile on their lips, they recall their favorite moments with Olvido, most of which involve food. Olvido made birthday cakes, late night café con pan, last minute lunches, Christmas dinners for one, and two wedding cakes. She helped people come to terms with the loss of a loved one, the end of a relationship, entering old age, and marriage proposals.

"Last summer was one of the most difficult moments of my life," Itzel Huerta declared to the crowd. "I came back from college engaged and with a bachelor's degree ready to start working and form a family, but I was so unhappy, I—I was not myself as y'all may recall. In the middle of the summer, Olvido invited me over to her house. She knew what was wrong without even asking. She brewed some hot fruit punch and patiently waited with me for an hour until I was brave enough to take a sip. Together we figured it out. I wasn't ready for marriage; I wasn't ready to start a job I didn't love. And now," she cries, "I'm back in school, and I know you don't like graphic design, Mami, but I'm so happy. I'm doing what I love, and I'll find love when I'm ready, and— And I miss Olvido, and I'm so grateful for her."

Angustias's fingers anxiously play with Felicitas's braid. Talking? Listening? When did her mother learn to do that? What if Olvido had sat with her for just an hour when she confessed she was pregnant? What if instead of forcing her to leave they had figured things out together?

Angustias lets go of the braid. It doesn't matter anymore. As people keep reminding her with their stories, Olvido is gone.

The sea of the townspeople's dark gray clouds becomes tinted with a content cool, pale yellow, and peaceful dusty pink. At the front, like a lighthouse on a shore, is Felicitas's cloud. Slate, just like in the restaurant the evening of their arrival. Angustias pulls her close. *I'm sorry if I've been distant these last few days*, she wants to say. *I'll do better.*

Eventually, the only person left to speak besides Angustias is Felicitas, but before her cheeks can turn red with embarrassment, Angustias steps toward the river and bends down so that she's as close to the water as she can be without getting in it. Carefully, she opens the box and tilts it down.

A flicker of disbelief crosses Angustias's face. She didn't want to point it out before, but she'd noticed that Felicitas didn't cry when she heard the news of Olvido's death. At first, she thought Felicitas didn't care. Her daughter has no memories of her grandmother other than of her voice through short shallow phone conversations. Now she's unsure of what her daughter feels. Her cloud keeps flickering between dark gray and slate, dark and rusty brown, burgundy and crimson.

This is too much for her. They need to leave. Tomorrow, they'll be gone by tomorrow.

chapter 25

Olvido

As Olvido's ashes hit the edge of the river, a gray-brown cloud forms and swirls in the water. The ashes soon disperse, and the water is clear again. Perhaps that is the solution to fixing a tainted relationship, Olvido thinks. Space.

No, that cannot be. She tried giving Angustias space. She tried giving herself some space. Just a few hours. Just a short distance. It was an impulsive act, a consequence of Angustias startling her with life-altering news on the most normal of days.

Olvido sat at the kitchen table across from Angustias, who gobbled up her chorizo and eggs as if she hadn't eaten in days. "Slow down," Olvido ordered. "You're going to choke." Angustias nodded but she didn't obey. Her hands moved quickly from her fork to her napkin to her mug and back. "What's wrong with you?" Olvido asked, her face scrunched up with concern.

"I'm pregnant," Angustias blurted. It took her a couple of seconds to realize what she'd done. She pressed her lips between her teeth and closed her eyes. Her body became so still, a visitor would have mistaken her for one of the many figures of la Virgen de Guadalupe that guarded the house.

Signing a cross over her heart, Olvido scooted out of her chair and marched to her room. She walked back to the kitchen a minute later with her purse in her hand and announced. "I will be gone for a while. Don't worry. I'll be back before it gets dark."

"Where are you going?" Angustias asked, still frozen in her chair.

"Out," Olvido said in the same tone Angustias used when leaving the house on weekend evenings. She stepped out of the house and locked the door behind her. Clearly, las vírgenes had not been vigilant enough.

After driving to a gas station and buying a pack of cigarettes, Olvido drove to the parking lot at the southern end of S. International Blvd., parked her truck, and walked to the canopy at the bottom of the walkway that led to the US-Mexico bridge. She lit a cigarette, which she hid every time someone passed by, and sat staring at the walkway for an hour.

She could stride up the walkway. No one would ask her any questions if she stayed on US soil. She could walk up to the entrance of the bridge and step up to the tripod gate. She could slide two quarters in and push the metal arm with her thighs. She could keep walking until her feet bled. She could reach the end of the world, and what came after Earth? Heaven.

Olvido put out her cigarette and walked back to her truck. She started the ignition and forced the motor to take her far away from where her feet wanted to run. *Don't go south. Don't go south.* If she reached Mexico, if she reached Heaven, she would be unable to see to it that her pregnant daughter ate right. Hot Cheetos and cheese were not appropriate pregnancy food unless Angustias was looking to birth a child the color of a ghost pepper.

Without Olvido, Angustias wouldn't know to attach a red thread to the cloth over her protruding belly to ward off evil. She wouldn't know to cut the leaves of an aloe vera and rub the sábila over her stretched skin after giving birth. She would try to sweep during her postpartum quarantine, and the broom would make a whirlwind of air and dust, and it would make Angustias sick, and the doctors wouldn't know how to help her because they were diablos but not viejos like Olvido, and Angustias would die remembering her mother by a single word. "Out."

Olvido would not be able to return because God would keep her in Heaven if she walked far, and la Migra would keep her in Mexico if she walked near. Border Patrol agents would lead her into their office and keep her there for a while, maybe just a few minutes, definitely not a whole day. Then, they would drag her out as she kicked and scratched and screamed, "Please! Let me go! My baby is having a baby!" They would not have mercy on her. Not even God would have mercy on her and her baby and her baby's baby.

"I gave you a gift," He would bellow. "And you ran away."

"You gave me a curse!" Olvido would shout back. "You and my mother, and her mother who was cursed by her mother. Will You curse my baby's baby, too?" Olvido did not find out within her lifetime.

"Eat this," Olvido said to Angustias a few hours after she arrived back at the house.

Angustias looked down at the plate Olvido dropped in front of her. "Salmon?" she said. "We can't afford salmon."

"We can't afford an unhealthy baby. Salmon is cheaper than a hospital bill. No! Don't eat yet." Olvido untied her apron, threw it over her chair and hurried to her bedroom.

"Where are you going?" Angustias called after her. "Why won't you talk to me?"

It was not her mouth Olvido was trying to keep shut. It was her ears. Olvido had not intended to get any truth out of Angustias when she served her breakfast that morning, but God had given her a curse disguised as a gift.

Olvido cooked her first truth-inducing food at age twelve. It began with a pregnancy scare.

"It's a baby. I know it is. We're doomed," Victoria cried, clutching her stomach.

"We've been doomed since before I was born," Olvido pointed out. "It's probably just indigestion or gas."

"I know what a baby feels like," Victoria snapped, but Olvido had been right. Her pain was simply gas.

Olvido soothed her mother's emotional and physical pain with a tea she made using the leaves of a mint plant Doña Ginebra had gifted her for Christmas. It was a sad excuse for a plant when it arrived at the Olivares home. Its stem drooped impossibly low. Its dull leaves refused to give off an appetizing scent. Olvido nursed it back to health by feeding it all the love and patience she could not give her mother. A few weeks later, the healthy plant was willing to return the love. "Take my leaves," it said with its vibrant green hue. "Use me for something good."

Olvido carried the boiling drink to Victoria, and said, "Careful. Don't burn your tongue." Victoria gulped the tea as if she were drinking agua de jamaica on the hottest day of the year. "Why did you think you were pregnant?" Olvido asked. "Who have you been seeing?"

"Javier," Victoria responded. The teacup slipped through her fingers with the same ease as the name had rolled off her tongue.

"Which Javier?" Olvido said with trepidation. "Doña Ginebra's husband, Javier?" Victoria's silence answered for her. "I wish you were pregnant," Olvido said softly as she picked up the ceramic pieces dripping with tea and tears. "I wish you had another child to deal with your sins. I would escape as soon as the umbilical cord was cut."

"Do it!" Victoria shouted. "Escape. Run away like your father. I should have given you his last name!"

It wasn't until she had a child of her own that Olvido realized she could force the truth out of those she cooked for. In the time between Victoria's disappearance and her wedding, Olvido didn't have anyone to share home-cooked meals with but herself. She didn't have the opportunity to observe how the truth escaped the mouths of those who sat across from her at the kitchen table.

Once she could afford a house and her garden flourished with mint and rosemary, tomatoes and nopales, and limes and oranges, Olvido was able to create the most delicious and frustrating dishes to ever touch her family's tongues. "I'm seeing another woman," Angustias's father confessed one evening over dinner. "Other women," he added during dessert.

"I'm failing calculus," Angustias admitted after she scooped up a dollop of icing from her birthday cake behind her mother's back. "But I'm the top student in my art class! Swear to God."

Olvido frowned and snatched the cake off the counter. "Do not swear," she said even though she'd done plenty of swearing to the Father, the Son, the Holy Ghost, and any saint willing to listen.

"If you take away this curse, I swear I will become a nun and worship you until my palms fuse and my knees bleed."

"What if instead of making people tell me things, you help me make them shut up? I swear I'll shut up, too. You'll never hear another plea from me."

"How about you help me force people to do what's right? What good is it to know people's terrible secrets if I can't do anything about them? Please. I will crawl to church and confess every wrong I have ever done, and if I'm ordered to pray until my lips fall off, I swear I will do that and more."

God, Jesus, the Holy Spirit, and every saint Olvido knew of did not listen, and if they did, they ignored her. When she gets to Heaven, Olvido decides as she sits at the edge of the water, she's going to cook up a feast for God. With every dish He tastes, she's going to demand an answer for the unfortunate events in her life, and when He scoops up the last forkful of tres leches, she'll flip the table over so He is forced to look at her when she asks, "Why did You force me to stay for so long? Why do You hate me?"

Or, Olvido thinks, suddenly fearful that God can sense her plans for retribution. *I'll stay quiet if You show mercy. You must show mercy. You're a good God. You're a good God.*

Angustias and Felicitas follow the townspeople out of the clearing. They cry softly as they walk back to the car. With their backs turned, they don't notice how with every tear they shed, the river slowly rises until it soaks the bottom of Olvido's dress.

Olvido closes her eyes and imagines the wind caressing her cheeks, God's soft hands calling to her. She will be with Him soon, and He will take away any pain or fear she ever felt. In Heaven, there is only peace and joy, all she ever wanted. He will let her take a peek at Angustias from time to time and help her send gentle signs to guide her decisions on love and work and parenting.

Standing at the edge of the water, facing the Devils River, she waits patiently with a smile for God to welcome her home. She waits there until nightfall, and when she accepts that He will not show, she weeps like she has done for too many nights in a row.

part
two

part
two

chapter 26

Felicitas

At one point in their lives, each of the women in the Olivares family were certain they were going to Hell, though no one alive knows where they went in the end.

Justa Olivares believed divorce was a sin. When one married, they were making a pact with their spouse *and* God, so if you divorced your spouse, you divorced God. Who in their right mind would allow their ex into their home, into paradise, for eternity? God did crazy things, but He wasn't genuinely insane. Justa's husband didn't see marriage this way, but he pretended to agree. While she signed the divorce papers, he whispered, "See you in Hell." He could feel the knife twisting deeper into her gut. It was more satisfying than the separation itself.

Calamidades Olivares believed her reason for going to Hell was far more significant. When she was five years old, she stole a lollipop from Don Enrique's candy shop, and she never asked for forgiveness. There were far more Bible verses regarding the immorality of stealing than divorce, but if Justa had been alive to witness her daughter's turmoil, she would have called her an idiot.

Victoria Olivares did not think her mother was an idiot nor a sinner. When Calamidades died, Victoria cried for a week straight, day and night, until her eyes swelled so much, she couldn't see for half a month. Calamidades was practically a saint, and everything Victoria did was a sin. They would never be reunited in the afterlife.

Olvido Olivares agreed. Victoria was going to Hell, and perhaps she would, too. One who does not provide for their relatives, and especially for members of their household, is worse than an unbeliever (1 Timothy 5:8). She'd done so well. Even when Victoria put her at her wit's end, Olvido did not abandon her, yet with Angustias . . . Technically, Angustias had abandoned Olvido. Yes, that seemed right. Olvido was free of sin.

Angustias Olivares was not, and she did not care.

Felicitas Olivares did. Olvido had rambled on about Heaven and Hell so much, she'd begun to question every action she'd ever done. Was killing a fly a sin? Was leaving the faucet open while brushing her teeth a waste of resources, and thus, immoral? Olvido clearly didn't care whether Felicitas landed in Hell. If Olvido was burning in the everlasting fire pit below, she was taking her granddaughter with her. So, even when it was clear that neither God nor Satan wanted to take her spirit, she continued to force Felicitas to lie and sin.

"Niña," Olvido pleads to Felicitas. "You need to do something. You can't leave." Felicitas glares at her grandmother. So, she is back to being called *niña*.

"Can't I have a little privacy? I'm in the restroom," Felicitas whispers with exasperation.

"Your clothes are on and the toilet cover is down."

Felicitas throws her arms up in the air. "Listen, I don't want to leave either, but what can I do? Nothing. As my mom always says, she's the mom. I'm just the daughter who gets dragged around. I mean, she doesn't say the last part, but that is what happens, isn't it? And why do you even want us to stay here? Can't you go stay with your neighbors or something? They liked you—" Felicitas stops herself. Olvido knows. After that funeral, she must know. The entire town liked her better than her own family.

"No. I cannot. I don't want you two to stay just to keep me company. I need you to stay so we can figure out how to help me to cross over. Believe me, I want to leave more than you want me gone. I don't want to stay here, not with you constantly speaking ill of me."

For a moment, Felicitas feels remorse. Then, her grandmother opens her mouth again. "So, this is what we are going to do, you're going to pretend to get injured—"

"What?" Felicitas's voice is low, but she hopes her grandmother can discern her disbelief and anger.

"Not a real injury! I said pretend. Sickness is an effective excuse to get you out of doing things you don't want to do. I learned that from your mother."

Felicitas knows what her grandmother is talking about. In second grade, Felicitas pretended to have a fever to miss the first day of school. Angustias agreed to let her stay home and even brought her a pint of ice cream when she came home after work, but as they silently ate their icy treat, Angustias confessed. She knew Felicitas was perfectly fine.

"I let you stay," Angustias said. "To allow you one day of rebellion to get it out of your system, but no more. You can't lie to me again. You couldn't even lie to me today. Trust me, I know every trick. I once drank spoiled milk to make myself truly sick just so I wouldn't have to take a calculus exam."

"What's calculus?" Felicitas asked.

"You know, I'm still not entirely sure, which is why I wanted to miss the test, but that is not the point. The point is, don't ever think you can fool me. En lo que tú vas, yo ya fui y vine."

"But I'm not going anywhere," Felicitas says, confused by the saying. "The whole point is that I don't want to go anywhere."

"Not literally go some—forget about the phrase. You're plenty smart. You know exactly what I mean. Now, I just want you to remember it." And Felicitas does remember, so she informs her grandmother that her idea won't work.

"Just try," Olvido says. "If your mother believes it just enough to take you to the hospital, it will work. I have a plan. I know—"

"The hospital! We can't afford the hospital! And if I go to the hospital, won't the doctors know I'm pretending right away?"

"Yes, they will, but as I said, I have a plan. I know someone who can help us."

"No! I'll help you cross from wherever we go."

Olvido raises a brow at Felicitas. "So, you've given up?" she challenges.

"You're willing to go just like that. You said you didn't want to leave either. Why is that?"

"I have my reasons," Felicitas says, and hopes that without having to say anything, Olvido can move through the barriers around her heart to see what is inside of it. Olvido wouldn't need to dig deep to discover that Grace has given her a feeling Felicitas didn't know she was missing: true hope.

She can imagine herself attending Grace Elementary until she graduates from fifth grade, growing closer to Estela and Gustavo, and becoming a regular visitor at the public library and discovering other places around town. Maybe Emilio will learn her literary taste and hold books for her without her asking. Maybe Estela and Gustavo will introduce her to other people, and one day she'll have more than two friends and a couple of crushes and a boyfriend.

She'll take road trips to Mexico. She'll improve her Spanish. She'll belong. That's never been a possibility before, not with her mother choosing to live in towns where they were the minority, where they stuck out like sore thumbs. Maybe Angustias was avoiding the border and any resemblance to her home, or she simply wasn't bothered by the lack of familiarity. It doesn't matter. Now Felicitas knows that feeling like an outcast does not have to be the norm. She can peacefully float in a sea of wide-ranging skin tones. Her voice can blend in with those of others, seamlessly transitioning between English and Spanish and creating new words in the process. She'll have friends who understand her Latin pop culture references, and with them, she'll discover new music and films and try new dishes. Maybe they'll understand her disconnect from Olvido, at least partially. They'll understand how frustrating it is to hear, "Didn't your mom teach you Spanish?" when she fails to understand a word, or her accent slips out without warning. "It's not your fault," they'll tell her. "She could have taught you Spanish. She could have raised you in Mexico if she had stayed."

"I want to stay for the possibility of happiness," she can say, but Olvido probably doesn't care about the answer, so Felicitas throws the question back. "Why don't you?"

"Because I have a plan. I know people at the hospital that can help us."

Olvido ignores Felicitas's persistent protests and walks out into her bedroom, looks around, and walks to the nightstand. She pushes and lifts, and the nightstand tumbles, but it doesn't fall.

With a wave of her hand, Olvido gestures for Felicitas to help her. Felicitas shakes her head. Even if she doesn't get hurt, Angustias will worry, maybe not for long, but even just a few minutes seems cruel. But not helping would be cruel toward Olvido. Her eyes look desperate. She doesn't have Angustias's nonchalant heart.

Felicitas sighs, frowns, and walks toward her grandmother. With Felicitas's small hands and Olvido's translucent ones, they easily knock down the nightstand. The wood hits the tile floor with a loud thump. The items on the stand bounce when they strike the cold surface. The glass of the photo frames and the body of the ceramic lamp shatters, creating a sea of jagged, sharp debris.

"Felicitas?" they hear Angustias call out.

"Scream," Olvido commands. Felicitas sighs but obeys once again. "Hurry. Put your arm underneath the nightstand. I'll hold it up."

"No," Felicitas protests. "You could barely push it."

"I'll concentrate. I can do it. I've lifted it before, and I remember the feeling. I promise. I only have to do it for a few seconds."

There's no time to think. They can hear Angustias calling Felicitas's name. Felicitas helps Olvido lift the nightstand and slides her arm underneath.

"Felicitas?" Angustias shouts. As she opens the door, Felicitas lets go of the nightstand.

Olvido was wrong. She can't lift the furniture on her own. The heavy wood comes crashing down on Felicitas's arm. There is a crack and three screams.

chapter 27

Angustias

Problems keep piling on top of Angustias, burying her, trapping her in an anxiety-filled chamber. Angustias's first and greatest concern is Felicitas's well-being, of course, but spending two hours in the emergency room has given her enough time to think about the financial consequences of the accident. Her eyes move around the small space they've been assigned to. The hospital will charge them for the most minute things—the light above their heads, the air they are breathing, simply existing.

Her eyes land on Felicitas whose frown is more pronounced than usual. "Are you angry at me?" Angustias asks, astonished.

"No," Felicitas responds, but she is surrounded by a cloud of red. The color cannot be misinterpreted. Her face looks angry. Her voice sounds angry, and who else can she be angry at but her? Well, Angustias is angry, too. The initial shock and worry she felt upon seeing Felicitas's arm under the fallen nightstand has not left her, but she can fit many feelings into her heart.

To avoid taking her anger out on Felicitas, Angustias stands up. "I'm going to buy something from the vending machine, and by the time I get back, I hope you've fixed that frown on your face. What do you want?"

"Nothing," Felicitas mutters.

"Fine. I'll buy you a Sprite. Gosh, why do the doctors here take so long?" Angustias furiously opens the privacy curtain to reveal the rest of the emergency room and is met with a sea of burgundy and navy blue clouds. Despite the evidence, she feels no one in the room understands what she's experiencing, and she's not entirely wrong. No one else's life is about to be drastically altered by the ghost of their mother.

chapter 28

Olvido

Out in the hallway of the hospital, Olvido wishes she could advise Angustias on how best to care for Felicitas in this moment. She digs into the mental catalog of home remedies she developed from years of caring for Victoria and Angustias. Some lime and honey for the throat, eucalyptus oil for the head, a limpia for the soul. It is pointless. Felicitas's problem cannot be cured with tea or herb-aided prayers, at least none that she's aware of. And how can Olvido help if Felicitas won't let her come within two feet?

When Angustias stepped out of the emergency room, Olvido moved from the corner of the curtained-off area to the side of Felicitas's bed. "I didn't know this would happen," she said, her voice full of shame. "I truly thought—"

"That's the problem," Felicitas snapped. Despite the thinness of the curtain separating her from the nurses' station and the patients to either side of her, Felicitas did not lower her voice. "You thought things through, and you still didn't care about the possibility of me getting hurt."

Olvido's mouth opened and closed until she found her words. "I did care."

"No. You didn't, and now my arm hurts, and my mom is worried, and we are probably going to have to pay some crazy amount of money we don't have. Aren't you the one who's always worried about money? Where's that worry now?"

"I am wor—"

"Leave!" Felicitas shouted as a nurse drew back the curtains and asked if she was all right. "Just leave! Leave me alone! Leave!" Olvido left. Now, all she can do is squeeze her daughter's shoulder. Angustias feels nothing.

As they cross the waiting area on their way back to the emergency room, the Olivares women can't help but notice how families sit in packs, huddled, leaning in. They comfort each other as they wait for their names to be called. Parents rock their babies, couples rub each other's backs, children hold their parents' hands and whisper in their ears that it will all be all right.

Must be nice, Olvido and Angustias both think. But an additional thought pops into Olvido's mind that most certainly does not occur to her daughter. *This. This is what Angustias needs.*

Olvido smiles as she follows Angustias through the expansive doors of the emergency room. She knows what she must do. Then, dread strikes Olvido like a lightning bolt to the heart as they return to Felicitas's side. Laying before them is Felicitas, red-faced and unconscious.

"Wha—Felicitas?" Angustias says out of breath as if someone has punched her in the gut and looks around frantically for a doctor or a nurse who can explain, "What's wrong with my baby?!"

chapter 29

Felicitas

Even as her mind slips into darkness, Felicitas's expression remains crossed. "What's wrong with my baby?" she can hear her mother shout. Soon, she'll move beside Felicitas's bed, rub her thumb across her forehead and demand, "Felicitas, remove that frown." Such a typical response. That's all Felicitas wants, normalcy. But nothing is ordinary besides Felicitas's face.

She wanted to appear more cheery, even tried to look at the bright side of the situation. *The nurses will give me a cast*, she thought as they led her into the emergency room. *Perhaps it will be a cool color, like fluorescent green or neon pink, and I'll be able to cover it in doodles and signatures.* But the bright side dimmed when Felicitas worked up the courage to open her eyes and realized that her arm was covered in a plain white cast that would remain plain and white because she had no one to sign it but her mother.

"Tomorrow," her mother had said on the drive back from Olvido's funeral. "We will leave tomorrow."

Neither Estela nor Gustavo will get a chance to visit and leave her a farewell message with permanent markers and gel pens. They will spend the summer with all the other children who get to continue their normal days reading and watching TV and making friends and definitely not moving to the first place their mother pointed to on a map.

Maybe not even Angustias will sign the cast. Felicitas saw her hands tremble uncontrollably and noticed the effortful rise and fall of her chest. *I'm sorry*, Felicitas wanted to tell her. *I didn't mean to. I'm sorry. I'm sorry. I'm sorry.* But Felicitas doesn't say she's sorry because no one ever apologizes to her, and she's tired of it. Why must she be the biggest person when in reality she's the smallest?

It's so unfair, she thought. *It's so unfair. It's so unfair.*

Her anger grew with the repetition of the phrase as if she were summoning a monster within her. Her skin felt hot, her cheeks were burning. It was a sensation that came from within. No matter how much she fanned herself, the feeling did not subside. Her blood was boiling inside her veins, como leche para chocolate. Her world was blurring and dimming. Felicitas saw the nurses rush toward her. Then, there was nothing but the sound of Angustias's voice demanding an explanation for Felicitas's concerning state.

"She has a fever," Felicitas can hear one of the nurses say to her mother. "We're giving her medication to bring it down." Felicitas feels water drip onto her face and evaporate in an instant.

"But she was fine when I left," Angustias cries. "I shouldn't—I shouldn't have left."

"The fever should go down soon. Ma'am. Ma'am? Can you hear me?"

"What that girl needs is a cold bath," Olvido says.

"Can't I give her a cold shower or something?" Angustias asks.

"You may. We're moving her to a room. For now, you can continue to soak the towels in water and press them to her skin. I will be back in a moment to move her upstairs. Her temperature has already begun to go down. She'll be okay."

Clinging to the nurse's promise, Felicitas falls fully into unconsciousness, but if Olvido isn't gone by the time she wakes up, she doubts she'll be okay or even close to it.

chapter 30

Olvido

Olvido remembers the moment she first laid eyes on her granddaughter as vividly as the moment they met again. It occurred hours after Felicitas's birth and her first feeding and her first diaper change. Olvido missed it all. Her manager at the time, a pathetic, grouchy man who lasted only a month on the job, had confiscated all employees' cell phones on account of a cook accidentally dropping his into the soup of the day. When Angustias called the restaurant and asked him to inform Olvido that she was in the hospital, the manager said, "With pleasure," and hung up before Angustias could say which hospital. They lived equidistant from two.

When Olvido finally arrived, she refused to leave Angustias's side until the nurse asked, "Are you sure you don't want to see the baby?" for the fifth time with an unnecessarily disapproving tone. "I just—usually, grandparents won't leave me alone about it." Olvido huffed and followed the nurse out of the room.

Through the window of the hospital nursery, Olvido inspected Felicitas for any resemblance to Angustias's boyfriend, but it was too soon to tell. Newborn Felicitas was pink, wrinkled, and hairy, and she was beautiful.

A nurse smiled at Olvido as she approached Felicitas's crib and jumped in surprise when she looked down at the baby. Olvido frowned.

The nurse looked up and smiled nervously. "I can see the resemblance," she said.

Grown Felicitas is not pink nor wrinkled, though maybe a bit hairy, and she is beautiful. When she wakes up to find Olvido sitting on the edge of her bed, her distinctive frown reappears. The nurse was right about the resemblance.

"How are you feeling?" Olvido asks and reaches out to touch her.

Felicitas recoils her leg. "Fine," she responds coldly. She looks around for her mother and sees her curled up in a chair beside the bed, her head hanging at a dangerous angle and her limbs bent in a painful-looking way.

"So, what do we need to do to get you to leave?" Felicitas whispers hostilely. "You said you had a plan?"

Olvido is no longer taken aback by her granddaughter's cruel straightforwardness. "Well, yes," she says. "I had a plan to buy us more time."

"That's it? Buying time to make a plan is not a plan." Felicitas raises her eyebrows and waits for a different response.

"Well," Olvido says. "Let's think of ideas together. What do you think will get me out of here?"

"Well," Felicitas says, imitating Olvido's appeasing tone. "What will get you out of here is clearly not your original brilliant idea."

Olvido drops her head and twirls the edge of her blouse with her fingers. "Yes, I suppose I was wrong about that. My body didn't have to be in Mexico for me to go to Heaven."

"Or Hell."

"Excuse me?"

"I didn't say anything."

Olvido stands, back straight, chin up. "You know my hearing is a lot better now that I'm dead."

Felicitas rolls her eyes. "I think it's time for us to accept that I can't help you," she says. "I don't know how the afterlife works. Whenever I see a ghost, I say, 'Hello,' and that's it, swear to God. Don't tell me to not swear to God. You're not allowed to tell me anything right now." Olvido closes her scold-ready mouth. "The point is spirits don't ask me to help them cross over to wherever it is that they go. They don't ask me to give a message to their loved ones. They don't ask me to rewrite their will or find a hidden treasure in their house. They just talk to me and go, so I have no idea what you need. I just don't."

Olvido tilts her head and pretends to give Felicitas's speech some thought. What her granddaughter needs, Olvido has realized, is a sense a power, not fear nor pity like she originally thought. Attempting to incite those emotions has ended in disaster. But power, that is all Olvido wished for when she was Felicitas's age living in her own mother's house under her rules. Sixty-two years old and Olvido still feels powerless. She can definitely see the resemblance.

"I once had a neighbor back in Matamoros who claimed to see spirits," she says. "I think she was a phony, but she must have gotten her tales from somewhere. All tall tales have some truth to them. She said that spirits stay because they need to attend to unfinished business. They need to right their wrongs. Maybe that's what I need to do."

Felicitas laughs sarcastically. "Seriously? Why didn't you think of that before making me do . . . literally everything you've made me do?"

"I was sure the Mexico thing would work. It was an old woman's intuition. One day you'll understand. Besides, I didn't think I had any wrongs to right."

Felicitas shakes her head with disbelief. "So, what are your wrongs?"

"Your mother," Olvido says. Felicitas raises her eyebrows. "I need to make her life right. She is all alone taking care of you. I ruined her life by not forcing her to stay."

Felicitas's frown returns. "I don't think—"

"I need to make sure her life is set before I leave."

"Set?" Felicitas questions.

"Right." Olvido says, pacing around the room. "What needs to be well and stable in a person's life to make it right? Think. Family, obviously. Family always comes first." Olvido turns to Felicitas to make sure she's listening. "A husband. It's not the end of the world to not have a spouse, but parenting should be a job of two. There are moral, emotional, and financial responsibilities that are difficult to carry out on your own. And for financial responsibilities, you also need a job. You cannot survive without money. But that's just for physical needs. The word of God is what feeds your soul. God always comes first."

"You said family comes first," Felicitas reminds her.

"Well, we are God's children. So, family, husband, job, God, but not necessarily in that order."

"I don't think—"

"I make sure all those things are in order and my duty as a mother will be complete, and poof," Olvido says, jumping as if attempting to disappear in a cloud of smoke. "I go to Heaven."

Felicitas sighs. "I'm her family," she points out. "Do I have to be 'in order'? You think there's something wrong with me?"

"Other than the fact that you can see me and that your manners are lacking? I suppose not. One down, three to go."

"I can make her go to church every Sunday."

Olvido shakes her head. "One's relationship with God is not just about going to church. It is about reading the Bible, praying every night, following His commandments every day, worshiping Him, believing in Him."

Felicitas stares at Olvido, straight-faced. "Uh, I can make her go to church every Sunday," she repeats.

Olvido stares back. "Ugh, fine," she eventually accepts. "That will do. Now a husband."

"Let's talk jobs," Felicitas interjects. "She has experience working as a waitress and a secretary."

Olvido scrunches her nose. "We can find something better."

"Better than a secretary? In this economy? I don't think so. She was lucky a friend of a friend of a friend helped her out. Finding a good job is hard, not like it was back in your day."

Olvido glowers at her granddaughter. "That is how it was in my day," she says. "I am not that old."

"You're right. You're not that old. You're dead," Felicitas reminds her.

"Fine! Secretarial work it is," Olvido says. "What do you know about the economy?" she adds under her breath. "Now, a husband."

Felicitas moves around the bed unable to make herself comfortable with the weight of the cast and her grandmother's persistence. "Shouldn't she get a boyfriend first?"

"Fine, we will get her a nice boyfriend. Someone fit for marriage. We'll see where it goes."

Felicitas's jaw drops. "You won't leave until she's married? That could take years!"

"We'll see. I also don't know how any of this works, but I am sure this is what we need to do to make sure your mom is okay. Now, you will be happy to know I have another plan to right my wrongs."

Felicitas sinks into her pillow. "What else?"

"I'll tell you on the way," Olvido says moving toward the door. "Hurry. I don't know how much longer your mom will be asleep."

"Hurry?" Felicitas says, dumbfounded, and glances down at her injured arm when Olvido turns around. "I have this thing slowing me down, remember?" She swivels to the edge of the bed and braces the side rail with her free hand. "And I have to do everything myself because you can't help me, remember?" Her hand shakes as it takes on her weight. Her knees bend as her feet hit the ground. "And this is all your fault, remember?" Olvido nods remorsefully, but she no longer feels as guilty as she did back in the emergency room. Her new plan will fix everything. She knows it will. Olvido is always right.

chapter 31

Felicitas

Felicitas Olivares's quiet nature tends to be viewed negatively as often as it is viewed positively.

"It must be so easy to take care of her!" Angustias's coworkers marvel.

"Follow Felicitas's example," teachers instruct her classmates.

"You're good company," chatty ghosts compliment her. "You listen."

But kids never compliment Felicitas's quietude. They point and sneer and laugh. Felicitas views her quietness as neither good nor bad. Sometimes, she thinks to herself, things are neither good nor bad, they just are. But if she's going to live with things that just are, she might as well use them to her advantage.

Felicitas isn't just quiet in the sense that she doesn't speak often. She also moves around silently. Her feet barely make a sound as she walks, quiet as a tree on a windless day, unless she's frantically running around, pressuring her mother to get ready to take her to school. Felicitas has accidentally snuck up on Angustias more times than Angustias cares for. The first time she heard her mother scream, "Felicitas! You scared me. I didn't hear you," Felicitas knew how to turn a boring, neutral trait into a talent.

Felicitas can quietly get up, make coffee, and drink a whole cup without waking her mother. She can sneak past lunch monitors in the school cafeteria to sit in the library and read while her classmates eat and socialize without her. On the days Felicitas doesn't have to go to school but her mother can't get out of work, she is able to inconspicuously walk into Angustias's workplace and hide behind her desk all day without her coworkers noticing.

The night of the nightstand incident, Felicitas learns that she can be twice as stealthy if she has a spirit to help her move about. To sneak out of the second floor of the hospital, all Felicitas has to do is wait. Olvido moves ahead of her and gives her a signal when all nurses are facing away. Felicitas speedwalks toward her and comes to a halt behind a desk or wall when a nurse turns in their direction. She waits until the nurses look away and continues. She repeats this process until they make it down to the first floor and into the hospital's cafeteria. The serving station is closed, but the dining tables are available. Two chatting nurses sit at one end of the room. A woman in a business suit sits near the entrance, staring intensely at her phone and sipping from a Styrofoam cup. A man in a white coat sits at the farthest end, nonchalantly munching on a granola bar. He is so invested in the book he is reading that Felicitas has to clear her throat twice before he takes notice of her.

"Hello," he greets when he finally looks up.

"Hello. Are you Dr. Gutiérrez?" Felicitas asks, though Olvido already told her he is.

"He was part of my original plan," her grandmother said. "Which you would have heard if you had stopped interrupting me."

"Yes, I am. And you seem to be a patient," Dr. Gutiérrez says, pointing at her cast. "Should you be here?"

"Yes," Felicitas responds and sits down directly in front of the doctor. "You knew my grandmother, Olvido Olivares."

Dr. Gutiérrez coughs, choking on the granola. "You're Doña Olvido's granddaughter? I did hear you and your mom were in town. I am so sorry I couldn't make it to the funeral today. When it was originally set for Sunday, I had every intention of attending and paying my respects, but I've been in the hospital since early this morning, and I don't get out until a couple of hours from now. I sent flowers, though, white roses."

"I'm sure we got them," Felicitas says. "Dr. Gutiérrez, do you believe in ghosts?" Felicitas knows she is being too direct, but there's no time for small talk. If her mother wakes up and sees the empty hospital bed, she'll have the National Guard searching for her in an instant.

"Excuse me?" Dr. Gutiérrez says, accidentally spitting out a piece of granola.

Felicitas grimaces. "My grandmother's spirit is here," she says. "She— We have a favor to ask of you."

Dr. Gutiérrez looks over his shoulder and around the dining room. "Where are you supposed to be right now? Where is your mom?"

"I'm supposed to be in room 205 on the second floor. My mom is sleeping, I hope. Dr. Gutiérrez, I have a message for you from my grandma. She says—"

Olvido looks at Dr. Gutiérrez as she speaks. "Me da mucha vergüenza tener que pedirle esto."

"I'm really embarrassed to have to ask this of you," Felicitas translates. "My daughter is going to wake up to a large hospital bill she cannot afford, and it's my fault. She cannot get into debt. She'll never get out of it. Is there—"

"Okay," Dr. Gutiérrez says with a clap. "Let's take you back upstairs."

"Is there a way you can write it off? I'm not sure how the US medical system works. I know there's a lot more paperwork and less autonomy, but I'm sure—"

"Miss," Dr. Gutiérrez interrupts, putting his palm up. "What's your name?"

"Felicitas."

"Felicitas, give me one second, and I'll take you upstairs so we can talk there with your mom." Dr. Gutiérrez walks over to the nearest trash can, throws away the wrapper of his granola bar, and brushes crumbs off his beard.

"I'm not lying," Felicitas maintains. "She's here. I can prove it."

"I don't want to have to call security," Dr Gutiérrez warns with a nonthreatening tone.

"Your wife died five years ago," Felicitas states. Dr. Gutiérrez freezes. "Her name was Linda, but you called her Gordita even though she was really skinny. You never had any kids because you both said you didn't want any, but you have a dog named Tortita who you do treat like a kid. My grandma says 'que la chiflas mucho.' Sorry, I don't know how to translate that. Every year, you take Tortita to the mall to get her picture taken with Santa, which my grandma says is ridiculous."

"Anyone can know those things," Dr. Gutiérrez says.

"The first time my grandma prepared food for you was a few weeks after your wife died. Sorry, 'passed away.' My grandma says it's rude to say 'died' just like that. She noticed you one day at the grocery store. You were buying too much canned food. She figured you were too sad to cook a proper meal. You were. She pretended to feel sick, too sick to move so that you would go over to visit her. She made chiles rellenos. You pretended to like them, but they were too spicy for you, so after that, she made sure to not put any chile on your food. Instead of enchiladas, she made entomatadas. Those were your favorite. It wasn't until a few months ago that you started to cook again."

"Anyone can know those things," Dr. Gutiérrez repeats softly. He looks down at his hands instead of Felicitas even when she continues to speak.

"She's saying, 'I'm very sorry I'm telling my granddaughter about this. Please forgive me. This is an emergency.' You confessed to my grandma one evening that you were glad you never had children. Before, you had lied. You had said that you didn't want any kids because that's what Linda always said, but after she passed away, you really were glad that you didn't have any because that meant it was only you who had to miss your wife. There were no kids at home missing their mother and missing their dad who still worked too much. You didn't tell anyone else that, did you? Only my grandma."

Dr. Gutiérrez frowns as he studies Felicitas's face, searching for a sign of bluffing, a twitch on her lips, a glimmer in her eye. "Did she tell you that before she passed away?"

"No," Felicitas asserts. "Why would she tell me about some random man? No offense."

Dr. Gutiérrez nods to himself. "Sorry," he says, shrugging. "I don't believe in ghosts. Now, let's get you back to your mom."

"Open your book to a random page," she orders.

"Felicitas."

"Just do it, please."

Dr. Gutiérrez sighs, grabs his book, and opens it to page three hundred and forty-seven. Behind his shoulder, Olvido reads the text out loud, phonetically. Felicitas repeats the words. Despite the errors, she can see seedlings of belief sprouting within the doctor.

Dr. Gutiérrez puts his left hand behind his back. "How many fingers am I holding up?" he asks.

"One, three, five, two, zero," Felicitas repeats after Olvido.

Dr. Gutiérrez removes his hand from behind his back and raises it to his mouth. His trembling fingers fail to cover his shock.

"So, will you help us?" Felicitas asks. Dr. Gutiérrez nods slowly. He cannot say the words out loud.

"My grandma wants me to tell you again that it's truly very extremely embarrassing and inappropriate to ask for money, but maybe we can pay you back little by little. You directly, not the hospital or the government because they'll never leave us alone, and . . . and we actually need your help with something other than hospital bills." Felicitas leans forward. "This might get you in trouble," she whispers. "Dr. Gutiérrez, are you a good liar?"

chapter 32

Angustias

Angustias Olivares's body experiences a peculiar reaction to being told a lie. It is not as physically obvious as an allergic reaction to food or cheap makeup, but Angustias would argue it's just as consequential. Like most people who feel threatened, Angustias experiences an activation of her freeze, fight, or flight response. However, unlike most people, her body does not choose only one response. It will freeze, which feels bad; fight, which looks bad; and fly, which *is* bad.

Lies embarrass Angustias, and because things rarely embarrass her, the feeling is impossible to ignore. Lies consume her thoughts. They gnaw at her brain. They render her unable to think about anything else until a new, and hopefully not embarrassing, issue arises. Only then does Angustias realize she has far more important things to attend to and is able to return to her default carefree self. Because embarrassment feels so awful for Angustias, it brings along anger, and when Angustias is angry, she runs away.

Olvido and Felicitas must be careful. They planned to have Felicitas back in bed before Angustias awakened, but Dr. Gutiérrez takes just three steps past the doorway and Angustias is on her feet, eyes wide, asking what's wrong. Dr. Gutiérrez assures her everything is all right. Felicitas was simply unable to sleep. She paid him a visit, and they chatted for a while.

"And you are?" Angustias inquires.

Dr. Gutiérrez extends his hand. "Dr. Christian Gutiérrez. It's very nice to meet you. I'm in charge of Felicitas's case."

"Case?" Angustias looks back and forth between the doctor and her daughter. "She has a case? She just broke her arm. She looks completely fine."

Felicitas does not look completely fine. Her hair is a greasy mess, tangled up in an anxious midnight blue cloud. Her skin looks dry, and there are unusual dark circles bordering the bottom of her eyes. She looks like Angustias on her most exhausting days, and this would be acceptable if Felicitas wasn't a child who didn't have to pay taxes nor raise a kid of her own.

Angustias gasps internally. Maybe there is something wrong with her daughter.

Lack of sleep and an empty stomach make Angustias susceptible to believing almost any lie. She interprets the doctor's cobalt cloud of determination as a desire to get her to understand Felicitas's diagnosis. Thus, she believes him when he informs her that Felicitas's unusually high fever is of great concern. She believes him when he says Felicitas needs to rest and remain in Grace for at least a month until they are sure of what the problem is and how they can fix it.

"A month," Angustias shouts, and quickly lowers her voice. "A whole month?"

"At least," Dr. Gutiérrez repeats.

"Is it really that bad? How do you know it will take a month?"

"There's no way to know for sure how long it will take, but I would like to personally oversee how her arm heals."

"Personally?" Angustias narrows her eyes at the doctor. "Why?"

"I knew your mother and—"

"Oh my God," Angustias lets her face fall into her cupped hands and takes in deep breaths. Of course, he knew her mother. The nurses outside in the hallway probably knew her mother, and the cafeteria staff probably knew her mother, and the security guard probably knew her mother. She will have to keep hearing that phrase for a whole month if they stay. "We can't stay. I'm sorry. We simply can't."

"Why not?" Felicitas asks. "It's not like you have a job you need to go to. And you haven't sold Grandma's house yet. And you don't even know where we're going to go after this."

Angustias stares incredulously at her daughter. "Yes, I do."

Felicitas crosses her arms in front of her chest. "Where?" she challenges.

"Harlingen," Angustias says, drawing a random city's name from her mind.

"Liar."

"Felicitas!"

"I'm not sure about the details of whatever it is that you're discussing," Dr. Gutiérrez interjects. "I'm just informing you of what is best for Felicitas's health."

"Yeah," Felicitas taunts. "Don't you want what is best for my health?"

Angustias scrunches her nose and pouts, but she nods. The clock on the wall reads 1:06 a.m. It's too early to argue. She thanks Dr. Gutiérrez for his help, and secretly vows that when it is time to leave the hospital, she will disobey his orders.

Then, the morning sun and bad cafeteria coffee bring some clarity to Angustias's mind. As she waits in the elevator on her way back to the second floor, she considers all the home remedies her mother taught her that could cure Felicitas, but what is there to cure?

"You're going to stay, mijita," Olvido whispers in her ear. "Y punto."

Angustias stomps her foot and huffs. The other elevator passengers turn to look at her. She smiles at them but stops as soon as they turn away. Life is not going according to Angustias's plan. It's not like she had a plan to begin with, but if she did have one, this was most certainly not it.

However, not everything is for the worst. When she attempts to pay a portion of their hospital bill at the cashier's window, Angustias learns that Dr. Gutiérrez paid for all their expenses.

"He—he did what?" she stammers. She asks to be led to his office or for him to meet her in the lobby, but her requests are denied. The cashier states, as per Dr. Gutiérrez's orders, that he has taken the rest of the day off.

"At least let me speak to him," Angustias demands. "He must have a phone number." And he does, but the doctor only answers Angustias's call after practicing for a fifth time what he has been carefully instructed to say.

"Hello?" he answers. "Yes, this is him. With whom do I have the pleasure of speaking? Oh, Angustias. Hello again." Dr. Gutiérrez sounds unnatural except for when he explains that the cost of the food Olvido made for him over the years most likely surpassed that of the costs they accumulated overnight.

Angustias taps the phone as she swallows her questions. *Why are you lying to me, and if you're not, why did my mother show such kindness to you? Or did she pay for her own medical expenses with home-cooked meals? No, because then she would owe you and not the other way around. That means you're telling the truth. Why then? Why did you get to experience her goodwill? Why couldn't I?*

"Hello?" she hears Dr. Gutiérrez say. "Ms. Angustias? Are you there?"

Yes. *She* is here. Olvido is not. The past doesn't matter. Only the future, the present, and Felicitas matter. In the present, Angustias is in no position to refuse help. Hesitant but thankful, she accepts both the doctor's favor and advice. She informs him they will stay in town as he suggested, but she tells herself that their stay won't be a whole month. That's too long. Maybe a week or two. If Dr. Gutiérrez can't figure out what was wrong by then, maybe she can take Felicitas to Mexico, maybe they can toss some flowers in the river on the way. Felicitas's cloud will lose those distressing colors and develop a bright yellow. Angustias will never let it fade.

But Angustias has never had absolute control over her daughter's emotions, and in the ensuing weeks, she doesn't have control over her own. The scheme her mother and daughter conduct behind her back is too grand to fight on her own. One by one, the people of Grace become involved in Olvido's plan. Gossip spreads quickly, so quickly that by the night Felicitas is discharged from the hospital, all but three residents of Grace know of Felicitas's ability and of Olvido's return.

chapter 33

Olvido

Olvido learned early on in her pregnancy that she would never be considered a perfect mother. She was either eating too much or not enough. She needed to stay active but also rest. Prenatal supplements were a must, but it was better to obtain nutrients through a balanced diet. According to some women of her church, she needed to start eating dates immediately. It would help ease the labor. Others said to not do that until the third trimester. Olvido was on her first.

Olvido learned, but she did not accept. She followed every suggestion. Always wear socks. Always! Don't wear socks. Eat more fish. Stop eating so much fish. A cup of coffee a day is all right. Don't drink coffee. Are you trying to kill your baby?

It wasn't until Angustias was born that she stopped trying. When Olvido yanked away a bug Angustias was trying to devour, and Angustias burst into tears and shrieks, Olvido accepted fate. Her own daughter would never see her as a faultless mother. What did other people's opinion matter?

When Felicitas explained to Dr. Gutiérrez why they needed his help, and his concern grew more and more evident, Olvido didn't care. He could squint his eyes and tighten his lips all he wanted. *She* was Angustias's mother, and she knew best how to take care of her.

"Go on," Olvido said. "Ask."

Felicitas pouted and turned to the doctor. "This is so embarrassing to ask," she said "And this time, I'm the one who is saying it's embarrassing, not my grandma. Do you, um ..." She looked down at her feet and twirled her index fingers around each other.

"Go on," Olvido encouraged.

Felicitas sighed. "Do you know of any single doctors or nurses looking for a girlfriend?"

"Excuse me?" Dr. Gutiérrez was not confused. He just couldn't hear Felicitas. Her lips had barely moved when she spoke. Felicitas repeated the question, and Dr. Gutiérrez let out a loud, hearty laugh. "Is Doña Olvido trying to set your mother up?"

Felicitas's head hung. "You laugh, but it's true, unfortunately." She proceeded to tell the doctor a condensed version of Olvido's theory regarding why she remained among the living and what needed to happen for her to move on. "Family, job, husband, God. But not necessarily in that order," she concluded. Olvido nodded approvingly.

"I see," Dr. Gutiérrez said. "No offense, Doña Olvido, but those ideas sound a bit outdated. However, I have been told that mothers know best. Usually, it is mothers who say this, which may make it a biased statement, but I believe it based on personal experience."

"So ... ?"

Dr. Gutiérrez shrugged. "No, no one comes to mind. I'm sorry," he said.

Felicitas held in a sigh of relief.

"Tell him everything else I said," Olvido urged. Felicitas shook her head. "Please."

"Is she saying something else?" Dr. Gutiérrez asked, noticing Felicitas's scowl.

Felicitas nodded. "Again, this is really embarrassing, but could you ask around? My grandma thinks we need help carrying out this 'fix my mother's life' plan. Not just the boyfriend thing, but the job thing and the church thing, too."

"Sure," Dr. Gutiérrez chuckled. "I'm terrible at keeping secrets, so I was going to tell everyone everything that you told me anyways."

Felicitas frowned. "I can't tell if you are being sarcastic or not, and that's not a good trait to have if you're a doctor. Doesn't matter. What does matter is that you do not let my mom find out about what I said, and do not, under any circumstance, let her know that I can see spirits. It's crucial. Please."

"I will try my best," he assured her, and he meant it.

That afternoon, as they walk toward the hospital parking lot, Dr. Gutiérrez spills the news to Dr. Aguilar. Olvido is still in town, a spirit among the living, and she has a request.

"Which is?" Dr. Aguilar's husband, Tom, asks her while buying groceries for dinner.

"For us to help her," Tom tells their neighbor, Mr. Salazar, when they bump into each other while taking out the trash.

"Help her how?" Mrs. Salazar asks Mr. Salazar during dessert.

"Family, job, husband, God. But not necessarily in that order," Mrs. Salazar tells her sister who tells their cousin who tells his mother-in-law who tells the rest of the town. Because Dr. Gutiérrez, a respected man of science, begins the rumor, the story gains credibility. With very little doubt, the people of Grace tell and retell the tale.

"It's truly a miracle," Doña Francesca says to her husband while they wash dishes. "I heard that little girl was able to tell Dr. Gutiérrez all about Linda. Do you think she would be able to contact Aunt Trinidad?"

Three streets away, Doña Sofia updates her daughter, Vanessa, on the gossip. "I heard that Olvido wasn't able to go to Heaven because she had problems with her family," she says. "Her daughter got pregnant as a teenager. Never married. Never went to college. No wonder Olvido couldn't die peacefully. I would be rolling around in my grave, too, if that happened to you."

By the next day, the townspeople are all well informed and quite excited about their not-so-silent agreement to follow Olvido's plan. They discuss it over breakfast, during their lunch breaks, during work hours, while in school, while running errands, while grocery shopping, and while out on dates.

Keeping the secret from Angustias is no problem. Olvido's daughter keeps mostly to herself. She rarely smiles. She barely says hello. She is very different from how Olvido described her, but what mother doesn't enhance their daughter's reputation? The townspeople decide not to take Angustias's reclusive behavior personally and attribute it to her mourning instead. Poor girl. She truly needs their help.

"Family, job, husband, God. But not in that order," Olvido repeats to Felicitas at least once a day. Felicitas rolls her eyes every time. She knows the plan well and so does the rest of the town.

When it comes to God, the people of Grace are anything but subtle. They make a point of saying "Have a blessed day" and "God bless you" as they pass by Angustias in the streets.

"You could at least say 'igualmente,'" Olvido reproaches.

At least three people walk up to her and ask her if she's been baptized. She gives them a forced smile and a nod and pushes her grocery cart forward as fast as she can.

Two days after Felicitas is discharged from the hospital, Angustias discovers a church pamphlet plastered to the windshield of her car. When she arrives back at the house, she finds a stack of Bibles on the rocking chair on the front porch. Some books have sticky notes that say, "To bring you comfort" and "We would love to have you over for Sunday service this week" and "Have you accepted Jesus into your heart?"

One person decides to kill two birds with one stone and brings marriage into the religious phase of the plan. Between the pages of their Bible, they've slipped in a bright pink paper with a verse written in black marker. "Ecclesiastes 4:11 If two lie down together, they will keep warm. But how can one keep warm alone?" Olvido isn't particularly fond of this verse, but she can't be picky.

Angustias crumples the paper and the rest of the notes and stuffs them in her pockets. She carries the Bibles inside, ambitiously all in one trip, and hides them in the back of Olvido's closet.

"What are you doing?" Olvido asks. Standing at the entrance of the room, Felicitas repeats her question.

Angustias quickly closes the closet door. "Nothing," she replies a little too fast. "Are you hungry? We finally have fresh food to cook. No more takeout!" Angustias walks over to Felicitas and gently touches her cast. She frowns with confusion. "Felicitas," she says.

"Hmm?"

"When we were at the hospital, how did you get to Dr. Gutiérrez by yourself?"

"I called a nurse," Felicitas says before Olvido can help her formulate a credible response. She sounds completely natural. Olvido's heart pangs with guilt.

"I figured, but why didn't they wake me?"

"I . . . asked them not to. You were really tired."

At least Felicitas spoke one truth. Angustias is exhausted, and Olvido cannot tell if she is the cause or the effect. The longer Olvido is in the world, the more troubles Angustias faces, but the more troubles Angustias faces, the more support Olvido needs to provide. Family, job, husband, God. Those aspect of her daughter's life were flawed before her passing. Olvido is not the problem. She is the solution.

chapter 34

Felicitas

Family, job, husband, God. But not necessarily in that order.

Because Angustias's family consists of only Felicitas, she bears the burden of being the center of the town's attention. Everyone has differing opinions of what is necessary to "fix" her. Some say that they should focus on finding Angustias a husband. Felicitas needs a dad. Others disagree and suggest they focus on strengthening the Olivares girls' relationship with God. They need to get Felicitas baptized. The most popular opinion is that they must get the Olivares girls to stay. Felicitas needs stability.

Samara attempts to convince Angustias to enroll Felicitas at Grace Middle School for the fall semester. When Angustias refuses, Samara considers doing it in secret. "It will be a wonderful surprise!" Felicitas advises against it. "I think we need to limit our lies, or we'll be found out. My mom says she has a sixth sense called motherhood, but I think she's part witch."

"You wish she was part witch," Gustavo teases.

Felicitas sighs. "Yeah, that would be cool." If Angustias was part witch, Felicitas's ability wouldn't seem so strange. She could tell the truth, and her mother wouldn't feel differently about her. But Felicitas is ten, almost eleven. She is sure that witches do not exist as much as she is sure that she is simply a freak.

Luckily, Estela and Gustavo don't seem to mind. The week after the accident, Gustavo invites Felicitas over to his house almost every day except Wednesday. "I have soccer practice," Gustavo says glumly. His parents, especially Samara, believe he spends too much time staring at screens.

"We could summon the spirits from the great beyond instead," Felicitas suggests over lunch. "We don't need electronics for that. Just a couple of candles, maybe a knife."

Samara laughs nervously. "Oh, Felicitas, you are so . . . creative, but I think the scents of the candles I have right now don't mix well. Y'all could just play some video games today. We'll think of something else tomorrow." Felicitas nods understandingly. Gustavo smiles so wide, he reminds Felicitas of the Cheshire cat. It's horrifying, and she loves it.

Estela's parents allow her to visit Felicitas on weekday evenings after her afternoon ballet practice. "Don't laugh," she says the first day she shows up at Olvido's house in a black leotard and beige tights.

"Are you going to a funeral?" Felicitas teases.

"I look like a giant baby," Estela fumes and plops onto the couch with as much familiarity as if she were in her own house. "I'm too old for ballet."

"Aren't there adult ballerinas?" Felicitas questions.

Estela squints her eyes and purses her lips. "Whatever," she says, and sinks further into her seat. "No, you know what the difference is? Adult ballerinas dance because they love it, not because their parents make them. I tell my mom I want to quit, and she says, 'Oh, just one more summer, just one more recital. I wish I could have gone to dance class when I was your age,' and then I feel bad and get roped in for 'one more summer, one more recital.'"

Felicitas nods because she truly understands. Her mother promises just one more move, one more town. With how annoyingly bitter Olvido is, it is likely Angustias wished she could run away as easily as she does now back when she was Felicitas's age. But there is no Olvido that Angustias needs to escape from now, none that she is aware of. When Felicitas tells Estela this, she expects her to say, "Yes, finally someone who comprehends my struggle!" but she expresses the opposite.

"Your mom may force you to be somewhere else but not someone else."

Felicitas supposes this is true, but only to an extent. Angustias cannot force her to be someone else if she doesn't know who Felicitas is, and Felicitas can't know who she is if she never stays in one place long enough to grow into it. When Pepe grew from a sprout to a small plant, Felicitas had to transplant him to a different pot, and she chose a bigger one, one she knew his roots would like. If she had chosen a pot of a different color or shape but similar size, Pepe would have been miserable, and miserable he would have died.

In Grace, Felicitas knows she can expand her roots. She's already met more people in the span of two weeks than she did in months in other cities, and with the exposure Olvido has given her, she's not just the new girl, the kid who wears the same color every day, the loner in the cafeteria. She's that girl with the unique ability, a potentially offputting ability but special, nonetheless. And if they stay, by her own merit, she'll become a beloved neighbor and cherished friend.

Like a good friend, Felicitas tries to make Estela feel better about her situation. "I thought you would love something like ballet," she says. "It's so . . . pink."

"Um, hello?" Estela exclaims jumping off the couch. "Ballerina Barbie is not the only Barbie."

"I don't know what that means."

"Good. We are also too old for Barbies. But you know what we're not too old for? The occult. Tell me, what's it like to speak to the dead?"

Estela was elated to learn about Felicitas's ability. Each day, she trades an activity for a ghost story. Estela's mom has gotten into and lost interest in every hobby imaginable, which has rendered her house impossible to walk through without stepping on an abandoned knickknack. A puzzle is exchanged for the spookiest encounter. Watercolors are traded for the saddest way someone has died. Scrapbook pages are swapped for most memorable spirit, and jewelry-making tools for the funniest-looking ghost. Has anyone died in their underwear? Ugly pajamas? Crocs? She wants to know everything. How do ghosts look? Do ghosts know they're ghosts? Can Felicitas communicate with anyone she wants? Can she call them from the great beyond? Estela is only slightly disappointed when Felicitas informs her that she cannot. Her encounters are random and unexpected.

"That's good," Estela says, placing a pink bead onto the string of her necklace, and handing Felicitas a gray one. Felicitas places it next to the pattern she's laid out on the table. Unlike Estela, she feels the need to plan out her design before putting it together.

"Why is it good?" Felicitas asks.

"Because some people want you to contact their loved ones. They just haven't asked you yet because we're not supposed to stress you out right now. We're supposed to make sure you're comfortable for Doña Olvido."

"Gee, thanks."

Estela gives her an apologetic look.

"They haven't put it off, though," Felicitas tells her, fuming at the memory. "Tons of people have called the house asking me if my grandma has any messages for them from the great beyond, but how can she have any messages from the great beyond when she hasn't gone to the great beyond? It doesn't make sense!"

"I hadn't thought of that."

"Apparently no one has. The calls have helped me prove that I'm not lying, though. I've told people facts about themselves that only my grandma knows, which I guess is not too much trouble for me but only when my mom's not around. Whenever she is here and someone calls, I have to run to the phone, hang up, and tell her it's a telemarketer calling about a free trip to the Bahamas. Why can't my grandma just answer the phone herself?"

"Can she do that? Is she here right now?" Estela looks around, as if she could actually see Olvido if her eyes land on the right spot.

"No. Thank God. She tends to stay with my mom." Despite Felicitas's uttered appreciation for God's doing, Estela can't discern whether her friend is disappointed or not. "No," Felicitas says when Estela asks her about it. "I'm glad she hangs around my mom and not me. She . . . doesn't like me very much."

Estela pauses her crafting. "What makes you say that?"

Felicitas nonchalantly continues working on her pattern as she vents. "All she ever does is talk about my mom. 'Tell your mom this. Do that for her. Ask how she's feeling.' Even though there are probably a million stories we can tell each other because, well, we never really talked before she died, she never asks about me. Like ever, ever. 'How are you, Felicitas? How are you dealing with the move? What's your favorite song? What's your favorite book?' Nope. No questions. I'm sure she would avoid me altogether if I wasn't the only person she could talk to."

"That doesn't sound like Doña Olvido."

"So I've heard." Done with her pattern, Felicitas begins to place beads into her plastic string using only one hand. She tightly holds the end of the string, and with a quick motion, attempts to scoop up a bead off the table. She fails and fails but eventually succeeds.

Estela stares at her, concerned that Felicitas is feigning indifference. "So, her and your mom did get along?"

"Not really. From what I know, they were always fighting."

"But fighting with someone doesn't mean that you don't love them. My mom and my sister used to fight all the time, but then when my sister left for college, my mom cried for like a whole week straight. I thought her eyes were going to fall out."

Felicitas frowns. She's never heard of anyone else being in a similar situation as that of her mother and grandmother. Then again, she's never had the opportunity to learn much about other people's relationships. "How can you act like you hate someone and love them at the same time?"

Estela shrugs. "I don't know," she says. "But now that I think about it, I also fought with my sister almost every day, and I miss her. And then when she comes home, we fight again. But then she leaves, and I miss her all over again."

There's the difference, Felicitas thinks. There came a point in which they missed each other. "Well, my grandma never missed me."

"Did she say that?"

"She doesn't have to."

"Do you miss her?"

Felicitas gapes at Estela as if she's grown two heads and four arms. "She's still here. How can I miss her?"

Estela puts her necklace down, claps her hands and brings them up to her chin. "Hmm. Maybe *miss* isn't the right word. Don't you ever get that feeling that—"

"Hi, Estela!" Angustias greets as she walks in through the front door shaking off the raindrops adorning her hair. She stomps down on the doormat with her soaked shoes and moves her legs and torso as if dancing the twist.

"Hi, Ms. Angustias!" Estela greets back.

"What are you girls making? Ooh, necklaces. I want one."

"I'll make you one. Did you find anything?"

Angustias shakes her head. She sheds her rain jacket and tennis shoes and lunges onto the living room couch.

"What were you looking for?" Estela asks.

"A job. I went to the library to search online, but nothing is available here nor in the next town. Emilio says hi, by the way. There are literally no jobs here, not even at McDonald's."

"Maybe people here don't post jobs online. Maybe you can find something in person," Estela suggests. "We're kind of old school."

Angustias sighs. "Yeah, maybe. Wait, how old school are we talking here? Will I need to go knocking door to door to find employment?"

Estela shrugs. "I don't know. Maybe the job will knock on your door."

"What do you mean?" Angustias says, suddenly alert.

"Nothing," Estela says dismissively. "Ms. Angustias, could you give me a ride home? It's going to rain a lot harder soon."

Wait! Felicitas wants to shout. *What were you going to say? What feeling were you talking about?* But Felicitas lets Estela go. She no longer fears that she'll never see her friend again. Although she wishes Olvido's original plan had worked, that she'd lifted the nightstand and used the nurses and doctors' long-held secrets to manipulate them into helping her fake the injury, she has accepted her situation to an extent. As long as she's weighed down by her grandmother's mistake, Angustias can't carry her away. If only mistakes could anchor Angustias without drowning her, she wouldn't be so determined on sailing the unknown sea.

chapter 35

Angustias

Angustias believes in signs, but that does not mean she appreciates seeing them. Some signs indicate tragedy will strike, others indicate that what she wants is not what is best for her, and others are just too loud and clear for her liking. Receiving an extraordinarily obvious sign about something she recently thought or talked about makes Angustias feel as if someone is watching and controlling her every move. And not a gentle observer like God or a guardian angel. It feels like this someone has a little too much power and too little regard for her opinion. This someone feels like her mother.

On the ride to her house, Estela gives Angustias two gifts: a guided tour of Grace and a heads-up about the strangest sign Angustias has witnessed. "That yellow house over there is where Doña Marta lives," Estela says, pointing out the windshield. "She has a three-legged dog that only eats chicken. Turn left at the stop sign. And that blue house over there is where Vanes—I mean miss Ms. Cazares lives. She's our math teacher. She used to babysit me when I was little. Turn right and then another right." It's been years since Angustias has had such a talkative passenger in her car. She decides that out of all the people she has met in Grace, she likes Estela the most.

"Ms. Angustias, do you believe in signs?" Estela says before getting out of the car when they arrive at her house.

"Two hundred percent," Angustias beams.

Estela looks out the window and toward the sky. "The rain," she says. "Is a sign of prosperity."

Glancing out the windshield, Angustias studies the still sky. "Yes, it is," she concurs with hesitation. She looks back down and jumps back at the sight of Estela staring intently at her. The salmon-colored excitement and curiosity floating above her do not reflect on her unsmiling face.

"It's going to hail," Estela declares ominously. "You should put your car in the garage."

"Okay," Angustias says, nodding rapidly.

Estela mimics Angustias's movement. "Think about it," she says. "Bye!" She jumps out of the car and runs up to the front door of her house where her mother stands, waving to Angustias. Angustias waves back. "Mom," Angustias can faintly hear Estela say. "Guess what I learned about Felicitas's mo—" The door shuts behind her.

Before driving away, Angustias turns on the data on her phone, which she promised to save for an emergency. She checks the weather app and searches the news. No mention of hail. But the apps are wrong. It hails in Grace that night, just like Estela predicted, and the next morning, the job offers came pouring in.

Having re-accustomed herself to the Texas heat, Angustias decides to spend the day out and about downtown along the main street. She could use a day of mindless window-shopping. She doesn't go far before coming to a sudden halt. Angustias walks backward, retracing her steps, and turns. She rubs her eyes to clear her vision, but her eyes are not deceiving her. There are, in fact, not one, not two, but *fifteen* Help Wanted signs posted on the doors of the businesses along the street.

Thinking this is a bewildering sight, she walks over to the next street and finds twenty more signs. She repeats the process the next street over and the street after that until she reaches the end of the downtown area. She pivots and quickens her pace until she is running back toward the main street. Fifteen minutes later, when Angustias reaches the Grace Public Library, she is panting, sweating, and pressing a hand to her forehead to relieve the excruciating pain above her right eyebrow.

"Are you okay?" Emilio asks when he sees her. He stands frozen with caution near one of the bookshelves.

"Yeah," Angustias laughs at his panicked expression. She walks around the front desk and lets herself fall into his chair. When her heartbeat has slowed down to a normal rhythm and she has enough air in her lungs, Angustias shakes her head. "No. I'm not okay. I'm going crazy," she admits. "Or this town is going crazy? Yes. That's it. This whole town is crazy. No offense."

Emilio waves the comment away. "Only partially taken. Is this a realization you had this morning, and did you run all the way here just to tell me this?"

"No," she responds defensively. "I ran here because—I mean, I came over because . . . something crazy happened out there," she whispers, pointing out the window. When Angustias describes the rows and rows of Help Wanted signs that chased her down every street, Emilio does not appear concerned or surprised. This is not, however, because he is aware of what is happening in town. There are only three people in Grace who are unaware of Olvido's plan: Angustias, for obvious reasons; Emilio, because everyone knows he is a terrible liar; and Don Fulgencio, who lives on the outskirts of town with no neighbors and few visitors who can inform him about the gossip of the week.

"You don't look freaked out. Why aren't you freaking out?" Angustias demands. Emilio raises his palms and shrugs. Angustias shrugs back, mocking his gesture. She stands and paces around the front desk chair. "I need a job and, all of a sudden, everyone needs help? And I mean *everyone*. That's just too weird."

"People can't always plan when they're going to need help, can they?"

Angustias stops pacing. "I suppose not, but—"

"Did you know you were going to need help?"

"What do you mean? I don't need help." Angustias attempts to toss her hair back to show her indignation, but the strands get caught in her fingers. Between the humidity and the running, her hair has tangled in multiple places as if various birds fought to make a nest on her head. The sweat caused her makeup to run down her face and her clothes to awkwardly stick to her skin. She may not need help, but she certainly looks like she does.

"You just said you need a job," Emilio points out.

"Yes. So?"

"So, you do need help." This time he shrugs to mock her. "Just pick a job."

"Excuse me? Pick one of the jobs out there?" Angustias glances at the display window and shudders. "No. Not out there. Not anymore."

"So then pick a job here."

"What?"

"Pick a job here," he repeats. Emilio walks over to the front desk, takes a stack of blue sticky notes and scribbles Help Wanted on the top one. He pulls it off the pad and sticks it to Angustias's forehead.

"Here?" Angustias asks, removing the note and examining the words. "As a librarian or a custodian?"

"A librarian, but be warned, that does entail custodial work."

Angustias shakes her head and hands the note back to Emilio. "I'm not a librarian. I'm not trained. I don't even like reading."

Emilio laughs. "You don't have to like reading."

"Do you even have a position open?"

"No, but I could make one. There's enough in the budget." Angustias raises an eyebrow and crosses her arms. "I could even pay you right away," Emilio insists. "I've been saving in case of an emergency."

"An emergency? What, are your books going to spontaneously combust?" Angustias throws her arms up in the air and waves them like flames in a bonfire.

"No, but those computers are so old, they might."

It's not just the computers. Angustias examines the ceiling's fissured tiles, which are all clearly from different decades. Some are white as snow; others, a concerning yellow color. The bookshelves are splintering. The floor tiles are cracked.

"Well, I'm glad you are at least aware of that." With her hands behind her back and her eyes narrowed, Angustias walks up and down an aisle, inspecting the bookshelves. "I could help you organize this place," she says.

"You most definitely could, and I could teach you the system."

Angustias whips her head out from between the stacks to look at Emilio. "There's a system?"

"Of course."

Angustias stares at him, dumbfounded. "Okay," she says calmly the way she does when explaining something to Felicitas. "How about instead of you teaching me the system, we update the system together?"

"What for? I know where everything is."

"Yeah, that's the problem. Only *you* know where everything is."

It is Emilio who now appears dumbfounded. "I don't know what you mean, and I'm offended," Emilio says, but there is no red in his cloud.

"Do you still want me as an employee, then?"

"Yes. I do. It's only for a month, right? I don't have to deal with you longer than that?"

"Ha-ha, very funny. So, it's official? I work here?"

"It is." Emilio stretches out his hand. Smiling, Angustias runs over to shake it. She is working at a library! Felicitas will be so happy and proud.

Has Angustias ever done anything worthy of those feelings? Self-pride is not foreign to her. She's a good mother. She's put a roof over their heads and food on the table, entertained Felicitas's interests and hobbies, emotionally supported her through conflicts in school and with other children, even moved across states just for Felicitas's peace of mind. But supporting her daughter's needs is a basic requirement of motherhood. Felicitas does not need to be proud of Angustias for that.

Is there anything else, not a fancy job title or a difficult-to-earn diploma but at least a positive personal attribute? No one would talk about Angustias the way the residents of Grace talked about Olvido, maybe not even Felicitas. Olvido never held a high-paying position, didn't finish high school, but she was certainly worthy of accolades.

"Hey," Emilio says, startling Angustias when he places a hand on her shoulder. "Are you okay?" Angustias flashes an unnecessarily large smile and nods. "Good. You might not be after I tell you that your first assignment is to clean the toilet."

"Yay," Angustias responds sarcastically, but it feels good to be needed for something trivial, to step away from matters of life and death and of an unrelenting higher power.

chapter 36

Olvido

Olvido is afraid. Her daughter is on the brink of running away again because the people of Grace are too forward. They are pushing her away. No wonder Olvido fit in so well. Those who try to be subtle speak as if they're engaging in their first human conversation. Those who want to be friendly come off as crazed. Then there's the priest, who is in a league of his own. He enters the library with a Bible in his hand. His freshly-polished rosary shines so bright it almost blinds Angustias when she looks up at him from the front desk.

You brought props? Olvido wants to yell at him. *My goodness. You're not preforming an exorcism.* If he were, Felicitas would love to be present.

"¿Cómo va tu día, hija?" Padre Alfonso asks Angustias.

She answers honestly. "Bizarre, but very good, Father. How can I help you?"

"Just good or unusually good?" he pushes.

"Um, unusually good, I suppose."

Padre Alfonso nods to himself. "We don't know why God is so good to us sometimes, but He is. Right?"

"Right," Angustias says, nodding sarcastically.

"And when very good things happen, when our prayers are answered, it is important to give thanks." The priest raises his eyebrows at her, challenging her belief in his statement.

"Yep. I'll let Him know I'm thankful. By the way, do you need help? With library matters, I mean."

"It is also important," he continues. "To not only give thanks but to actually show Him our appreciation."

"Ay, Padre Alfonso," Olvido says, covering her face to hide her embarrassment. So many years in the priesthood and he still has such terrible social skills. "You see. This is why people came to talk to me instead of you."

"What do you have in mind, Padre?" Angustias sighs. Padre Alfonso smiles and turns toward the window facing the church.

Angustias stands to follow his line of vision. "What?" she asks.

"It's important to give thanks," he repeats.

Angustias frowns as she tries to decipher what the priest is saying. "Oh, you mean now? Go give thanks now?"

"Sure, now. Or perhaps on Sunday?"

"Ah, Sunday. I can't Sunday," she says shaking her head apologetically. "I'm working here on Sunday, actually." She smiles and points at her name tag, a Post-it note Emilio scribbled on before he went out for lunch.

"Oh, wonderful! But I'm sure Emilio can let you miss Sunday mornings. He's run this place by himself for years. Most public libraries don't even open on Sunday mornings."

"But this one does," Angustias asserts.

"Ay, Emilio," Olvido reproaches. Only she knew he opened Sundays because he didn't want to attend church either.

"I'll talk to him," the priest assures her.

Angustias smiles awkwardly. "I don't feel comfortable getting time off when I've only been working for . . . literally three hours."

"I'll talk to him," the priest insists as he moves toward the exit. "Don't you worry."

"Well, I wasn't going to, but maybe I should?"

"Don't worry," Padre Alfonso repeats, waving a hand through the window.

When Emilio arrives, he informs Angustias that she must attend Sunday service or he will be forced to fire her. "It was you or me," he says.

"You sacrificed me?" Angustias says, putting her hand up to her chest.

"Yes. Sorry," Emilio says though he does not sound apologetic at all. "What did you expect? The man tracked me down during my lunch break. That's kind of terrifying, no?"

Olvido shakes her head disapprovingly. "You need to find the Lord, too, mijo."

"Don't ask me how," Angustias whispers. "But I know, I just know, that somehow my mom is behind all this. She called almost every Sunday just to ask if I was going to church. I was honest and said that I wasn't. Now that she's dead, she's somewhere up there finding little ways to get me to do what she wants."

Emilio looks up as if he can see Olvido looking down at them, but she's standing by the entrance of the library. "I'm still going to ask you how you know, though," he says. "How do you know?"

"Because when I die," Angustias admits. "I'll probably do the same to Felicitas."

Olvido beams with pride. "I told you one day you would understand."

chapter 37

Felicitas

Felicitas Olivares's first church-going experience occurred during her eighth year of life. During one of her weekly phone calls with Angustias, Olvido complained about a pain in her throat. She had been coughing for a month, but whenever Angustias asked about it, Olvido dismissed her worries by saying she just needed to clear her throat with some water or she had left the air-conditioning on too long or she had walked barefoot on the cold tile floor. However, because Olvido rarely spoke about how she was doing, the complaint indicated to Angustias that the problem was not as insignificant as her mother made it out to be.

"Grandma doesn't sound good," Angustias whispered to Felicitas as she covered the phone with her hand.

"Really?" Felicitas said. "Let me talk to her."

Angustias put the phone back up to her ear and said, "Ma, Felicitas quiere hablar contigo. Te la paso." Then, she frowned and nodded and said, "Hmm," and "Mhm," and "Okay, bye." Felicitas held out her hand for the phone, but Angustias did not hand it to her. "Sorry, mijita. Grandma said she was really busy. She'll call you some other time."

It was always the same routine. Olvido called. Olvido talked to Angustias. Olvido hung up. Although Felicitas was a tad bit hurt by her grandmother's actions, she asked how serious the cough was. "She could barely speak," Angustias said.

All day, Felicitas quietly attempted to think of a solution. There was not much they could do from multiple states away. "We should go to church and pray," she declared. "We can light a candle for her. You said that's what you used to do when you were little, right?"

Angustias shook her head. "I don't know. It doesn't feel right after all these years. We can pray and light a candle here. And frankly, I don't know if I believe—"

"Does Grandma believe?" Felicitas interrupted. She knew the answer to her own question. She had heard enough stories about Olvido to be aware of the extent of her religious devotion. Olvido ended every phone call by reminding Angustias to go to church and pray, and in the instances sprinkled throughout in which Olvido actually spoke to Felicitas, she made sure to remind Felicitas to remind her mother to go to church and pray.

The trip to save Olvido was quick and uneventful. The one Catholic church they found in the town they were living in at the time didn't have any candles to light, so the Olivares girls simply sat in one of the middle pews and silently prayed. Felicitas panicked for a second. She'd never prayed before and didn't know if there was a proper way to do it. She turned to Angustias to ask for guidance, but her mother's eyes were already closed, so Felicitas improvised. "Hello, God," she silently began her prayer. "My name is Felicitas Olivares, currently living at 547 18th Street."

Felicitas wasn't sure if she prayed correctly that day, but she supposed she had because the next week, Angustias informed her that Olvido's cough was gone. There were a few other instances in which Felicitas prayed, but her requests were never fulfilled again. Sitting among the Grace townspeople in the pews of Nuestra Señora del Carmen, Felicitas makes a new attempt.

"En el nombre del Padre, del Hijo y del Espíritu Santo. Amén," she begins like Olvido taught her to during her funeral. "Hello, God. I'm not sure if You remember me. My name is Felicitas Olivares, no official address, but currently staying at 2045 Maple Road, Grace, Texas, 78455. I have a favor to ask of You. My grandma is dead, but she is still with us, and I don't know why. I would like for You to please take her to Heaven if that is where she belongs, and if that is not currently possible, I would like for You to get the idea that she needs to 'fix' my mom's life out of her brain. I think my mom's perfectly fine. Well, sort of. My grandma wants her to get married, and there's nothing wrong with marriage, but I think she's rushing things, and my mom is not going to be happy. What if she forces her to marry some weirdo? I don't want to live with a weirdo. The worst part is—"

"Psst! Felicitas!"

Felicitas opens one eye and finds Estela in the pew across the aisle with her hands cupped around her mouth. "Felicitas!" Estela whispers again. Felicitas closes her eyes. She needs to finish her prayer.

"The worst part is that she's making me a part of this, and I don't like it. But, if You are able to put an end to her crazy ideas, can You still find a way to make us stay here in Grace? I really don't want to move again. You didn't—"

Felicitas feels a tap on her shoulder. She looks up at Estela now standing next to her. Estela points inconspicuously to the left and walks away. No one else sees the gesture. Everyone's eyes are down as the priest leads them in the closing prayer. Felicitas watches Estela reach the end of the aisle, point to the right toward the restroom, and gesture for her to follow her. *Come on*, Estela mouths, but Felicitas closes her eyes and speeds through the end of her prayer instead.

"You didn't prevent our move last time I asked You to, but hopefully You'll listen to my petition today. Pretty please. Sincerely, Felicitas Olivares. Wait. I already told You my name. Okay. Bye."

Felicitas makes the sign of the cross and turns to inform Angustias that she's going to get a drink from the water fountain. "But you don't need to come with me," Felicitas assures her. "I'll be right back." Angustias gives her a single nod. She doesn't open her eyes. Either she's attempting to take a nap or what she is praying for is of great importance.

"They're trying to set up your mom!" Estela squeals as soon as Felicitas enters the restroom. She grabs Felicitas's uninjured arm and pulls her toward her.

"What? Who is 'they'? With who?"

Estela looks around the empty restroom, leans in, and says, "'They' are the whole town, but now that I think about it, it's really just Doña Ybarra. As soon as she heard that Doña Olvido really, really wanted your mom to get married, she immediately offered up her son. I don't know if she actually believes in your ability or just saw it as the perfect excuse." Estela's last words drift off as if she's lost herself in the mystery she's created in her mind. Felicitas snaps her finger and calls her attention back.

"Right. His name is Claudio, but we just call him Cayo. I don't know how old he is, but in my opinion, he looks super old, like as old as my parents. Anyways, he lives with his mom, Doña Ybarra, our neighbor. I don't think there is anything wrong with living with your parents, I mean I live with my parents, right, but he doesn't seem very . . . helpful? I don't know if that's the right word. Basically, he's a Mama's Boy, although maybe he's not if his mama wants to get rid of him."

Felicitas frowns as she pictures her mother's potential date. The Cayo she has conjured up in her mind is short and stubby and has long, greasy hair. He has a beer belly, which he rubs as if he's carrying a baby, and he's missing a couple of teeth, a trait Felicitas can see when he lets out a breathy laugh. "Eew. I don't like that."

Estela agrees. Suddenly, her eyes grow wide. In one quick motion, she pushes Felicitas against the door, blocking a woman attempting to enter the restroom.

"The restroom is out of service," Estela yells. "Felicitas threw up in here. It's really gross. You don't want to come in." Behind the door, the woman scrunches up her nose and scurries away. The girls can hear the clicking of her heels growing fainter.

Felicitas glares at Estela. "You could have said you threw up!"

"But she saw me, and I look perfectly fine."

"And I don't?"

Estela shrugs. She continues to fill Felicitas in on the town's latest news. There aren't too many eligible bachelors in Grace, but Don Aguirre's nephew is visiting and is a potential suitor, and Doña Susana knows a guy two towns away with lots of money and no wife although plenty of girlfriends.

Felicitas's frown deepens with every sentence Estela utters. She knows she should view the town gossip positively. It will propel Olvido's plan, and the faster the plan is completed, the faster she'll get rid of her grandmother's spirit. Still, she doesn't like the fact that people are talking about her mother behind her back. She doesn't like that they are controlling her dating options, and she doesn't like that the dating prospects they have deemed worthy of her sound so terrible.

Before Felicitas can say "ew" again, Estela runs to block the door with her body and repeats her lie. "Felicitas, you threw up?" they hear a very concerned Angustias ask. "Do you have a fever again?"

"Say yes," Olvido instructs as she makes her way into the restroom, brushing off nonexistent dust before her body is fully inside. "Go on, so she can continue to believe you are unwell."

"Yes," Felicitas replies, and moves Estela out of the way.

Angustias barges in and bends down to inspect Felicitas's head, which is cool to the touch, but Angustias plays along for some reason. "Then we should get home right away," she says. "Service is over anyways. Estela, your parents are looking for you."

Angustias grabs Estela and Felicitas's hands and drags them out of the restroom. She takes Estela to her parents, respectfully greets and says goodbye to multiple churchgoers including Samara, who is very concerned about Felicitas's health, and eventually makes it out of the church.

"Mamá, the car is that way," Felicitas says, pointing to her left.

Angustias ignores her and drags her forward into the street. "I know, but we're going to hide at the library for a bit first."

"Hide?" Angustias does not elaborate.

Felicitas quickens her step as her mother hurriedly pulls her by her uninjured arm. She closes her eyes, startled by the honk of a nearby car. She can't see, but she can feel. They're flying, and she's sure if they weren't being weighed down by gravity, her mother would fly them home, wherever that may be.

chapter 38

Angustias

Angustias knows the importance of setting a good example for her daughter, but good is a vague term, and it is difficult to be good in a bad world. Wisdom and courage, they don't always go hand in hand. Sometimes it is wise to be a coward and courageous to be foolish. Acting wisely, Angustias hides from her mother's intrusive neighbors. If they are anything like Olvido, the battle against their meddling will not end until someone has a mental breakdown or drops dead.

"Jaywalking is illegal in all fifty states," Felicitas shouts when they enter the library.

"Is it?" Emilio asks cheerfully from the front desk.

"It is, and so is child abuse. You threw me into the path of moving cars!"

"There were no cars," Angustias assures Emilio, holding one hand up as if delivering an oath in court. From the corner of her eye, she catches movement outside the window and runs behind the front desk, pushing Emilio out of the way. On the desk's left side is a pile of books so high it blocks most of the display window. Angustias stands on her toes to peak over the pile and looks out into the street. Emilio copies her.

"What's out there?" he whispers.

Angustias shushes him and ducks when she spots Claudio Ybarra and his mother standing across the street, squinting their eyes at the library. Angustias pulls Emilio down with her. "We need to lock the door," she instructs, inches away from his face. "Now!"

Emilio follows her orders. He marches over to the entrance, locks the door, and flips the Open sign so that it signals that they're closed. "Are we being attacked by aliens?" he asks Felicitas, who refused to go into hiding.

"I sure hope so," she responds, but they are not. From Angustias's perspective, the truth is far worse than extraterrestrial beings. People in town are trying to set her up on dates. Strangers, friends of her mother, are trying to set her up on dates!

It's all her fault. She shouldn't have gone to church. She foresaw trouble since Thursday morning at the pharmacy. While waiting in line, an old woman who stood behind her tapped her shoulder and asked her if she was Olvido's daughter. Angustias smiled and responded that she was. She didn't remind her that they'd met once before at Olvido's funeral. She didn't want to start a conversation about her mother.

The woman tapped her shoulder again. "And you're looking for a husband, right?" the woman said in a deep, hoarse voice.

Angustias turned around. "Excuse me?"

"A husband," the woman enunciated loudly.

"No, ma'am. I'm looking for cortisone," Angustias said, raising her arm to display her wounds from a battle with a vicious Texas mosquito. The cashier called Angustias up and saved her from the impending doom of the woman's response. Angustias paid as fast as she could and ran out, but the woman's voice chased her to the parking lot. "Do you like younger—?"

On Friday afternoon, as Angustias walked from the library to her car, she was stopped by an old man accompanied by a much younger one. "Angustias, so good to see you!" the man said as if he were a lifelong friend. Angustias smiled, echoed the remark, and tried to continue walking, but the man spoke again. "How is your daughter? Felicitas, right?"

It was odd to hear a stranger talk about Felicitas, but she figured the man knew Olvido, and she'd mentioned her granddaughter. The man did not wait for Angustias to answer before presenting to her his nephew who was visiting from El Paso, and unsurprisingly, was single. That was all the information he gave her. He was from El Paso, and he was single.

Angustias smiled at the nephew whose name she did not know and said, "Good for you," in reference to the latter piece of information. She hopped into her car and sped away.

Then, on Sunday before church, she encountered Cayo and Doña Ybarra, who, like every other person in town, lacked subtlety and shame, and like the woman in the pharmacy and the man near her car, wore matching sky-blue clouds of determination. Angustias could sense as the mother and son duo walked up to her that she would not be able to escape them as easily. Their clouds were more opaque. Their intentions to get her to listen were stronger. They were also far more absurd. Cayo was very direct. "Hi, I'm Cayo. I'm single," is how he introduced himself after his mother interrupted Angustias's conversation with Samara with a brief introduction of her own. Angustias snorted in an attempt to keep in her laughter. "I was wondering—"

The power of God saved Angustias with a request from a church-goer. "Please take your seats. Service is about to begin."

Genuinely happy, Angustias excused herself and pushed Felicitas toward the pew that Samara's family sat in. They'd reserved a space for her, and it was fortunately very far away from Cayo and Doña Ybarra.

During the final prayer, Angustias asked God to quickly heal Felicitas from whatever it was that Dr. Gutiérrez thought she had, to help her sell Olvido's house quickly, to let her find a nice affordable home in the Valley, and to scare away anyone who wanted to figure out if she was single so they could throw their relatives at her. Unfortunately, she forgot to ask Him to scare the relatives themselves.

She silently cursed her prayer's loophole when Cayo briskly and determinedly walked up to her after service and asked her out on a date. She then thanked God again when a woman interrupted him to inform Angustias that she needed to go to the restroom immediately. Felicitas had thrown up. Angustias silently rejoiced then cursed herself for feeling thankful for her daughter's misfortune. She excused herself and made her grand escape. She couldn't go home, though. The mysterious

Bibles left on the porch told her that Olvido's house was not a safe space, but the library was. No one ever went to the library.

She—they couldn't live like this. They needed to leave Grace and soon. *Con la voluntad de Dios*, Olvido would say in such a situation, but if Angustias waited around for God's will to reveal itself, she risked a whole town's will dictating her fate first.

chapter 39

Felicitas

Felicitas is torn. She wants Olvido's plan to succeed if only to stay in Grace, but she knows it's not right. Despite her grandmother's insistence and her long-winded excuses for her insistence, Felicitas feels bad for her mother. Gone are the days in which she was jealous of Angustias, when it seemed like everything worked out in her favor. That is not normal.

"I think she's scared," Felicitas says, as she runs her hands across the spines of the books in the children's section of the Grace Public Library. "Or weirded out."

Gustavo, who sits at the top of a short bookshelf he climbed, purses his lips, and shakes his head. "Moms should never be scared. It's like a doctor being sick or a dentist having a cavity."

"Exactly," Felicitas says. "It's not right. And that's the problem. Everyone is acting . . . abnormal." Her fingers freeze and pull out a book. "It seems paranormal!" she says with a smile, lifting up a copy of *Night of the Living Dummy.* "The way we go back to my grandma's house after her death and suddenly all the things she wished for my mom start being pushed onto her."

"I think it's normal," Estela says from the other end of the bookshelf. "Moms are the scarediest people in the world. Is that a word?"

Felicitas shrugs and studies the cover art of her book. "It's my favorite word. *Paranormal.* It sounds almost the same in English and Spanish and Portuguese and Italian and French and even Filipino."

"Mine's *extraordinary*," Estela says, pausing between syllables. "*Extra* means very, and *ordinary* means, well, ordinary. So, you would think that *extraordinary* means very ordinary, but it means the exact opposite of that! It's totally not what you expect it to be."

"Well with *paranormal* you can figure out the definition just by looking at it. *Para* means stop in Spanish, and when adults say, 'stop,' they also mean 'don't do that' or 'no.' So, *para* and *normal* must mean not normal. And isn't it better to know what things are just by looking at them? Like, why do you want secrecy?"

"What about paramedics?" Gustavo asks. "Are they not supposed to give you medicine? And what about parasites? What are they stopping?"

Estela marches over to Gustavo and holds down his swinging legs. "Technically, paramedics can't give you medicine. That's why they take you to the hospital where the doctors are. Duh! And parasites attach themselves to a specific *site* in your body and make it *stop* functioning." She lifts her right hand like a claw and strikes it down on Gustavo's ankle.

"You're wrong," Gustavo says, looking up from his phone. "*Parasite* means 'feed beside' because *para* can also mean beside. Wow! *Para* can mean a million things. Between and around and beyond and—"

Taking advantage of Gustavo's rambling, Felicitas taps Estela's shoulder and motions for them to face away from him. "Can I ask you something?" she whispers. Estela throws a quick glance over her shoulder and nods. "Remember when you asked me if I missed my grandma and that maybe *miss* wasn't the right word?" Estela nods again. "What's the right word?"

Estela purses her lips and taps her index finger against her chin. "I don't know," she sighs after a moment. "I'm sorry. Have you tried googling it?"

"Yeah," Felicitas says, her shoulders slouching forward. "I clicked on this site called Quora and people said it was insecurity or obsession or infatuation, which basically means obsession."

Estela frowns. "You don't seem obsessed with Doña Olvido."

"I'm not! And I don't feel insecure around her either. I just feel . . . not good." Estela wraps one arm around Felicitas's back and squeezes her shoulder. The gesture is far from comforting. "I don't even miss her, actually," Felicitas quickly clarifies. "I just want to know what the word is. I was just curious. Swear to God."

"I know," Estela says, but the upturned inner corners of her brows tell Felicitas she does not.

"I'm serious. I know what I'm feeling toward my grandma, and it's just anger because she's so . . . she's so annoying. But the word sounded strange, and I like strange things."

"What word sounds strange?" Gustavo whispers into the space between Estela and Felicitas's heads, causing them to break their huddle in a jump.

"We don't know," Felicitas answers as Estela says, "Supercalifragilisticexpialidocious."

Gustavo crosses his arms. "Why are you guys lying? Is it a secret? You can tell me. I love secrets!"

"You love them, but can you keep them?" Estela argues.

"Yes, I can! I haven't told Ms. Angustias about Doña Olvido, have I?" Felicitas runs to cover Gustavo's mouth.

"Not yet," Estela reproaches. "But you might end up telling Emilio with that big mouth of yours."

"And we're not lying," Felicitas adds, removing her hands. "We don't know the word. We barely know the definition."

"So, we can't google it?" Gustavo says, shifting his weight from his heels to his toes and back. Estela and Felicitas shake their heads. Gustavo's pout transforms into a bright grin in an instant. "Then we should ask Emilio! He's a librarian. He has to know every word ever written."

Estela slaps her palm on her forehead. "No, he does not."

"Yes, he does. To get your librarian diploma, you have to read and memorize every book in your school's library, including the dictionary. I don't know what he did for the sections in other languages, though. Do you guys think there are Dr. Seuss books written in other languages? Where are the books in Spanish?"

Estela waves her hand as if she can blow away Gustavo's comments and leans in toward Felicitas. "Gustavo has a point. Do you want to ask Emilio?"

Felicitas's eyes grow wide. Her head shakes vigorously. "What if he tells my mom I miss my grandma?"

"So, you do miss her?"

"No," Felicitas shouts. Her hands shoot up to her lips, but they're unable to push the word back into her mouth. "I don't know. Maybe I'll know if I hear the word." Now would be the perfect time to ask, she admits to herself. Emilio sent Angustias on a mission to the Las Flores Public Library to pick up some donated books. Well, she volunteered.

"They'll try to give you some copies in appalling conditions as well. Don't take those or we'll have to go through the trouble of getting rid of them," Emilio instructed. "We are not a dumping ground no matter what everyone else thinks."

"Sir, yes, sir," Angustias roared, lifting her hand up to her forehead like a cadet. Felicitas is sure her mother is taking her sweet time going through each book they hand her, anything to buy herself a few hours away from Grace.

"He said he can help us!" Felicitas hears Gustavo's voice boom through the shelves.

"Gustavo!" Estela shouts disapprovingly as they make their way through the labyrinth of books. They find him sitting on top of Emilio's desk, swinging his legs innocently. Emilio waves them over.

"Gustavo tells me you're looking for a word," he says when they reach his desk.

Felicitas nods. "What else did he say?" she asks, shooting daggers at Gustavo with her eyes.

"Nothing," Emilio assures her. "I'm waiting for the details. Is there something you didn't want him to tell me?"

"No. Nothing." Felicitas shakes her head suspiciously fast. She can't help herself. Her heart is pounding against her ribs. Her stomach is twisting into a knot. She's going to throw up.

"She's writing a story," Estela interjects.

"Yes," Felicitas says hesitantly. This is a lie, but it doesn't have to be. And she shouldn't feel guilty about lying to Emilio. She's been deceiving him on matters of Olvido for weeks. "Yep, I am. I'm writing a story."

Emilio nods, stands, and pats his chair for Felicitas to take it. Then he moves to sit next to Gustavo and asks, "What about?" while Felicitas makes herself comfortable in his too-large chair. She wiggles back so that her body is one with the backrest, causing the chair to swivel. When she turns back around, she finds her friends staring intently at her, waiting for her to feed them words of wisdom or love or suspense, whatever this unwritten story may bring. She braces the armrest for strength. She's in charge. She's the storyteller. What's her story about?

"Death," she declares. "It's about death."

Estela claps encouragingly and nudges Emilio with her elbow to disrupt the million questions of concern reflected on his grimacing face. His face unfreezes, and his eyebrows fall back to their usual place. "That's nice," he squeaks.

"Yes, and in the story, Death is the Devil's daughter, and she feels like she misses the Devil, but she doesn't know why since she doesn't really know him. He's forcing her to stay here on Earth, snatching souls." Felicitas pretends to lunge at Emilio with clawlike hands.

Emilio jerks back but smiles tightly. "Mhm. Okay. I'm following."

"We want to know what that feeling is called when you miss someone you never met or when you miss someone who's not really gone."

Emilio hums as he thinks, turning slowly toward each child's eager face. "*Yearning*?" he suggests.

"Wait! I got it." Gustavo whips out his cell phone from his pocket, types, and says, "*Yearning*," with pride as if he thought of the word on his own. "A tender or urgent longing. Example, a yearning for justice." He puts the phone down on his lap. "Tender like chicken tenders?"

Estela laughs. "Honestly, how did you skip a grade?"

Felicitas shakes her head. "That doesn't sound right."

"No," Estela agrees. "Because tender doesn't mean tender like chicken tenders."

"I meant *yearning*," Felicitas says softly. "The definition doesn't sound right. And what's—"

"*Tender*," Gustavo reads. "One. Marked by, responding to, or expressing the softer emotions. Two. Showing care. Three. Easily chewed. Ha! I was right. That's how I skipped a grade. I can keep more than one definition in my brain."

"Yeah, but you don't know which one's the right one in this case," Estela scorns.

"Okay, okay," Emilio says, patting the air. "I know you kids like to play around by being mean and sarcastic, but—"

"What if Death doesn't feel soft emotions?" Felicitas asks him. "What if she's a little bit angry at the Devil?" She can picture Death, perplexed at the tornado spinning inside her cold heart. Lines form on the pale skin between her black-bead eyes.

Gustavo snorts. "Why would Death miss the Devil if she's angry at him?"

Embarrassed at her lack of knowledge, Felicitas shrugs and folds into herself as best as she can with her injured arm. These are her story and characters. Why can't she just turn on a light switch in her mind and find what they're doing, what they want and what they feel?

"Emotions are complex, and they don't always make sense," Emilio explains. "Did Death ever meet the Devil in this story?"

"Um, yes," Felicitas says. "For a little bit when she was a baby."

Emilio nods in understanding. "Was Death happy during the time they spent together?"

"No," Felicitas laughs as if the answer is obvious. "He's the Devil, so he wasn't very nice."

"I see. Does Death wish he was nicer or that they had a better time together?"

Felicitas takes a deep breath as she searches for the answer. Where's that stupid light switch? "I think so. Yes. Yes, she does."

"Hmm. Gustavo, look up the word *longing*."

"*Longing*," Gustavo reads. "A strong desire, especially for something unattainable. Another word is *craving*—like craving chicken tenders!"

Estela lightly punches his arm. "Would you stop with the chicken tenders? Does your mama not feed you?"

Gustavo ignores her. "Ooh! Does Death want to eat the Devil? That would be a good revenge story. She eats him because he was so mean to her and made her work instead of letting her go home, and then, she absorbs all his evilness and power and becomes the new ruler of Hell!"

MY MOTHER CURSED MY NAME 203

"Death does not eat the Devil," Estela shouts. "He's her father. That's cannibalism."

"Does *longing* fit better?" Emilio whispers, kneeling beside Felicitas.

Felicitas nods. "Yeah, I think so."

A desire did not have to be positive. She had a strong desire to see Olvido gone, to regain her peace. And Olvido's spirit certainly felt and was unattainable. She came and went as she pleased and stuck to Angustias like a roach on a flypaper trap. She never let Felicitas in on her thoughts and emotions. She told her what to do but not why she had to do it. Why did she feel the need to "fix" Angustias's life? Why did she look at her with tender eyes but speak with sharp words? Why were her eyes so different when she looked at Felicitas?

"Is this story inspired by anyone?" Emilio says. "Do you maybe miss your dad?"

Felicitas jumps back in the chair. "No! Definitely not. It's not about my dad." At one point, the story could have been about her dad. She's longed for him before. Well, not him specifically, but a father, a family. She's looked around the cafeteria during her school's Donuts for Dad events, browsed the crowd during talent shows, and glanced up at parents' faces during parent-teacher nights and wondered what it would be like to have a father, two parents to love you and tell you how proud they are of you. It's called *longing*, she now knows, but it's not the same as her longing for her grandmother. Thoughts about fathers were triggered randomly and rarely, but thoughts about grandmothers, about Olvido, came with every story about Angustias's youth, every phone call and refusal to speak to Felicitas. And every time they moved, Felicitas couldn't help but think that Angustias's first escape was her fault. She was responsible for her own lack of family.

Who knows where Felicitas's father is now. He could have a picture-perfect house, an amazing job, a loving wife, and a daughter whom he adores. It doesn't matter. He's not here. Olvido is. Olvido has met her and still doesn't want her. She is simultaneously absent and present, and Felicitas longs for her interest, maybe even love. "It's not about him," she repeats.

"Okay, I believe you."

"It's not!" Her stomach twists tighter. Tighter. It's so tight, it might never come undone. This isn't guilt, and it isn't about lies regarding Olvido. This is fear, and it's about her. *There's nothing to be afraid of,* Felicitas repeats to herself. *Emilio did not see through you.*

"If you say it's not, then it's not."

Felicitas frowns and tugs on Emilio's shirt to keep him from standing. "Please don't tell my mom about the story, especially not about you thinking it's about my dad because it's not, and she would get worried about the dad thing and about me writing about death. These aren't her favorite kinds of stories, especially not right now."

Emilio puts his right hand over his heart. "I promise I won't say anything. Your mom doesn't seem like the judgmental type, though."

Felicitas shakes her head. "My mom is predictably unpredictable." And because she's known Emilio for only a couple of weeks, his actions are unpredictable as well, but Estela assures her that he'll keep his word. "He's usually not good at keeping quiet. He once snitched on me and told my mom I had checked out *The Exorcist* behind her back, which I was not supposed to do because I was eight, but I am three hundred percent sure he'll try his best to keep quiet this time. I slipped him a note," she says with a wink before Samara starts the car to drive them home.

"Saying?" Felicitas whispers although she doubts Samara will hear their conversation. Gustavo's unmelodic voice is loud enough to engulf the sound of the latest pop hit playing on the radio.

Estela cups her hands around Felicitas's ear and leans in. "Keep the secret. Return Doña Olvido's favor." She leans back. "He'll definitely do it for her. It's a tiny secret. I don't think his Goody Two–shoes heart could handle anything bigger."

"What favor?"

"What?"

"What favor did my grandma do? Do you mean her food? Emilio said he wasn't really in need of it."

"Oh." Estela frowns. "Right. Sorry. It makes sense that you don't know."

Felicitas frowns back. "Know what?"

Estela holds up her index finger, requesting a moment to think. "I have an idea," she says a second later, her eyes twinkling with excitement. "I could tell you, but what if you ask your grandma instead?"

"Ask her what?"

"Ask her how she knows so many people's secrets! That's *her* secret. How does she know?"

Felicitas shrugs. "Small town, big gossip is what my mom always says."

Estela shakes her head. "If people's secrets were town gossip, everyone would know them, and they wouldn't be secrets anymore. Have you really never wondered why Doña Olvido knows so much about everyone?"

The lines between Felicitas's brows deepen. "Excuse me. I had bigger things to worry about like my near-death experience. And I had an explanation. Didn't people go to her house all the time? Sounded to me like they just had a lot of private conversations over dinner."

"I have dinner with my parents every night, and I never tell them about my crushes," Estela argues. "But Doña Olvido knows about all of them, even the half one."

Felicitas's jaw drops. Olvido's presence knows no boundaries. She already has Angustias and their history. Does she have to take Estela, too? Her conversations, her secrets? Did Olvido ask for them? When? Why? And why didn't she ask for Felicitas's secrets?

"Will you tell *me* about the half crush, whatever that means?"

Estela holds out her pinky to make a promise. "I will if you talk to your grandma first."

Felicitas crosses her arms and bangs the back of her head against the headrest. "Why are you insisting?"

"Because that weird feeling, longing, or whatever it's called, I know it doesn't feel good. I've felt it, too. But your grandma isn't unattainable. She's still here. You can get rid of that feeling before she leaves, before it's too late."

"But," Felicitas says, picking at the edge of her shirt. "What if we talk and she still acts unattainable?"

Estela shakes her head. "I doubt it. That's what the Devil would do, right? Doña Olvido doesn't like cosas del diablo."

Exactly, Felicitas thinks. *She doesn't like* me.

chapter 40

Olvido

Olvido, like most middle-aged Mexican women, declared everything to be a miracle. Felicitas visited the library after school? "Miracle to see you here. Did you come to see me?" Felicitas quietly greeted her in the morning? "Miracle to hear from you. Who taught you such good manners?" Felicitas brushed her teeth in the proper direction? "Miracle to see this! What wise woman instilled this good habit?"

So, when Felicitas enters the house and says, "Milagro verte por aquí," Olvido lets out a short but sincere laugh and can't help but feel a bit proud. Felicitas *has* been listening to her. "Milagro verte aquí," she repeats in a mocking tone. "You weren't lying. I really do talk too much, don't I? You're starting to sound like a middle-aged woman."

"Middle-aged?" Felicitas taunts.

"Watch your mouth," Olvido warns through gritted teeth. "I've been practicing every night, and I'm getting much better at holding things, and know that if I throw that spatula at your head, I will not miss. But you are right. My presence is a miracle, a blessing for your eyes."

"What are you doing here?"

"Ah, there's that rude tone I'm so fond of. I'm here to make sure you're all right. Your mother wasn't thrilled about you staying alone in the house while she drove back. She still has to stop by the library, so she'll be gone for a while."

Felicitas narrows her eyes as she makes her way into the kitchen.

"If my mom was worried, she would've forced me to wait with Mrs. Samara," she says, carefully taking a seat.

Olvido rolls her eyes. "Fine. It was me. I wasn't thrilled. You still need to practice using only one arm. What if you couldn't turn the key? La puerta tiene maña. You have to jiggle the key—"

"I know. I know. You have to jiggle the key a certain way and pull the knob at the same time to get it to open."

"And what if you got hungry and decided to cook up something that requires a knife? What if you cut yourself? Would we have to take you to the hospital again? I don't want to ask for any more favors."

"The first trip to the hospital was your fault," Felicitas reminds her.

"As you and your mother like to say, 'Whatever.' Let's change the topic. I was thinking, Las Flores. We could expand our search. I don't know why I didn't think of it before—"

Felicitas takes in a deep breath and grips the seat of the chair. "Actually," she says. "I want to ask you something, aprovechando that my mom isn't here."

Olvido frowns. "There you go, interrupting me again. What is it? Do you have a better idea?"

"No," Felicitas says hesitantly. "It's not about my mom. It's about you."

"About me?" Olvido's frown dissolves into an irritated, phony smile. "Oh, I know what it is. The answer is no."

Felicitas scoffs. "You don't even know what I was going to say."

"Yes, I do. You were going to ask me to help you use a Ouija board for next week's homeroom show and tell. I saw you eyeing me while you were watching that disturbing show last night. I told you, esas son cosas del diablo."

"That is an amazing idea," Felicitas exclaims with genuine surprise and admiration. "I can't believe you thought of it all on your own, but that is not what I was going to say."

"No?" Olvido says, turning up her chin and glancing at Felicitas from the corner of her eye. "Then what is it?"

Straightening her back to give herself one more centimeter of authority, Felicitas clears her throat and says, "I want you to tell me why you know so many townspeople's secrets. Are you a mind reader? Are you psychic?"

"Psychic?" Olvido laughs. "That's just silly. People can't read minds. Why do you want to know all of a sudden?"

Felicitas huffs. "Because suddenly it's starting to seem like a big secret, and I don't like not being in on secrets."

Olvido's expression softens. "Well, it is not a secret. You can get your answer from anyone really. But let's say it is a secret. If I tell you, what do I get in return?"

"Do you have to get something in return? I think I've been helping you plenty."

"I know you are helping me for your own benefit. You don't want to listen to me telling you how to brush your teeth anymore, do you?"

"Fine," Felicitas says, leaning in. "I'll trade you a secret for a secret. You can ask me anything you want, and I'll answer honestly. I swea— promise. Don't! I corrected myself."

Olvido nods. "Seems reasonable. I accept. Answer this question, and answer it honestly, because I will know if you're lying. Remember—"

"Yes, yes. You're old and wise and a mom or whatever."

Olvido closes her eyes in frustration. "Does," she begins to say, but hesitates and trades her ensuing words for absolute stillness. She stares at the space above Felicitas's head as if her words are written there, hidden in plain sight. "Does your mother hate me?" she asks abruptly.

Felicitas sighs. "No," she says, monotone. "She loves you."

Olvido slams her hand on the table. "Why do you sigh? It is a very important question. Your mother hasn't exactly shown that she loves me these past few weeks."

"She's cried countless hours for you. Is that not enough?"

"No! Of course, it isn't. I don't know why she's crying. Is it because she misses me? Because she regrets not saying sorry? Because she's angry? Or is she just hungry and tired?"

Felicitas rolls her eyes. "Last time I asked her, you ran away."

"Because she was angry!"

"Well, then, there's your answer. But," Felicitas adds when she sees

Olvido's eyes glisten with tears. "It is not the right answer. She loves you. I know she does. I answered honestly."

Olvido gives her a weary smile and stands. "Follow me," she commands, walking across the kitchen and to the hallway. She waits for Felicitas in the backyard, her hands gently clasped behind her back. "This," she says, when Felicitas steps up to her. "Is mint, freshly picked." She holds a small, vibrant green leaf out to her, and drops it gently into her hand.

Felicitas frowns. "Okay, and?"

"Have you ever had mint tea before? Fresh. Not store-bought."

Felicitas shakes her head. "Are you avoiding my question? I answered—"

"And I am answering, too. Oh, look! I interrupted you. How did you feel? It's annoying, isn't it? Here," she says, patting down the brim of the mint's pot. "Pluck a few more leaves and meet me in the kitchen. I will get the water started."

"Here," Felicitas mutters once she's back inside. With a flick of her wrist, she tosses the leaves on the countertop beside the screeching water kettle. "Is that enough?"

Olvido gasps, scooping up the leaves with the care one would give to a wounded bird. "What did you do? Did you leave nothing but the stem?" Felicitas shrugs. "How do you keep that plant of yours alive?"

"You mean Pepe?"

"You named it?"

"Of course," Felicitas says nonchalantly. "He's part of the family."

Olvido shakes away her bewilderment. "Forget it," she says. "Just observe."

Felicitas eyes Olvido's hands as they move between the ingredients and utensils. The process is slow and dull. The mint gets washed, smashed, placed inside a mug, and covered with boiling water. It sits in its ardent ocean, swirling and then floating, reaching out to escape, but it cannot do it without help.

"Then, we sweeten it," Olvido says as she gently fishes out the leaves with a spoon. "Bring me the honey, please." After wiping the spoon on a towel, she digs into the glass jar Felicitas opened for her and scoops out a teaspoon of gold. "Is this enough?" she asks as she stirs in the honey. "I know you don't like your coffee sweet, but I think you'll like this."

"Sure, whatever," Felicitas mumbles.

"Okay, here," Olvido says, handing her the cup. "Careful. Grab it by the handle. It is very hot. Now, before you taste it, what is one thing you don't want me to know?"

"What?" Felicitas sets down the cup and rubs her burnt fingertips on her shirt. Olvido repeats her question. "Why would I tell you something I don't want you to know if I don't want you to know it?"

"Because," Olvido shouts, exasperated. "You don't have to tell me what the actual answer is, just tell me the general topic. For example, is there a boy that you like?"

Felicitas frowns, confused.

"Drink the tea," Olvido instructs. Felicitas obeys. "Now, is there a boy that you like?"

"No," Felicitas shrieks. "Wait, is this some sort of love potion? I knew it! You're a bruja!"

Olvido slides a towel out from the stove handle and smacks it against Felicitas's uninjured arm. "How dare you. Witches are devil worshipers. And if I could make love potions, don't you think I would have used that on your mother and Cayo? You know what? Forget it. I tried to show and not tell because I thought you wouldn't believe me, but now I'm sure you would believe me if I told you the Pope is a vampire."

Felicitas gasps. "The Pope is a vampire?"

"No!" Olvido pulls out a chair and dramatically lets herself fall into it. "The tea. It's supposed to make you tell me the truth."

Felicitas takes a seat across from her grandmother and says, "I'm listening."

Olvido sits up and drags the chair closer to the table. "When people eat something I've cooked, they tell me things," she explains. "Sometimes they want to tell me those things, sometimes they don't, but whatever they say, it's always the truth."

"Yeah, right," Felicitas says, and stretches out her hand toward her grandmother. "Pass me the tea. I'm going to think of a number from one to ten and tell you the wrong number." She blows on the tea and sips. "I'm thinking of six," she blurts. Eyes wide, she gently sets down her cup. "I wanted to say eight," she whispers. Olvido nods dismally. "What is it? Do you not like being told the truth?"

"Not always. Sometimes the truth hurts."

Felicitas frowns. "I guess, but I would rather be told a truth than a lie because truths hurt sometimes and lies hurt always. Is this why people came to visit you?" Felicitas asks, holding up the cup.

"Yes. People began to suspect what my food could do, and they kept coming back."

"And did *you* tell them the truth?"

"Yes, I did if they asked, but most people didn't feel the need to know. They felt it, the relief of letting out all their emotions, the pain or sadness they were feeling. They released everything they were too ashamed to say out loud. They could tell me anything, and they didn't have to worry about shame or guilt because it was beyond their control to speak. They wanted to get rid of the one thing that was holding them back: themselves. So, this house, this kitchen, became sort of a confessional. Do you know about confessionals?"

"Yes. I've seen them in plenty of horror movies, but you're not a priest. You didn't have to keep any secrets. Did people not worry about you telling their truths?"

"No, because I promised I wouldn't, and not everything people confessed was bad or shameful. They just felt that it was. Dr. Gutiérrez, for example, was grieving for his wife. He cried all the time. He couldn't sleep. He couldn't cook. Sometimes, he couldn't even shower or brush his teeth. He couldn't find the motivation to take care of himself. He felt ashamed because he was a grown man. He believed he had to push down his feelings and focus on his patients who had plenty of problems of their own. But that's not right, is it? He was allowed to feel sad, right?"

Felicitas nods.

"Once he admitted it, well, that was it. He admitted it. It was the truth, and he couldn't avoid it. He could allow himself to feel."

"I think I understand," Felicitas says, but Olvido isn't sure she does. What could she know about missing someone with such ardor, she can't bring herself to admit it? "Back to the magic, though."

"It's not magic," Olvido corrects her. "Magic is witchcraft, and witchcr—"

"How does it work? Does it have to be food with ingredients from your garden? Does it work with store-bought things? When did you first start doing it? Did you ever use it to get my mom to tell you things? Does it work on yourself? Are there things you're too ashamed to say, and can you force yourself to say them by drinking your own tea?"

Olvido exhales deeply through her nostrils. "No, it doesn't work on me, and— Ay, I already forgot all your other questions."

"How does—"

"One question at a time. Oh, look! There I go interrupting you again. I've learned so much from you," Olvido says sarcastically. "Thank you."

Felicitas flashes a bogus smile. "You're welcome." She looks down at the teacup and traces the rim with her finger. "Do you want to ask me the question again? About my mom?

Olvido shakes her head. "No. I believe you," she lies. Felicitas is wrong. Truths hurt always because they are true, and once you know something is true, you cannot pretend that it is not. Lies hurt sometimes because the act of lying is upsetting, but the lie isn't.

"Do you want me to give her the tea?"

"No," Olvido says before Felicitas's question is fully out. "Don't give her the tea. Don't ask her anything. Tell you what. Instead of continuing with this, would you like to learn something else?"

"Another secret? Another recipe?"

"No. There's not much in the fridge at the moment, and your mother would become suspicious of you cooking a whole dish in that," Olvido says, pointing at Felicitas's cast. "It's a game. It's fun."

Felicitas snorts. "What do you know about fun?"

"I know more than you," Olvido snaps. "All you do is read and sit in front of a TV screen."

Felicitas's brows furrow. "You sound like my mom."

Olvido mirrors the expression. "Well, now you sound like your mom," she says.

"No, *you* sound like my mom."

"No, *you* sound like your mom!"

They continue this argument well into the third round of their game. If Felicitas and Olvido drank her tea, and if the tea could work on Olvido, they would admit to themselves three things. The first is that they both sound like Angustias, and the second is that neither is truly upset over this fact. They both, at some point, wanted to be like her happy, carefree self, but they were not named Angustias, and are therefore burdened to exist with perpetual downturned lips and furrowed brows. It is because of these bothersome scowls that the third fact is apparent and true. They don't just sound like Angustias. They sound like each other, they look like each other, and they are part of each other.

chapter 41

Angustias

Angustias has grown accustomed to leaving Felicitas alone in the house. Before Grace, she tried to limit these instances. Cities, suburbs, rural towns, everything was riddled with crime. She was friendly with her neighbors and trusted most of them to keep an eye out for Felicitas when Angustias had to rush out to cover for a coworker or made time to go on a short coffee date, but she was never gone for long. When it came to her daughter, friendliness is not a strong enough trait to provide full peace of mind.

Saying that Samara's family was friendly was an understatement. They pressured Angustias to visit them so often and with such enthusiasm, their invitations drove her away. Her alone time felt vital in Grace, and she didn't care if her rejection came off as impolite. She was never rude, however. She still needed them to look in on Felicitas while she was out. When Samara told her she would check up on her every half hour and her cloud filled with a determined sky blue, Angustias knew her words were true.

Angustias doesn't worry about Felicitas's safety, but she does feel guilty about leaving her alone all day. The older kids get, the more aware they are of the slowness of time.

"What are you doing?" Angustias asks when she enters Olvido's house and finds Felicitas scrambling through a drawer in the living room. "What's in your hand?" Felicitas moves back to reveal a board game. It's damas chinas, Olvido's favorite. "Were you playing by yourself?" Angustias asks, walking up to her and taking the board in her hands.

"Yes," Felicitas says. "I was bored, so I looked through some of the living room drawers."

"How did you figure out how to play?" Angustias caresses the wooden wells, her fingertips filling their emptiness.

"I didn't. I just made up my own rules."

"How very you," Angustias teases. "I'm sorry, mijita."

Felicitas gives her a puzzled look. "For what?"

"You're so bored you've resorted to playing board games by yourself. That's so sad."

Felicitas rolls her eyes. "I also considered exploring the house," she says. "I almost went into your old room." Angustias raises an eyebrow at her. "I'm in the mood for discovering secrets, and I want to know what you're hiding in there."

"I'm not hiding anything," Angustias says nonchalantly.

"Then why do you refuse to go in there? You're hiding something."

"I am not." Angustias walks around Felicitas toward the bedroom to prove she isn't lying. "A teenagers' room is simply private."

"You're not a teenager anymore," Felicitas points out.

"But this room does not belong to me," Angustias contests, opening the door. "It belongs to my teenage self."

Stepping into her old bedroom makes Angustias forget why she was so intent on avoiding it. Yes, she does feel some disconnect to the photographs on the nightstand, the sketches tacked to the wall, the knick-knacks on the dresser, and the overly girly comforter. Its pink ruffled lining is a far cry from what she would consider buying today. But to Angustias's surprise, the room does not feel like it belongs to an entirely different person. It may belong to some naïve, happy version of herself, but not a stranger, and certainly not the girl she remembers, the one who is miserable despite not yet encountering the most difficult obstacles of her life.

"My iPod!" Angustias exclaims and rushes to her vanity. Between the nail polishes and hair ties, rests the tiny pink metallic device. She delicately picks it up with the tips of her fingers and holds it out to her daughter as if presenting a gift to a queen. "Look! It still turns on! I was so upset about forgetting it here."

Felicitas leans forward and inspects the device. "How much do you think we can sell it for?"

"Sell it?" Angustias gasps.

"Yes. Sell it. It's an antique."

Angustias falls back against her vanity and puts her hand on her chest as if she's been stabbed. "An antique! This is not an antique! Are you implying that I'm ... I'm ... old?"

Felicitas shrugs playfully and slowly moves around the room. Angustias follows her with her eyes and tries to guess what details Felicitas perceives. The CDs on the shelf are not in alphabetical order nor are they grouped by genre. The nail polishes on the bureau are not arranged by color, and there is no rational system in the closet. Short-sleeve shirts are crammed between dresses, long sleeves, jackets, and jeans. In one corner rests a pile of shoes with missing partners. At the other is a pile of textbooks with withered spines and graffitied edges.

"Will I have a room to myself when I'm a teenager?" Felicitas asks.

"Of course," Angustias says, but she is not sure they will ever be able to afford a two-bedroom apartment.

"What's that?" Felicitas says, pointing to the top shelf in the closet. Beside disorganized purses and belts sits a box covered in glitter and stickers.

Angustias follows her finger. "That's private," she says.

Felicitas turns to face her mother. "Show me," she demands. Angustias shakes her head. "Show me."

"No," Angustias whines, but she knows what's coming when she sees the bright orange cloud over her daughter's head.

"Show me. Show me. Show me. Show me. Show—"

"Fine!" Angustias stomps over to the closet. After a few jumps, she manages to bring the box down. She presses it against her chest and looks at Felicitas. "You promise to not laugh?" she says.

Felicitas sticks out her left pinky finger and crosses her right index and middle finger behind her back. "Promise."

Angustias sighs as she hooks her pinky finger around Felicitas's. "Please understand that I was young. I was a completely different person back then."

"Oh my God! Are there drugs in here?"

Angustias gasps and bursts out laughing. "No. Of course not." Although the idea of having done any sort of drug under Olvido's roof seems ludicrous to her, she realizes it's not absurd for Felicitas. Angustias lets her daughter in on her life before motherhood in small bursts. She's never sat her down to tell her life story, about her grandfather and the day he left, about her dad and how they fell in and out of love, and she's never spoken about her grandmother other than to say she was strict. She'll do it, Angustias decides. She'll tell her daughter everything, but not tonight. Rambling about one's life is an Old Lady thing to do, and tonight is a night of remembrance for her teenage self.

chapter 42

Olvido

Olvido left Angustias's room untouched for ten years, but she considered rummaging through its contents on three separate occasions. The first occurred when Taliah's house flooded on account of a burst pipe. She stayed with Olvido for a week. Olvido thought of setting her up in Angustias's room, but she could not bring herself to open the door. Her hand stayed glued to the doorknob on the first day, made a turn on the second, and gave a weak push on the third. "It's okay," Taliah said. "We don't even have to talk about it if you don't want to."

The second instance occurred when the local schools hosted a drive for the victims of Hurricane Harvey. Olvido knew there had to be something in Angustias's room that could be donated. She opened the door, just an inch, but did not step through. She donated items from her room instead.

The final instance occurred a week before her death. "She wants to get rid of me," Sarai sniffled, looking down dismally at her birthday cake. "Can't even wait until I'm dead."

"Mother," Samara sighed. "I don't want to get rid of you. I want to get rid of our excess items. It's called spring cleaning, and it's good for all of us."

"I am the items," Sarai cried. "Without my belongings, there won't be any evidence left of my existence."

"What about me?" Samara shot back. "What about Gustavo?"

Olvido was tempted to call Angustias that night, but they'd talked the day before. What would she say? I miss you? I want to know that you're still here? Embarrassed, Olvido opted for looking into Angustias's room instead. She opened the door, peaked her head in and quickly stepped back. That was enough at the moment, but it isn't anymore.

Angustias sets the box down on Felicitas's lap. Carefully, Felicitas lifts the tattered lid and slaps her hand over her mouth to stop herself from laughing. "What is this?" she says, lifting a magazine cutout of a young, blond man. A poorly trimmed picture of Angustias is glued beside him. Her bangs and lack of framing strands give her hair the appearance of a bowl cut.

"That is Ryan Gosling when he was younger. I had a very intense crush on him," Angustias explains between clenched teeth. "Stop laughing."

"I can't!" Felicitas says, holding her belly. "You had a crush?"

"Yes," Angustias replies, dignified, with her chin up. "Back in my day, if you had a crush on a celebrity, you cut out pictures from magazines and made collages. It was the equivalent of creating Instagram fan pages."

Felicitas holds up the picture again and laughs. "It could be worse."

"How so?" Angustias and Olvido ask.

"You could have given yourself a wedding gown. What's this?" Felicitas asks, digging through the box. She pushes past more magazine cutouts, movie tickets, and friendship bracelets and takes out a lined sheet of paper. "Dear Angustias, I've noticed you in math class—"

"Stop! No!" Angustias throws herself on the floor and covers her face with her hands.

"And," Felicitas continues between giggles. "I think you're kind of cute."

Olvido gapes at Angustias. "¿Qué?"

"Stop tormenting me!" Angustias screams, her words muffled by her hands.

"Mamá," Felicitas says, her tone suddenly serious. "Is this letter from my dad?"

"No," Angustias and Olvido shout simultaneously. Felicitas accidentally turns toward Olvido, who although she refused to step into the room minutes before, now stands one step past the doorway. "Your dad was not one to write letters," Olvido explains.

"Your dad was not one to write letters," Angustias repeats. Her tone is less accusatory, more disappointed. "That," she says, inching closer to Felicitas. "Was written by a boy named Francisco in my sixth grade math class. And this letter was written by a boy named Diego in ninth grade chemistry. And this poem was written by Ignacio who I think was in my gym class? I can't remember. Oh my God, and the song on this napkin, which isn't very good by the way, was written by Juan Pablo."

"Juan Pablo from church?" Olvido asks.

"From church," Angustias adds, scrunching her nose.

"That's a lot of boys," Felicitas says.

"Yeah," Angustias sighs. "But I was not allowed to go out with any of them. Your grandma didn't let me, and I obeyed my mother, as should you."

Olvido huffs. "I wish!"

Felicitas rolls her eyes. "You did not always obey your mother."

"Well, almost always. I guess I kept these to remember that although I didn't have a lot of boyfriends, I was worthy of attention. I mean, I had a song written about me. How many people can say that?"

Felicitas takes the napkin and reads through the song's verses. "This guy rhymed *love* with *love* five times."

"I said it wasn't very good."

"Your mother," Olvido says, moving closer to Felicitas, "is still worthy of attention, don't you think? Is there something you want to say to her? Hmm?"

Felicitas inhales deeply. "Mamá," she says, twirling her fingers, unable to look directly at Angustias. "Why don't you go on a date with Cayo?"

Angustias slams down the lid on the box and stands to store it back in its original place. "Because I don't like him."

"She doesn't even know him," Olvido protests.

"But it could be fun."

The box falls out of Angustias's hands. "Excuse me?"

"Aren't you lonely?"

Olvido's stomach churns. She heard that question too many times while alive. *Yes,* she wanted to yell sometimes. *So, what? I'm not lonely every hour of every day.* Even people in relationships felt lonely. Having a partner was not a cure. Being in a romantic relationship was like taking pharmaceuticals. Your symptoms could improve or worsen, and you had no control over being one of the unlucky few who dealt with the latter. Olvido had been unlucky once. She was not willing to risk her peace of mind again. Angustias's situation was different, though. She was too young to give up on love and too irresponsible to face life's challenges by herself.

But Angustias doesn't seem to think so. When she turns, the lines between her brows are as deep as the ones Felicitas's face usually carries. "Felicitas, where is this coming from?" she asks, picking up the box again.

"I was just wondering."

"No, I'm not lonely," Angustias declares. She jumps up and pushes the box onto the shelf. It doesn't budge. The neighboring purses fell and blocked its place. "I have you," Angustias says, giving up and tossing the box on her bed.

"What about when I'm gone? When I go to college?"

"I'll move in with you," Angustias reasons. Felicitas frowns. "I'm just kidding. But honestly, I will be okay. Just because I'm alone doesn't mean I'm lonely. I'm plenty good company. Everyone else is dull in comparison."

"What about Emilio?"

Olvido gasps. "What are you doing?"

"What about Emilio?" Angustias asks.

"You could go on a date with him," Felicitas suggests.

Angustias laughs. "No. I can't."

"No, she can't," Olvido agrees.

"Why not?"

"Because I don't want to. You may be a little too young for me to be giving you this lesson, but here it goes. You should never ever go out with someone simply for the sake of going out. You should go out with

someone because you actually like them. Otherwise, you'll have a terrible time, and they'll have a terrible time, and then you'll feel pressure
to go on a second date, and then, you'll have a second terrible time, and
you'll be caught in an endless loop of dates and terrible times."

Olvido plays with the edge of her shirt. Angustias is not wrong.

"So, you don't like Emilio?"

"Emilio is not part of the plan!" Olvido stomps her foot.

"I like Emilio but not like that," Angustias says, leading Felicitas out
of the room.

"I think he likes you," Felicitas insists.

"He does not," Angustias singsongs.

"Just try it."

"Nope."

Olvido shakes her head as her daughter and granddaughter move
farther and farther away. No one ever listens to her. Even if she were
alive, they would not listen to her.

But at some point Angustias had listened. *Thank God*, Olvido thinks
as she sits on the edge of Angustias's bed and reads through her past
suitors' letters. Otherwise, her daughter would have been stuck with
Francisco or Diego or Ignacio or Juan Pablo. Well, maybe Juan Pablo
wouldn't have been so bad.

Olvido sets the box down on the nightstand below the window.
She looks around the room with a scowl on her face. The room has
been closed for too long. It doesn't smell right.

Olvido pulls the window latch and pushes up. *There*, she thinks
when she feels the night's breeze. *That should do it.* She leaves the room
satisfied, and because she refuses to revisit her daughter's past, she
never witnesses the damage she caused. For the next three nights, it
rains over Grace. The water makes itself at home in Angustias's room.
It rots the feet of the vanity and the base of the nightstand. It soaks the
pink bedspread and leaves it smelling like a wet dog. It swallows Angustias's forgotten letters and washes away all evidence that she once
obeyed her mother. Olvido never sees the damage. She does not enter
the room again because in the ensuing weeks, Felicitas doesn't give her
time to think of what could have been, only what is and what can be.

"I have a proposition for you," Felicitas declares when Olvido steps out into the hallway. Olvido looks both ways as if she were about to cross a street. "My mom's in the shower."

"What is it?"

Felicitas straightens her back and lifts her chin. "This whole time, I've been giving and not receiving. You forced me to help you with your plan by threatening me with your stay, but I think I've gotten used to you."

"Oh?" Olvido says, surprised.

"To the point where I can ignore you, at least."

"Oh."

"So, I've decided that I will no longer help you unless you give me something in return."

Olvido crosses her arms. "And what would you like from me? You've inherited all my belongings."

"I want cooking lessons," Felicitas says. "I want to play with magic."

chapter 43

Angustias

Angustias did not plan to get pregnant at the age of sixteen. She did, however, plan to fall in love. The idea blossomed when her aunt Rosa, Angustias's absent father's sister, stopped by one New Year's Eve a couple of months before Angustias turned fifteen. Tía Rosa, like Olvido, was a devout Catholic, and she believed her brother would go to Hell for abandoning his wife and child. His sin brought her immense guilt, although Angustias never really understood why. She hadn't done anything wrong, at least not regarding child and wife abandonment, but Tía Rosa felt guilty nonetheless. As a result of this guilt, Tía Rosa made a point of visiting Angustias and Olvido once a year and gave them everything from money to food to socks. Olvido always refused Tía Rosa's gifts, but Angustias accepted them when her mother wasn't looking. Tía Rosa would lift her index finger up to her lips, place the gift in Angustias's hands, and send her off running to her room.

On her New Year's Eve visit, Tía Rosa came bearing only one gift: a basket of miniature grapes. "For tonight's wishes," she said to Angustias. "You're becoming a woman now, which comes with far more problems than being a girl. You'll need all the help you can get."

"What kinds of problems?" Angustias asked.

"Well," she said, rubbing the back of her neck. "A lot more pain for one. You're also going to have to start making more decisions, very important decisions that will shape the rest of your life."

Angustias could detect by her aunt's nosy orange cloud that a conversation about her future was approaching, and she was not in the mood for it. "What do you want to do when you grow up?" was her least favorite question in the world along with "How do you pronounce your name?" and "Where's your dad?"

Pretending to understand what Tía Rosa meant, Angustias smiled and took the grapes.

Mexican tradition says that if you eat twelve grapes in the first twelve seconds of the year—one for each chime of the clock at midnight—you can make twelve wishes and they will come true for you in the ensuing year. But eating one grape per second is a very difficult task, and very few accomplish it. Tía Rosa's miniature grapes, however, completely changed the playing field.

Angustias began drafting her wishes during dinner, an unusual occurrence for her since she so rarely planned ahead, but these wishes needed to be perfect. She was becoming a woman. She couldn't wish for frivolous things like getting Becky Anzaldua to stop teasing her about her terrible haircut or convincing her mother to allow her to attend the midnight screening of a movie. She needed to make her wishes count. But what counted? Angustias regretted not questioning Tía Rosa further before she left for her New Year's Eve party, but she had one other adult she could turn to.

"Mamá," Angustias said between bites of green spaghetti.

"Hmm?" Olvido responded.

"What is one thing that changed the entire trajectory of your whole adult life?"

"Meeting your father," Olvido said dryly as she cut a piece of brisket.

Angustias sighed and copied her mother's action. She should have asked her mother something easier like "What should I wish for this New Year's Eve?" Instead, she'd conjured up the memory of her father, which meant her mother would carry around a crimson cloud for the rest of the day. The rest of the day consisted of just a few more hours, but in the Olivares house, hours could feel like days and days could feel like weeks. Fortunately for Angustias, the hours went by quickly that night. She had pressing matters occupying her mind.

Why had meeting Angustias's father changed the trajectory of Olvido's life for the worse? Olvido hadn't said it'd been for the worse, but Angustias was certain of it. If it'd been for the better, Olvido wouldn't have a perpetual frown.

Was it because the encounter had led to Angustias? No. That could not be. Angustias was a ray of sunshine, un pan de Dios. Olvido loved her. She had to.

Was it because he had left her? No. Olvido had said she was glad Angustias's father was gone. He hadn't helped her emotionally or financially when he was home, and Olvido preferred to be alone than in bad company.

Was it because he hadn't loved her and she hadn't loved him back?

That was it! Olvido hadn't found true love. The disillusionment of discovering that Angustias's father was not her One and Only must have been so jarring to Olvido, she had completely given up on the idea of love. Had Olvido fallen in love before getting married and before getting pregnant, her life would not have turned out so miserable.

Angustias didn't want to be a miserable adult, which meant she needed to fall in love. The sooner the better.

Grape 11. I want to fall in love.

Grape 12. I want Zac Efron to fall in love with me.

"Happy New Year!" Angustias shouted as the clock struck twelve and accidentally spat out her half-eaten twelfth grape. Olvido reprimanded her for speaking with food in her mouth and wrapped her arms around her so tightly, Angustias's eleven other grapes threatened to come back up.

One month after her fifteenth birthday, Angustias met Felicitas's father, the sweetest, kindest boy Angustias had ever met, although she hadn't really met many boys before him. (Olvido rarely allowed her to go out.) One year after their meeting, Angustias was pregnant, and one year after that, Felicitas's father was screaming, and Felicitas was crying, and Angustias was throwing her hair straightener out the window to alert the neighbors that she needed help. And that was that.

Angustias learned that falling in love is not the same as finding true love. Although she still believes her One and Only is out there in the world, she is in no particular hurry to find him; and if they never meet, that is perfectly fine by her as well. She's not in a hurry for anything other than to get out of town.

"I might have to call in sick tomorrow," Angustias informs Emilio as he locks up the front door of the library. Locking up is supposed to be her responsibility, but Emilio insists on staying well after his shift. Angustias likes his company, so she doesn't fight about it more than what is politely appropriate.

"You don't feel well?" Emilio asks.

"No," Angustias says. "I don't. I feel . . . uncomfortable."

Emilio freezes. "What did I do?" he asks with trepidation.

Angustias rolls her eyes. "You didn't do anything. Everyone else, on the other hand, has obviously crossed a line." Emilio tilts his head. His eyes wander as he attempts to recall the events of the previous days, searching for evidence of line-crossing. "Hello! They keep trying to set me up with that guy Cayo, or whatever his name is. They've even convinced Felicitas to pressure me to go on a date with him. My own daughter. Ugh, it's so—it's so infuriating!" Angustias shouts, punching the air like a speed bag.

"Well," Emilio says calmly, taking one step back. "Let's find a solution that doesn't involve you going into hiding or accidentally giving me a black eye."

"The solution is them understanding that *no* means *no*."

"I understand, and they should understand, but, um, maybe! Maybe it's not about you, it's about Cayo. They really want him to date someone. Poor guy."

"Duh! Of course, it's not about me," Angustias says, flipping her hair with the back of her hand. "But why are they making him *my* problem?"

Emilio pats her shoulder gently until her agitated breathing subsides. "Don't skip work tomorrow," he says. "Everyone knows where you live. At least if they find you here, you can say you're working and that you're busy. I can even give you more things to do if that'll help."

"Haha," Angustias says sarcastically, but she remembers the Bibles and she shudders at the idea of people searching for her at Olvido's house. She nods and says, "Fine. I'll be here for my shift. But you have to help me find a better solution, one that doesn't involve me working more than I have to."

"I'll try my best," Emilio says as he backs away.

Angustias catches him doing a short two-step skip on his way to his car. He's proud of himself for keeping Felicitas's potential longing for her father out of the conversation and so has done the right thing and repaid Olvido's favor. True to herself, Angustias misinterprets his skip and the watermelon pink pride in his cloud as warnings that she needs to distance herself. She can be Emilio's employee, neighbor, and friend, but no more. Pink is dangerous, especially if it transforms into magenta, because magenta makes you want to stay.

chapter 44

Felicitas

Felicitas's desire to stay in Grace grows stronger every day. She's glad her mother is almost back to her usual self, that their dynamic at home is almost back to normal, and she is thankful for the things that are not. In deviation from the norm, Felicitas gets to leave the house to play, not sit in her room and read, not sit alone and write, but actually play with other kids. She doesn't fully understand the point of Gustavo's video games, but she enjoys the screaming, the laughter, the cheering, and the complaining.

Yes, even the complaining and the fighting. She doesn't feel the same pain in her heart that she gets when she fights with her mother or grandmother. When she fights with Angustias and Olvido, she knows they're not on an even playing field. Angustias can tell her what to do. She can take away her books, her movies, her freedom. She can force her to move to a new town or state. Even Olvido feels more powerful. She knows things about Angustias and her past that Felicitas may never know. She shows off her gray hairs and the crinkles at the corners of her eyes with pride. Those signs of aging taunt Felicitas with wisdom, maybe not wisdom about good family relationships, but about independence, hard work, and not being treated like a baby.

Gustavo and Estela are her equals. Whoever wins the fight will be proven to be right. It will have nothing to do with being older, bigger, or stronger. And if the fights ever become more consequential than determining if someone cheated in a video game, they can part ways in a manner that daughters and mothers will never be able to do.

Felicitas can't imagine ever wanting to part ways. Even if Gustavo is a bit childish, he's fun to be around. He always has a story to tell, and these stories seem to race in his mind so quickly, he stumbles over his words as if his brain has already reached the finish line while his mouth is barely trying to piece together the racetrack with the building blocks of the alphabet.

Estela is anything but childish. In addition to being more emotionally aware, she has knowledge on boys, bras, and periods. "You already got your period?" Felicitas asks with amazement when Estela explains why she keeps taking her purse to the restroom.

"Yes," Estela whispers back. "Four months ago. Luckily, it didn't happen while I was in school. Can you imagine?"

Felicitas's eyes grow wide. "What if I get mine while I'm in school?" She has yet to formulate a plan of action for her period. Angustias told her the Olivares women were late bloomers, so she probably wouldn't get hers until she's twelve, but there's a whole other family they hadn't thought about. Were the Castañedas late bloomers, too?

"Don't worry," Estela says. "I always have an extra pad in my backpack. I can start carrying two, one for you and one for me." Felicitas sighs with relief and decides that she'll take some pads from Angustias and carry two in her backpack as well, one for her and one for Estela, in case her friend ever forgets hers at home. "We just have to be sneaky when I hand them to you. Some boys act so annoying when they see one, especially Ricky."

"Who's Ricky?"

"A horrible boy in Ms. Collins's class," Estela says, making a retching sound at the word horrible. "Every time my bra straps show, he sneaks up behind me and snaps them. Oh, it makes me so mad!"

Felicitas's hands move reflexively to the thick, soft straps of her training bra.

"Like, hello? I'm already uncomfortable enough with these stupid wires. I don't need your nasty, Cheeto-stained fingers making things worse. You want to know a tragic secret?" Felicitas nods. Estela cups her hands around Felicitas's ear and whispers. "I used to have a crush on him." She pulls away and scrunches her nose. "Well, half crush. Half because I only liked him when he didn't speak or do anything. Basically, I just liked his face."

Felicitas's face brightens. She's so delighted to be trusted with Estela's secret, without thinking, she admits, "I've never had a crush on someone before."

Estela's jaw drops. "Really? Never?" she says, as if it's an admirable feat rather than an embarrassing flaw. "That sounds amazing. All my crushes have ended in heartbreak."

"I'm starting the next round," Gustavo yells from across the room. "Are you guys ready to lose again, or are you going to sit there and talk about boys?" Estela throws a pillow at Gustavo's face to stop him from making kissing sounds at them. Felicitas follows her closer to the television. She loses first. Her mind is not with the characters on the screen.

We are not the same, she keeps repeating in her mind, *but she's my friend*. Felicitas has a friend. She has a person she doesn't feel nervous around; someone who she can confess embarrassing secrets to, who won't judge her; someone she can actually talk to. *I have a friend, and we are not the same, and it is wonderful.* If Estela wasn't so different, Felicitas wouldn't have someone to warn her about her period and mean boy's bra-snapping.

Angustias would have warned her eventually, but she would have been too late. She's forgotten what it's like to be ten. She's twenty-seven, over a quarter century old. She's begun to say things like, "When I was your age," and "Back in my day." Gustavo and Estela will never say that. They won't reminisce about the past because they can experience the present together.

"Did you talk to your grandma about the secrets?" Estela asks as Gustavo runs around his bedroom, cheering his own victory. Felicitas smiles shyly and nods. "And?"

"She's going to teach me how she does it," Felicitas says. "How she cooks magic food."

"Ooh, the power we'll have! Who should we use it on first? Oh my

God, we can bring food to school. We're going to know everyone's secrets."

Felicitas shakes her head apologetically. "She's going to teach me how to cook, but I think the magic only works for her."

Estela shrugs. "Then we'll ask her to cook for us."

"She can't. She's leaving," Felicitas explains. "That's the whole point of me being here, to help her go. And when she leaves . . . I might leave, too."

Estela sighs. "Yeah, but only maybe. Maybe you will, maybe you won't."

"When—*if* I leave," Felicitas says, "can I call you? You know, not all the time, but sometimes, or I could text you from my mom's phone."

"Of course!" Estela responds. "And I will call and text you. I'll update you on any new crushes, and you'll let me know when you get your period."

"I'll probably call you crying. With my luck, it'll happen during lunch or P.E."

"If it does, it'll be okay. Just ask to go to the nurse right away. Your black clothes will hide any stains. Why do you wear black all the time anyway?"

"Why do you always wear pink?"

"I don't *always* wear pink, and I asked first."

Felicitas picks at the frayed hem of her dress as she pictures her mother frantically putting on and taking off clothes. *Nothing fits! Angustias yells. I think I gained weight. Ugh, this is too bright. This is too dull. Is this shirt see-through? When did I buy this? Oh. It was a gift. Maybe we can sell it.*

"Have you ever wished your school had a uniform?" Felicitas asks.

Estela sticks out her tongue in disgust. "No, why would I want that?"

"Because you wouldn't have to think about what to wear. Everything would be the same. You would save time, and you would also save money because you could just add layers in the winter and take off layers in the summer."

Estela scrunches her nose. "Sounds practical, I guess, but kinda boring. Couldn't you make your uniform a different color? I bet green looks great on you."

"There's many shades of black but not as many as there are for other colors," Felicitas points out. "Does olive green go with neon green?"

"Absolutely not!"

"Exactly. Even white has too many shades, and it gets dirty easily."

Estela turns to Felicitas with admiration. "Your brain is strange but amazing. I guess black is also good for fancy parties and most weddings and funerals." Felicitas sighs and nods.

"Well, maybe when you come back to visit, we can go shopping and try on bright-colored clothes, just so you can see how good it feels to wear pink. I mean, you are going to visit me, right? You promised me an unauthorized trip to the movies, remember?" Estela says, nudging Felicitas with her elbow.

"Mhm," Felicitas says, and grabs the remote control. "Gustavo, are you ready to lose?" she shouts, though she knows that with only one arm and little to no experience, she's at a disadvantage.

During their next round, Felicitas contemplates wearing pink once they leave Grace. She's willing to try anything to make herself feel a bit better, just enough to get through the drive to wherever it is that Angustias wants to go. Olvido would hate to see her in such a happy shade so soon after her death. "How dare you," she'd growl. "I can't stand to see this." If she did it before Olvido leaves, maybe Olvido will think the "family" part of her plan isn't complete. Felicitas is still a brat. Olvido needs to stay to change her ways.

Felicitas reaches out to Estela and strokes the collar of her light pink blouse and asks, "Could I borrow this tomorrow?"

chapter 45

Olvido

Olvido spent the first six months of her daughter's pregnancy refusing to think about her granddaughter. In the seventh month, when it became impossible to pretend Angustias's large belly was a symptom of indigestion, she began to brainstorm baby names. The first name she thought of was Concepción. Simple. Literal. The baby was not yet a granddaughter.

A month later, when the women of her church asked her if she had any names in mind, Olvido responded, "Milagros or Caridad," inspired by the taste of the symbolic blood of Christ lingering in her mouth.

Then, Felicitas was born.

"Paz," Olvido shouted at Angustias over Felicitas's piercing cries. "You should have named her Paz."

"Her name is Felicitas," Angustias said, bouncing her baby in her arms.

"Well, I'm not very happy and neither is she," Olvido said. Felicitas shrieked in agreement. "You see."

The night before Angustias and Felicitas left the Valley, Olvido suggested the name Soledad. "Really?" Angustias hissed. "After what you just asked me to do? I was right. You do hate her."

"I don't mean Soledad as in loneliness," Olvido explained. "I want her to grow up to be independent, to know how to be on her own. I want you to understand that she'll be fine without you."

"Without her mother?" Angustias said, trembling. Another wave of tears threatened to wash over her.

"Without *you*."

"Your mom should have named you Fe," Olvido tells Felicitas during their first cooking class, or as Felicitas prefers to call it, potion lesson. "You're lacking it."

"What am I supposed to have faith in, you or the food?" Felicitas asks, picking at her burnt rice.

"Yourself," Olvido says. The response sounds more like a reproach than gentle encouragement.

"Faith is not why this happened. I just suck at cooking. Or maybe, your dishes are too complicated."

Olvido lets out a short laugh. "I had you make rice! The most basic part of a dish."

"Yeah, but my mom usually uses a powder for seasoning. You made me do some fancy sauce."

"It was three ingredients!"

"Four! And your pan is too old. The usual fifteen minutes of cooking time burned the bottom."

"That's why I said to keep an eye on it. No. Stop. I know what you're going to say. 'I don't know what it's supposed to look like,'" Olvido whines to mimic Felicitas's voice. "But you'll learn."

Felicitas crosses her arms and lets out an angry exhale. "No, I won't. Not if you teach me like this. I ask you, 'When is it ready?' You say, 'Eyeball it.' How much water? 'Not too little.' How much salt? 'Just enough.' What kind of instructions are those? I thought we were going to start off easy, like with spaghetti and meatballs or something."

Olvido frowns. "Meatballs?"

"Yes." Felicitas says, falling back into her seat. "But would we have to make the pasta from scratch for it to work? Wait, you don't know what meatballs are?"

Olvido shakes her head. "Dilo en español."

Felicitas taps her chin as she thinks. "Um, bolas de carne?"

"¿Bolas de . . . ? ¡Ah, albóndigas!"

"Albo—what?"

"Al-bón-di-gas," Olvido repeats slowly. "Sure, we can make that. We just need cilantro, tomatoes, onion, garlic, eggs, meat, rice, potatoes, carrots, and squash. And like always, oil, water, and salt. Close your mouth. You're going to swallow a fly."

Felicitas stares, confused. "I don't think we're talking about the same thing."

"Albóndigas, yes. Mexican albóndigas are different. It's a broth dish, and you don't pair it with spaghetti. Mexican spaghetti is different as well. For example, the sauce for green spaghetti—"

"Green?"

"Do not interrupt me. The sauce for green spaghetti is made with poblano peppers, garlic, onion—"

"And cilantro," Felicitas concludes.

Olvido tsks. "Did your mom never make it for you?"

Felicitas shakes her head. "If it's as complicated as the other things you've described, she didn't have time."

"We'll do green spaghetti tomorrow," Olvido says quickly. "Today, let's focus on the rice. Do you have faith in your ability to do the next cup correctly?"

"No," Felicitas says, following Olvido to the stove where she burns the next two cups. They don't have time to dwell on her failure. The kitchen clock's hands signal Angustias's impending arrival. Olvido and Felicitas store the edible outcomes of the day's lesson in Samara's Tupperware and Felicitas carries them over to the neighbor's house while Olvido begins to clean. It is only fair that her neighbors keep what Olvido and Felicitas cook. They paid for the ingredients.

Olvido was mortified when Felicitas asked Samara to help them, but Samara began to dig through her pantry before Felicitas could make a case for herself. "I think it's lovely that you're learning how to cook," Samara said as she filled up a paper bag with tomatoes, onions, peppers, and cilantro. "And I can't wait to taste your salsa again, Doña Olvido. Mom is always complaining that mine is not spicy enough."

"It tastes like tomato soup," Doña Sarai argued. "Do you think you could do patitas de puerco sometime this week? This one gets grossed out by anything that looks like a body part."

"If it looks like it belongs in an animal's body, it should remain in the animal's body," Samara fought back. "You know what? Starting next week, I will only be cooking vegetarian meals."

"Are you trying to kill me?" Doña Sarai shouted. "Now you must cook for us, Olvido. My daughter is trying to become a *vegan* again." She gave the word *vegan* the same intonation of disgust Olvido gave to the word *bruja*.

"I don't think I'll ever be ready for patitas de puerco," Felicitas tells Olvido as they watch Angustias step out of her car.

"Not with that attitude," Olvido says, and smiles. Despite Felicitas's sentiments, Olvido considers their first cooking class a success. She refrained from asking personal questions even when Felicitas opened windows into her life.

The ensuing lessons are not as easy. Felicitas's comfort around Olvido grows slowly like a cake filling up its pan as the clock ticks above the oven. The batter rises with every question. They must not go over the specified time. What if the questions spill over and make a mess?

At first, Felicitas limits the topic of their conversations to Olvido's new state of being. She asks once again where Olvido goes when she isn't with Angustias. "Just around," Olvido says. "The tortilla is burning. Flip it."

"Around where?" Felicitas presses.

"Around town. I visit friends. Sometimes I go to church," Olvido admits, no longer seeing a reason to withhold that piece of the truth.

Felicitas rolls her eyes. "How saintly of you."

Olvido mimics her gesture. "It's peaceful," she says.

"Peaceful? Do you know how many scary movies take place in churches, how many involve priests and nuns?"

"No, and you need to learn how to use your fingers instead of a spatula, like this."

"Do you spook your friends when you visit them?"

"No, but I'll spook you if you continue dipping that spoon you just licked into the sauce."

Felicitas licks the wooden spoon and drops it into the saucepan.

"Could you travel anywhere in the world? Could you travel to the center of the Earth or the inside of a volcano or a cloud?"

Olvido narrows her eyes. The inside of a volcano? Who would travel to the inside of volcano? Earth. Volcanos. Clouds. Maybe Felicitas will become a scientist. "I don't know," she says. "Careful. That's hot."

"Can you try?"

"No."

"Why not?"

"What if I can't come back? I don't want to be stuck in the center of the Earth for eternity. Here, taste this."

"Needs salt. If you reached into someone's chest and squeezed their heart really tight, could you kill them?"

Olvido sighs. "I will not answer that."

On the fourth week, Felicitas's curiosity focuses on the very distant past. She asks Olvido what it was like growing up in the 1800s. "I was born in the sixties!" She asks what Olvido's mother was like. "A drunk." And what was that like? "Bad." Why?

What? Why? What? Why? What did you do for fun when you were my age? Why were you so boring? What was Mexico like? Why did you leave? What do you miss most about it? Why are you crying?

For every ten questions Felicitas throws at her, Olvido tosses one in return. She's curious as well and has been for a while, but she can't work up the courage to ask too much.

Keep it simple, superficial, safe, she reminds herself. If you dig deep, she'll dig deeper, and she won't like what she finds. And you? What will you find? It doesn't matter if it's bad or good, you'll eventually hit a gusher, and you'll drown in guilt and regret. It is dangerous to feel guilt and regret when you're dead. It makes you wish you were alive, and then you become miserable. You can't be miserable and go to Heaven. God will kick your ungrateful butt back down, farther down than you were before. You will *be* una cosa del diablo. That is, if you aren't one already. Just focus on the food. Smash the tomatoes. Crumble the cheese. Slice the thorns off. Quick. Away from your face. Slice. Slice. Slice. Away. Away. Away.

"What did one nopal say to another nopal when it started growing too close to it?" Olvido asks as she dices the thornless cacti that Felicitas hands her.

"What?"

"Quítate, baboso." Olvido slaps the countertop and cackles until the sound becomes deafening in the quiet kitchen. Her smile slowly fades. "Did you not understand?"

"I understood," Felicitas says. Slice. Slice. Slice.

"No, you didn't," Olvido teases. "What did I say?"

"Move." Away. Away. Away.

"Move what?" Olvido persists. "What about baboso? What does that mean?" Felicitas stays quiet. "Babas means drool," Olvido explains. "So baboso means drooly."

"You mean slimy?"

"Yes, that's the word. Slimy like a nopal. But really, baboso means stupid. It has a double meaning."

Felicitas scrunches her nose. "Your joke wasn't funny. It was baboso."

Olvido shakes her head. "No. That's not how you would use that word."

"Is it a bad word?"

"No."

"Can you teach me a bad word in Spanish? I know the ones that start with *p*. What's your favorite bad word? Is it *pu—*"

"Do you know what 'tiene el nopal en la frente' means?" Olvido interrupts and holds up a piece of nopal to her forehead. She doesn't wait for Felicitas to answer. "It means that someone is obviously Mexican. Some people use it as an insult, but I say it about myself with pride. What do you think. ¿Tengo el nopal en la frente?"

Felicitas studies Olvido's face. Deep lines form between her brows. "Is it true you crossed the border secretly?"

"Secretly?" Olvido says, dropping the nopal back on the cutting board. How long had she been waiting to ask that?

"Yeah, secretly, like *illegally*?" Felicitas says, whispering the last word.

"No, I did not. I came here legally. I just didn't leave when the law said I was supposed to. Don't touch that. It's hot."

"Were you scared that someone would find out? Ouch!"

"I told you not to touch that," Olvido yells, attempting to grab Felicita's injured finger. Her hand moves through it.

Felicitas quickly sticks her finger in her mouth and mumbles, "So is it true?" Her curiosity seems to outweigh her pain, but her eyes are brimming with tears.

A pressure appears in Olvido's chest as if her rib cage were pressing down on her lungs. It's a feeling she knows well, but she hasn't experienced it in a while. *Why now?* Olvido thinks. *I'm not in danger.* "I was scared certain people would find out," she says. "Here. Wrap some onion around your finger so it won't blister."

"What do you mean, certain people?"

"Well, some people would have called the police if they'd known I was here . . . secretly. And then the police would have sent me to jail or back to Mexico. I would, um, I would have been separated from your mom." *Why can't I breathe?* Olvido wonders. *Was I breathing before? My lungs don't need oxygen.* "The onion, Felicitas."

"But by saying *certain* people," Felicitas says, wrapping a thin layer of onion around her finger, "it means there are other people that wouldn't have done that?"

"Mhm, that's right. Okay, let's put everything away and clean up. I think we can end early today."

"How did you know who were the good people and who were the bad people?" Felicitas asks as she washes the dishes.

Olvido hesitates to answer but figures there's nothing wrong with discussing this particular part of her past. It has nothing to do with Felicitas. She can focus on the facts. "You simply talk to them, get to know them. I wasn't very chatty, though. Usually other people would talk, and I would find out they were in a similar situation first."

"So, you knew other people who could get in trouble with the police?"

"Yes, a few."

"I see." They finish cleaning up the kitchen in silence. The pressure in Olvido's chest subsides. Then, Felicitas speaks again. "There were a lot of Mexicans in the Valley, right?"

"Yes," Olvido says, holding back a sigh of relief. Yes or no questions.

Facts. These are good. "I didn't even have to learn English there. All done? Let's go to the bathroom."

Olvido forces Felicitas to search for an ointment for her burn even when Felicitas insists that she is fine. It takes her a while to dig through the drawer full of expired medication.

"It must have been nice to have lived with other Mexican people," Felicitas says. She picks up a box. Olvido shakes her head. "It probably felt like you never left home."

"I suppose it was nice," Olvido says, and although she knows she could leave it at that, a sudden urge takes over her. She needs to make Felicitas understand. "It wasn't exactly like home, though. Not at all, really. Everything was different: the language, the people, the buildings, the roads. I didn't understand the health care system or the school system or the political system. It was a lot to navigate, to learn about, and I'm not sure I learned all of it to be honest. It frustrated me that I couldn't just magically know everything. Oh, there! It's that one."

Olvido looks away in shame as Felicitas spreads the ointment on her finger. She was wrong. This conversation is dangerous. It does involve Felicitas. Her life wouldn't be what it is now if Olvido hadn't made that one decision decades ago. But it was a good decision, wasn't it? It was an act Felicitas should be thankful for or proud of, or at least understanding of. Olvido once said and did things Felicitas wouldn't comprehend, but this, this Felicitas should know. *I did good once*, she wants to say. *See how a difficult decision can lead to a better future. The bad doesn't last forever.*

"Maybe there's someone out there who can cook magic food that can give you knowledge about anything and everything," Felicitas says, and blows on her finger.

Olvido sighs. "I doubt it."

"Then it is not fair to expect to know everything. Whenever I move to a new school, I have to learn my new teachers and classmates' names, where all the different classrooms are, and who I should avoid and who it's okay to sit by. It takes me a while to figure things out, and it's scary to think that I won't learn fast enough and get in trouble. I

242 ANAMELY SALGADO REYES

can't imagine suddenly moving to France and having to learn all that *and* French at the same time."

"Yes," Olvido says. "Except I wasn't in France. I was only a couple of miles away from home. It was the distance some people travel for work or to go to the mall. Yet, it was the same land beneath my feet, the same air flowing in and out of my lungs. Birds came and went and didn't know the difference between here and there."

"Maybe because it's not here and there. Texas used to be Mexico, right?"

Olvido nods. "Yes, it was, but it also wasn't. At one point there were no countries. Land was just land. It didn't belong to anyone, but people drew lines. And although those lines are not real, in a way they are because now there are differences between here and there. There is home and—"

"And home isn't here?" Felicitas asks with a puzzled look. "My mom is here."

Olvido smiles. "Yes, home for me is where your mom is, but there are other things that make a home a home."

"Like friends and family?"

"Exactly. A community."

"Is Grace not your community?"

"Yes," Olvido says, suddenly feeling guilty for appearing ungrateful. "People here became my community, but there's more to it. I—I was never completely at ease. I was constantly . . . anxious, expecting for something bad to happen, waiting to be separated from your mom. Every person I met, I had to wonder, would they be as kind to me if they knew the truth? It doesn't matter if someone is friendly or unfriendly, Mexican or not Mexican, you just never know what they might think or do. And I couldn't help feeling disconnected from people who weren't Mexican immigrants. They didn't always understand my comments or references."

"They didn't understand your jokes?" Felicitas asks with raised eyebrows.

"Yes, exactly," Olvido says, realizing who Felicitas is referring to.

Felicitas sighs. "I know what you mean."

Olvido lets out a short laugh. "Do you?"

"Well, not all of it, but a lot of it, yes. I know you don't think I'm Mexican—"

"I never said that."

"But I have el nopal en la frente, too, right? Except, it's hard to be proud of it when it's the thing that makes you stick out and not in a good way. And that doesn't mean I'm not proud or that I want to look different, it's just my mom keeps moving us to states and towns where people didn't look like us and—"

Olvido runs and cuts off a piece of toilet paper as soon as she sees Felicitas's bottom lip quiver. "Go on," she could say. "Let it all out." Instead, she holds the paper up to Felicitas's nose and simply says, "Blow." Maybe Felicitas doesn't know, but this is Olvido's doing. If she had forced Angustias to stay, if she had helped her make better choices, Felicitas wouldn't be feeling this way. She'll figure it out if they keep talking. "Let's go check the time," Olvido says, throwing the dirty tissue in the trash. "Your mom will be home soon."

"Sometimes, I'm also afraid of being separated from my mom," Felicitas whispers between sniffles. "You know of—"

"Oh! Did you hear that? I think your mom just pulled into the driveway," Olvido lies. "I'll go check. Wash your face. Cold water will fix those red, puffy eyes."

Olvido sits on her porch facing the dark, empty yard for an hour. Felicitas does not search for her. Olvido is glad but ashamed and angry. She has reached into her granddaughter's chest, squeezed her heart, and left a bruise that may never fade. *I should have been named Dolores*, Olvido thinks. Despite what Grace believes about Olvido, all she causes is pain, and she can't even fix it the way she fixes other people's problems. She can't drink a self-brewed cup of tea and regurgitate her thoughts. She can't even light a cigarette to sooth her racing heart. Is she cursed or is she simply a mother?

chapter 46

Angustias

Angustias can admit that her curse is, at times, a blessing. Visualizing what others were feeling brought her high school popularity, job offers, free drinks, supermarket discounts, multiple love letters, and warnings instead of tickets for driving over the speed limit. Her gift, however, has not brought her a better love life, it did not improve her relationship with her mother, and it appears it will not help her understand her daughter. Angustias can analyze people's colors and change her words and actions to obtain a desired reaction, but her ability has its limits. When it comes to romance, she can say the right phrases to make a man fall in love, to taint his cloud with magenta so that he wants to take her out to dinner, buy her flowers, and kiss her before she says goodnight, but there is nothing she can say to convince herself to want to kiss him back.

A month and a half after they arrive in Grace, Angustias has an epiphany. She'll never see the shade of fuchsia that surrounds the teenagers she finds making out at the back of the library. She's too old. At least that's what the kids seem to think when Angustias slams her hands on one of the bookshelves and startles them. They look at her the way she used to look at her mom whenever she came back home late from a date and Olvido yelled, "¿Dónde has estado? Me tenías con el Jesús en la boca."

"In the children's section? Really?" she reproaches the teens. "Don't you have a school librarian you can go bother instead of me?"

"School's closed," one points out with an annoyed tone Angustias does not appreciate. "It's summer?"

"Well, then break in or go literally anywhere else."

The teenagers roll their eyes at her as they pick up their backpacks and head out. "Maybe if we help get her a date, she won't be so bitter," she hears one of them mutter under their breath.

"I heard that," she shouts.

"Cayo's nice. You should call him," the other teen yells back. They run out in a sprint, laughing with their clouds now tinged with red orange.

Angustias gasps. "Did you hear that?" she says to Emilio.

Emilio shakes his head, oblivious. "No."

"Ugh!"

Miraculously, Angustias has a second epiphany that day thanks to the most unexpected person. Blanca, the woman who shamelessly asked if she was looking for a husband weeks earlier, walks into the library pulling a cart with a stack of books. As she struggles to get through the front door, Angustias instinctively crouches behind the desk.

"Hello," Blanca says, her voice clearly only one foot away. "I saw you through the window." Angustias slowly rises and greets her as if she did nothing wrong. "I came here to sell some books," Blanca says, and slams down a paperback in front of Angustias. It's a romance novel, the kind with a shirtless man and a woman in a flowy dress clinging to his muscled arms on the cover. "How much for thirty?"

"Um, I don't know," Angustias stalls as she takes in Blanca's outfit: a long-sleeve, high-neck, knee-length dress, pearl earrings, and cat-eyeglasses. "I don't think we buy books, but we accept donations."

"Donations?" Blanca gasps. "These are first editions in mint condition. Can't you tell?"

"No, I can't. Sorry. I don't know much about books, but I believe you. I'll go get Emilio. He'll help you."

"You don't know about books, but you're a librarian," Blanca questions. "How did you get this job, then?"

"Emilio!" Angustias calls.

Blanca gasps again and bends down to search through her cart. When she pops back up, she holds out a newer looking book, this one with just a black-and-white photo of a shirtless torso.

"Oh," Angustias says, shocked at the pairing of the book and Blanca's salmon-colored cloud.

"So, you're still single?" Blanca asks. Angustias sighs. "You know, I have a grandson—"

"Nope, not single," Angustias says quickly. "And look at that. It's time for my break. Emilio," she shouts. "Customer!"

"They're not customers. They're patrons," Emillio clarifies before they close for the day. "And we're not coworkers. I'm your boss."

"Just one date," Angustias pleads.

"It would be inappropriate."

"It wouldn't be a real."

"Mm, no."

"Please," she says with the voice Felicitas uses to convince her to rent a gory film. "I can't be set up if I'm not available. Please, please, pretty please." With hopeful eyes, Angustias rushes to Emilio's side, puts her hands up in prayer, and smiles as his olive-green cloud begins to develop salmon pink at the edges. She knew it was wrong to rejoice. The pink could transform into magenta, but she felt lime green with desperation.

Emilio looked down at his book. His lips formed a thin hard line, but they rose at the ends. "Fine," he replied. "One date."

chapter 47

Felicitas

Felicitas knows it is disrespectful to raise your voice toward your elders. And sometimes—*often* with Olvido—disrespectful is exactly what she wants to be. For one night only, however, Olvido doesn't call out Felicitas's loudness. She welcomes it, encourages it by yelling back. Competition isn't fun when its muted.

"You're ruining my move!" Felicitas shouts at Olvido as she searches for a way around her grandmother's play. Olvido's green marble blocks the path Felicitas so carefully set up for her blue one.

"Good," Olvido shouts back. "You're ruining mine."

"Are you talking about the game or my mom's life?" Felicitas challenges, moving a blue marble one well to the left.

"Both," Olvido admits. "And don't think I don't know what you're doing by asking me that question."

"What am I trying to do?"

"Distract me," Olvido accuses and moves one of her green marbles over Felicitas's.

"Your friends are freaking her out," Felicitas says, still pretending to be more interested in discussing Olvido's plan for Angustias than their game of damas chinas. Felicitas does not like to lose, and she is most certainly losing. "Dr. Gutiérrez was right. Your ideas are old and wrong. My mom doesn't need a boyfriend. Definitely not a husband. She's fine all by herself."

"If you move that one over there, you can jump all these spaces," Olvido advises, tracing a path on the wooden board with her finger.

"Don't help me!" Felicitas shouts, throwing her free arm in the air. "I know how to play!"

Olvido rolls her eyes. "It's okay to need help."

"Don't change the subject."

"You're the one who changed it first. We were talking about the game. Now, play."

Fuming, Felicitas moves one of her marbles, one very far from the one Olvido suggested she move. Olvido scoffs. "You are too young to understand," she says as she studies the board and finds a new path. "And you need a dad."

Felicitas gasps so intensely she almost falls back on her chair. "A dad! I don't want a dad. And I do not want that man to be my dad, for sure. Besides, you don't have a husband, and you raised mom all right."

A genuine laugh escapes Olvido. "All right? If I had raised her all right, I wouldn't be doing all of this while I'm supposed to be enjoying my restful eternal sleep. Besides, my situation was different."

"Different how?" Felicitas presses, hoping to distract her grandmother as she drafts her next move.

"Just different." Olvido squints her eyes as they sweep the game's board. "I'm me, and she's her, and I know what she needs."

Felicitas raises an eyebrow at her grandmother. "And she doesn't know what she needs?"

"No," Olvido responds without looking at her.

"And I don't know what she needs?"

"Most certainly not." Olvido carries her last lone marble to its designated winning section, slowly to prolong the sweetness of her victory. *Plop*. The marble triumphantly falls into its well. Olvido folds her hands in front of her and beams. "I won."

Felicitas crosses her arms and sinks into her chair. "I don't like this anymore. She has a job, she's going to church, and I'm this close to asking her to enroll me in school here. Is all that not enough?"

Silently, Olvido rearranges the marbles on the board. "Try again."

"Can you haunt your town friends and tell them to chill?" Felicitas insists that night as she gets ready for bed.

"Do not speak with toothpaste in your mouth," Olvido reprimands. "And the front teeth are supposed to be brushed in an up, down motion. Up. Down. Up. Down." Olvido demonstrates with an imaginary toothbrush. "And, no, I cannot haunt people. And what is 'chill'?"

"To back off. They're scaring my mom."

"Up, down! Up, down!"

"I know! Gosh!" Felicitas brushes her teeth properly but brusquely as she glares at her grandmother.

"Do not rinse your mouth with tap water. You're going to get sick."

Felicitas narrows her eyes, bends down so that her face is an inch from the faucet, and tosses handfuls of water into her mouth.

"Fine! If you get sick, I won't care," Olvido says, and disappears. Two minutes later, she walks into the restroom holding a glass with what Felicitas presumes is filtered water. Olvido says nothing as she sets it down on the counter.

"If your plan fails, don't blame me," Felicitas says, and takes a gulp.

"I won't because it won't. Don't worry. I will be out of your greasy hair in no time."

Felicitas spits out her water. "It's not greasy!"

"Yes, it is," Olvido teases and disappears before Felicitas can defend herself.

Suddenly, Felicitas feels an uncomfortable sensation in her chest, like a thorny rose wrapping itself around her heart and lungs. It's painful. It doesn't let her breathe properly. It's similar to the rose that blossomed every time Felicitas reached for the phone and she heard a *click* instead of Olvido's voice, whose stem elongated and tightened its grip when she saw her kindergarten classmates decorate cards for Grandparents' Day, who grew a new thorn with each observation of a child and grandparent playing in the park, shopping for groceries, or visiting the library. Similar but not the same.

What's it called when you miss someone who is right in front of you? This doesn't feel like longing because Olvido is no longer completely out of reach. She's simply at arms' length. But if she's right, she'll disappear soon, forever. What is this feeling called? Felicitas can only come up with one word: *misery*.

chapter 48

Angustias

Angustias can admit that she is not miserable living in Grace, but she does often feel uncomfortable around its residents. At the grocery store, people throw concerned glances at her across aisles and between checkout lanes. In the library, patrons give her pitying looks before they greet her or tell her what they need. On Sundays, churchgoers walk up to her after service and inform her that they're praying for her. The thought of this does not bring peace. Angustias can imagine them at the kneelers of the pews or the edges of their beds, bowing their heads with their eyes closed and whispering. Their lips move slowly and then faster and faster, and when they speak, she recognizes the voice. It's her mother's.

"Please keep Angustias safe," she says. "Give her wisdom and good judgment." Those are the things Olvido always requested for her. Is she still lacking them? She's safe. She has a roof over her head and a job and good health. Most importantly, she has the ability and means to make sure Felicitas is safe as well.

Felicitas is more than safe. She's happy. Most days, she carries around a daffodil yellow cloud. Sometimes it brightens. Sometimes it dims. Sometimes it's tinged with maroon and burgundy and different shades of blue. The slate gray never fully disappears. But there's yellow! And when Estela visits and they watch a movie or scroll through her phone or just talk, Felicitas's cloud looks like cherry-flavored cotton candy. When she walks back from Samara's house after spending all afternoon with Gustavo, her cloud is baby blue and salmon pink. How can she be tired and excited at the same time? Why does she want to go back the next day and the day after that? Why does Angustias want that for her, too? Why has she stopped asking Samara for advice on how to sell Olvido's house? She hasn't put in any effort toward that task.

I have to wait until Felicitas's arm heals, Angustias thinks. Just a few more weeks. There's still a month left until the start of the school year. And with how reckless Felicitas is acting, they might have to pay Dr. Gutiérrez another visit soon. Gustavo convinced Felicitas to learn how to ride a bike with only one arm. She's scraped her knees and right elbow, but by some miracle, has not fallen on her injured arm.

"Mom, look!" Felicitas yells from the street as she propels herself forward on Gustavo's bike, one hand on the handlebar and the other tucked toward her torso. She doesn't get very far before she has to stick her leg out to balance herself and prevent a fall, but Gustavo cheers as if she's conducted the most daring stunt. Angustias doesn't worry much. She did far more dangerous maneuvers when she was Felicitas's age, and she was fine.

Angustias is not fine now. She's tired of indigo clouding her sight. That color will never disappear, not in Grace, not where people remember her mother and still cherish her and for some reason revere her. "Do you know what your mother did for me?" someone asks her at the post office, but they don't go into detail about what Olvido did other than she listened to their problems or gave good advice. "Do you know how special she was?" a woman says to her while they wait in line at the gas station. She follows the question up with the most generic compliment. "She was a gifted woman."

"Are you as exceptional at cooking as she was?" a man asks her when she sits at a bench in the town square park during a lunch break. "No," Angustias replies curtly, and bites into her bland ham and cheese sandwich. She stands and walks back to the library.

Even without her colorful sight, Angustias would not be able to stop thinking about her mother. She sleeps in her living room and showers in her bathroom and eats in her kitchen every day. And Samara has begun to bring over all kinds of traditional Mexican dishes with an oddly familiar taste. Angustias has kindly asked her to stop, using the excuse that she doesn't want to take advantage of Samara's generosity, but Samara insists that she accidentally made too much food and doesn't think it's right to throw it in the trash. Felicitas hurries to the entrance and accepts the dish on Angustias's behalf. Angustias doesn't resist much. They need to eat. Who cares if the familiarity of the flavors makes her a bit sad?

Felicitas has become extra chatty during dinner. Every evening, she briefly and hurriedly recounts the events of the day as if she can't wait to get to the next part of the conversation, the one in which she asks Angustias a million questions about her childhood. Did you like your hometown? What was it like? What did people do for fun? Did you like your school? How were the teachers? Who were your friends? Did you like your neighbors? Were they anything like the people here? Do you like the people here?

"Not all of them," Angustias admits, and drops her fork in surprise. She didn't mean to say that. She was supposed to be respectful and say, "Sure."

Orange fills Felicitas's cloud. "Who don't you like—no, wait! Who *do* you like?" she asks.

"Well," Angustias says. "I like Samara and her family. I like Taliah. I like Emilio. Not like that, Felicitas. Do not give me that look. Don't frown either. Just eat." She shoves a forkful of rice into her mouth to keep herself from saying anything else, but the words slip out. "I don't dislike people here," she says. "I just . . . People keep reminding me about your grandma. It's not like I'm trying to forget her or anything, but I am trying to forget that I'm sad."

"So," Felicitas says. "Being here makes you sad?"

Angustias nods. "Sometimes."

"So, are we going to leave?"

"I don't know," Angustias responds, and when she sees Felicitas's cloud darken and develop a grayish shade of blue, she wants to add, "Probably not." But she cannot. The words get stuck at the back of her throat. She coughs and drinks water and coughs some more, but the sensation remains. "Don't worry about it," she says, and stands to clear her plate.

Here is her reason to leave Grace, the one she knew would come sooner or later. The town makes her sad.

Felicitas is happy, though. Can't she make a small sacrifice for her? She can. Of course, she can. The reason why they never stay in one place for too long *is* for Felicitas's happiness, even if Felicitas doesn't see it that way. But in the same way in which Angustias can't ignore the bright yellow hue of her daughter's cloud, she cannot pretend she can't see the indigo around her. She needs to fix that. She needs to make the townspeople see that she doesn't need their help. They can keep their prayers, comments, and "good" intentions to themselves. If she can get rid of the indigo, of the discomfort that the town's pity brings, she won't feel so bad about her decision to stay. Because that's what she's decided. They are going to stay.

The next day, soon after Emilo locks the entrance to the library but before he can say goodnight, Angustias steps up to him with furrowed brows and tight lips. "Emilio," she says. "Do you remember our promise, the one about our date?" Emilio puts away his keys and nods. "I think we've put it off long enough. Does Friday after work sound good?"

chapter 49

Felicitas

Felicitas Olivares will never forget the first time she watched a horror movie with her grandmother, but she will hardly remember the movie itself as every piece of crucial dialogue is interrupted by Olvido's complaints.

"I cannot believe your mother is on a date with Emilio. Emilio! Of all people!" Olvido says.

Felicitas throws a cushion over her face and yells into its rough fabric. "And I can't believe you're here and not there. Of all days! Today!"

Olvido shakes her head. "I can't watch such a disaster."

"And I can't watch my movie!" Felicitas says, thrashing her uninjured arm against the couch. "I have no idea what's going on."

Olvido repositions herself to face her granddaughter. Back straight and chin up, she eloquently recounts to Felicitas the plot of the film. "So, now Andrea's spirit won't rest until Bernarda pays for forbidding her from seeing her dying mother," she concludes.

Felicitas stares at her grandmother with an open mouth and bulging eyes. "You've seen this before?"

"Of course," Olvido responds. "Everyone my age has seen *Hasta el viento tiene miedo*. I was maybe ten or twelve when I saw it. Terrible experience. But not as bad as *The Exorcist*."

"You like horror movies?" Felicitas shouts with a hint of a smile.

"Absolutely not," Olvido huffs. "I just said it was a terrible experience. You know who I hope is having a terrible experience? Your mother."

Felicitas rolls her eyes and goes back to staring at the screen. "Why are you so against Emilio? I thought you liked him."

"Of course, I like him. He's a smart, kind, respectful boy, but he is a boy. Meaning, he is too young to take care of a child."

"Again," Felicitas says, lifting her torso up so her grandmother can see the weight of her statement. "I don't need a dad. Period." She lets her body drop back onto the couch and goes back to staring at the screen. "How old is Emilio anyways?"

"Your mother's age."

Felicitas throws her arms up in the air. "Then he's fine!"

Olvido mimics Felicitas's gesture. "He is too young. He's still in school."

"He's getting a master's. Do you know what a master's is?" Felicitas says.

"Not really. Do you?" Olvido taunts back.

"It's school," Felicitas responds.

"Exactly. Isn't that what I said?"

"Ugh. Just let me watch the movie," Felicitas cries.

Olvido sits silently beside Felicitas for a few minutes but bothers her once more to cover her eyes during an inappropriate scene. "Let me see!" Felicitas demands, pushing away the cushion her grandmother holds over her eyes. "Let me see!"

"Not until this scene is over. Okay, now you can watch." Olvido drops the pillow to reveal a fuming Felicitas. She chuckles at the sight but quickly changes her expression. She makes a point of positioning herself between Felicitas and the television, hands on her hips, feet slightly apart. "If your mother does not end up with the right man, I won't feel at peace. If I don't feel peace, I won't be able to leave," she warns.

"I can see through you," Felicita says. Olvido looks down at her semitranslucent body. Her face twists into a grimace. "What are you doing?" Felicitas asks. Olvido shakes her head and covers her face with her hands. Muffled sobs escape through her fingers. Felicitas sighs and turns off the television. "Who is the right man according to you?"

"Claudio Ybarra," Olvido says, all traces of sadness and worry gone from her voice. "He is older, Catholic, has a stable job, and I know his mother."

"Yeah, unfortunately, I know his mother, too. What do you want me to do, call him, tell him to go interrupt my mom's date?"

Olvido seems to consider the option but shakes the thought away. "No, no. That would just make her angry, and she could run away. But you could bring him here, make them talk."

"I doubt hearing Cayo speak is going to make my mother like him. Actually, she might dislike him more."

Olvido smiles so wide, she gains a few extra wrinkles around her eyes. "I know what to do. Call him, please. Doña Ybarra's phone number is in the phone book in my room."

Felicitas groans, begrudgingly stands, and heads to Olvido's bedroom. "This is wrong," she says before dialing.

Olvido places her right hand over her heart. "If they talk, and she absolutely hates him, I'll dismiss my idea entirely."

"No more talk of Cayo?"

Olvido bends down to come face-to-face with Felicitas. "No more talk of men."

Felicitas's eyes grow wide. She quickly dials Doña Ybarra's phone number on Olvido's landline. "Hello?" she says when she hears a voice on the other end. "Is this Doña Ybarra? This is Felicitas, Olvido's granddaughter. Yes. No. Yes, she's standing right beside me."

chapter 50

Angustias

Angustias shakes her head disapprovingly as she looks around the diner. "I think you chose the wrong restaurant," she says to Emilio and takes a bite of her pancake.

Emilio turns to inspect their surroundings as he chews. "*We* chose the wrong restaurant. We both thought this place would be more crowded."

Angustias rolls her eyes, refusing to take any blame. Above her chewing, she can hear crickets. They'll have to rely on the diner staff to spread rumors about them. "How was I supposed to know this place would be so empty? I'm not from here," she contends. "You have way more knowledge of this town than me."

"No, I don't," Emilio insists. "Not by much."

"You've been here, what, five years?"

Emilio shrugs. "Never went out much. It wasn't until your mother invited me over for dinner that I began to meet other people."

"Emilio, your only friend was a cranky sixty-two-year-old woman? That is so sad," Angustias says, with no real pity.

"I said that's when I started meeting people," Emilio fights back. "Not that she was my only friend. And it was either a sixty-two-year-old or an eighty-year-old. How many people our age have you seen around here?"

"Hmm, maybe three?" Angustias says. "No, wait. Um, five!"

"Exactly, and they're all married with children."

"I have a child," Angustias points out. She scrunches her face and pretends to cry as she says, "Am I not good enough to be your friend?"

"No," Emilio responds, dragging out the word. He widens his eyes and darts them side to side. "We're not friends. We're dating."

Angustias's mouth forms an *o*. "And *so* in love!" she shouts. Emilio spits out his coffee, a perfect shot at Angustias's face. Angustias laughs so hard, she is unable to thank the waitress when she comes around with a stack of napkins. Above the waitress is a white cloud. She's bored, not curious. They've failed.

"I'm friendly with people here," Emilio says once he has blown all the coffee out of his nostrils. "But I wouldn't say I've made tons of close friends."

Angustias sinks into her seat. "Yeah, making close friends in your twenties is hard."

Emilio nods. "Probably harder when you have a child."

"In a way," Angustias says, genuinely giving the remark some thought. "But maybe it's also supposed to help me. I think I'm supposed to meet Felicitas's friends' parents? Maybe meet people through her school community or something like that?"

"But you've never really had a community."

"I guess not."

"Because you keep moving?"

"I guess so. Why did you move here?"

Emilio wags his index finger at her. "We were talking about you."

"But now we're talking about you," Angustias says, pointing at him with a pancake-stuffed, syrup-filled fork. She quickly takes a bite of her pancake so that she's unable to speak. Emilio follows her example and prolongs his chewing for as long as possible, but Angustias wins.

"My great uncle worked at the library," he finally says. "He worked there since its inception actually. He moved here decades ago. He was kind of a nomad until he settled here. I'm not sure what made him stay, but I, um, had a falling out with my family after I graduated from college. I couldn't find a job, so I moved back home, and I . . . felt worthless, I guess. My parents, they weren't supportive in a moral sense. They were constantly telling me that I was unemployed because I wasn't trying hard enough or I secretly did not want to succeed, that I was lazy, and that made me feel worse, so I left. I called my great uncle knowing he lived the farthest away out of all my relatives, and I asked him if I could stay with him for a bit, and that's that. There's not much to my story."

Angustias frowns and shakes her head. *It's your story*, she wants to say. *It can't be weighed or measured.* "Where is he now?"

"Uh, he passed away about a year after I moved here."

"I'm sorry." Angustias reaches over and squeezes Emilio's hand. Though he smiles reassuringly, his gray cloud darkens. It's frustrating, Angustias thinks, to see a persons' emotions and not be able to do anything to improve them. If time has not mended Emilio's heart, how can she do it with a gentle touch or phrase? Is he living proof that her heart will remain unhealed as well?

"Me too," Emilio says. "I wish I had spent more time with him. I thanked him for taking me in when I first arrived, but I'm not sure if I sounded genuine enough because, at that time, I don't think I knew how good I had it."

Angustias nods. "Are you on better terms with your family?"

"Nope."

"Too proud?" Angustias questions. "Doesn't seem like you."

"Too embarrassed," Emilio admits.

"Ah, that seems more like you."

Emilio sticks his tongue out at Angustias. She returns the gesture. "But I should reach out to them," Emilio says. "I know I should."

Angustias narrows her eyes and taps her chin as the gears in her brain turn. "It seems like," she deduces, "this town attracts prideful people looking to escape from their family. That and death." She holds up her butter knife in a threatening position. Emilio doesn't laugh.

"Why did you have a falling out with Olvido?" he asks, his cloud a shade of concern but not pity. Angustias would have been thankful for that once, but now wishes she could make it disappear along with Emilio, the rest of the diner, and herself. "And," he says before Angustias takes another bite of her pancake. "You have to answer because I shared something personal with you. It's only fair."

Angustias sprawls against the booth's backrest and slides down until she's lying on the seat. Emilio peeks beneath the table and waits for a response. "It was gradual," she says. "We were very different. She was very strict, and I wasn't a fan of her rules."

"And?"

Angustias sighs and slowly rises. "And I got pregnant. She was livid. It was a huge sin. She was worried about what people would think, and—and she was also worried about money. My mom grew up in a very financially unstable household. My grandma had a lot of debt. My mom made a lot of sacrifices to escape it. I guess she felt like she was falling back into it, and it was all my fault."

This is the first time Angustias has spoken her thoughts about it out loud. Confined to the walls of her brain, her ideas were unable to grow. The possibilities of why her mother was the way she was ranged from *She is simply a terrible person* to *She hates me*. Angustias does not want to divulge these potential causes to Emilio. Being back at Olvido's house has revived her Catholic guilt, and as Felicitas said the day after their arrival, not honoring your parents, which includes speaking ill of them, son cosas del diablo. Olvido's past, however, is a safer territory. History, unlike inherent evilness, is complex and unavoidable. Olvido was no guiltier of being born to a negligent mother than Felicitas was of being born to a blithe one.

"I can't imagine Olvido angry," Emilio says.

"Well, then you didn't know my mom," Angustias laughs. "It seems like no one here knew my mom." The words feel wrong in her mouth. Perhaps it was the other way around.

"So, she kicked you out?"

"Yes and no. She told me to leave. She demanded it, but I know that if I hadn't left, she wouldn't have physically forced me out of the house. At that point, though, she had already emotionally shut me out, so."

"I'm sorry," Emilio says, reaching across the table and giving Angustias's hand a reassuring squeeze. "It must have been difficult to leave with a baby and not have anywhere to go. Or did you have somewhere to go?" Angustias shakes her head. "And Felicitas's dad? Don't answer if you don't want to."

"Felicitas's dad left the picture the same day I left home," Angustias says, fixing her posture. "We got into an argument. Someone told him I was cheating on him, which was *not* true, but it didn't matter. I think that was just an excuse. He had been distancing himself for a while. His parents did not approve of me nor my pregnancy, and I don't know . . . I guess once my belly started showing, it hit him. His parents were right, we were going to have a baby, his life was going to be difficult, blah, blah, blah. We had little fights toward the end of my pregnancy, and they escalated once Felicitas was born, until our final fight, the one when he—" Angustias's breath catches in her throat. "He hit me. *Hard.* Just once, but once is too much. I was afraid that he was going to hurt Felicitas."

"Did he?"

"No, but I wasn't going to risk it. I alerted the neighbors, and they called the police. It was a mistake. I didn't mean for the police to get involved. I told them it was all a misunderstanding, just teenage drama. I needed them to leave before my mom got back. I didn't want them to ask her questions and risk—

"My mom was so angry at me even though the argument was not my fault. She kept saying 'Who chose him? Who slept with him?' And then she suggested—she—" Tears trickle down Angustias's cheeks. Her lips tremble, yet she can't stop talking. She's not sure if her retelling is comprehensible. A new sentence begins before the last is completed. Her pitch is high and low and everything in between. Her words are wet and bubbly like Felicitas's first. "She said it would be too difficult for me, that—"

Angustias's hands shoot up to her face. She holds them there for a moment as she tries to stop her crying, but the weeping does not subside. Her memories flow out in raging currents, carrying the sadness and anger out of her overflowing heart.

"I'm sorry," Emilio repeats.

Angustias nods as if she agrees, but she is not sorry for her present self. She is fine and will continue to be fine. She is at a diner eating breakfast for dinner with a kind friend who is willing to listen to her and her daughter is safe at home with a fridge full of food and a book on her lap. It is a good life. It is her teenage self who is stuck in an endless loop of fights. It is her world that is filled with reds and blues. It is too late to save her, and it is too late to save her mother.

How much did Olvido yearn to save her teenage self that she made returning to Mexico her dying wish? What good could that do? Victoria was gone. Her house had most likely been sold, destroyed, or neglected to the point that it had become one with the flora and fauna. There was nothing there. There was no one.

Angustias cannot make the same mistake. She needs to move on from the past. There will be no more spiraling thoughts of her childhood or her mother or her mother's childhood. She still has someone, and she loves Felicitas more than her own life.

"Well," Angustias says with a smile. She blows her nose on a napkin and wipes away her tears with her fingertips. "If what we wanted was attention, I think we got it." She peeks over her seat's backrest and slides back down so that she can no longer see the dreadful splashes of indigo throughout the room.

"Do you want to leave?" Emilio whispers.

Taking a deep breath, Angustias sits up and says, "Nope." Pity and judgment cannot control her and plans to control her cannot scare her. She is not one to run away. "Let's get another round of coffee. My treat."

chapter 51

Olvido

Olvido Olivares craved nopales every morning and evening throughout the first eight months of her pregnancy. It began as a small seedling of an emotion. The seedling's roots settled deep within the pink walls of her stomach, trying to blend in with its veins. Olvido welcomed the discomfort. She understood what was happening perfectly well. Before the seedling grew arms and legs and was given the name Angustias, it tasted the earthy flavor it so strongly desired with additional spices and textures to complement. The seedling enjoyed nopales with egg, nopales in tacos, nopales in salsa, tlacoyo de nopales, nopales in soup, nopales with ground beef, nopales with chorizo, and plain nopales. The seedling was happy.

Olvido was, too. Her baby was already eating vegetables without being asked to do so. If the cravings weren't a sign of health, then they were a sign of a prickly personality, which most parents would have seen as a warning sign of trouble ahead, but not Olvido. A bad temper would save her baby from being taken advantage of, overlooked, or ridiculed. She would wear armor made of the sharpest thorns.

Then, on the first day of the ninth month, when Olvido's belly looked bigger than a full moon, her craving for nopales was replaced with a craving for the cactus's tuna, its bright, sweet fruit, prickly on the outside and mushy on the inside. *Ah*, Olvido thought. *You were just blooming. This is the real you.*

Filled with sweetness, Angustias was born with a smile on her face, an expression the doctor quickly wiped away with a smack to her bottom. The pain sent her into a wailing fit. Her voice did not stop trembling until she was placed in her mother's arms. "Ru, ru, ru," Olvido sang until she felt her seedling's heart calm down.

The nurses struggled to take Angustias away to clean her properly. She clung to her mother's hair with the strength of a tree threatened by a hurricane's wind. "Let me try," the doctor said. Angustias squirmed, opened her little jaw, and let it come down hard.

"She's trying to bite you," Olvido laughed proudly. "She thinks you're going to hurt her." Her little seed was a quick learner, but not a good judge of character. She didn't understand that although the doctor had hurt her, he hadn't done so with bad intentions, and he did not intend to do it again. He was trying to help her.

Olvido still wishes her daughter had been born a nopal instead of a tuna. Angustias is always misjudging people. Her thorns poke those who want to help her, and her sweetness invites those who want to harm her. She is astoundingly good at perceiving people's emotions, but concerningly terrible at guessing their thoughts. What good are emotions? Angustias's father loved them at some point, and that didn't make him stay. Maybe Angustias had loved Felicitas's father, and that didn't make her stay. And Olvido. She was livid when Angustias told her she was pregnant, but Angustias didn't understand that her anger had been directed at herself, at her own failure.

That's fine, Olvido assures herself. It's not an unsolvable problem. Olvido can serve as her guide. She can make Angustias listen to her own thoughts at least. *Be honest*, Olvido can push her to think. *You don't want to run away. You desire the same things that I want for your life.* Olvido has revised her tactics based on her observations of her daughter and granddaughter. If you tell your child what to do, they will not do it. However, if you help them come to their own conclusions, the right conclusions, they will obey.

"You understand. You are plenty smart," Angustias often says to Felicitas when she is being overly stubborn about rejecting Angustias's perspective. Angustias is plenty smart, too. She's just obstinate, nothing her mother can't fix, especially now that she has two allies: God, who's given her additional time, and her granddaughter, who's given her an extra set of hands to complete her mission.

"Pass it through the fire," Olvido says, inspecting Felicitas's work over her shoulder. "Make sure all the thorns burn."

"I know," Felicitas mutters under her breath, and Olvido smiles because she knows she does. Felicitas's first attempt at burning the no-pales' thorns was a disaster. The arms of the metal tongs twisted in opposite directions. The nopal fell. Flames erupted.

"Your fire alarm needs batteries," Felicitas says matter-of-factly after Olvido put out the fire with a pot.

"I don't have an alarm," Olvido says, inspecting the damage on the nopal. It was burnt beyond repair.

"What?" Felicitas exclaimed. "That's not safe. What if there's a fire?"

"What if there is? I'm not going to die again. The salsa needs salt."

"But I will," Felicitas insisted. "It's dangerous."

"Then you should buy an alarm, but you don't have a job nor money to buy it with, do you? So, let's focus on not starting a fire for now. Does that sound good? Hold the tongs like this, like you're grip-ping a bicycle's handles. Do you know how to ride a bicycle?"

"Yes, I do," Felicitas states proudly. "One of my neighbors taught me. She was dead and couldn't catch me, so I fell a lot. I have a bunch of scars on my knees because of it. Wanna see?"

Olvido gags. "No. I do not. And I thought you didn't know ghosts struggled to hold on to things."

"I didn't know then. I thought she avoided helping me because she had arthritis. Do you know what arthritis is?"

"I do. No, stop! Stop right there. Do not explain it to me as if I don't know. What I do want to know is why you're holding the tongs wrong again." Felicitas frowns and modifies her grip. Her nails dig into her palms. "Better. But calm down. They're not going to run away."

"Do you think Cayo will remember to bring the Tupperware?" Fe-licitas asks. "He seems a little stupid."

"Yes, he will, and don't be rude. Now, help me clean. Leave no trace behind." Olvido gathers the utensils, cutting boards, and pans and places them closer to the sink. Her finger moves quickly.

"What if when my mom spills all her truths, she doesn't feel relief? What if she feels angry?"

Olvido turns on the faucet and lets the water pressure wash away everything her fingers leave behind. "That may happen at first, but I doubt it will last long. She'll come around. Come help."

"Why?" Again. What? Why? What? Why?

"Because Cayo is on his way and I'm sure your mother is, too."

"No. Why do you think her anger won't last? Why do you think she's looking for someone to spill her truths to?"

Olvido is able to scrub much faster now that she's not afraid of cutting herself, but it's still not fast enough. There's a pile of empty, dirty bags and open containers lying about. "She hasn't had anyone to spill her truths to in a while," Olvido says. "It's not easy to live like that. Clean the table. Actually, no. Clean the stove."

"She has me," Felicitas points out.

Olvido lets her explanation wash down the drain. Felicitas doesn't need to know now. She'll eventually become a mom and realize that her children should be the last ones to hear her truths.

chapter 52

Angustias

Angustias is rarely surprised by men's audacity to disrespect her. Her father lied to her for years, and the father of her child took zero responsibility for their mutual action. Male coworkers with an air of superiority could not hurt her feelings. Men hitting on her in the streets could be ignored. But a man disrespecting her in front of her child? That was inexcusable, maddening enough to break the curse of a carefree heart.

When Angustias sees Claudio Ybarra sitting in Olvido's kitchen alone with Felicitas, her combat reflexes immediately kick in. Above him is a mix of guilty rusty brown and anxious midnight blue. He did something to Felicitas. He must have. "What's going on?" she asks as she moves her shoulders back and stretches her neck. Cayo stands. He's only an inch taller than Angustias, but she feels like a giant and hopes that Cayo is not stupid enough to disregard the enormity of her anger.

"Buenas noches." Cayo rushes toward Angustias to give her a kiss on the cheek. Angustias dodges him, but she is not entirely without manners. "Buenas noches," she greets, and stares intently at Felicitas to force an explanation out of her.

"I invited Cayo over for dinner," Felicitas says, and presses her hands over her stomach, highlighting the navy blue cloud of stress above her.

"Yes," Cayo pipes in and proudly stands next to a neat display of Tupperware on the kitchen table. "Felicitas told me about all your favorite dishes. I brought these from home. Made everything myself. Please sit. Try it." He attempts to take Angustias's arm to usher her to the table, but she snatches her arm back.

"Thank you, I already ate," she says. "Felicitas?"

"Yes?"

"What is going on?"

"I heard so much about Cayo," Felicitas says, and licks her lips nervously. "I just wanted to talk to him myself, see what all the fuss is about."

"Did you know she was alone?" Angustias asks Cayo, her hands on her hips as if she were interrogating a misbehaving child.

"Yes. I—"

"Did she tell you I was okay with inviting you over?"

"Mamá," Felicitas tries to interject.

"No," Cayo admits. "Not exactly."

Angustias takes a step toward her unexpected guest. Cayo retreats. His already pale face loses the only brush strokes of color it held on his cheeks. "Do you think it's prudent to accept the invitation of a ten-year-old child, a ten-year-old child who is home alone?" Angustias challenges.

"Mamá, let's just eat."

"I'm—I'm sorry?" Cayo stutters.

"Apology accepted. Please leave."

"But—"

"Leave!" Angustias barks. She stomps her way to the front door and throws it open. "Now."

"Angustias—" Cayo begins to protest, but he is already walking out with his tail between his legs and a cloud of fear over his head.

Angustias doesn't feel like a giant anymore. She's one inch tall, embarrassingly minuscule, a sad excuse of a mother who left her child alone for too long. And for what? A date? A fake date she planned because she let her mother's friends get in her head. Grace has changed her for the worse. She needs to put an end to this. They'll leave tomorrow, bright and early, to a town where they won't have the threat of Cayo and his mother and Olvido's bizarre friends looming over them.

Tomorrow.

Tomorrow.

chapter 53

Felicitas

Felicitas's heart does somersaults as it attempts to figure out what it should feel. Guilt, definitely. Embarrassment, perhaps. Relief? Yes. Her grandmother's plan is falling apart right in front of her eyes, just like Felicitas knew it would. Olvido will finally let it go. She'll focus on other things like teaching her new recipes and telling her stories about Mexico and her life before she came to the US. Maybe, she'll even begin to ask Felicitas more questions, and once they know each other deeply, the way grandmothers and granddaughters should, Felicitas will have the courage to ask her what she has always wanted to know.

It's too bad about the casualties. Cayo was only trying to make his mother happy. Felicitas knows how hard that can be. She would battle demons for Angustias. Cayo would face a ghost.

"So, she died here, right?" he said to Felicitas while he helped her transfer the dishes into his Tupperware.

"Yes," Felicitas responded. "But she doesn't like to be talked about as if she weren't here."

"Here? She's here? As in this kitchen?"

"Yes." With her fork, Felicitas pointed at the other side of Cayo where all he could see was a floating spoon dumping rice from a pot to a plastic container. He jumped back, spilling sauce down the front of his shirt.

"Don't worry," Felicitas said when she noticed the hair standing on his arms. "She's only mean to me." The person she should have warned him about was her mother. Felicitas had become too comfortable listening to Olvido, living in her house as if it were a home. She forgot who the real boss was, who was still alive.

"Are you okay?" Angustias asks when they're finally alone. Felicitas nods. "Did he do anything to you?"

Felicitas shakes her head. "*I* was the one who invited him," she says. "Honest. I wanted you two to talk."

Angustias's concerned expression hardens. Clenched jaw. Furious eyes. She looks like Olvido when they first met. "What for?" she hisses. "I've told you how I feel about all this."

"I'm sorry," Felicitas says sincerely.

"I am humiliated!"

Felicitas frowns. "But why? Because of how you acted? You humiliated yourself. You didn't have to yell."

"That's not why. Why did you call that man?"

"All you had to do was sit down and eat with him, and it would've all been over. Like this." Felicitas marches to the table, rips off the lid of a container and scoops up its contents with her fingers. They clumsily shove nopales into her mouth. A papery seed hits the back of her throat. "Did you see?" she coughs. "Did that look difficult?"

"What would have been over?" Angustias cries. "Why did you invite him here? Why doesn't anyone listen to me? Why doesn't anyone care about what *I* want?"

"Grandma told me to," Felicitas shouts and gasps at her own confession. A second gasp escapes her, one that is far more joyous and appreciated. The truth has brought a strange and wonderful feeling. Felicitas feels light and calm and free. She feels like she can float away into the night sky and reach the moon. To ground herself, she walks over to her mother and wraps her arms around her waist, closing the distance between them warms her heart.

Angustias stiffens. "What?"

"Grandma told me to," Felicitas repeats, pulling away to look up at her. "I can see her ghost. She's right there."

Angustias doesn't follow Felicitas's finger. She looks at no one but her daughter as she shakes her head with disappointment. "I don't know what's going on with you. You've been acting strange, and now you're making up horrible lies. Why? What's wrong? Talk to me."

Felicitas takes a step back. "It's not a lie."

"Felicitas, just tell me the truth," Angustias pleads, going down on one knee. "Whatever is going on, whatever you're feeling, just tell me the truth. I can help."

"It's not a lie. Grandma's spirit is here. Look," Felicitas spins around to face Olvido. "Tell me something only you would know about my mom."

"We're leaving Grace," Angustias announces before Olvido can respond. "Tomorrow."

"What?" Felicitas and Olvido shout. "No!"

"Yes. It's final."

"What difference is leaving going to make?" Felicitas screams. She feels twice her weight again. She's not going to float into the sky. She's going to sink. A hole is going to open beneath her feet, and she will fall. She'll be buried deep within the town her mother so desperately wishes to escape.

"It's final, Felicitas."

"I hate you," Felicitas bellows before she runs to her grandmother's bedroom and locks herself in. She doesn't see her mother cry herself to sleep in the living room or her grandmother caress her hair in an attempt to sooth the hushed cries. All she sees is the ceiling of her grandmother's bedroom, faintly lit by the moonlight passing through the curtains, the outline of the fan blurred by the tears in her eyes.

That night, Felicitas cries for eight hours straight, flooding her grandmother's bedroom with salt and sorrow. When she finally falls asleep, she dreams she is lost at sea.

Off in the distance, she can see two pieces of land. Between them is the mouth of a river. It grins like the Cheshire cat. It's terrifying, but Felicitas doesn't love it. It laughs at her pleas for help. Its breath pushes her farther away until the river is nothing but the imprint of a memory.

Felicitas reaches out to no one, and then, to God. By the time she awakens, the sea around her has evaporated, but a salty taste remains in her mouth.

chapter 54

Felicitas

Felicitas Olivares wished for psychic abilities for so long, she did not expect to be startled when they appeared, but she also did not expect to see Mr. Kelley standing in the corner of the room covered in dirt and leaves. "I'm sorry," he said. "I must have entered the wrong house. This mud won't let me see properly, but I can't seem to clean it off." Felicitas let out a piercing shriek. Mr. Kelley scoffed. "Well, there's no need to be rude."

By the time Angustias rushed into their bedroom, toothbrush still in her mouth, Mr. Kelley was long gone. "What is it?" Angustias asked, bending down beside Felicitas. "What's wrong?"

"A ghost," Felicitas panted. "I saw Mr. Kelley's ghost."

Angustias banned her from watching television for a week.

Three months later, Felicitas came across Mr. Campbell's ghost. She was far calmer then, mostly because she didn't know Mr. Campbell had passed away until he explained his situation to her. After Angustias's dismissal of her ghost-seeing claims, Felicitas began to believe her encounter with Mr. Kelley had been a dream. Therefore, Mr. Campbell's slight translucency had to be a trick of the eyes, a mistake from her brain, an illusion of the sunlight. But then, Mr. Campbell caught her staring and he practically danced toward her. "Can you see me?" he beamed.

"Yeah," she said. "Can you see me?" When Mr. Campbell laughed and raised his fists in triumph, she asked why their sight was so marvelous. He explained the religious way, and Felicitas found it odd that he was happy even though he knew he was dead. Felicitas decided that she liked Mr. Campbell because she liked odd things. Too bad he was dead. They could have been friends.

"Well, I'm not happy I'm dead," Mr. Campbell said. "But I was sick for a while, and that wasn't very pleasant. Now I don't feel any pain! And I'm really excited that you can see me. What an extraordinary ability. I get to witness a miracle before I go with God."

"You think my ability is a miracle?" Felicitas questioned.

"Of course! I've never met anyone who can do what you can."

"But why do I get to have this miracle? Why do I get to see you? You probably wish it was your son, don't you?"

"No," Mr. Campbell laughed. "My son is a scaredy cat. You are a brave girl. Maybe only really brave people are able to see spirits."

With her newly discovered bravery, Felicitas informed her mother about her encounter over dinner. "Felicitas, it's not right to make jokes about dead people," Angustias reprimanded. "Poor Mr. Campbell. He was so nice."

"*Is* nice," Felicitas corrected.

"That's enough."

When she came across Mrs. Reed's spirit, Felicitas couldn't help but tell her mother. She had no one else to speak to about it, and she really needed to get her thoughts out of her head. Her brain hummed like a beehive. "Strange. Crazy. Wrong," the bees sang. Felicitas liked watching ghosts on TV but not in her bedroom. Real ghost-seeing girls didn't embark on perilous but thrilling adventures. They got locked up in a hospital or bullied at school.

"I saw another ghost today," Felicitas whispered in the middle of the night.

"Just scare them away," Angustias mumbled, unable to open her eyes. "Boo."

"I'm not scared," Felicitas said. "Should I be?"

Angustias did not respond.

Felicitas considered waking her mother up and forcing her to pay attention, but first she thought through Angustias's potential reactions. If she attempted to convince her mother that she was telling the truth and provided some proof, her mother would either believe her or not believe her. If she believed her, she would either become afraid of her or for her. Helping her figure out her abilities was not an option, Felicitas realized. Her mother couldn't see ghosts. She wouldn't understand.

Felicitas did not like the idea of her mother being afraid of her. She did not want to be shunned by the only person who loved her. She also did not like the idea of her mother being afraid for her. Her mother reserved worrying for extremely terrible situations. Extremely terrible situations were things to run away from. If Felicitas fell into that category, and her mother ran away from her, where would Felicitas go?

If Angustias did not believe her, she would either worry, which Felicitas had already established was bad, or she would not care. This was the most terrifying scenario. Felicitas had heard of mothers who didn't care about their children. Scary men and women in suits knocked on their doors and took them away. Felicitas did not want Angustias to be one of those moms, and she most certainly did not want to be taken away. Felicitas could not think of any other scenarios that could occur if she said something, so she didn't say anything at all. Mr. Campbell was wrong. Her ability was not a miracle. It was a curse.

This is how Felicitas has spent her life: assessing possible outcomes and remaining quiet. Angustias cannot know about Felicitas's thoughts and feelings. Felicitas has Estela and Gustavo now, and she should have Olvido, but her grandmother has remained inaccessible despite how much she's changed. Their conversations have been a one-way street, and until Olvido builds a bridge to reach her, Felicitas does not feel safe enough to ask what is truly on her mind. *What happened between you and Mom?* she wants to shout across the kitchen table. *What did it have to do with me? What did I do wrong?*

Either Olvido will answer her questions or she will not. Regardless of which way she potentially reacts, Olvido will be forced to remember why she hates Felicitas, and her resentment will float back up. Olvido will once again be the cold shell of a being she was when she first appeared in their apartment kitchen.

Answering Felicitas's questions delicately is not an option. Olvido has slowly warmed up, but not like leftover Christmas tamales toasted in the comal, more like a tamal reheated in the microwave. Where Felicitas wishes there were toasty, crunchy edges, there is unevenly distributed heat. She has no way of knowing if the next piece she bites into will be scalding or frozen, but either way it is bad.

"You're very quiet this morning," Olvido says, setting a cup of coffee in front of Felicitas.

"I'm always quiet."

"I know, but a lot happened yesterday. You don't have anything to say about it? What are we going to do? What is your mother going to do? Look." Olvido points to a piece of paper held down by the empty flower vase in the center of the table. Felicitas snatches it out and reads it. "What does it say?"

"She went to the library to tell Emilio that we're leaving," Felicitas translates. "She's also stopping by Dr. Gutiérrez's and Ms. Taliah's to deliver yesterday's dinner to them. She doesn't want the food to go bad."

"But those containers don't belong to us."

"She says she can take me to say goodbye to Gustavo and Estela before we . . ."

"Don't cry," Olvido orders. Her tone is somewhere between that of a military commander and of a concerned Angustias. "We'll think of something, and this time, it will not involve a trip to the hospital. I promise. That girl needs to stop running away from her problems. I know she thinks that's what I did. She was always rubbing it in my face, but I had a good reason for my own actions. She does not. What is it? It looks like you want to say something. Let me guess. Another question. Is it 'what' or 'why' this time? 'What do you mean you ran away? Why did you run away?'"

Felicitas shakes her head. She already asked those questions, and Olvido answered, but does her grandmother know she's left a window open? What questions can Felicitas fit through it? *What if she's running away from you?* she thinks. *What if she's running away from me?* These questions feel massive, but Felicitas is unwilling to let go of this opportunity, so she asks Olvido to tell her about her father instead. She's curious, but doesn't truly care about the answer to that question, and what she doesn't care about can't hurt her.

"I didn't know him very well," Olvido says with a shrug. "He was ugly and skinny." She hesitates for a moment as if she's holding something back.

"Did you want to say like me?" Felicitas says, and takes in a gulp of coffee so large, her cheeks puff out like a chipmunk's.

"No. You have my good looks," Olvido says, gently tapping her own cheeks.

Felicitas rolls her eyes and gulps. "Whatever you say." She slams her cup down on the table. "Why did my mom leave him?"

Olvido pretends to be absorbed with inspecting the cleanliness of her kitchen counter so she doesn't have to look at Felicitas. "Did your mother never tell you?" she says.

"No."

"Well then, that is something she should talk to you about," she responds.

Felicitas narrows her eyes. *Unattainable, but not cold.* She carries her dirty cup to the sink and decides to wash the rest of the dishes. Every few seconds, she glances at her grandmother from the corner of her eye. Olvido has moved on to inspecting the cabinets and the fridge. Felicitas takes a deep breath. *Do it,* she commands herself. If Olvido has the worst possible reaction, then Felicitas can just ignore her. Maybe Olvido will be so upset, she'll decide to stay in Grace without them. No, Felicitas is kidding herself. She wouldn't do that, but she would disappear for a while like she did the day before her funeral.

Felicitas takes a deep breath, marches to the fridge, and takes out a jar of lemonade Olvido prepared days earlier. "Ask me what it is that I really want to say," she commands as she pours herself a glass.

"What?"

"Ask me what it is that I really want to say."

"What do you really want to say?" Olvido repeats with trepidation.

Felicitas chugs the lemonade until there is not a drop left in the glass and involuntarily speaks. "Why did she leave? My mom. Why did you kick her out?"

"I did not kick her out," Olvido says, still refusing to make eye contact. "And that is also something *she* should talk to you about."

Felicitas stomps her foot to get Olvido's attention and yells, "Hey!" when her grandmother tries to turn her back on Felicitas. "As you may have noticed, my mom doesn't tell me anything."

Olvido laughs. "It seems like she tells you plenty. You act more like friends than mother and daughter."

Felicitas frowns. "No, we don't. You just think that because you two didn't act like friends at all. She only tells me things that I'm 'old enough to understand,' but I don't know how she determines what those things are."

"There's no criteria," Olvido says earnestly. "You just know. When you become a mother, you will understand."

Felicitas scrunches her nose. "I don't think I want to become a mom. Ever."

Olvido rolls her eyes and signals for Felicitas to move so that she can inspect the fridge. "You don't know what you're talking about," she says, opening the door and bending down to check the fresh produce drawers.

"Yes, I do," Felicitas says. She straightens her back to make herself larger, but she feels one inch tall. "I know plenty. I know what being too distant and too close to your daughter looks like. I know moms lie and convince themselves they are making the right decisions without ever asking their daughters what *they* want. I know being a daughter and a mother means nothing."

Olvido frowns and stands. "What do you mean it means nothing?"

"Mother and daughter are just titles," Felicitas explains. "That's what they're called, right? Titles? Like Mrs. and Mr. and husband and wife. They're just words. They don't tie you together forever."

"Yes, they do," Olvido snaps.

Felicitas smirks. "You think you and my mom were tied together?"

"Of course. Why do you think I called her all these years? Because I enjoyed fighting with her? No. Because she is my daughter, and I have a responsibility to make sure she's all right."

"You are obsessed with her," Felicitas says, enunciating every word so that it can push through her grandmother's stubbornness and into her brain.

"All mothers are obsessed with their child's well-being."

"She's not a child," Felicitas contends.

"She's my child," Olvido says. "And you are getting on my nerves."

"You don't know a thing about her well-being."

"Neither do you."

"Tell me something I don't know. No, I'm serious," Felicitas insists. "Tell me something I don't know. Why did she leave?"

"You really want to know?" Olvido says, slapping down a kitchen towel on the counter to stand her ground.

"Yes."

Olvido takes a step back, her impeccable posture gone. She twirls the corner of her blouse and looks down at her hands before answering. "Very well then. She got into a fight with your dad and—" She stiffens for a moment but continues. "I suggested she give you up for adoption. I believed it was the best option. She was too immature to take care of a child. She refused, and I threatened to call child protective services."

Felicitas ignores the first part of Olvido's confession. She knew about the fight. Of course, there'd been a fight. It was an easy thing to guess. Angustias told her that her father wasn't dead, and one does not leave someone because they're happy and in love. But her grandmothers' actions? Those were impossible to ignore.

"She should have known I wasn't really going to do it," Olvido continues. "I couldn't risk—it was just to get her to understand the severity of the situation."

"Child protective services," Felicitas repeats. A bitter taste floods her mouth. "Those are the people that take kids away when their parents don't care about them."

"Not necessarily," Olvido says. "It's not because their parents don't care. It's because they can't provide their children with an adequate life, a safe life."

"My mom has always kept us safe."

"Not according to that," Olvido says, lifting her chin to point at the taped-up window.

"Was that from the fight?" Felicitas asks. Olvido nods. "That wasn't her fault, though, right?"

"In a way, it was. She let him in."

Felicitas's brows furrow. "You don't believe that."

"No, I don't," Olvido says. Tears stream down her cheeks to match Felicitas's own. "It didn't matter what I believed, though. What mattered was what other people would believe."

"You said," Felicitas says softly. "You said abandoning your child son cosas del diablo."

"Yes. I know, and it is," Olvido acknowledges. "But you weren't my child. She was. I wanted to make sure she was all right."

Felicitas nods with resignation. She is, as she suspected, una cosa del diablo, an ugly, bothersome, wretched thing that ruined her mother's life. Olvido wasn't stuck on Earth because she needed to find her way home or fix Angustias's situation. She was there to punish Felicitas, but hadn't she been punished enough?

chapter 55

Olvido

Olvido can see in her granddaughter's warped expression that her words are not getting through to her. She knew it. She knew Felicitas would not understand. She wasn't the mother of a reckless girl or the daughter of a selfish woman. She couldn't see what future Olvido had envisioned for all of them. But that future does not exist. Angustias and Felicitas's life is difficult but not hopeless. They are a team in a way she never thought she and Angustias could be or should be, in the manner that she and Felicitas have become.

"It was wrong. I know that," Olvido says. "You are my granddaughter. I was wrong. I'm sorry."

Felicitas shakes her head somberly. "No," she says.

"Yes, it was wrong. It—it was a sin."

"No, I mean, you're not sorry. And I'm not your granddaughter."

Olvido's eyes narrow with confusion. "Of course, you are. You have my face," she says, extending her hand to caress it. *Those are my eyes,* she wants to say. *Those are my lips and my cheeks and my frown.*

Felicitas slaps her hand away. "My father is not my dad, is he? I have his blood, but he's not my dad. He didn't raise me. He doesn't know me, and I don't know a thing about him, and I don't care. And you didn't raise me. You don't know me, and I don't know a thing about you, and I don't care."

Olvido scoffs. She wants to mock Felicitas, tell her she's being as ridiculously dramatic as Angustias, but she can't. Felicitas meant what she said. She can see it in her impassive eyes. "Wha—we can get to know each other." The hard truth is out in the open. Olvido will no longer have to worry about saying the wrong thing or Felicitas asking a difficult question.

"Are you serious?" Felicitas says incredulously.

"What?"

"You've had plenty of time to get to know me, but you never tried, even when I tried to get to know you."

"We were busy trying to get me to cross," Olvido reminds her.

"Yet you had plenty of time to give me instructions on how to take care of my mom."

Olvido lifts her arms up in surrender. "Well, I am apparently staying with you two for a little bit longer, so now we can focus on you."

Felicitas's jaw clenches. Her nostrils flare and her hands form tight fists at her sides. "I don't want you to come with us. I want you to stay here."

Olvido shakes her head. "I cannot do that."

"You're not coming with us," Felicitas growls.

"Yes," Olvido declares, puffing out her chest. "I am."

"Fine!" Felicitas shouts. "Then, I'm staying." Storming out of the house, she leaves an indignant Olvido sitting at the kitchen table. Olvido refuses to chase after her or even look at her, so she doesn't see her granddaughter steal her neighbor's bike and clumsily ride off toward the river where a storm awaits her with welcoming arms.

chapter 56

Angustias

Angustias is aware of her inability to accurately decipher people's colors. She sees this potential defect as a blessing. One can deceive themselves more easily if there is no physical marker of the turmoil in their heart. The night of her semipermanent departure from Olvido's home, Angustias was able to look in the mirror, smile, and tell herself she would be all right even though she felt every terrible emotion imaginable, and a cloud should have been crowning her with the most chaotic-looking piece of abstract art. Scarlet rage. Black sorrow. Gray loneliness. Dark brown fear. A minuscule sliver of silver hope.

As a teenager, she was able to tell the right lies to soften her mother's angry scarlet and lighten her anxious midnight blue, but she was unable to pretend that there was no yellow in her cloud when Angustias brought Felicitas home from the hospital. She couldn't unsee Olvido's pearl white halo of indifference when people pointed out what a beautiful baby Felicitas was, when they said, "She has your eyes," and "You must feel so proud."

It feels strange to not be able to see Olvido's cloud anymore. *It's because she's not here*, Angustias tells herself. *Her mother is gone no matter how much a part her wishes Felicitas's lies were true.*

"You're lying," Emilio says when Angustias informs him that she and Felicitas are leaving Grace. Angustias shakes her head. "Joking? Bluffing? Should I continue with the synonyms?"

Angustias continues to shake her head, afraid that if she opens her mouth to speak, she'll start to cry.

"Is there anything I can say to convince you to stay?"

Angustias shakes her head more forcefully.

Emilio's cloud darkens in an instant. "Not even saying I'll miss you?"

Angustias bites her lips and shuts her yes, but it's hopeless. A rush of tears falls down her cheeks to the ground. Will she drown this time? She's not going to wait and find out. Angustias hugs Emilio and runs out into the rain.

chapter 57

Olvido

Olvido's earliest memory of a hurricane is as fragmented as her childhood home's kitchen ceiling. A tree branch borne by the hurricane's breath had broken through the roof and ceiling, exposing the interior of the house to unrelenting rain and natural debris. She remembers the suffocating heat that enveloped her when her mother opened the living room windows during a brief pause in the downpour. Olvido remembers how the water clung to the hem of her dress the way she would cling to her mother when she was afraid. She remembers how she and her mother bent over to collect rain in steel pots and how they threw the water out into their already drowning garden.

Mostly she remembered the gray sky, how she felt as if her world had transformed into a black-and-white movie but was aware that her reality was a lot less glamorous than that of a movie star. If María Félix's roof had caved in like Olvido's had, she could've demanded for it to be fixed in less than a week, and in the meantime, she could've stayed in a fancy hotel in Mexico City where specially designated staff could grant her every wish. She could've bought new clothes to replace those destroyed by the rain, and she could've eaten to her heart's content and not worried if there would be any food left for the next day.

Olvido could not afford to do any of those things, and her ceiling was never fixed. Her mother simply covered it with a wooden board that fell down every few years when a new hurricane hit. The fix was flimsy and rotten and useless.

Decades later, despite the lack of natural disasters, Olvido's home is still falling apart, and she can't cover it with a piece of wood. She can't mask it at all.

Olvido can no longer bear to see the hatred in her granddaughter's face nor hear how much resentment her daughter still keeps in her heart. So, she runs away to her neighbors' house, a cowardly move, she knows, but who will judge her? No one but her granddaughter can see her repeating her mistakes. She won't hide forever. She'll find them and follow them wherever they go, but there's no need to stay and be present when Felicitas and Angustias return home. There's no need to witness them pack their belongings, load their car, and drive off to another new start. What good will it do to see how easily they leave her behind?

"We're in the eye of Hurricane Sage which is making landfall right now on the coast of south Texas with ninety-six miles per hour winds. The first hurricane of the season, Corpus Christi is hit hard as Sage makes her way inland," the news reporter yells over the rain. His voice is so faint, Samara must raise the volume on the living room television to its highest level. Behind the reporter, scenes of imminent destruction play out, palm trees on the brink of flight, currents on a paved road propelled by the wind.

Doña Sarai puts her hand over her chest and shakes her head. "Dios cuide a esa pobre gente," she says.

Normally, Olvido would agree and send out a prayer for those being threatened by the monster she's encountered numerous times, but she is preoccupied with her own problems. She sits hunched over in one of the dining room chairs wishing she could take a sip of Doña Sarai's hot tea to spook away the inexplicable cold she feels.

"I never understood why they make reporters stand outside in weather like that. We can see things just as well from inside a building," Alberto says moments before the television screen displays the roof of a house being ripped away from its base. It disappears piece by piece as if the wind is having too much fun and wants to prolong its destruction. "Or not."

"Will that happen to our house, too?" Gustavo asks. While Doña Sarai looks on at the television with worry, Alberto with confusion, and Samara with fear, Gustavo appears curious and eager. He wasn't lying when he said he hadn't been scared since he was seven.

"No," Samara assures him and herself. "We live too far inland for the hurricane to get to us. We're hundreds of miles away."

"Aw, man," Gustavo whines. "I wanted to see . . ." He jumps on the couch and shouts, "Destruction!"

The adults turn to him with disapproving looks. Samara's frown conveys such intense discontent, Olvido can't help but think of Felicitas. She looks away, ashamed.

"It seems like we're already getting a storm," Alberto says looking out the living room window. The drizzle of the previous hour has transformed into fat, rapid-falling drops. The neighbors' house is barely visible behind the curtain of rain. "Wasn't that too fast?" he whispers to his wife. "Shouldn't it have taken a little longer to get here?"

The camera cuts back to the studio. The reporter takes a second to speak. "It appears the winds are picking up. Hurricane Sage is now a Category 3 with winds of one hundred twenty-five—"

"How did it change so quickly?" Alberto says to no one in particular.

"It appears to be moving inland at a faster pace," the reporter continues.

"Can it do that? Can it get worse as it moves inland?" Doña Sarai asks. "Gustavo, google it."

Olvido does not hear Gustavo's answer. The sound of the rain thunders in her ears as she stares out the window, eyes wide with horror.

chapter 58

Felicitas

Felicitas knows that when Mrs. Thompson's spirit said, "Just do what your mother does," she did not mean to act impulsively. That, Felicitas knew, was not a trait anyone would suggest she adopt from her mother. People thought Angustias was fun and adventurous, but they would also give her a funny look when she shared how they had up and left their previous apartment one night and moved into this new-to-them town. "Oh," they would say. "I thought you moved here because of work."

"Nope," Angustias would respond nonchalantly.

"You didn't have a job lined up before coming?"

"No."

"Oh."

Angustias caught the judgment in their tone, but she didn't particularly care. Everyone judges. "It's human nature," she says. It's what one does with their judgment that matters, and what Felicitas does is attempt to avoid it. So, she makes sure to always have a plan.

Felicitas's plans started off small. She planned her outfits for the week, her after-school schedule and the book she would read before going to bed. She planned at what time she would do her homework, shower, and turn off the lights, and the number of sheep she needed to count in her head in order to fall asleep. She planned when and what to eat, the ingredients needed for the meal and the amount of time it would take to make it. She accepted no mistakes and no deviations from her plan, afraid of a disastrous domino effect.

"We can't eat milanesas tonight," she once exclaimed as if Angustias had chosen not to read through the plans she'd drafted in her mind. "I already planned for you to make spaghetti. See?" she said, pointing to the ingredients she had set on the kitchen counter.

When her plans were small, Felicitas was able to accomplish them with few resources and just a bit of determination. It was when her plans grew more ambitious that she realized making plans when you're a child is tiring and pointless. Adults don't stick to your plans. Other children don't stick to your plans. And life? Life laughs at your plans. Felicitas planned to make friends. She planned to like her new town. She planned to never have to move again.

All her plans failed. But with less rigidity and more creativity, she continued to plan things out in the hopes that one day, one plan, just one plan, would succeed.

Felicitas has abandoned all hope. She'll never get her mother to stay put. She'll never get Olvido to be the nice grandma she longs to have. She probably won't even make it out of the hurricane alive.

Felicitas drops Gustavo's bike and runs to seek shelter beneath a low tree. She braces the trunk with her free arm, claws her nails into the wood, and digs her shoes into the soft ground to keep the wind from blowing her away. Her legs shake with exhaustion. *If I had planned to run away*, Felicitas thinks, *instead of just escaping, this would not be happening*. If she had planned to run away, she would've taken a backpack and a jacket. She would've packed snacks, water, and an umbrella. She would've checked the weather.

Despite the impetuosity of her escape, Felicitas knew where she was heading. She wasn't sure, though, why she was heading there. The river had already failed to save her from her grandmother once. There was nothing else it could offer her.

Maybe she thought she could swim away from her problems. Maybe she thought she could wash away her sorrow. Maybe she thought she would find her grandmother's ashes, clumped and stuck to a rock, preventing Olvido from reaching her home.

No, that was silly. That's not how ashes worked, and that was not what Felicitas thought as she had pedaled away from Maple Road. Felicitas had simply not thought of anything at all. Just like Angustias, she ran away knowing where she was heading but with no idea what she would do once she got there. It was all Olvido's fault then, and it's all Olvido's fault now. Felicitas feels as if she understands her mother now, to an extent at least. Olvido's heartlessness can make you act crazy and imprudent. It will make you do anything to get away from her. Unlike Angustias, however, things have not worked out for Felicitas. She has come across a monumental obstacle in her nonexistent plan. She has encountered a hurricane.

Is this a sign? Is God or the universe telling her she needs to accept her mother's wishes? Stop that, Felicitas orders herself. First, she acted impulsively and now she's interpreting signs. *I'm turning into my mother. God, just strike me dead,* she pleads.

Looking up at the webbed crown of the tree, Felicitas considers the possibility of God finally granting her a wish. Is she supposed to hide beneath a tree or avoid it? The tree's leaves provide some protection from the rain, but if a branch strikes her, she's as good as dead.

Out of the eight schools Felicitas has attended, none have prepared her for this moment. They've taught her how to survive fires and school shootings but not hurricanes. She'll have a word with Gustavo's dad when she makes it back to Olvido's house. Maybe he can let other school principals know that they really need to add a "Surviving a Natural Disaster" unit in their physical education classes. But first, she needs to make it back to Olvido's house. She needs to find open land. Was the house to her right or her left? Have her right and left traded places?

"De tin Marín, de do pingüe—" Felicitas sings until her finger lands in fate's direction. She lets go of the tree and moves to her left. The rain is far worse than the wind, which she supposes is a good thing, but she can't see more than a few feet in front of her. The water has turned the dirt to mud, and she slips every few steps.

Forward.

Forward.

The sound of the river's current tells her she's made another mistake.

"Don't go any further," Olvido shouts. "You'll fall in."

"I'm not even close to the edge," Felicitas shouts back. "Go away!" She knows it's not the time to start a fight with her grandmother, but really, there should never be a right time, and she's not starting a fight. She's simply continuing one Olvido began before her birth.

"Can you not see through the rain?" Olvido yells.

"Not really. And I'm glad 'cause I don't want to see you right now."

"Head the other way!"

"I know! I'm going." Felicitas pivots and pushes her body against the wind.

The wind. She should have known. The river is east, the house is west, and the wind is coming from the east because Texas hurricanes are born in the east. She should not have fought the wind.

Felicitas takes a step forward and feels a light pressure against her back. "Don't push me!"

"Well, move faster. You're too close to the edge."

"I said stop pushing me!" Felicitas turns to swat her grandmother's arm away. Her hand goes straight through it.

Olvido stomps her foot. "Fine. You want me to drag you instead?"

"You could barely hold up a nightstand. You think you can drag me?"

"If it will get you to move away from the river's edge, I'll give it a try."

"I am not close to the—ah!" Felicitas puts her good arm forward to break her fall, but it provides no assistance as she slides across the mud. The pain in Felicitas's knee takes a while to kick in, but the pain in her face is instantaneous. She lifts her hand up to her forehead. She cannot tell whether the warm, viscous liquid she feels is blood or rain or mud.

"Don't move!" Olvido orders, kneeling at her side. "You're hurt."

Felicitas lifts her muddied, bloodied face just enough to show her grandmother her annoyance. "No. Really?"

"Your mom is on her way. Do you think you can reach the tree?"

Felicitas looks forward and squints to catch a glimpse of the tree she moved away from a few minutes before. "Aren't I *not* supposed to hide under trees during a hurricane?"

Olvido nods. "Yes. You're right."

"What do you mean my mom's coming?" Felicitas shouts.

"I'm going to let her know you're here."

"Let her know? As in she doesn't know yet?" Felicitas says, disobeying her grandmother's orders and inching forward to a nearby bush. "So, she's not coming?"

"She's coming. Stay here. I'll go check on her."

"Where else am I supposed to go?" Felicitas screams, but Olvido is already gone.

chapter 59

Angustias

Angustias enters Olvido's house unzipping and throwing her soaked jacket on the ground, eager to rid herself of the cold rain. "Felicitas, are you done packing?" she calls out and sees the note she left that morning lying facedown on the ground. "Felicitas? Change of plans. We're not leaving until the storm is over. Felicitas?" The house responds with silence. "Felicitas?" Silence and emptiness in the living room. Silence and emptiness in the kitchen. "Felicitas?" Silence and emptiness in her bedroom. "Felicitas?"

Expecting it to be locked, Angustias turns the knob of her mother's bedroom with force. She topples into the room with her own momentum as the door opens with ease. "Felicitas?" Silence and emptiness in the bedroom. Silence and emptiness in the bathroom.

Angustias's breath quickens. She can feel her heartbeat pounding against her chest as she checks beneath the bed and in her mother's wardrobe. "Felicitas, this isn't funny," she yells, failing to mask her fear with anger. The backyard is empty. The front yard is empty.

She calls Samara. She calls Estela's parents. She calls Emilio, even though he is the last person who would know where Felicitas is. She just drove back from the library. Why did she go to the library? Was it truly necessary to say goodbye?

A high-pitched shriek escapes Angustias as the glass of the kitchen window abruptly shatters into a million pieces. A rock bounces off the kitchen table and lands on the floor with a *thud*, barely audible over the howling storm. Angustias runs to the window and sees nothing but rain. "Felicitas?"

The front door bursts open, letting in water and soiled leaves. Angustias rushes to close it. The wind fights her for control, but Angustias wins the first round. She closes the door and locks it. *Click.*

The door unlocks and bursts open once again. Angustias closes it and locks it. The door unlocks. She locks it. It unlocks. She locks it.

As Angustias observes the slow turn of the lock, she comes to accept what she's feared since she heard "México lindo y querido" inexplicably blast in her mother's living room. "¿Mamá?" she whimpers as she slides down to the ground, her back against the wall.

A framed photograph flies from the living room. Angustias hears the shatter of its glass before she sees it. She crawls to it and lifts it by its broken frame. Her own unhappy face stares back at her. Behind her five-year-old self is Olvido, proudly smiling at her daughter on the day she graduated from kindergarten.

Angustias can't contain her tears, but she has no time to dwell on her sadness and confusion. "Do you know where Felicitas is?" she yells out into the empty house.

The door swings open. Angustias's hand shoots up to her mouth to cover her gasp. "Is she outside? Where? Where is she?"

The vivid sounds of trumpets announce an answer. Guitars and violins join in on the response. Angustias runs into the living room and crouches in front of the record player. "Fuck," she screams. Another song? Is there no simpler way for her mother to help her? She can't speed up the record to get through the intro. "Hurry up," she barks at the machine, impatiently patting the floor with her hand. "Can't you just show me?"

Finally, she hears Vicente Fernández's booming voice. "Crucé el río Grande nadando," the mariachi sings.

Angustias springs to her feet and dashes out of the house.

"Angustias," Samara shouts from her porch, her hair flying wildly around her face, tangling in her dark blue and tangerine cloud. Her feet slide across the wet floor of her porch. Alberto catches her by her arm. "Did you find Felicitas?"

Angustias can't hear her over the raindrops hitting the roof of her car. It doesn't matter. Angustias has no time to address her neighbors' worry and confusion. She has her own midnight blue to worry about.

chapter 60

Angustias

Angustias Olivares can't remember her first hurricane. She was too young to retain any memories, but she remembers her second hurricane with fondness. Olvido gave her a million and one responsibilities. "Help me move the sandbags. Help me tape the windows. Fill those jugs with water. Have you checked the flashlights? Did you disconnect everything but the fridge?" Angustias felt like a grown-up, like she wasn't a nuisance her mother had to keep out of trouble or even just keep alive. She'd been promoted to her mother's second-in-command of the great ship Olivares.

When Angustias became the chief officer of her own ship, she applauded Felicitas's signs of maturity, her efforts to be responsible, her attempts to be independent. Sometimes Felicitas got a little carried away and worried about unnecessary things, but Angustias reeled her back and assured her everything would be all right. She was still trying to find that balance between encouraging Felicitas to think for herself and discouraging her from worrying. It's likely, Angustias knows, that she'll have to seek this balance for the rest of her life because no matter how much her daughter thinks she can survive on her own, she will never stop needing her mother. Angustias wishes this wasn't true, but it is. She knows from experience. Her mother is dead, and Angustias is still depending on her.

"¿Mamá, sigues aquí?" Angustias shouts inside her car. The radio turns on, blaring the guitar of a country song. The stations switch rapidly. Voices and melodies blend into one. Then, there is static.

Angustias lets one hand go from the steering wheeling to turn down the volume. The other keeps its tight grip. The paleness of her bones is visible through the stretched skin of her knuckles. "If the answer is yes, turn up the volume," Angustias instructs in Spanish. "If the answer is no, turn it down. Okay?" The volume rises.

"Am I on the right path?" The volume rises.

"Is she where we held your funeral?" The volume lowers.

"Near it?" The volume rises.

"How close? Wait, you can't answer that. Very close as in less than half a mile?" The volume rises.

"Okay. Thank you. Thank you."

Angustias leans over the steering wheel to get a better view of her path. She's made it to the outskirts of town. There are no buildings or street signs in sight, but she knows she's heading the right way. She paid close attention to her surroundings when she drove to her mother's funeral. If she concentrated on where she was going, she wouldn't have to think about her mother or how much she missed her or how much she wanted to tell her she was sorry and how much she wanted her mother to echo her sentiment.

The sound of static and rain fills the car, but all Angustias can hear are the unnerving thoughts running through her mind. Olvido can see the anxiety consuming her daughter. "It's going to be okay," she tells her, putting her hand on her shoulder. Angustias doesn't feel a thing. "You're close. It's going to be okay. You know what you should do? You should pray."

Angustias takes in deep breaths and tightens her grip on the steering wheel. Olvido tunes the radio until she finds the station she's looking for.

Angustias rolls her eyes at the chorus of the church hymn, but she finds comfort in the sound. It truly is her mother who sits beside her. "Fine," Angustias says as if she heard her mother's suggestion directly from her lips. Frantically, she prays.

Angustias finds the area where the funeral attendees parked their cars and moves further east. "Do I turn right—" Angustias's head springs forward and back as the car comes to a halt. She presses down on the accelerator. She can feel the wheels of the car struggling to turn, but there is no movement forward. "Shit!" She tries to reverse. Nothing. Press. Nothing.

She opens the door and sees her front tires have landed in a hole, its edges greased by mud. "I'm getting out," she announces. "Am I near?" The volume rises.

"Thank you, God. Thank you," she says softly then raises her voice to ask, "Is she straight ahead?" The volume lowers.

"Left?" The volume rises.

Angustias turns off the ignition and steps out of the car. "Felicitas!" she calls out as she distances herself from the car and reaches more solid ground. "Felicitas!" Left, she repeats to herself. She's near. Left. Angustias feels a sudden pressure against her arm and gasps. Forward and left.

"Felicitas!" Angustias continues to scream for what feels like an eternity.

"Mamá," she hears a faint voice respond. "Mamá. I'm here! Can you hear me?"

"Yes!" she shouts. "I can hear you. Keep talking! Keep talking, bebé."

"I can see you. Walk forward. More. Straight ahead. I'm in front of you!" Felicitas shouts. "Look down."

Angustias uselessly wipes the rain off her face. Squinting her eyes as they sweep the land in front of her until they find Felicitas on the ground holding on to the branches of a bush. The vomit pooled at her side slowly washes away with the rain.

"Felicitas!" Angustias rushes to her daughter and wraps her arms around her. "Oh my God," she cries, caressing her head. "I found you. I found you. Can you stand?" Felicitas nods. "The car is near. That way."

Holding on to each other, Angustias and Felicitas move against the water and wind and head toward the car. Angustias opens the door for Felicitas and makes sure she's safely inside before going around the car to enter through the driver's seat. They each take a minute to catch their breath. Angustias reaches into the glove compartment and rummages through paperwork and broken phone chargers until she finds some napkins. She soaks one with the water of an old plastic bottle she keeps forgetting to throw out and presses the damp paper against Felicitas's forehead. Felicitas winces, but she doesn't complain. "Let me look at your arm."

Felicitas moves her injured arm toward the door. "It's fine. I can clean it myself."

Angustias allows Felicitas to take charge and falls back into her seat. Her twitching muscles ache. She's never felt such exhaustion. *That's not true*, she remembers. *I gave birth. I am invincible. I have to be.*

chapter 61

Olvido

Olvido, for once, decides to stay quiet during her daughter and grand-daughter's conversation. There's nothing she can say that can improve their situation but there are a million things that can worsen it.

"Why aren't you driving?" Felicitas asks, frowning at Angustias's resting hands.

"The car's stuck. I would push it, but I think it's best we wait this out." Olvido agrees silently.

"How long will we have to wait?"

Angustias shrugs. "How should I know?"

Several hours. A day or more.

"Uh, you should know because you've actually lived through hurri-canes," Felicitas responds, mimicking her mother's nonchalance.

"This isn't a hurricane. Hurricanes don't reach this far in. It's just a storm . . . I think." A thin, long branch crashes against the hood of the car to challenge Angustias's statement.

"Looks like a hurricane," Felicitas says matter-of-factly. It is.

"Okay, Felicitas, we are sitting in the middle of a hurricane. Happy? Let me see your forehead again." Felicitas moves her head out of her mother's reach. "What's wrong?" Angustias demands.

"I'm mad at you."

Angustias's jaw drops. "Why?" Felicitas stares straight ahead and does not respond. "I know you don't want to leave," Angustias says. "But it's for the best. I promise. Wherever we end up in the Valley will be our permanent home, okay? No more moving after that."

"Why can't Grace be our permanent home?" Felicitas says, still refusing to look at her mother.

"Because it—it just can't," Angustias stammers. But why? "People here are strange, and they keep pestering me, and they look at me like—because I said so."

Oh no. Not that phrase. As soon as one becomes a parent, they forget how that sentence means nothing yet causes the most hostile reaction. Felicitas whips her head away from Angustias and her hair splashes everyone in the car.

The Olivares women sit in silence, each staring out a window, observing the undying storm. Nothing sits still outside, not even the earth that liquefies more and more with every droplet that crashes into it. Soon, it won't be able to hold the tree's roots. Pebbles roll away from the green giants in fear. The Olivares women aren't as fearful. They each wish they could step out into the rain, extend their arms, and let the wind carry them wherever it desires, hopefully somewhere far away from where they now sit.

"Are you sure you're okay?" Angustias asks after a few minutes.

"Yes," Felicitas mutters, staring at her muddied shoes. "I already told you I'm fine, but it doesn't matter what I say. You never believe me."

"I believe you," Angustias sighs. Felicitas turns to her with doubt in her eyes. "About everything," Angustias clarifies. "I'm sorry. Is she here right now?" Her shoulders tense up at the potential response. Her gaze locks on the fallen branch ahead.

"Yeah, she's right behind you."

"Ah!" Angustias screams. Felicitas and Olvido jump in their seats. "Sorry. I don't know why I did that."

"Weren't you, like, communicating with her or something?" Felicitas says.

"Yeah," Angustias replies, combing her wet hair with her fingers.

"How?"

"The radio, among other things. When did you start seeing her?"

"Since the morning after she died."

"Passed away," Olvido corrects.

"OMG, passed away!" Felicitas exclaims. "You can talk to her, you know," she says to Angustias.

Angustias ignores the suggestion. "You weren't lying about Mr. Campbell and Mr. Kelley either," she says. Felicitas shakes her head. "Have there been more?" Felicitas nods. "Is it scary?"

Not for Felicitas.

"No."

"Would I be scared?"

Probably not.

"Probably not."

Angustias nods as if rattling the ideas inside her brain will somehow fuse them into a digestible explanation. "Why didn't you tell me?"

"I did."

"About your grandma." Curious, Olvido perks up.

"Would you have believed me?" Felicitas says, head tilted down and eyebrows raised.

"Yes. No," Angustias admits after seeing Felicitas's look of suspicion. "I would have, eventually."

Felicitas looks down at her twisting fingers. "Do you think there's something wrong with me?"

"No," Angustias says earnestly.

Felicitas shakes her head at Angustias and rolls her eyes. "I knew it."

Knew what?

"What?"

Smearing the seat with the dirt stuck to her legs, Felicitas positions herself so that her full body is facing her mother. "You never worry about anything. You never worry about me."

Angustias frowns. "That is the most untrue statement I have ever heard."

"But there is something wrong with me," Felicitas contends. "I'm weird."

Angustias chuckles. "Felicitas, there's something wrong with everyone, which means that you are, in fact, perfectly normal."

Felicitas narrows her eyes. "Oh, yeah? What's wrong with you?"

"Nothing. I'm perfect."

Frustrated, Felicitas slumps in her seat and casts a sidelong glance toward the backseat. Olvido raises her eyebrows. What?

"Is she saying something?" Angustias asks Felicitas, following her gaze.

"No. She's sitting quietly."

Olvido whips her head toward Felicitas. "Do not talk about me as if I'm not here."

"Now she spoke."

"What did she say?"

"To not talk about her as if she isn't here."

"Sorry," Angustias yells to the backseat. "Is she supposed to—" she begins to say. "Sorry," she shouts. "Aren't you supposed to be in Heaven or whatever?"

Olvido's eyebrows furrow. "I'm dead, not deaf."

"She's not deaf," Felicitas repeats. "And you can't ruin her hearing, but you can definitely ruin mine."

Angustias apologizes again, this time more quietly. "So . . . ?"

"I'm not speaking as if you aren't here. I'm just answering a question," Felicitas clarifies to Olvido before responding. "She can't cross. She doesn't know why."

"Do *you* know why?"

Felicitas sneers. "If I knew, I would have gotten her to leave a long time ago."

"Felicitas, do not use that tone with your grandmother," Angustias reprimands.

It's fine. Olvido is used to it.

"You used that tone with her," Felicitas points out.

Angustias opens and closes her mouth. "I—" She exhales. You what? "Do you see a light?" Angustias finally asks, turning around to look at the backseat.

"No," Felicitas says before Olvido can answer. "She doesn't."

"Do you want to see a light?"

"Duh," Felicitas sasses. "She hates being here."

"I wonder why," Angustias says. "Can we help you cross?"

"No, we cannot. Now, this," Felicitas says, pointing to her mouth. "Will be out of service because I really don't feel like talking right now. Is there something you two would like to say to each other before I become unavailable? Nothing? Nothing? Didn't think so."

Olvido knows she should say something before it is too late. They should all say something. The storm could rip the car apart and thrash their bodies against a tree and then a rock and then the river. Olvido died without any apologies, and it is how Felicitas and Angustias may die as well. They all carry their mother's last name for a reason. They are tied, one and the same, always repeating the same mistakes.

chapter 62

Felicitas

Felicitas Olivares wishes she could talk to God. Many people share this wish, but no one feels as much urgency as Felicitas does at this moment. Hours have passed, and the storm shows no sign of dwindling. It must be a deluge. God is punishing them.

"So, God killed everyone? He committed murder?" Felicitas asked Olvido during one of their potion lessons. She slammed her knife down on the cutting board, slicing a carrot in two uneven halves.

"Well, no," Olvido responded. "People were being bad, so they died. If they had been good like Noah, they would have lived."

"You mean, He wouldn't have killed them."

Olvido sighed as she stirred the chicken broth. "Yes," she said, defeated. "He wouldn't have killed them."

Who exactly are You punishing right now? Felicitas wants to ask God. Is it her grandmother for trying to separate Felicitas from her mom all those years ago, for doing una cosa del diablo? No. Olvido is dead. She's received the ultimate punishment.

Is he punishing Angustias for being cruel, for wanting to take Felicitas away and destroy her happiness? No. God was a father. He is probably on Angustias's side. Although He is supposed to be a son, too. He should understand Felicitas. And He is a spirit as well. He could be on anyone's side, really.

Or not.

No. God is definitely not on Felicitas's side. No one is ever on her side. He is most likely punishing her for being una cosa del diablo, for being the result of the bad thing her mother did, for ruining her life like Olvido suspected she would.

The car shakes as it attempts to withstand the wind's blows and God's punches. Felicitas looks up at Olvido for a brief second. Her grandmother's gaze locks with hers. A fleeting, white light frames the lines between Felicitas's brows. Thunder voices her thoughts and emotions, those she's too exhausted to audibly convey.

"Is she asleep?" Olvido asks.

"Are you asleep?" Felicitas repeats. Angustias responds with silence.

"I'm sorry," Olvido says. She's been apologizing every fifteen minutes or so, but this time, she continues beyond that sentence. "I really am. You may understand what I did, what I tried to do, when you become a mother, but maybe you won't. I hope you don't. Our lives have been so different. Our mothers were so different. You don't see the world like I do, and because of that, you won't make the mistakes I did, but you will make mistakes. That, I can guarantee."

Felicitas closes her eyes. It is unfair that only her mother gets to sleep and avoid the world around her. "Do you hate me?" Olvido asks.

Felicitas lets her grandmother's question linger in the hot air for a few seconds. "No," she says, and opens her eyes. She hates that her answer is true, but lies are draining, and her most exhausted muscle is her heart. "But I am mad at you. Leave me alone."

Olvido disobeys. "Did you hate me? Before everything? Before knowing what I did?"

Felicitas considers letting her lack of response signal an affirmation, but her grandmother seems a bit dense in matters of emotions, so she shrugs and says, "Yes." Her heart's thorny rose tightens and forces her to correct herself. "Maybe. A little. I don't know. I . . . longed for you."

"¿Qué es 'longed'?" Olvido asks.

Felicitas takes a moment to assess Olvido's potential reactions if she were to speak candidly. None seem too terrible. They're going to die anyway. "I don't know what the word is in Spanish," she whispers to not wake her mother. "But it means that I wanted to have you. I wanted to have a grandmother, someone who would love me unconditionally, someone to always be on my side and not get mad at me like a parent would."

Olvido frowns and nods. "I think I understand," she whispers back. "I'm sorry I didn't give you that. I would have liked to have had a grand-mother, too, I suppose. No one was ever on my side either."

"A granddaughter could have been on your side."

Olvido smiles. "Do you really think so? You weren't on my side these last few weeks."

"Your ideas were insane!" Felicitas says, accidentally using her nor-mal volume. She quickly turns to her mother and is happy to see her chest rise and fall in the same rhythm as before. "And you didn't treat me like a granddaughter anyway. You think I'm una cosa del diablo."

"What?" Olvido exclaims. "No. I do not think that. You have it all wrong."

"No, I don't. Your actions don't lie. It's not just that you wanted me completely gone when I was born. You wanted my mom to give me up for adoption, and then you realized it was a mistake. So what? You didn't want me in your life for ten years after that. I can count the number of times we talked with one hand."

"I know. I'm sorry."

Felicitas rolls her eyes. "I heard you the first one hundred times."

I know. Everyone seems to know things. If someone knows things, and still acts improperly, then they don't deserve forgiveness.

"You are not una cosa del diablo," Olvido says. "I did think it was wrong for your mother to get pregnant at her age and without God's blessing, but I did not think it was your fault. I thought it was my fault for not taking proper care of your mother. I should have talked to her. I should have asked her about her life, what she was doing, who she was spending time with, what she was thinking. When she told me she was pregnant, I felt like a failure. I felt like I was repeating my mom's mistakes."

"The drunk lady?"

"Yes," Olvido laughs. "The drunk lady."

"You didn't get pregnant when you were in high school, did you?"

"No. I did not."

"Then, how were you repeating the same mistakes?"

"Well," Olvido sighs. It's a long, heavy breath, and for a moment Olvido does seem as wrinkly as a dried prune. "She also didn't really talk to me. She acted like she didn't really care about my life unless it concerned my ability to clean or cook or earn money."

"But you cared about my mom."

"Yes, but as you said, it is my actions that matter, and I'm sorry about my actions toward you. Talking to you made me feel ashamed and guilty, and I acted selfishly. I'm so sorry. If I had a time machine, I would go back and fix it."

"If you had a time machine, wouldn't you rather stop my mom from getting pregnant?" Felicitas gasps. "You hesitated! You wanted to say yes!"

"No," Olvido says with a dishonest tone. "Yes, but time travel is not real, so just know that I don't think you are una cosa del diablo, and I am truly sorry you felt that way, and I am thankful that Angustias has you because if you were anyone else, I don't think her life would be as good as it is right now. I *swear* I'm glad you're my granddaughter."

Felicitas looks out the window at the unceasing storm. She knows she should return the compliment. She should be kind in her last hours of life just in case Heaven and Hell are real. Instead, she says, "I can't say the same about you."

"That's understandable and fair." From the car's side-view mirror, Felicitas can see Olvido narrow her eyes. "Hmm. What does a good grandmother do? Other than speak to their granddaughters of course."

"Hmm," Felicitas says to mock her. She should tell her. She should let Olvido understand how easy it would have been to be a good grand-mother, and maybe that will make her feel exceptionally terrible. "They sit with you while you watch TV even when they don't like what you watch."

"Ugh, I can't do that," Olvido says. "What you watch is too ugly."

"You just have to sit there! You can close your eyes. I mean, grand-mothers just have to sit there. They can close their eyes."

"Ok, I'll try that. What else?"

Felicitas slowly turns around to fully face the backseat. Her eyes are wide with disbelief. Olvido used future tense. Olvido is asking questions. "They tell you stories."

Olvido clasps her hands gleefully. "Easy. I've already told you plenty of stories about my life."

"But they have to have magic."

"Oh, I have many magical stories. I can tell you the one about the mayor and how I was able to blackmail him into donating two million dollars to the children's hospital. Or the one where I was able to expedite one hundred and seventy-three marriage proposals in the span of two years."

Felicitas frowns. "You did what?"

"What else?"

"They give you candy."

Olvido crosses her arms and shakes her head. "Candy is bad for you, and you are terrible at brushing your teeth." Felicitas throws herself back into her seat. She should have known everything was sounding too good to be true. "But, I can give you arroz con leche," Olvido adds.

Felicitas rolls her eyes. "I told you," she says. "Rice is not a dessert." Feeling a scratch on her triceps Felicitas looks down and finds a Tupperware beside her.

"She must have not gotten a chance to visit Taliah before the storm began. Go on. Try it," Olvido urges, poking Felicitas's arm with the edge of the lid.

It's a trap, Felicitas knows. Her grandmother wants her to spill her truths, but there are no more truths left to spill, and she's starving, so she opens up the car console, and digs through her mother's stash of essentials. Ibuprofen. Band-Aids. Plastic forks and spoons. Felicitas opens the Tupperware's lid, digs in, and shoves a spoonful of the dessert into her mouth. The rice is soft and sweet, better than any dessert Felicitas has ever tasted, better than a grandmother's candy. The wonderful taste is ruined by a raisin that gets stuck between her teeth.

"Do you forgive me?" Olvido asks.

The question brings scorching tears to her eyes. *It's the raisin*, Felicitas lies to herself. *I must be allergic.* "No," she says, wiping away her tears with the back of her hand. She turns away and spits out the raisin into a napkin. "But I want to," she adds. Her words are slow and cautious. They don't bubble out of her like they usually do with Olvido's truth-inducing food. She is purposely spilling her truths in an attempt to save her heart. She needs to keep it from overflowing with emotion before it drowns her. "Maybe I will one day."

"I hope so," Olvido says. "Maybe when I become a better grand-mother."

"Yeah. Maybe." The floating sensation that disappeared the night before returns, and although it is softer, just a whisper of a feeling, it is better than anything Felicitas has ever felt before. This is not magic or manipulation. This is autonomy, self-induced freedom. Maybe the hurricane won't be able to lift her. Maybe her mom won't be able to take her away if they survive. Felicitas will float right through the rain and lightning. She'll float through the clouds, maybe make a stop at the moon, and she'll wave down at Olvido and Angustias and shout, "You can't catch me. I am invincible!"

But for now, Olvido keeps her in the stuffy car. "What else do grand-mothers do?" she asks.

"Um, they give you advice," Felicitas says, her voice still shaky. "But they don't pretend to be better than you for knowing things that you don't."

"Well, I have plenty of advice to offer, and I think it's very clear that I am not better than you. May I give you a suggestion right now? You don't have to do it if you don't want to." Felicitas hesitates but accepts. "Wake your mom up and tell her everything you're feeling. She can't run away, not right now."

Felicitas shakes her head. "She already knows what I'm feeling."

"I don't think she does. She knows what you want but not why you want it. You never told me either, why you don't want to move."

Felicitas shakes her head more aggressively. "I can't. I can't. I can't." She can't even think about the possible reactions such a confession would elicit. What if her mother catches her and ties her down? Felici-tas will never make it to the moon.

"Yes, you can," Olvido says softly.

"No," Felicitas cries. "I'm scared."

"Use the arroz. It will give you strength, and I will be right here."

"You promise?"

"No," Olvido says, suddenly fixing her posture and staring straight ahead. Though she doesn't smile, her eyes are bright. "I cannot promise you that. I'm sorry." Guilt flashes across her face. "I have to go."

"What? Now?" Felicitas whispers when she realizes what Olvido means. She frowns as she examines her grandmother. She doesn't look different. The world around her doesn't look different. "How do you know? Do you see a light? Do you hear angels? Do you see God? Do you see Satan?"

Olvido smiles tightly, clearly trying her best to not reproach her for the last question. "I'm not going to spoil the surprise for you. But do you see? I was right. The hurricane must have washed my ashes over Mexico."

Felicitas rolls her eyes. "Your ashes would have reached Mexico by now. You are so stub—" Felicitas gasps. "Wait!" she shouts.

Angustias wakes up in a startled jolt. "What is it?" she says, patting her surroundings. "What happened? Are you hurt?"

"She's gone," Felicitas says, and opens her arms to catch her mother. Switching between pats on the back and light squeezes on the shoulders, Felicitas holds Angustias as she cries until the clouds stop weeping and the birds begin to chirp. This time she joins her in her sorrow.

chapter 63

Angustias

The rain ceases long before Angustias's tears dry and her breathing stabilizes. It's her rumbling stomach that brings her back to the present. It's time to leave. She takes in a deep breath and reaches for the car keys, but Felicitas places her hand over hers to stop her from turning on the car. "There's something I need to tell you," Felicitas says. She reaches for the Tupperware of arroz con leche that Angustias had left on the backseat.

"You're hungry," Angustias says. "Me too. I'm sorry. I also have what I was going to drop off to Dr. Gutiérrez."

"This will suffice," Felicitas assures her and bites into a spoonful of rice. She chews for an unnecessary amount of time, swallows, and says, "I don't want to move."

Angustias gives her a quizzical look. They were not talking about moving. "I know you don't, but—"

"I don't want to move because I'm happy here." Felicitas eats another spoonful. She chews faster this time, as if someone is going to tear through her teeth and snatch the rice right out of her mouth if she doesn't get it down fast enough. "I haven't been happy anywhere else. Ever."

"That is not true. You—"

"Yes, it is. It's true. I've hated every town we've ever lived in, every school, every neighborhood. Every time we move you say that whatever problem we face in our new home won't matter as long as we are together and we're healthy and we're happy. But they matter to me, and I don't feel like we're together. How many hours a day do I actually get to spend with you? When I'm not in school, I'm studying, and when you're not working, you're sleeping. And I'm not okay. I can see ghosts. I feel closer to old, dead people than kids my age. That's not okay, right? Before we came here, I had no friends. None. And I wasn't happy, and I'm still not happy. I'm lonely." Angustias reaches out to wipe Felicitas's tears, but Felicitas slaps her hand away. "I have no one," she screams.

"That is not true."

"Yes, it is. I don't even have Estela or Gustavo or Emilio because you're going to take me away."

"You have me." Angustias intended for her words to come out as a reaffirming statement, but they sounded more like desperate plea. *Please have me. Please be okay with having me.*

"No, I don't. I couldn't even tell you what I was feeling without this stupid rice."

Angustias frowned. "What are you talking about? You can always talk to me."

"No. I can't, just like you couldn't talk to Grandma and she couldn't talk to you, not even with her magic food. This," Felicitas said, holding up the arroz con leche. "Grandma made this yesterday. Cayo didn't bring it. She was teaching me how to cook."

"When—"

"And while we cooked, she told me stories. Stories about her life and stories about truths. Her food, it could make people tell the truth. Try it."

Angustias pushes the Tupperware away when Felicitas shoves it in her face. There are more important matters to address than fantastical stories from Olvido. "You have me," she repeats with more confidence. "You can always talk to me. You don't have to feel lonely."

"But I *only* have you. I know it sounds mean, which is why I didn't want to tell you, but it's not enough. When Gustavo fights with his mom, he can talk to his dad or his grandma. When Estela fights with her mom, she has her sister and her dad."

Angustias raises her arms in defeat. "I'm sorry you don't have a lot of family members. I didn't either. Everyone was in Mexico—"

"But you had other people, didn't you? At school? In your neighborhood? You had friends who looked like you and talked like you and ate the same food as you."

"People who look—you mean Mexican friends?"

"Yes."

"I suppose I did," Angustias admitted as she remembered her friends, her classmates, even Felicitas's father. "But I didn't know that's something you needed, something you wanted."

"How could you not? Didn't you feel like a weirdo?"

"No, not really, and I thought since you were born here and grew up here—"

"You're saying I'm not Mexican?" Felicitas asked, her voice drenched with disbelief.

"That's not what I'm saying."

"Then, what are you saying?"

"That—I just," Angustias lets out a frustrated sigh. She could try to analyze her upbringing and how it shaped her current views and decisions, but it would take years to get her thoughts straight, to figure out the right words to say. Felicitas was her child, not a therapist. "I'm sorry. I was inconsiderate. I didn't think you would miss something you never really grew up with."

"It's called longing," Felicitas says. "I'm always longing, but I don't want to long anymore. I want to have friends and a home. I want to be happy."

"I want you to be happy, too," Angustias says, and reaches out to touch Felicitas's face, but she moves away again. From the corner of her eye, Angustias looks down at the arroz con leche. "How does it work? Your grandma's food. What did she say it did?"

Felicitas twirls the spoon over the rice. "You eat it," she says. "Any amount, even just a bite or a sip, and all your truths will spill out, even the ugly, embarrassing ones."

"Alcohol can do the same trick," Angustias jokes.

"So, you believe me?"

Angustias does not. Magic food felt as unbelievable as a pregnant virgin and a woman being created from a man's rib. "I think Maria was lying," she had once told Olvido after Sunday service. "I bet she hooked up with some guy and told that lie to not get in trouble. Now that I think about it, she is pretty cool. Maybe I should start worshiping her. Maria, Patron Saint of Lies. What? I believe in God. Is that not enough? Do I have to believe everything in the Bible?"

"Ay, niña. ¿Qué voy a hacer contigo?" Olvido had said, shaking her head. "Why do you believe in God but not the Bible? How do you decide which unexplainable things are true and which are not?"

Angustias had grinned at her mother's tangerine cloud. "I can see them."

"You can see God? Can you tell Him to send nicer customers and bigger tips?"

"No, I cannot see God, Mother. I know He's real because I'm cursed."

"Are you now? And what is this curse I haven't heard of?"

"Neither my mother nor Maria, Patron Saint of Lies, ever listens to my pleas. I am doomed to always be grounded."

Angustias reached for the Tupperware and settled it on her lap. The arroz con leche couldn't force the truth out of her, she was sure, but there was a possibility that it could help. Getting a barrida de huevo helped, not because having someone rub an egg over your body and praying the evil away could actually cure you, but because the comfort of someone taking care of you, of fighting your battle for you, truly healed the soul. It is why babies stopped crying when their parents picked them up and sang "ru, ru, ru, ru." Everyone needs to feel loved.

Angustias takes the spoon from Felicitas, scoops up no more than four grains of rice, and chews on them cautiously. She doesn't feel any different, but in the rearview mirror she can see that something has changed. Hovering above the crown of her head and blending with her hair is a black cloud.

It's hideous, Angustias thinks. But it is not permanent. A dark gray will remain at the core of her cloud for decades until she develops senile dementia and forgets that Olvido is dead. When she calls for her mother, and her daughter reminds her that she is gone, the dark gray will return. It will disappear and reappear until her death, but at this moment, Angustias cannot fathom such a thing. The cloud feels everlasting and heavy. It pushes down on her head with such force, it drags down the rest of her features, her brows, her eyes, her lips.

"Why do we keep moving?" Felicitas asks. "Why do you run away?"

"Because," Angustias sobs, keeping eye contact with her newly visible cloud. "Because I'm scared."

"Of what?"

"Everything. I was scared of not being a good mother. Of you not being happy. I kept trying to find a good place, a happy place, but instead I made every place unhappy. I kept wanting to leave because every place we went to, I felt miserable, too. Every town made me wish I was home, but I couldn't go home. I couldn't."

Felicitas squirms in her seat. "Can't we make this place our home?"

Angustias shakes her head. "No. Everything reminds me of my mom. The people, they remind me of my mom and they pity me, and they make me feel," Angustias squints at her cloud, trying to discern its colors through the blur of her tears. "Miserable. Desolate. Just . . . sad."

How long have I had this color? Angustias thinks. *Has it always been so dark and opaque? The cloud won't change when we leave, will it? I will still miss my mother and mourn the life that we had and could have had if we'd been honest. I will never stop wishing I was home. When will I be home?* Felicitas offered a solution. They can stay. They don't have to long anymore.

"What are you staring at?" Felicitas asks.

"I have a confession to make," Angustias says. "No, thank you. I don't need the arroz. I can do this on my own." She takes in a deep breath and begins her confession. "I lied earlier, when I said that there was nothing wrong with me, that I'm perfect."

Felicitas's eyes narrow with suspicion when Angustias tells her about the clouds, and her nose scrunches with confusion when she tries to explain what each color means. But her face softens when Angustias admits that she often misinterprets people's colors. Flaws are something she can believe in. "What color is my cloud?" Felicitas asks as if she's testing her.

"It's many colors," Angustias says. "It's sad, but hopeful, and it's full of curiosity. I can see that you're tired, and I can see that you're lonely." Angustias takes in another spoonful of rice. "I'm sorry," she cries. "I'm so sorry. I could see it before. I could see that you felt abandoned, and I blamed it on how your grandmother acted toward you, but it was me. It was me who made you feel that way. I'm so sorry. That's why I didn't tell you about the colors. I was so embarrassed. I should have known better than any mother how you felt and what I needed to do to make you feel better, but I didn't know, or I didn't want to know. I don't know which it is, and that's the truth. I'm sorry. Look at me, please. Please forgive me."

Felicitas turns to her. "I forgive you," she says as tears roll down her cheeks. "Because sometimes I can see that you're sad, too, and I also don't know what to do." She's unable to speak for a moment. Her words get pulled back as her sobs are pushed forward. Angustias rubs Felicitas's hand with her thumb. "Do you forgive me?" Felicitas manages to say in bursts.

Spilling the arroz con leche over her lap, Angustias pulls Felicitas toward her and wraps her in a hug. "I don't need to forgive you. It's my job to make you happy, not the other way around."

"Was it not your job to make Grandma happy?" Felicitas's voice is muffled by Angustias's arms.

"I don't know," Angustias says. She'd often wondered this herself. Olvido sometimes acted as if it was Angustias's job to please her, to follow her every command. At what point had Angustias made Felicitas feel what she'd fought so hard to escape? The question brings tears to Angustias's eyes. "If it was, I failed, but it's different. I'm—"

"An adult. I know. I know."

Angustias laughs. It's such a normal response, so childish. That's all Felicitas should strive to be. "You're the adult, and you make the decisions, and I'm the child, and I have to follow what you say."

If Angustias had failed to improve her parenting style from the type that was inflicted on her, now was the time to right her wrongs. Another hurricane could come around and whisk them away. The ground could open beneath them and swallow them whole. They could simply cease to exist at the snap of a finger. Stranger things had happened. She couldn't leave Felicitas the way Olvido had left her. Two months. Olvido had been with Angustias two months and had not apologized for . . . the past. It was all in the past. But Angustias and Felicitas were in the present, and they had a future. So, Angustias grabs Felicitas's hand and says, "No. *We* make decisions. I have the final say, of course, but we are a family, and I want us to be together and healthy and happy. I'll take your input. Do you really think we should stay?"

Felicitas smiles and says, "Yes."

chapter 64

Felicitas

"You lied! You said we were staying!" Felicitas shouts when, a week after Olvido's departure, she sees her mother dragging their suitcases out of their house.

"We are," Angustias assures her. "I just want us to take a little trip, that's all."

"To where and for how long?" Felicitas says, glaring at her mother and then the suitcases. They aren't bursting at the seams like they were when they arrived at Grace.

"The Valley. McAllen. I want you to see where I grew up. Just for the weekend. I promise." Felicitas rolls her eyes and sighs, but she trusts her mother's promise.

Three hours into their drive across the state, Felicitas lowers the volume of the radio and clears her throat. "I'm going to name my daughter Mariazul," she announces, lifting her chin up to show her mother and the universe that she means business.

"Okay?" Angustias snorts. "Why?"

"So she'll never be blue," Felicitas says. "We're always the opposite of what we're named, right?"

"Of course," Angustias sighs. "Of course you would figure out a pattern by yourself." She drums the steering wheel with her nails as she mulls over Felicitas's declaration. "What if you just give her a name that doesn't mean anything? Wouldn't that be better?"

Felicitas shakes her head. "Impossible. Think of a name, any name, and google it. Everything has meaning."

"What if you have a boy?"

Felicitas gasps and signs a cross over her chest. "¡Ni lo mande Dios!" It is more of a demand than an expression or request.

Angustias laughs so hard, she has to pull over to the side of the road and park the car.

"What?" Felicitas says. "What's so funny?"

Angustias gasps for air and manages to say, "You sound like my mom," before doubling over in pain.

"*You* sound like your mom," Felicitas argues.

"No," Angustias insists. "You sound like my mom."

Felicitas slams back against her chair. "Whatever."

"Oh, no! Now you sound like me." Angustias seems to find this fact much funnier than the last. She laughs so hard, she slaps her leg with one hand while holding her belly with the other, a stitch forming in her side.

Felicitas frowns. Sounding like your mother is no laughing matter. She turns to the backseat, forgetting Olvido is not there to argue with Angustias. She smiles mischievously because she knows just what will make her mother stop. "Wanna know what Grandma was up to for the last few weeks?" she asks. Her words slice through Angustias's laughter, killing it in an instant. "You're not going to like it," Felicitas singsongs. "Not one bit."

acknowledgments

This book was a labor of love, and I am eternally grateful to everyone who helped bring it out into the world.

Thank you to my agent, Cecilia Lyra, for her editorial guidance, faith, and emotional support. CeCe, thank you for believing in this story from the beginning, for understanding its message, and for championing honesty and authenticity. Thank you for guiding me through every step of the publishing process, for believing in me and my potential as a novelist, and for constantly reminding me to believe in myself. None of this would have been possible without you. I am incredibly lucky to be represented by you.

Thank you to the P.S. Literary Agency team, as well, for their work in helping bring this book into existence and for promoting it since its early stages.

Thank you to my editor, Melanie Iglesias Perez, for her editorial insight, wisdom, and trust. Melanie, you have made this novel the best that it can be. Thank you for handling this story with care and good humor. You are forever my dream editor.

Thank you to the publishing team at Simon & Schuster and Atria Books for giving this book a home. To Elizabeth Hitti, you have been a wonderful editorial assistant. Thank you for your kindness and support and for answering all my questions with enthusiasm, even when I perhaps sent too many. Thank you to my cover designer, Chelsea

McGuckin, for creating a beautiful depiction of this story. Chelsea, thank you for your patience and willingness to explore new ideas and for sharing your undeniable talent. Thank you to my editor-in-chief, Lindsay Sagnette; managing editorial assistants, Shelby Pumphrey and Lacee Burr; and managing editor, Paige Lytle. Thank you to my publisher, Libby McGuire; associate publisher, Dana Trocker; and associate publisher assistant, Abby Velasco. Thank you to my test designer, Dana Sloan; marketers, Maudee Genao and Jolena Podolsky; senior production editor, Sonja Singleton; publicist, Megan Rudloff; and director of subsidiary rights, Nicole Bond.

A special thank you to those who champion books and diverse stories, to readers and to those who dedicate their time to spreading the word about literary works through social media and personal interactions. I am honored and thankful to each and every person who has picked up this book.

To my friends, thank you for hyping me and this book up from the moment I told you I had written a novel. Your enthusiasm and encouragement were vital for overcoming moments of self-doubt. I'm lucky to have y'all in my life.

And finally, thank you to my sister for her support and tough love, for her excitement in each stage of the writing process, and for checking in to ensure that I was meeting all deadlines. Jessica, you annoyed me sometimes, but I also couldn't have this without you.

Gracias a mi mamá, por su apoyo y amor incondicional. Mamá, sé que la industria editorial es algo nuevo para nosotras. Gracias por no tenerle miedo a lo desconocido, por siempre creer en mí y por decir "tú puedes" y "te amo". Yo también te amo.

about the author

Anamely Salgado Reyes grew up on both sides of the Mexico and Texas border. Currently based in the Rio Grande Valley, she writes about what she cherishes most: family, friendship, and finding magic in everyday life.